Murder Came Easy

The killer had been at large in the dead man's room, feverishly searching ... searching in all the cupboards and drawers for Penhallow's secret. ... But perhaps the lifeless figure of Penhallow lying on the bed had outwitted this desperate man. Perhaps the secret would be sealed in the dead man's tomb.

By the same author

Georgette Heyer

Penhallow

A PANTHER BOOK

GRANADA
London Toronto Sydney New York

Published by Granada Publishing Limited in 1964
Reprinted 1966, 1967, 1969, 1971, 1972, 1973, 1976,
1979, 1982

ISBN 0 586 02767 X

First published in Great Britain by
William Heinemann Ltd 1942

Granada Publishing Limited
Frogmore, St Albans, Herts AL2 2NF
and
36 Golden Square, London W1R 4AH
866 United Nations Plaza, New York, NY 10017, USA
117 York Street, Sydney, NSW 2000, Australia
100 Skyway Avenue, Rexdale, Ontario, M9W 3A6, Canada
61 Beach Road, Auckland, New Zealand

Printed and bound in Great Britain by
Cox & Wyman Ltd, Reading
Set in Intertype Plantin

Granada ®
Granada Publishing ®

The characters in this book, who have been given place
names, are entirely fictitious and bear no relation to any
living person. The village of Polzant exists only in the
author's imagination.

A man that apprehends death no more dreadfully but as a drunken sleep; careless, reckless, and fearless of what's past, present, or to come; insensible of mortality, and desperately mortal.

Measure for Measure Act iv Scene 2

CHAPTER ONE

JIMMY THE BASTARD was cleaning boots, in a stone-paved room at the back of the house which commanded, through its chamfered windows, a view of the flagged yard, of a huddle of outhouses, and a glimpse, caught between the wing of the manor and the wood-shed, of one of the paddocks where Raymond had some of his young stock out to grass. Beyond the paddock the ground rose towards the Moor, hidden from Jimmy's indifferent gaze by a morning mist.

The room in which he worked was large, and dirty, and smelt of oil, boot-polish, and must. On a table against one wall a variety of lamps had been placed. Jimmy paid no attention to them. Theoretically, the cleaning and filling of the lamps was a part of his duty, but Jimmy disliked cleaning lamps, and never touched them. Later, one of the maids, driven to it by Reuben Lanner, would polish the glass chimneys, fill up the bowls with paraffin, and trim the wicks, grumbling all the time, not at Penhallow, the Master, who had never installed electric-light at Trevellin, but at Jimmy whom no one could force to perform his duties.

Under the windows, a wooden shelf accommodated the long row of boots and shoes awaiting Jimmy's attention. Several tins of polish and blacking jostled a collection of brushes and rags. Jimmy dipped a brush into one of these tins, and, with something of the air of an epicure making his choice, picked up from the row one of Clara Hastings's worn, single-barred, low-heeled black glacé slippers. He began to spread on the blacking, without haste and without enthusiasm, but thoroughly, because he rather liked Mrs. Hastings. When he came to them, he would clean Raymond's gaiters and Bart's top-boots just as thoroughly, not from affection, but from the knowledge, born of experience, that neither of these sons of Penhallow would hesitate to lay their crops about his back if he cleaned brown boots with brushes last used for black ones, or left a vestige of mud upon the soles.

Clara Hastings's slippers were worn out of shape, the thin leather cut in places, and in others rubbed away. They were large, roomy slippers, and had never been any smarter than their owner, who went about Trevellin from year's end to year's end in ageless garments of no particular cut or style, with skirts uneven, and often muddied about the hems from Clara's habit of wearing them at ankle-length, and trailing them over her garden-beds, or through the untidy yards. Vivian Penhallow had said once that Aunt Clara's name conjured up a vision of gaping plackets, frowsty flannel blouses, gold chains and brooches, and wisps of yellow-grey hair escaping from a multitude of pins. It was a fair description, and would in no way have perturbed Clara, had she heard it. At sixty-three, a widow of many years' standing, a pensioner under

7

Penhallow's roof, and with no apparent interest in anything beyond the stables and her fern-garden, Clara was as indifferent to the appearance she presented as she was indifferent to the jealousies and strifes which made Trevellin so horrible a prison to anyone not blessed with the strongest of nerves, and the most blunted of sensibilities.

Jimmy, uncritical of her deplorable shoes, did his best by them, and laid them aside. He was her nephew, by blood if not by law, but the relationship was unacknowledged by her, and unclaimed by him. Relations meant nothing to Jimmy, who was rather proud of being a bastard. Clara, accepting his presence at Trevellin without expostulation or repugnance, treated him as one of the servants, which indeed he was; and, beyond observing to Penhallow that if he took all his bastards under his roof there would be no end to it, never again referred to his parentage. The young Penhallows, with the robust brutality which still, after twenty years amongst them, made their stepmother wince and blush, did not attempt either to ignore or to conceal Jimmy's relationship to their father. They called him Jimmy the Bastard. Excepting Ingram, Penhallow's second son, who was married, and lived at the Dower House, and so did not come much into contact with him, they all disliked him, but in varying degrees. Eugène complained that he was insolent; Charmian knew he was dishonest; Aubrey was fastidiously disgusted by his slovenly appearance; the twins, Bartholomew and Conrad, objected to him on the score of his laziness; and Raymond, the eldest of Penhallow's sons, hated him with an implacability that was none the less profound for being unexpressed. Jimmy returned his ill-will blatantly, but in silence. If he had dared, he would have left Raymond's boots and gaiters uncleaned, but he did not dare. Penhallow might, in his peculiar fashion, be fond of his baseborn son, but Penhallow would only laugh if he heard of his being flogged. Penhallow had flogged and clouted all his legal offspring – not, indeed, into virtuous behaviour, but into some sort of an obedience to his imperious will – and although his great, bull-like frame was now rendered more or less quiescent by gout and dropsy, his lusty spirit had undergone no softening change. He had lived hard, intemperately, and violently, scornful of gentleness, brutal to weakness; his body had betrayed him, but his heart had learnt neither tolerance nor pity. He certainly showed a liking for Jimmy, but whether he encouraged him from affection, or from a malicious desire to enrage his legitimate children, no one, least of all Jimmy himself, knew.

There were eight pairs of shoes or boots laid out upon the shelf. Jimmy ran his eyes along the row, noting Eugène's elegant patent-leather shoes, with their pointed toes and thin soles; the neat brogues, belonging to Vivian, his wife; Raymond's stout boots and serviceable gaiters; Bart's and Conrad's riding-boots; a pair of cracked black shoes belonging to Reuben Lanner, who had lived and worked at Trevellin for as long as anyone, even Clara, could remember, and called himself Penhallow's butler. Jimmy had no particular liking for Reuben, but he recognized the unique position he held in the house, and did not object to cleaning his shoes for him. But last on the row stood a cheap, jaunty pair of shoes, with high-heels and short toes, which instantly caught Jimmy's eye, and brought a scowl to his dark face. He picked them up, and tossed them under the shelf on to the stone floor, with a gesture of eneffable contempt. He knew very well that they belonged to Loveday Trewithian, Mrs. Penhallow's personal maid, and he wasn't going to clean that sly cat's shoes for her, not he! She was a saucy piece, if ever there was one, he thought, slipping about the house so quiet and pretty-behaved, with her soft, ladyfied speech, and her eyes looking slantways under her long lashes. She was Reuben's niece, and had started as kitchenmaid at Trewithian, of no more account than any other of the girls who performed ill-defined duties at the Manor. If it hadn't been for Mrs. Penhallow, who took a silly fancy to the girl, and had her out of the kitchen to wait upon herself, she wouldn't have learnt to ape the manners of the gentry, nor yet have got ideas into her head which were above her station.

Jimmy gave her shoes a little kick. He knew what he knew: he'd seen Loveday and Bart kissing and cuddling when they thought themselves safe from discovery. She wouldn't dare complain of him, not even to Mrs. Penhallow, for fear he should up and tell the Master what she'd been fool enough to boast of to him. Penhallow didn't give a damn for Bart's making love to the girl: he wasn't above pawing her about himself, if he got the chance; but let him but get wind of a marriage planned between the pair of them, and then wouldn't the fur fly! Jimmy hadn't told him yet, but he would one day, if she gave him any of her airs.

He gave Mrs. Eugène Penhallow's brogues a final rub, and set them down. He didn't reckon much to Mrs. Eugène: she was a foreigner; she didn't understand Cornish ways, nor, seemingly, want to. She didn't like living at Trevellin, either, and made no secret of it. Picking up one of Eugène's shoes, and spitting on its glossy surface, Jimmy grinned, and reflected that Mrs. Eugène wouldn't succeed in moving Eugène from quarters which he found comfortable, not if she tried till Doomsday. Jimmy was contemptuous of Eugène, a hypochondriac at thirty-five, always feeling the draughts, and talking about his weak chest. He was contemptuous of Mrs. Eugène too, but more tolerantly. He couldn't see what there was in Eugène to absorb her whole attention, or to make her so passionately devoted to him. She'd got spirit, too: she wasn't a poor downtrodden thing, like Penhallow's wife, who allowed herself to be bullied by the Penhallows as though she was nobody. She'd stand up to Penhallow, telling him off like a regular vixen, while he lay in his great bed, roaring with laughter at her, egging her on, saying things to make her lose her temper worse than ever, and telling her she was a grand little cat, even if she didn't know a blood-mare from a stallion, and hadn't had more sense than to marry a nincompoop like Eugène.

Jimmy turned his attention to Bart's riding-boots, which bore every evidence of Bart's having walked all about the farm in them, which he probably had. Bart, to whom the reading of a book was a penance, and the writing of a letter a Herculean labour, was going to be a farmer. No doubt, thought Jimmy, he planned to settle down at Trellick Farm with Loveday one of these fine days. Trellick was earmarked for Bart, but catch Penhallow handing it over to him if he married Loveday! He might whistle for it then: in Jimmy's opinion he wouldn't in any event make a do of it. He'd no head, not as much sense as Conrad, his twin, though from being the hardier and the more rollicking of the two it was he who always took the lead, and set an example for the other to follow. They were the youngest of Penhallow's first family, and had reached the age of twenty-five without having achieved any other distinction than that of being two of the most bruising riders in the county, and of having placed their parent in the position of having to pay an incredible number of maintenance-sums on their behalf at an age when most young gentlemen were innocently occupied at school. Not that Penhallow grudged the money. He himself, with a fine freedom from restraint which savoured of an earlier age, had done what lay in his power to perpetuate the distinctive Penhallow cast of countenance, and the sight of an unmistakable Penhallow amongst a knot of village brats seemed to afford him a degree of amusement which scandalized, and indeed alienated the more virtuous of his acquaintances.

The wonder was, thought Jimmy, turning it over in his curious mind, that Bart, whom anyone would have thought the spit and image of his father, should have taken it into his head to marry a girl like Loveday. She was a cunning one, sure enough, looking as though butter wouldn't melt in her mouth, and twisting Bart round her impudent finger.

Jimmy picked up Bart's second boot. His dark glance fell on Conrad's, standing next in the row, and the sight of them, setting up a train of thought, made him smile to himself with a kind of malign satisfaction. Conrad, the cleverer yet the weaker of the twins, had for his brother a jealous devotion which, though it was undisturbed by Bart's many casual village affairs, would be likely to prove a thorny barrier in the way of his marriage to Loveday or any other young woman. Maybe Conrad already guessed what was in the wind: Jimmy didn't know about that, but it wouldn't surprise him if he found that Bart had taken his twin into his confidence. In Jimmy's opinion he was fool enough for anything, too thick-headed to realize that Conrad, adoring him, vying with him, quarrelling with him, would be ready to play any dirty trick that would rid him of a rival to his possession of him.

He was turning over in his mind the possible results of telling Penhallow what was going on under his roof when a footfall sounded on the flagged passage, and Loveday Trewithian came into the room, carrying the lamp from her mistress's bedroom.

Jimmy scowled at her, but said nothing. Loveday set the lamp down on the table beside the others, and turned, smiling, towards him. Her warm brown eyes flickered over the shelf; he knew her well enough to be sure that the absence of her own shoes from the row had not escaped her, but she gave no sign. She watched him, at work on Bart's second boot, and said presently in her rich, soft voice: 'You do polish them clean-off, Jimmy.'

He was as impervious to her flattery as to the seductive note in her voice. 'I won't lay hand or brush to yours,' he said unamiably. 'You can take 'em away.'

Her smile grew. She said gently: 'You don't need to be so set against me, my dear. I won't do you any harm.'

He made a sound of derision. 'You do me harm! That's a good 'un!'

Her smile became a little saucy. 'Aw, my dear, you'm jealous!'

'I ain't got nothing to be jealous of you for, you dressy bit! If I was to tell the old man the tricks you're up to with that Bart you'd smile t'other side of your face!'

'*Mister* Bart!' she corrected mildly.

Jimmy sniffed. He turned his shoulder on her, but watched her out of the corners of his eyes as she bent to pick up her shoes from under the shelf.

'To be sure, I do be forgetting you'm in a way related, my dear,' she murmured.

The taunt left Jimmy unmoved. He said nothing, and she went away, carrying her shoes, and laughing a little. It annoyed him that she showed no resentment of his churlishness; he thought she was a poor-spirited girl, or else an uncommon deep 'un.

He had not quite finished polishing Conrad's boots when he heard Reuben Lanner shouting for him. In a leisurely way he went out into the passage. Reuben, a spare, grizzled man in a rather worn black suit of clothes, told him that he would have to take the Master's breakfast into him.

'Where's Martha?' asked Jimmy, not because he didn't want to wait on Penhallow, but because he was naturally disinclined to obey Reuben.

'No business of yours where she is,' responded Reuben, who, in common with the rest of the household, disliked Jimmy cordially.

'I ain't finished the boots, nor I won't for ten minutes.'

'That'll do well enough,' said Reuben, rather disappointingly, and vanished through one of the doorways farther down the passage.

Jimmy went back to the boot-room. The command to carry Penhallow's breakfast to him did not surprise him, any more than a command to take up Mrs. Penhallow's tray would have surprised him. There were a number of persons comprising the domestic staff at Trevellin, but nobody had any very clearly defined duties, and no member of the family would have been in the least astonished to have found himself waited on at table by the kitchen-maid, or even by one of the grooms. Nor would the servants have thought of objecting, in any very serious spirit, to being obliged to do work for which they had not been engaged. Reuben, and Sybilla, his wife, had been in Penhallow's service for so long that they seemed to have no interests beyond the confines of the Manor; Jimmy was bound to the family by strong, if irregular, ties; and the maid-servants, all of them locally born girls, had only the vaguest ideas about their rights, and would not, in any case, have preferred to work in more orderly but stricter establishments than this sprawl-ing, over-large, ill-run, but comfortably lax house.

By the time an untidy housemaid had come clattering down the backstairs in search of Mr. Bart's boots and gaiters, for which he was shouting, a message had been brought to the kitchen by Loveday from Mr. Eugène, requiring Sybilla to send him up a glass of boiling water and his Bemax; and Jimmy had collected the various trays which were needed to accommodate the staggering number of dishes which made up Penhallow's breakfast, Raymond Penhallow had come in from the stables, and was pealing the bell in the dining-room. Reuben Lanner began to pile a number of plates, pots, jugs, and dishes on to a heavy silver tray, and without bestirring himself to any noticeable degree presently bore his load off, down the flagged corridor, round a corner into another, up three steps, through a black-oak door, across a large, low pitched hall, and so to the dining-room, a long, panelled apartment which faced south on to the front drive. That the dining-room might be somewhat inconveniently placed, having regard to the position of the kitchen, was a thought that had long since ceased to trouble his mind; and although the family often complained that food came cold to table, and were perfectly well aware of the cause, none of them ever made the slightest attempt to remedy it. Clara had indeed once remarked that they ought to cut a serving-hatch through the wall, but she had not been attended to, the Penhallows having grown up with this inconvenience, and preferring it to any revolutionary change.

Raymond Penhallow was standing before the great stone fireplace, reading a letter, when Reuben came in. He was a sturdily built, dark man, of thirty-nine, with a rather grim cast of countenance, a de-cided chin, and no small-talk. He had the strong, square hands of the practical man, the best seat on a horse of any man in the county, and a kind of rugged common sense which made him an excellent farmer, and a competent bailiff. It was generally thought that when Penhallow finally succumbed to the ailments which were supposed to beset him Raymond would make several changes at Trevellin, which, however disagreeable to the various members of the house-hold at present subsisting upon Penhallow's reckless bounty, would no doubt be extremely beneficial to the over-charged estate. In theory, he had managed the estate now for several years; in prac-tice, he acted as an unpaid overseer for his father, and was at the mercy of Penhallow's unpredictable whims. Penhallow showed a certain unwilling respect for his ability, but condemned his business like sense of the value of money as pettifogging, and, with a magnificent disregard for the drain upon his finances which the support of so many souls under his roof entailed, continued to maintain as many members of his family as could be brought under his sway with a careless but despotic open-handedness which savoured strongly of seigneurial times.

Reuben dumped the silver tray down upon an enormous sideboard of mahogany which occupied most of the wall-space at one end of the room. In a leisurely fashion, he began to arrange the plates and dishes. The fact that all three silver entrée dishes were tarnished disturbed his complacency no more than the discovery that one of the plates did not match its fellows. He remarked dispassionately that that was another of the Spode plates gone, and added that they were down to five now. As Raymond vouchsafed no reply to this piece of information, he placed a singularly beautiful coffee-pot of Queen Anne date on the table, and flanked it with an electro-plated milk-jug, and a teapot of old Worcester.

'Master's had a bad night,' he observed.

Raymond grunted.

'He had Martha out to him four times,' pursued Reuben, fitting a faded satin cosy over the teapot. 'Seemingly there wasn't much wrong with him, barring the gout. He's clever enough now.'

This piece of information elicited no more response than the first. Reuben thoughtfully polished a thin Georgian spoon on his sleeve, and added: 'He's had a letter from young Aubrey. Seemingly, he's got himself in debt again. That's done Master good, that has.'

Raymond made no objection to this unceremonious reference to his younger brother, but the intelligence thus cavalierly conveyed to him brought a scowl to his face, and he looked up from the letter in his hand.

'I thought that 'ud fetch you,' said the retainer, meeting his gaze with a kind of ghoulish satisfaction.

'I don't want any damned impudence from you,' returned Raymond, moving to the table, and seating himself at the head of it.

Reuben gave a dry chuckle. Removing the lid from one of the entrée dishes, he shovelled several pilchards on to a plate, and dumped this down before Raymond. 'You don't need to trouble yourself,' he observed. 'Master says young Aubrey won't get a farden out of him.' He pushed one of the toast-racks towards Raymond, and prepared to depart. 'Next thing you know, we'll have young Aubrey down here,' he said. 'That'll be clean-off, that will!'

Raymond gave a short bark of sardonic laughter. Reuben, having unburdened himself of all the information at present at his disposal, took himself off, just as Clara Hastings came in from the garden, and entered the dining-room.

It would have been hard for anyone, casually encountering Clara, to have made an accurate guess at her age. She was, in fact, sixty-three years old, but although her harsh-featured countenance was wrinkled and weather-beaten, her untidy locks were only streaked with grey, and her limbs had the elasticity of a much younger woman's. She was a tall, angular creature, and, rather unexpectedly, looked her best in the saddle. She had strong, bony hands, generally grimed with dirt, since she was an enthusiastic gardener, and rarely took the trouble to protect her hands with gloves. Her skirts never hung evenly round her, and since she wore them unfashionably long, and was continually catching her heels in them, their hems often sagged where the stitches had been rent. When enough of the hem had come unsewn to discommode her, she cobbled it up again, using whatever reel of cotton came first to her hand. She was always ready to spend more money than she could afford on her horses or her garden, but grudged every penny laid out in clothing. She had been known to watch, over a period of months, the gradual reduction in price of a hat in one of the cheaper shops at Liskeard, triumphantly acquiring it at last for a few grudged shillings in a clearance sale at the end of the year. As a bride of twenty-two, she had set out on her honeymoon in a new sealskin coat: as a widow of sixty-three, she still wore the same sealskin coat, brown now with age, and worn in places down to the leather. Neither her son, Clifford, a solicitor in Liskeard, nor any of the Penhallows paid the least attention to the deplorable appearance she so often presented, but her ill-chosen and occasionally frayed garments were a source of continual disgust to her daughter-in-law, Rosamund; an annoyance to Penhallow's wife, Faith; and even roused Vivian from her absorption in more important cares to comment caustically upon them.

She was dressed this morning in a voluminous and shiny blue skirt imperfectly confining at the waist a striped flannel shirt-blouse; a woollen cardigan, shapeless and tufty from much washing, and faded to an indeterminate hue; a pair of cracked shoes; odd stockings; and a collection of gold chains, cairngorm brooches, and old-fashioned rings. Two strands of hair had already escaped from the complicated erection on the top of her head; and a hairpin was dropping out of a loop of hair over one ear. She took her seat opposite Raymond, behind the cups and saucers, remarking as she did so that her grey had cast a shoe.

'I can't spare any of the men,' responded Raymond. 'Jimmy the Bastard will have to take him down to the smithy.'

Clara accepted this without comment, and began to pour out some coffee for him, and tea for herself. Having done this, she got up and went over to the sideboard, returning in a few moments with a plate upon which reposed a sausage, a fried egg, and several rashers of bacon. Raymond was studying a sheet of figures, and paid no attention to her. It occurred to neither of them that he should wait on her.

'Your father was on the rampage again in the night,' remarked Clara presently.

'Reuben told me. He had Martha out of bed four times.'

'Gout?' inquired Clara.

'I don't know. There's a letter from Aubrey.'

Clara stirred her tea reflectively. 'I thought I heard him shoutin',' she said. 'Aubrey gettin' into debt again?'

'So Reuben says. I shouldn't be surprised. Damned young waster!'

'Your father won't be happy till he's got him down here,' said Clara. 'He's a queer boy. I never could make head nor tail of those bits of writing of his. I daresay they're very clever, though. He won't like it if he has to come down here.'

'Well, nor shall I,' said Raymond. 'It's bad enough having Eugène, doing nothing except lounge on the sofa, and fancy himself ill all day.'

'Your father likes havin' him,' said Clara.

'I'm damned if I know why he should.'

'He's very amusin',' said Clara.

Raymond having apparently nothing to say in answer to this, the interchange ceased. The clatter of heavy feet on the uncarpeted oak stairs, and a loud whistling, heralded the approach of one of the twins. It was Conrad, the younger of them. He was a good-looking young man, dark and aquiline like all his family, and, although taller than his eldest brother, was almost as stockily built. Though not considered to be as clever as Aubrey, his senior by three years, he had more brain than his twin, and had contrived to pass, after a prolonged period of study, the various examinations which enabled him to embrace the profession of land agent. Penhallow having bought him a junior partnership in a local firm of some standing, it was considered that unless the senior partners brought the partnership to an end, on account of his casual habit of absenting himself from the office on the slimmest of pretexts, he was permanently settled in life.

He came into the room, pushed the door to behind him, favoured his aunt with a laconic greeting, and helped himself largely from the dishes on the sideboard. 'The old man's had a bad night,' he announced, sitting down at the table.

'So we've already been told,' said Raymond.

'I heard him raising Cain somewhere in the small hours,' said Conrad, reaching out a long arm for the butter-dish. 'Your grey's cast a shoe, Aunt Clara.'

She handed him his coffee. 'I know. Your brother says Jimmy can take him down to the village.'

'Bet you the old man keeps Jimmy dancing attendance on him all day,' said Conrad. 'I don't mind leading him down. I'm going that way. You'll have to arrange to fetch him, though.'

'If you're going to the village, you can drop that at the Dower House,' said Raymond, tossing a letter over to him.

Conrad pocketed it, and applied himself to his breakfast. He had reached the marmalade stage, and Raymond had lighted his pipe, before the elder twin put in an appearance.

Bartholomew came in with a cheerful greeting on his lips. There was a strong resemblance between him and Conrad, but he was the taller and the more stalwart of the two, and looked to be much the more good-humoured, which indeed he was. He had a ruddy, open countenance, a roving eye, and a singularly disarming grin. He gave his twin a friendly punch in the ribs as he passed him on his way to the sideboard, and remarked that it was a fine day. 'I say, Ray!' he added, looking over his shoulder. 'What's the matter with the Guv'nor?'

'I don't know. Probably nothing. He had a bad night.'

'Gosh, don't I know it!' said Bart. 'But what's got his goat this morning?'

'That fool Aubrey. Reuben says he's got into debt again.'

'Hell!' said Bart. 'That puts the lid on my chances of getting the Guv'nor to dip his hand in the coffer. Lend me a fiver, Ray, will you?'

'What do you want it for?'

'I owe most of it.'

'Well, go on owing it,' recommended Raymond. 'I'll see you farther before I let you owe it to me.'

'Blast you! Con?'

'Thanks for the compliment.'

Bart turned to Clara. 'Auntie? Come on, be a sport, Clara! I swear I'll pay it back!'

'I don't know where you think I could find five pounds,' she said cautiously. 'What with the vet's bill, and me needin' a new pair of boots, and—'

'You can't refuse your favourite nephew! Now, you know you haven't the heart to, Clara darling!' wheedled Bart.

'Get along with you! You're a bad boy,' Clara told him fondly. '*I* know where your money goes! You can't get round your old aunt.'

Bart grinned at her, apparently satisfied with the result of his coaxing. Clara went on grumbling about her poverty and his shamelessness; Conrad and Raymond began to argue about a capped hock, a discussion which soon attracted Clara's attention; and by the time Vivian Penhallow came into the dining-room the four members of the family already seated at the table were loudly disputing about the rival merits of gorse, an ordinary chain, or a strap-and-sinker to cure a stall-kicker.

Vivian Penhallow, Surrey-born, was a fish out of water amongst the Penhallows. She had met Eugéne in London, had fallen in love with him almost at first sight, and had married him in spite of the protests of her family. While not denying that his birth was better than their own, that his manners were engaging, and his person attractive, Mr. and Mrs. Arden had felt that they would have preferred for their daughter a husband with some more tangible means of supporting her than they could perceive in Eugéne's desultory but graceful essays and poems. Since they knew him to be the third, and not the eldest, son of his father they did not place so much dependence on Penhallow's providing for him as he appeared to. But Vivian was of age, and, besides being very much in love with Eugène, who was seven years her senior, she had declared herself to be sick to death of the monotony of her life, and had insisted that she hated conventional marriages, and would be happy to lead an impecunious existence with Eugène, rubbing shoulders with artists, writers, and other Bohemians. So she had married him, and would no doubt have made an excellent wife for him, had he seriously settled down to earn a living with his pen. But after drifting about the world for a few years, leading a hand-to-mouth existence which Vivian enjoyed far more than Eugène did, Eugène had suffered a serious illness, which was sufficiently protracted to exhaust his slender purse, and to induce him to look upon himself as a chronic invalid. He had naturally gone home to Trevellin to recuperate both his health and his finances, and Vivian had never since that date been able to prevail upon him to leave the shelter of the parental roof. Eugène declared himself to be quite unfit to cope with the cares of the world, and added piously that since his father was in a precarious state of health, he thought it his duty to remain at Trevellin. When Vivian represented to him her dislike of living as a guest in a household teeming with persons all more or less inimical to her, he patted her hand, talked vaguely of a roseate future when Penhallow should be dead and himself pecuniarily independent, and begged her to be patient. A tendency on her part to pursue the subject had the effect of sending him to bed with a nervous headache, and since Vivian believed in his ailments, and was passionately determined to guard him from every harsh wind that blew, she never again tried to persuade him to leave Trevellin.

Since she was not country-bred, knew nothing about horses, and cared less, she was regarded by her brothers-in-law with an almost completely indifference. Being themselves unable to imagine a more desirable abode than Trevellin, and having grown up to consider the tyranny of its master an everyday affair, they had none of them any conception of the canker of resentment which ate into Vivian's heart. They thought her a moody little thing, laughed at her tantrums, and mocked at her absorption in Eugène. Without meaning to be unkind, they teased her unmercifully, and were amused when she quarrelled with them. In their several ways, they were all of them imperceptive, and insensitive enough to make it impossible for them to understand why anyone should be hurt by their cheerful brutality.

Faith, their father's second wife, had been crushed by the Penhallows; Vivian remained a rebel, and had even developed a kind of protective crust which rendered her indifferent to their contempt of herself. She never pretended to take an interest in the subjects which absorbed them, and said now, as she walked into the room in time to hear Conrad ask Bart whether he remembered a herring-gutted chestnut Aubrey had picked up cheap some years ago: 'Oh, do shut up about horses! I want some fresh toast for Eugène.

Sybilla sent him up slices like doorsteps. I should have thought she must know by now that he likes very thin toast, not too much browned.'

She cast a frowning glance at the toast still remaining in the racks on the table, but Bart warded her off with one outstretched arm. 'No, you don't! Eugène is damned well not going to pinch our toast!'

She stalked over to the bell-rope, and tugged at it imperiously. 'That's cold, anyway. Sybilla must make some fresh for him. He's had one of his bad nights.'

Both twins at once made derisive noises, which had the effect of bringing a flush to her cheeks. Even Raymond's grim countenance relaxed into a faint smile. 'There's nothing the matter with Eugène, beyond a common lack of guts,' he said.

She said hotly: 'Because you've never known a day's illness in your life, you think no one else has a right to be delicate! Eugène suffers from the most terrible insomnia. If anything happens to upset him—'

A roar of laughter interrupted her. She shut her lips closely, her eyes flashing, and her nostrils a little distended.

'Now don't tease the gal!' said Clara. 'Eugène's got a bit of indigestion, I daresay. He was always the one of you with the touchy stomach, and if he likes to call it insomnia there's no harm in that that I know of.'

'I don't know how anyone can expect to get any rest in this house, with your father behaving as though there was no one but himself entitled to any consideration, and shouting for that disgusting old woman in the night loud enough to be heard a mile off!' cried Vivian furiously. 'You wouldn't like it if I said that there was nothing the matter with him, but nothing will ever make me believe that he couldn't be perfectly well if he wanted to be!'

'Who said there was anything the matter with him?' demanded Bart. 'He's all right!'

'Then why does he rouse the whole house four times during the night?'

'Why shouldn't he? His house, isn't it?'

'He's as selfish as the rest of you! He wouldn't care if Eugène got ill again!'

Raymond got up from the table, and collected his letters. 'You'd better tell him so,' he advised.

'I shall tell him so. *I'm* not afraid of him, whatever you may be!'

'Ah, you're a grand girl, surely!' Bart said, lounging over to where she stood, and putting an arm round her shoulders. 'Loo in, my dear, loo in! Give me a bitch-pack every time!'

She pushed him angrily away. 'Oh, shut up!'

At this moment Reuben came in. 'Was it one of you, ringing?' he asked severely.

'It was I,' said Vivian, in a cold voice. 'Mr. Eugène can't eat the toast Sybilla sent up to him. Please tell her to make some more, *thin,* and not burnt!'

'Sybilla's more likely to box his ears for him,' remarked Conrad, preparing to follow Raymond out of the room.

'I'll tell her, m'm,' said Reuben disapprovingly, 'but he always was a one for picking over his food, Master Eugène was, and if we was to start paying any attention to his fads there'd be no end to it. Many's the time Master's walloped him—'

'*Will* you kindly do as I tell you?' snapped Vivian.

'You're spoiling him,' said Reuben, shaking his head. 'I'd give him fresh toast! Master Eugène indeed!'

Vivian with difficulty restrained herself from returning an answer to this, and after giving one of his disparaging sniffs Reuben withdrew.

'Stop worryin' over the boy, my dear, and have your breakfast!' recommended Clara kindly. 'Here's your tea. Now sit down, do!'

Vivian took the cup-and-saucer, remarking that it was as black as ink, as usual, and sat down at the table. 'I don't know how you can bear that man's impertinence,' she added. 'He's familiar, and slovenly, and impossible!'

'Well, you see, he's been at Trevellin ever since he was a boy, and his father before him,' explained Clara mildly. 'He doesn't mean any harm, my dear, but it's not a bit of good expecting him to be respectful to the boys. When you think of the times he's chased them out of the larder with a stick, it's not likely he would be. But never you mind!'

Vivian sighed, and relapsed into silence. She knew that Clara, though sympathetic, would never take her part against her own family. The only ally she had in the house was Faith, and she despised Faith.

CHAPTER TWO

IT was Faith Penhallow's custom to breakfast in bed, a habit she had adopted not so much out of regard for her health, which was frail, but because she resented her sister-in-law's calm assumption of the foot of the table, behind the coffee-cups. She had no real wish to pour out tea and coffee for a numerous household, but like a great many weak people she was jealous of her position, and she considered that Clara's usurpation of her place at table made her appear ridiculous. She had several times hinted that it was the mistress of the house who ought to take the foot of the table, but while she was incapable of boldly stating a grievance Clara was equally incapable of recognizing a hint. So Clara, having taken the seat upon her first coming home to the house of her birth, kept it, and Faith, refusing to acknowledge defeat, never came downstairs until after breakfast.

It was twenty years since Faith Clay Formby, a romantic girl of nineteen, had been swept off her feet by Adam Penhallow, a great, handsome, dark man, twenty-two years her senior, and had left the shelter of her aunt's house to marry him. She had been very pretty in those days, with large blue eyes, the softest of fair curls, and the most appealing mouth in the world. Penhallow's age had lent him an added enchantment; he knew just how to handle a shy girl; and the knowledge that he was a rake did not in any way detract from his charm. She had been flattered, had pictured to herself the future, when she would be mistress of a Manor in Cornwall, moving gracefully about the beautiful old house, worshipped by her (reformed) husband, adored by her stepchildren. She had meant to be so kind to his motherless family. She was prepared to encounter enmity, but she would win them over by her patience, and her understanding, until, within a few months, they would all confide in her, and vie with one another in waiting on her.

At first glance, Trevellin had been all and more than she had imagined. Situated not many miles from Liskeard, the big Tudor house, with its Dutch gables, its tall chimney-stacks, its many mullioned windows, was large enough and lovely enough to draw a gasp from her. She saw it on a clear summer's evening, cool grey in a setting of pasture-land, with its walled gardens bright with flowers, its heavy oak doors standing hospitably open, and allowing her, before she set foot across the threshold, a glimpse of floors black with age, of a warped gateleg table, of a warming-pan hanging on a panelled wall. North of Trevellin, in the distance, the Moor rose up, grand in the mellow evening light. Penhallow had pointed out Rough Tor to her, and had asked her if she could smell the sharp peat-scent in the air. Oh, yes, it had quite come up to her expectations! Even the discovery that most of the bewildering number of rooms in the house were badly in need of decoration; that many of the carpets and curtains were shabby; that the most hideous examples of a Victorian cabinet-maker's art stood cheek by jowl with pieces of Chippendale, or Hepplewhite; that it would have needed an army of servants to keep so rambling a house in good order, failed to dash her spirits. She would change all that.

But she couldn't change Penhallow's children.

Whatever picture she had conjured up, faded, never again to be recalled, at that first sight of them, drawn up in formidable array for her inspection. It was forcibly borne in upon her that her eldest stepson was of the same age as herself, and a good deal more assured. Had Penhallow told her that Raymond was nineteen? She didn't know; probably he had, but she was the type of woman who found little difficulty in glossing over such information as did not fit into her dream-pictures, and she had forgotten it.

There they had stood, seven of them, ranging in age from nineteen to five: Raymond, scowling and taciturn; Ingram, taller than Raymond, and brusque in manner; Eugène, a slim edition of Ingram, but with a livelier countenance, and, even at fifteen, a quick, bitter tongue; Charmian, five years younger than Eugène, as black-browed as the rest of the family, and quite as hardy; Aubrey

looking, at eight, deceptively delicate; the twins, sturdy and un-
friendly little boys of five, resisting all her attempts to cuddle them,
and plunging after their great, rough brothers.

They showed no enmity towards their stepmother; they did
not appear to feel the smallest pang of resentment at her stepping
into their mother's shoes. It was some time before she had realized
that they had encountered, and taken for granted, too many of
Penhallow's mistresses to cavil at a second wife. She had had a
horrifying suspicion that they regarded her from the start as just
another of Penhallow's women, to be tolerated, but not admitted
into their charmed circle. She had pictured them as neglected: she
had never imagined that she would find them revelling in neglect,
impatient of caresses, tumbling in and out of scrapes, scandalizing
the countryside, dodging their father's wrath, never happy except
when astride plunging horses, the very sight of which terrified her.

She had never had a chance to mother them. You couldn't
mother a young man as old as yourself; or striplings who despised
the tenderer emotions; or a wild, wiry little girl who scornfully
rescued you from a field full of aggressive-looking bullocks, and
thought you a fool for calling a blood-mare 'a pretty horse'. As for
Aubrey, and the twins, their creature comforts were administered to
them by Martha, and whatever fondness they had for any female
was given to her. Her overtures had not been repulsed so much as
endured; she had never been able to flatter herself that her marriage
to Penhallow had made the smallest difference to any one of them.

She had tried, of course, to shape herself into the pattern Penhallow desired, even learning to ride under his ruthless instruction.
She endured hours of sick terror in the saddle, never achieving
mastery over any but the quietest old horse in the stable; and she
cried because Penhallow roared with laughter at her; and sometimes
wondered why she had married him, and still more why he had
married her. She had not enough perception to realize that Penhallow never weighed a question in his impatient mind, never sub-
ordinated his body's needs to the counsel of his brain, never
troubled to look to the future. He had wanted to possess Faith, and
since he could not get her without marrying her, he had married
her, leaving the future to providence, or perhaps not even caring for
it.

She had never understood him, probably never would; and
although his love-making frightened her sometimes, she was too
young and innocent to realize, until the knowledge was forcibly
borne in upon her, that she had married an incontinent man, who
would never be faithful to one woman all his life long. She was
shocked beyond measure, and bitterly hurt, when she first discovered that he had a mistress; and might have left him had she not
been pregnant at the time. Her son, Clay, was born, and after that
there could be no question of leaving Penhallow. But she did not
love Penhallow any more. She was sickly all through the months of
her pregnancy, nervous, and often peevish. Still living in a world

of make-believe, forming her expectations on what she had read between the covers of novels, she imagined that Penhallow would treat her with loving solicitude, waiting on her tenderly, begging her to take care of herself, and certainly pacing the floor in an agony of dread while her child was born. But Rachel Ottery, his first wife, had borne her children without fuss or complication, riding her high-bred horses to within a few weeks of her deliveries, and making no more ado over the whole business than she would have made over the extraction of a tooth. Penhallow, then, had little patience with an ailing, querulous wife, and no more sympathy with her nervous fears than he had with what he thought was her squeamishness. Faith, who believed that the more primitive functions of the human body were 'not nice', and could only be spoken of under a veil of euphemism; who called bitches lady-dogs; and who would certainly tell the twins that God had sent them a dear little baby brother felt her very soul shrink at Penhallow's crudities. On the day that he jovially informed the Vicar that his wife was breeding, she knew that she had married a brute; and on that day died her youth.

Clay was born at four o'clock on a damp autumn day. Scent was breast-high; Penhallow was hunting. He came into Faith's room at seven, mud-splashed, smelling of the stables and leather and spirits, singing out: 'Well, my girl, well? How are you feeling now? Clever, eh? Where's the young Penhallow? Let's have a look at the little rascal!'

But he had not thought much of Clay, a wizened scrap, tucked up in a cradle all hung with muslin and blue ribbons. 'Damme if ever I saw such a puny little rat!' he said, accustomed to Rachel's bouncing, lusty babies. 'Not much Penhallow about him!'

Perhaps because he saw so little of the Penhallow in this youngest son he permitted Faith to give him her own name, Clay. The child was inclined to be weakly, a fault ascribed by Penhallow to Faith's cosseting of herself when she was bearing him. He was a tow-headed baby, darkening gradually to an indeterminate brown, and with his mother's colouring he inherited her timid disposition. Nothing terrified him as much as the sound of his father's voice upraised either in wrath, or in boisterous joviality; he would burst into tears if startled; he early developed a habit of sheltering behind his mother; and was continually complaining to her that his half-brothers had been unkind to him. In defence of him, Faith could find the courage to fight. She dared her stepsons to lay a finger on her darling, and was so sure that their rough ways must harm him that she instilled into his head a dread of them which they had in actual fact done little to deserve. The twins certainly bullied him, but the elder Penhallows, who would have good-naturedly taught him to ride, and to fish, and to shoot, and to defend himself with his fists, had he shown the least spark of spirit, shrugged their shoulders, and generally ignored him. Fortunately for himself, he was intelligent, and managed to win a scholarship to a public school of good standing. Penhallow, who had allowed the younger sons of his first marriage to be educated locally, in the most haphazard fashion, said that as he didn't seem to be good for much else, he might as well get some solid book-learning into his head, and raised no objection to his taking up the scholarship. Later, he was to consent to his going on to Cambridge, where he was at present. For this, Faith had Raymond to thank. 'He's no damned good to anyone, and we don't want him here, eating his head off,' Raymond had said bluntly. Penhallow had seen the force of this argument. Clay was the only one of his sons whom he did not wish to keep at home. He said the sight of the boy's pasty face and girlish ways turned his stomach.

The boy's colouring had from the outset been a source of mortification to him. The Penhallows, with their usual forthrightness, animadverted frequently on the incongruity of light hair in a Penhallow; and casual visitors were all too apt to comment artlessly on it, saying that it was strange to meet a fair member of that family. Faith, resenting these remarks as much as Clay, wondered why the Penhallow in him should be expected to predominate, and would say in an aggrieved tone that as the first Mrs. Penhallow had been as dark as Penhallow himself it was not surprising that his elder sons should be all as dark as was apparently desired.

Faith used to stare at the portrait of Rachel Penhallow, which hung in the hall, trying to imagine what kind of a woman she had been, how she had managed to hold her own against Penhallow, or if she had not. She thought that she had : the painted face was strong, even arrogant, with hard challenging eyes, and a full underlip thrusting up against the upper. Faith felt that she would have disliked Rachel, perhaps have been afraid of her; and sometimes, in one of her morbidly fanciful moods, she would take the notion into her head that the painted eyes mocked her. She would have liked to have thought that Rachel's spirit brooded darkly over the house, for she was superstitious by inclination, but it was impossible to suppose that any other spirit than Penhallow's reigned at Trevellin. So curious was she about her predecessor that during the early years of her marriage, she was for ever trying to make those who had known Rachel intimately talk of her, even cultivating a friendship with Delia Ottery, who was Rachel's younger sister, and who lived with her brother Phineas in a square grey house on the outskirts of Bodmin. But the inconsequent stories Delia told of Rachel did not help her to form a composite picture, because it was plain that Delia, admiring her sister, had yet had no real understanding of her. She knew what Rachel did, but not what Rachel was. She had an unspeculative mind, and was, besides, stupid and very shy. She had developed into the old maid of fiction : there could be nothing in common between her and Faith; and the friendship languished. It had lasted for long enough to provide the young Penhallows with food for ribaldry, Delia having always been regarded by them as the Family Eccentric.

It would have been better for Faith could she but have found a friend, but this she was unable to do, being convinced that she could have nothing in common with her neighbours. They were country-bred, and she was never able to interest herself in country pursuits, always preferring to dwell upon the amenities of the life she had abandoned when she married Penhallow than to adapt herself to circumstances. Her relations with the matrons of the district never extended beyond acquaintanceship. She blamed the inelasticity of their minds: it was not given to her to understand that a craving for sympathy was no foundation for friendship.

This craving had grown with the years; because of it she had taken Loveday Trewithian out of the kitchen, and had promoted her to be her personal maid, and, later, her confidante. Loveday was gentle, and patient. She would listen to Faith's complainings, and agree that she was hardly used; and she invested her services with a tender cajolery immensely gratifying to a woman who all her life long had passionately desired to be cosseted, and considered.

'Oh, Loveday!' Faith said, in her fretful voice, when Loveday came into her bedroom. 'Has anything happened?'

Beside the fair, faded woman in bed, with the thin hands and dilating blue eyes, Loveday Trewithian seemed to glow with life and vigour. She lifted the breakfast-tray from her mistress's knees, and smiled down at her warmly. 'It's nothing,' she said soothingly.

'I thought I heard Mr. Penhallow shouting,' Faith said falteringly.

'Yes, sure,' Loveday said. 'My uncle Reuben's saying it's Mr. Aubrey that's made him angry. You don't need to upset yourself, ma'am.'

Faith relaxed on to her pillows with a little sigh, her mind relieved of its most pressing anxiety, that Clay, whose career at Cambridge was not fulfilling his early promise, might have done something to enrage his father. She watched Loveday set the tray down near the door, and begin to move about the room, laying out what clothes she thought Faith would wear. Her mind turned to a lesser care; she said: 'The bath water was tepid again this morning. I do think Sybilla might pay a little attention to it.'

'I'll speak to her for you, ma'am, never fear! They say it's the system that's wrong.'

'Everything's out-of-date or out-of-order in this house!' Faith said.

'It isn't fit for a delicate lady like you, ma'am, to have to live where there's so little comfort,' murmured Loveday. 'It's wonderful the way you put up with it, surely.'

'Nobody cares whether it's fit for me or not,' Faith said. 'I'm used to that. Trevellin never agreed with me. I never feel well here, and *you* know how badly I sleep. I had to take my drops last night, and even then I had a wretched night.'

'It's your nerves, and no wonder!' Loveday said. 'You ought to get away for a change, ma'am, if I may say so. This is no place for you.'

24

'I wish I could go away, and never come back!' Faith said, half to herself.

A knock sounded on the door, and before she could reply to it Vivian had walked in. Loveday set the brushes straight on the dressing-table, picked up the breakfast-tray, and went away. Faith saw from the crease between Vivian's brows that she was in one of her moods, and at once said in a failing voice that she had passed a miserable night, and had a splitting headache.

'I'm not surprised at all,' responded Vivian. 'Your precious husband saw to it we should all have thoroughly disturbed nights.'

'Oh! I didn't know,' Faith said nervously. 'Was he awake in the night?'

'Was he! You're lucky: you don't sleep on his side of the house When he wasn't pealing his bell, he was shouting for Martha. Disgusting old hag!' Vivian took a cigarette from a battered packet in the pocket of her tweed jacket, and lit it. 'Is it true that she was one of his mistresses?' she asked casually. 'Eugène says she was.'

Faith flushed scarlet, and sat up in bed. 'That's just the sort of think Eugène would say!' she said angrily. 'And I should have thought you would have had more decent feeling than to have repeated it to *me*!'

'Oh, sorry!' Vivian answered. 'Only Penhallow's affairs are always so openly talked about that I didn't think you'd mind. It's no use pretending you don't know anything about them, Faith, because of course you do. And for God's sake don't pretend that you mind, because I know darned well you don't.'

'Well, I do mind!' said Faith. 'You needn't think that because I say nothing I like having that old woman in my house, doing all the sort of things for Adam which any decent man would have had a valet for! But I think it's disgraceful of Eugène to go about saying she used to be Adam's mistress! Even if it were true, such things are better not spoken of.'

'I don't know,' Vivian said reflectively. 'Practically the only thing I like about the Penhallows – except Eugène, of course – is their way of having everything aboveboard and freely spoken of. I mean, there's nothing furtive about them.'

'I was brought up to consider that certain things were better left unsaid!' said Faith primly.

'So was I, and damned dull it was. If you wouldn't pretend so much—'

'You seem to forget that I'm Eugène's stepmother,' said Faith, snatching at the rags of her dignity.

'Oh, don't be silly! You're not quite eleven years older than I am, and I know perfectly well that you loathe this place as much as I do. But I do think you might do something to make it more possible! After all, you're Penhallow's wife! But just look at the servants, for a start! Sybilla's just been extremely insolent to Eugène, and as for Reuben, and that loathsome creature, Jimmy—'

'It's no use complaining to me,' interrupted Faith. 'I can't do anything about it. And Sybilla's a good cook. I should like to know who else would stay in a place like this, or cook for a positive army of people on a stove that was out of date twenty years ago! I'm only thankful she and Reuben do stay.'

'And then there's that maid of yours,' Vivian continued, disregarding. 'You'll have to get rid of her, Faith.'

'Get rid of Loveday! I'll do no such thing! She's the one person in the house who considers me!'

'Yes, I know, but Aunt Clara always says she's a double-faced girl.'

'I don't want to listen to what Clara says! She's a spiteful old woman, and just because I'm fond of Loveday—'

'No, it isn't that. They all say the same. Bart's at his old tricks again. It's absolutely fatal to employ good-looking servants in this house. I should have thought you must have known that.'

'Loveday Trewithian is a thoroughly nice girl, and I won't hear a word against her!'

'Eugène says she means to marry Bart.'

Faith's blue eyes started a little. She stammered: 'I don't believe it! Bart wouldn't—'

'I know he's never wanted to marry any of his other bits of stuff,' said Vivian, 'but honestly, Faith, he does seem to have gone in off the deep end this time. Conrad's livid with jealousy. You must have noticed it! Eugène says—'

'I don't want to hear what Eugène says! He always was a mischief-maker, and I don't believe one word of this!'

Any criticism of Eugène at once alienated Vivian. She put out her cigarette in the grate, and got up, saying coldly: 'You can believe what you like, but if you've a grain of sense you'll get rid of the girl. I don't know if Bart means to marry her or not, and I care less, but if it's true, and Penhallow gets to hear of it, you'll wish you'd paid attention to me, that's all.'

'I don't believe a word of it!' Faith repeated, on the edge of tears.

Vivian opened the door, remarking over her shoulder: 'You never believe anything you don't want to believe. I've no patience with people like you.'

After she had gone, Faith lay for quite half an hour thinking how brutal Vivian had been, and how rude, and how no one cared for her nerves, or hesitated to upset her when she had had a bad night. It was characteristic of her that she did not let her mind dwell on the unwelcome tidings which Vivian had imparted. If they were true, there would be the sort of trouble she dreaded; but she did not want to dismiss Loveday, and so she refused even to contemplate the possibility of their being true.

It was past ten o'clock when Faith at last got up and began to dress. Fortunately for herself, and indeed for the rest of the household, it was Sybilla Lanner who undertook the housekeeping at Trevellin. She had done so from the time of Rachel's death. An attempt by Faith, in the early days of her marriage, to take the reins

26

into her own hands had failed, not because Sybilla opposed it, or showed the slightest jealousy of the new Mrs. Penhallow, but because Faith had no idea how to cater for a large family, and was, besides, the kind of woman who could never remember people's individual tastes. Easy-going, slovenly, wasteful Sybilla, never planning ahead, always sending one of the maids running to the village to buy another couple of loaves of bread or a tin of baking-powder, yet never forgot that Mr. Raymond would not touch treacle, or that Mr. Conrad liked his eggs friend on both sides, or that the Master would not eat a pasty unless scalded cream were served with it, in the old-fashioned way. On the only two occasions that Faith's aunt, who had brought her up, visited her at Trevellin, she had exclaimed against Sybilla's extravagance, and had tried to introduce her to more methodical ways. She had failed. Sybilla, soft-spoken like all her race, agreed with every word she said, and continued to rule the kitchen exactly as she had ruled it for years.

By the time Faith came out of her bedroom it was eleven o'clock, and the family had dispersed. The maids were still making beds, emptying slops, and raising a dust with long-handled brooms; for since no one bothered to oversee their work they went about it in a cheerful, leisurely fashion, with a good deal of chatter, and singing, and no attention paid to the clock. Faith remarked, encountering a stout girl who had just come out of Raymond's room with a dustpan-and-brush in her hand, that the rooms ought to have been finished an hour ago. The girl agreed with her, smiling good-humouredly, and adding that they did seem to be a bit behindhand today. They were always behindhand. Faith passed on, down the wide, oaken stair, feeling irritated, knowing that she ought to look after the maids better, but telling herself that she had neither the health nor the energy to train raw country girls.

The stairs led down to the central hall, a low-pitched, irregularly-shaped space with several passages leading from it, and a number of doors. Rachel's portrait hung over the great stone fireplace, facing the staircase; a gateleg table, with a bowl of flowers on it, stood in the middle of the hall; there were several Jacobean chairs, with tall carved backs, and worn seats; a faded Persian rug; a large jar containing peacocks' feathers, which stood in one corner; an ancient oak coffer; a coal-scuttle of tarnished copper; two saddle-back armchairs; Chippendale what-not, its several tiers piled with old newspapers, magazines, garden-scissors, balls of string, and other such oddments; and a kneehole-desk, of hideous design, under one of the windows which flanked the open front door. Besides Rachel's portrait, the walls bore several landscapes, in heavy gilt frames; a collection of mounted masks and pads; four stags' heads; two warming-pans; a glass case enclosing a stuffed otter; and a fumed oak wall-fixture, from whose hooks depended a number of hunting-crops and dog-whips.

The season was late spring, and the air which stole in through the open Gothic door was sharp, and made Faith shiver. She crossed the hall to the morning-room, a pleasantly shabby apartment which looked out on to a tangle of shrubbery and flower-beds. There was no one in the room, or in the Yellow drawing-room which led out of it. She guessed that her sister-in-law was either gardening amongst the ferns which were her obsession, or driving herself along the hollow lanes in her high dogcart, behind the rawboned horse which Faith always thought so like her. She looked about for the morning's paper, and, not finding it, left the room, and went to look in the dining-room for it. She was returning with it in her hand when Reuben came into the hall from the broad passage which led to the western end of the house, and delivered an unwelcome message.

'Master wants to see you, m'm.'

'Oh! Yes, of course. I was just going,' she said. She always hoped that the servants were not aware of her dread of Penhallow, who seemed to her so much more monstrous now that he was confined nearly always to his bed. 'Loveday tells me that he isn't so well this morning,' she added.

'I knew how it would be when he was so set on having Sybilla bake him a starry-gaze pie,' responded Reuben gloomily. 'It never did agree with him.'

Faith barely repressed a shudder. Penhallow had suddenly taken it into his head, on the previous day, to demand a dish rarely seen now in Cornwall. He had wanted to know why starry-gaze pies were never served at Trevellin, had recalled those made under his grandmother's auspices, had reviled the modern generation for turning away from the customs of their fathers, and had ended by sending for Sybilla, and commanding her to make him a starry-gaze pie for his dinner. By God, they should all of them have starry-gaze pie for dinner, and know what good Cornish food could be like! He had got up from his huge bed, and had had himself wheeled into the dining-room to preside over this memorable meal, and had had the pie set down before him, so that he could serve it with his own hands. Since eight persons sat down to dinner, the pie was of generous proportions, a great mound of pastry through which protruded the heads of a number of pilchards. Faith had felt sick, but she had forced herself to eat some of it, lacking the moral courage which made Vivian reject it with loathing.

She thought privately that a bout of indigestion served her husband right; and hoped that it might prevent his again demanding this objectionable dish.

As though he read this thought, Reuben said: 'But no one won't get him to believe it was the pie, tell him till Doomsday, set in his ways, that's what he is.'

It seemed to her beneath her dignity to discuss her husband with his manservant, so she returned no answer, but laid the newspaper down on the table, and moved towards the corridor which ran along the back of the western end of the house.

A series of small windows, set deep in the stone wall, lit the corridor, which led past a winding staircase to a smaller hall with a door leading out of the back of the house into Clara's fern-garden. Beyond this, double doors gave on to a room which seemed to have been designed as a ballroom, and which had been for several years Penhallow's bedroom.

Faith hesitated for a moment, with her hand on the door, and her head slightly bent to catch any sound of voices within the room. She could hear nothing, and after drawing in her breath, rather in the manner of a diver about to plunge into deep waters, she turned the handle, and went in.

CHAPTER THREE

THE room into which Faith Penhallow stepped occupied the whole of the floor space at the western end of the house, and had windows at each end, those at the front looking out on to the sweep of the avenue leading down to the lodge-gates, and the lawn and fields beyond; and those at the back overlooking an enclosed garden, surrounded on three sides by a grey, creeper-hung wall. This wing of the house had been added to the original structure in the seventeenth century; Penhallow's room was wainscoted from floor to ceiling, and contained, besides some magnificent mouldings, a superb fireplace on the wall between the double doors through which Faith had come, and another, single door leading into a dressing-room at the front of the house. This fireplace was most richly carved, its lofty mantelpiece upheld, on either side of the big square cavity where a log-fire burned on a huge pile of wood-ash, by caryatids. The room was higher-pitched than the rooms in the main part of the house, and had a very fine plaster ceiling, somewhat damaged in places by cracks, and blackened by smoke, which would occasionally puff out from the hearth, when the wind was in the wrong quarter. The heavy wainscoting made the room dark, in spite of the windows at each end, but the first impression of anyone entering it was of colour, so varied and unexpected as to make the uninitiated blink.

The room was crammed with furniture, and ornaments jostled one another on the mantelpiece, on the tops of several chests, over several small tables which had been fitted into any vacant space that offered. These, like the incredible assortment of furniture, seemed to have been chosen without regard to period or congruity, which was indeed the case, Penhallow having crammed into the room every piece that took his fancy. Thus, a red lacquer cabinet, with an ivory figure of the god Ho-Ti on the top of it, stood between the two windows at one end of the room, and two repulsive plant-holders fashioned of bamboo and each containing some half-a-dozen pots of tropical greenery, stood under the corresponding windows at the other end of the room. Flanking the fireplace, were two enormous malachite vases, on consoles, which had been wrested from the Yellow drawing-room. In one corner, stood a marble-topped washstand of red mahogany, imperfectly hidden by a cheap Japanese screen which showed a covey of golden birds flying on a black ground. Close to this, on the wall opposite to the fireplace, was a marquetry chest, mellow with age, rubbing shoulders with a delicate table of yellow satinwood, squeezed between it and the bed. Beyond the bed, a walnut tallboy confronted a round table covered with a crimson chenille cloth, and a Carolinian day-bed of particularly graceful design, whose frayed cane seat and back were fitted with squabs of faded wine-red velvet. Penhallow's wheel-chair stood in the corner, and a long refectory table, piled with books, papers, decanters, medicine-bottles, and a canvas-bag from which several dog-biscuits had spilled, occupied most of the space behind the front windows. A mahogany corner-cupboard hung beside the door into the dressing-room; several armchairs of varied design and colour were scattered about the room, together with a pair of rush-seated ladder-back chairs; an early Chippendale stool, with cabriole legs and claw-and-ball feet; an angular seat of Gothic design and unsurpassed discomfort; and a large chesterfield, which was drawn across the foot of the bed. There were no pictures on the walls, but a convex mirror of Queen Anne date, set in a gilded frame, hung over the mantelpiece, and there were a number of candle-sconces round the room. On the mantelpiece, a gilt time-piece with an enamelled face, and supported by nymphs and cherubim, stood under a glass dome, and was flanked by a pair of Rockingham pheasants, one or two pieces belonging to an old chess-set, and two groups of bronze horses. The corner by the double doors was taken up by a grandfather clock of Chippendale-chinois; and, placed wherever space could be found for them, were some small, spindle-legged tables, covered with punch-spoons, snuff-boxes, patch-boxes, Bristol paper-weights; and Dresden figures.

But it was not the medley of ornaments, the crowded furniture, or the juxtaposition of wine-red and crimson and the hot scarlet of Chinese lacquer which instantly claimed and held the visitor's attention. Colour rioted in the carpet which almost covered the floor, grass-green curtains swore at chairs upholstered in peacock-blue, but they all faded into neutrality beside the blaze of colour thrown over Penhallow's bed in the form of a patchwork quilt sewn in multi-coloured hexagons of satin, velvet, and brocade.

The bed itself dominated the room. It might have been supposed that so massive and antiquated a structure had been in the family for generations: in actual fact Penhallow had bought it at a sale some years previously. It was an enormous four-poster of painted wood, hung about with curtains of mulberry velvet, much rubbed and faded with age, with a ceiling painted with a design of cupids and rose-garlands, and an intricate arrangement of cup-boards and drawers set in the tall headpiece. It stood uncomfortably high, and was wide enough to have accommodated four people without undue crowding. In the middle of it, banked up by a collection of pillows and cushions, and wearing an ancient dressing-gown over his pyjamas, lay Penhallow, a mountainous ruin of a man, with a hawk-nose jutting between bloated cheeks; fierce, malicious eyes staring beneath brows that were still jet-black and bushy; and an arrogant, intemperate mouth. His hair was grizzled, and it could be seen that he had developed a huge paunch. Around him, spread over the splendour of the quilt, were a variety of books, periodicals, cigar-cases, match-boxes, ledgers, letters, and a dish piled with fruit. At the foot of the bed, panting slightly, lay an aged and rather smelly cocker spaniel, as obese as her master. It was her amiable custom to growl at anyone entering Penhallow's room, and she made no exception in Faith's favour.

'Good bitch!' said Penhallow approvingly.

Faith shut the door behind her, and moved towards an arm-chair which stood at some distance from the fire. The room was uncomfortably warm, the pile of wood-ash in the hearth glowing red under a couple of smouldering logs. Except during the very few weeks in the year when Penhallow allowed his fire to go out, the ash was never removed. It made the dusting of his bedroom one of the labours of Hercules, but that was a consideration which naturally did not weigh with him.

'Good morning, Adam,' Faith said, her anxious eyes trying to read his face. 'I'm so sorry you had a bad night. I didn't sleep at all well myself.'

She knew from the curl of his full lips, and the gleam in his eyes, that he was in one of his bad moods. He was always like that after a disturbed night. She guessed that he had sent for her to make himself unpleasant, and felt her heart begin to thump against her ribs.

'Didn't sleep well, didn't you?' he said jeeringly. 'What have you got to keep you awake? You weren't worrying your empty head over me, at all events. Loving wife, aren't you?'

'I didn't know you were awake. Of course I would have come down if I'd known you wanted me.'

He gave a bark of laughter. 'A lot of use you'd have been! By God, I don't know how I came to tie myself up to such a poor creature!'

She was silent, her colour fluctuating nervously. He observed this sign of agitation with open satisfaction. 'Lily-livered, that's what you are,' he said. 'You've got no spirit. Eugène's little cat of a wife's worth a dozen of you.'

She said imploringly: 'I can't bear quarrelling, Adam.'

'My first wife would have cut my face open with her riding-whip for half of what you take lying down,' he taunted her.

She was aware that he would like her the better for storming at him; she was unable to do it: she would never, all her life long, overcome her sick dread of being shouted at by a loud, angry voice. With her genius for saying the wrong thing, she faltered: 'I'm different, Adam.'

He burst out laughing in good earnest at that, throwing his head back, so that his laughter seemed to reverberate from the painted ceiling of his preposterous bed. To Faith's ears, it held a note of savage gloating. She closed her thin hands on the arms of her chair, and sat tense, flashing. 'Different!' he ejaculated. 'By God, you are! Look at Rachel's brats, and at that whelp of yours!'

Her flush died, leaving her cheeks very pale. She looked anxiously at him. She thought that of course she should have known that he would attack Clay.

He shifted his bulk in bed, so that he was able to look more directly at her. 'Well,' he said abruptly, 'I can't discover that that precious son of yours is doing any good up at Cambridge, or likely to.'

It was true that Clay's University career had been, so far, disappointing, but he had not, to her knowledge, disgraced himself in any way, and she could hardly suppose that scholastic attainments would have interested his father. She said: 'I don't know what you mean. I'm sure—'

'I mean it's a waste of money keeping him there,' Penhallow interrupted. 'He's wasting his time, that's what he's doing!'

'I don't know why you should say so, Adam. It isn't as though he'd *done* anything—'

'Damme, woman, don't be such a fool!' he exploded, making her start. 'I know he hasn't done anything! That's what I'm saying! He doesn't row, he doesn't play a game, he doesn't want to join the Drag, he isn't even man enough to get into mischief. He's a namby-pamby young good-for-nothing, and I'll be damned if I'll keep him eating his head off there for the pleasure of seeing him come home a couple of years on with a Pass degree!'

'I'm sure I don't know why you should mind his not doing as well as – as we'd expected,' Faith said, plucking up courage in defence of her darling. 'You always said book-learning didn't run in your family.' It occurred to her that his attack on Clay was more than usually unjust. Roused to indignation, she said, 'I should like to know what Eugène did at Oxford, or Aubrey either, for that matter! It's simply because it's Clay that you go on like this!'

A sardonic chuckle shook him. 'You'd like to know, would you? They're a couple of young scoundrels, both of 'em, but neither of 'em spent three years at Oxford without leaving their marks, I can tell you that!' He stabbed a thick finger at her. 'But it didn't do them a bit of good! That's what I'm saying. They learned a lot of damned nonsense there, and I was a fool to send 'em. My other boys are worth a dozen of that pair. What use is Eugène, I should like to know, writing for a pack of half-baked newspapers, and keeping his feet dry in case he should catch a cold? As for young Aubrey, if I'd kept him at home, and set him to work under Ray, I'd have done better by him! I've had trouble enough with Bart and Con, but, by God, give me a couple of lusty young rogues who take their pleasures in the way they were meant to, rather than that covey of unhealthy intellectuals Aubrey runs with!'

'It isn't fair to blame Oxford for what Aubrey does,' Faith expostulated feebly. 'Besides, Clay isn't in the least like that. Clay's a very good boy, and I'm sure—' She broke off, for she saw by his face that she had said the wrong thing again.

'Clay's nothing,' he said shortly. 'No guts, no spunk, not a bit of devil in him! Takes after you, my dear.'

She turned away her eyes from the derisive smile in his. A black cat with a nocked ear, which had been curled up in a chair by the fire, woke, and stretched, and began to perform an extensive toilet.

Penhallow selected an apple from the dish of fruit on the bed, and took a large bite out of it. 'I'm going to put him to work with Cliff,' he said casually.

She looked up quickly. 'With Clifford,' she repeated. '*Clay?*'

'That's right,' agreed Penhallow, chewing his apple.

'You can't do that!' she exclaimed.

'What's to stop me?' inquired Penhallow almost amiably.

'But, Adam, why? What has he done? It isn't fair!'

'He hasn't done anything. That's why I'll be damned if I'll keep him eating his head off at college. You had a notion he was cut out for a scholar. *I'd* no objection. The hell of a lot of scholarship he's shown! All right! if he ain't going to be a scholar what's the sense in leaving him there? A country solicitor's about all he's fit to be, and that's what he shall be. Cliff's willing to take him.'

She stammered: 'He isn't cut out for it! He'd hate it! He wants to write!'

'Wants to write, does he? So that's his idea! Well, you can tell him to get rid of it! There are two of my spawn playing at that game already, and there isn't going to be a third. He'll study law with Cliff.' He spat out a pip, and added: 'He can live here, and Ray can see what he can do towards licking him into some kind of shape.'

'Oh no!' she cried out involuntarily. 'He'd hate it! He doesn't care for the country. He's much happier in town. This place doesn't agree with him any more than it agrees with me.'

He heaved himself up in bed, his countenance alarmingly suffused with colour. 'So that's the latest, is it? He doesn't care for Trevellin! By God, if you weren't such a spiritless little fool I should wonder if you'd played me false, my girl! Or is this a notion out of your own head? Do you tell me that a son of mine is going to tell me to my face that he doesn't care for his birthplace?'

She reflected that nothing was more unlikely. Passing her tongue between her lips, she said: 'You forget that he's my son as well as yours, Adam.'

'I don't forget he's your son,' he interrupted brutally. 'The only doubt I have is whether he's mine.'

The insult left her unmoved; she scarcely attended to it. With one of her inept attempts to divert him, she said: 'You aren't feeling well this morning. We can discuss it another time.'

He pitched the core of his apple into the fire, and licked his fingers before answering her. 'There's nothing to discuss. I've had it out with Cliff. It's all setttled.'

'You shan't do it!' she cried. 'I won't let you, I won't! Clay at least shan't be tied to this hateful place as I am! It isn't fair! You're only doing it to hurt me! You're cruel, Adam, cruel!'

'That's a good one!' he exclaimed. 'Why, you bloodless little idiot, a lad with an ounce of spirit in him would thank me for it! I'm giving him a damned good roof over his head, and the best life a man could ask! He can hunt, shoot, fish—'

'He doesn't care about that kind of thing!' she said, betrayed into another of her disastrous admissions.

His anger, which had so far been smouldering, burst into flame. 'God damn the pair of you!' he thundered. 'He doesn't care for that sort of thing! He doesn't care for that sort of thing! And you sit there boasting of it! He'd rather live in town! Then let him do it! Let him show me what he's made of! Let him set up for himself in London, and astonish us all with this precious writing of his! Let him send me to the devil, and cut loose! I'm agreeable!' He beat with one hand upon the patchwork quilt, upsetting the dish of fruit. An orange rolled off the bed, and a little way across the floor, and lay, a splash of crude colour, in the middle of the carpet. He looked savagely at Faith, out of narrowed, mocking eyes. 'Can you see him doing it, this fine son of yours? Can you, whey-face?'

'How can he get away, when you know very well he has no money? Besides, he isn't of age. He—'

'That wouldn't stop him, if he were worth his salt! Not of age! He's nineteen, isn't he? When Bart was his age he was the most bruising rider to hounds in two counties, besides being the handiest young ruffian with his fists you'd meet in a month of Sundays! Hell and the devil, he was a *man*, d'ye hear me? If I'd thrown him out on his arse, he could have got his living with his hands! And he would have! Why, he was younger than your brat when he fathered a child on to Polperrow's bitch of a daughter!'

'I believe you would like Clay better if he'd been as wild and shameless as Bart and Conrad!' she cried in a trembling voice.

'I should,' he replied grimly.

She began to cry, a suggestion of hysteria in her convulsive sobs. 'I wish I were dead! I wish I were dead!'

'Wish I were dead, more likely!' he said sardonically. 'But I'm not, my loving wife! Damn you, stop snivelling!'

She cowered in the depths of the chair, hiding her face in her hands, her sobs growing more uncontrolled. 'I don't believe you ever loved me! You'd like to break my heart! You're tyrannical, and cruel! You only want to hurt people!'

'Will you stop it?' he shouted, groping for the worsted bell-pull, and tugging it furiously. 'Slap my face, if you like! Stick a knife between my ribs, if you've the courage, but don't cringe there snivelling at me! You and your son! You and your son!'

She made a desperate effort to control herself, but she was a woman to whom tears came easily, and she found it hard to check them. She was still gulping, and dabbing at her eyes when Martha entered the room in answer to the bell's summons. The promptitude with which she appeared suggested that she had in all probability been within earshot of the room for some time.

Penhallow, who had not ceased to tug at the crimson bell-pull, released it, and sank back on to the bank of pillows, panting. 'Take that damned fool of a woman away!' he ordered. 'Keep her out of my sight, or I'll do her an injury!'

'Well, it was you sent for her,' Martha pointed out, unmoved by his rage. 'Give over, my dear, now do! You'd better go away, missus, or we'll have un bursting a blood-vessel. Such doings!'

At Martha's entrance, Faith had sprung up out of her chair, making a desperate attempt to check her tears. Penhallow's words had brought a wave of shamed colour to her cheeks; she gave an outraged moan, and fled from the room, almost colliding in the passage with Vivian. She ran past her, averting her face. Vivian made no movement to stop her, but walked on, into Penhallow's room, a purposeful scowl on her brow. Encountering Martha, she said curtly: 'I want to talk to Mr. Penhallow. Clear out, will you?'

This rude interruption, instead of adding to Penhallow's fury, seemed to please him. Some of the high colour in his face receded; he gave a bark of laughter, and demanded: 'What do you want, hell-cat?'

'I'll tell you when Martha's gone,' she replied, standing squarely in the middle of the room, with her back to the fire, and her hands dug into the pockets of her tweed jacket.

'Who the devil do you think you are, giving your orders in my room?' he asked roughly.

She pushed her underlip out a little in an aggressive way which tickled him. 'I shan't go till I've said what I've come to say. I'm not afraid of you. You won't make *me* cry.'

'Good lass!' he approved. 'Damme, if you'd the sense to know a blood-horse from a half-bred hack I'd be proud of you, so I would! Take yourself off, Martha. God's teeth, what are you standing there for like a fool? Get out!'

'And don't stand listening at the door either!' said Vivian, with a forthrightness to match Penhallow's own.

Martha gave a chuckle. 'Aw, my dear, it's a wonder, surely, Master Eugène chose you for his wife! You'll eat us all up yet you're that fierce,' she remarked, without rancour, and took herself off with her shuffling step, and shut the doors behind her.

The spaniel, which had greeted Vivian with her usual growl, now jumped down from the bed, lumbered over to the fire, and cast herself down before it, panting. The cat paused in its ablutions to regard her fixedly for a few moments, after which it resumed its toilet.

Penhallow flung one or two of the ledgers and papers which littered the bed on to the chenille-covered table beside him, and said: 'Pour me out a drink. Have one yourself.'

'I don't drink at this hour of the morning,' replied Vivian. 'You oughtn't to either, if you've really got dropsy.'

'Blast your impudence!' he said cheerfully. 'What's it to you, I should like to know? You'd be glad enough to see me underground, I'll bet my last shilling!'

She shrugged. 'It isn't anything to do with me, except that it'll make your gout worse, and that means that we shall all suffer. What do you want?'

'I'll take a glass of claret. Claret never hurt any man yet. My old grandfather never touched anything else, the last years of his life, and he lived to be eighty-five. You'll find the bottle in the corner-cupboard. Bring it over here where I can lay my hand on it.'

She brought him the bottle, and a glass, and set both down on the table, retiring again to her stance before the fire. Penhallow heaved himself round in bed to reach the bottle, cursing her in a genial way for not pouring the wine out for him, and filled his glass. He drank it off, refilled the glass, and disposed himself more comfortably against his pillows. 'Now, what's the matter with you, eh? Do you think I haven't had my fill of silly women this day?'

'You're nothing but a bully,' she remarked, looking scornfully at him. 'Why don't you take it out of someone more capable of defending herself than Faith?'

'Daresay I will,' he retorted. 'You, if you annoy me. You're as discontented as she is. Spoilt, that's what's the matter with you! Spoilt!'

'Spoilt! In this house? No one is considered here but you, and well you know it! That's what I've come to talk about. I can't and I won't stand it any longer. This isn't my home, and never will be. I want to go.'

'What's stopping you?' he inquired amiably.

'You are!' she flung back at him. 'You know very well nothing would make me leave Eugène!'

He lay sipping his wine, and grinning. 'He's his own master, ain't he? Why don't you get him to take you away if you don't like it here?'

She felt her control over her too-quick temper slipping, and exerted herself to retain it. 'Eugène isn't strong enough to earn his own living without help,' she said. 'He's never got over that illness.'

'You mean he's always fancyin' himself sick,' he jibed. 'I know Eugène! A lazy young devil he always was and always will be! For a sensible girl, you've made a mess of handling him, my dear. If you didn't want to stay here, you shouldn't have let him come down here in the first place.'

'I never guessed he would want to stay on and on!'

He gave a chuckle. 'The more fool you! Eugène's not one to leave a snug fireside. You won't shift him.'

'He wasn't living here when I married him!' she said.

'No, he wasn't. Trying his wings. I always knew he'd come back. I didn't mind.'

She looked across at him, under the straight brows which gave her the appearance of frowning even when she was not. 'Why do you want to keep us here?'

'What's that to do with you?' he retorted.

'It's just your love of power!' she said. 'You like to feel you've got us all under your thumb! But you haven't got me under your thumb!'

His smile taunted her. 'Haven't I? You try to move Eugène, and see! Think you're going to win against me, do you? Try it! I fancy you'll go on dancing to my piping, my girl.'

She bit her lip, knowing that it would be fatal to lose her temper. After a pause, she said carefully: 'If you think Eugène's lazy, you ought to want to encourage him to exert himself—'

'God bless the wench! I never do what I ought to do. Don't you know that yet?'

She ignored this. 'I've got a right to my own home, to have my husband to myself. It isn't fair to expect me to live in a house full of relatives!'

'Fair! fair!' he broke in impatiently. 'You're all alike, you women, bleating about what's *fair*! Think yourself lucky you've got a comfortable home to live in instead of having to rely on Eugène to support you! You'd fare badly if you had!'

'I'd sooner starve in a cottage with Eugène, than go on living here!' she said fiercely.

He laughed. 'Ho-ho! I'd like to see you doing it! Take him off to your cottage, then! You'll come back soon enough, with your tails between your legs, too!'

She said sullenly: 'Why don't you make Eugène an allowance? It needn't cost you more than it must cost to keep us both here.'

'Because I don't want to,' he answered.

She clenched her hands inside her pockets until her nails hurt her. 'You think you've beaten me, but you haven't. I'll never give in to you. I mean to get Eugène out of this house, and away from your beastly influence. You've got Ray, and Ingram, and the twins: why must you have my husband too? He belongs to me!'

He made a gesture with one hand. He was a hirsute man, and strong, dark hairs grew over the back of it, and on his chest too, where the top button of his pyjamas had come undone. 'Take him, then – but don't expect me to help you! The impudence of you!'

She said with a good deal of difficulty, because she had much pride: 'While you encourage him to hang about here, I can't take him away. We haven't enough money, and – all right, if you will have it, he *does* take the line of least resistance! But if you'd make him a small allowance, so that I could rent a little place in town, and keep him comfortable, I – I – I should be *grateful* to you!'

His smile showed her that he perfectly understood what an effort it cost her to make such an admission. He filled his glass a third time. 'I don't want your gratitude. I'd sooner keep you on the end of your chain, my lass. I've got a sense of humour, d'ye see? It amuses me to see you straining and struggling to break free. Think because I'm tied by the heels I haven't any power left, don't you? You try setting up your will against mine, and see whether I've still power to rule my own household!'

'O God, how I do hate you!' she said passionately, glaring at him.

His grin broadened. 'I know you do. I shan't lose any sleep over that. Lots of people have hated me in my time, but no one ever got the better of me yet.'

'I hope you drink yourself to death!' she threw at him. 'I shall dance for joy on the day you're buried!'

'That's the spirit!' he applauded. 'Damme, you've been badly reared, and you'd be the better for schooling, but there's good stuff in you, by God there is! Go on! Toss your head, and gnash your little white teeth at me: I don't mind your tantrums – like 'em! I shall keep you here just to pass the time away. It's a dull enough life I lead now, in all conscience: it would be a damned sight duller if you weren't here to spit your venom at me every time your liver's out of sorts.'

'I'll get the better of you!' she said, her voice shaking. 'You'd keep Eugène hanging round you until it's too late for him to pick up the old threads again. You don't care whether it's bad for him, or how miserable you make me! All you care for is getting your own way! You've tyrannized over your sons all their lives, and over Faith, too, because she's a weak fool, but you shan't spoil my life, and so I warn you!'

'Fight me, then!' he encouraged her. 'I know you've got claws. Why don't you use 'em?'

She did not answer him, for a soft knock fell on the door at that moment, and as Penhallow shouted 'Come in!' her husband walked into the room.

Eugène Penhallow, third of the Penhallow brothers, was thirty-five years old, and resembled his elder brother, Ingram, except that he was more slenderly built, and looked to be more intelligent. He had the sallow complexion that often accompanies black hair, and moved in a languid way. He enjoyed the convenient sort of ill-health which prevented his engaging upon any disagreeable task, but permitted his spending whole days following the hounds whenever he felt inclined to do so. He was adept at escaping from any form of unpleasantness, and extremely quick to detect the approach of a dilemma which might endanger his comfort. When he saw Vivian, standing stockily in front of the fire, with her chin up, he perceptibly hesitated on the threshold.

Penhallow, observing this, said derisively: 'Don't run away, Eugène! You've come just in time to see your wife scratch the eyes out of my head.'

Eugène had a smile of singular charm. He bestowed it now upon Vivian, in a glance which seemed to embrace her as well as to sympathize with her. She felt her bones turn to water, helpless in the grip of the love for him which still, after six years, consumed her. Her lip quivered as she looked at him; she moved instinctively towards him. He put his arm round her, and patted her. 'What's the trouble, little love?'

'It doesn't matter,' she said, her voice sounding sulky because of the constriction in her throat. She smiled tremulously up into his face, gave his hand an eloquent squeeze, and swung out of the room.

It was characteristic of Eugène that, when she had gone, he made no attempt to discover what had happened to upset her. He lowered himself into a chair by the fire, remarking: 'Yours is the only warm room in the house, sir. Has anyone told you that you ought not to be drinking wine, or would you like me to?'

'Pour yourself out a glass,' said Penhallow. 'Do you more good than the chemists' muck you pour into your belly.'

'I haven't inherited your digestion,' replied Eugène, stretching his long legs towards the fire. 'If you don't mind my saying so, Father, you ought to put central heating into this house. It's damned cold.'

'When I'm dead, you can start pulling the house about: you won't do it in my time,' responded Penhallow. 'What's brought you here this morning? Pleasure of my company?'

'Oh, I do get a lot of pleasure out of your company,' Eugène assured him. 'I like this room, too. It's utterly atrocious, artistically speaking – and that bit of so-called Dresden is a fake, though I don't suppose you'll take my word for it – but it has an atmosphere – er – not all due to that overfed bitch of yours.'

Penhallow grinned at him. 'She's old, like me. I'm overfed, too.'

'But you don't stink,' murmured Eugène plaintively, stirring the spaniel with one elegantly shod foot. He turned his head, and said with a faint lift to his brows: 'Are you really taking Clay away from college?'

'Oh, so Faith's been pouring out her grievances to you, has she? She hasn't wasted much time. Yes, I am.'

'Not to say *pouring*,' Eugène corrected. 'I don't mean that that wasn't the general idea – which just goes to show that she must be very upset, because she doesn't really like me: I can't think why, for I'm sure I'm very nice to her – but I can't bear listening to other people's troubles: they're always so boring. Besides, she's decidedly hysterical, which I find most unnerving. So I came to sit with you. But she says you're going to make Clay study law with Cliff?'

'It's about all he's fit for,' replied Penhallow. 'He isn't doing any good at Cambridge, and never would, if he stayed there for the rest of his life.'

'No, I feel sure you're right,' Eugène agreed. 'I shouldn't think he's doing any harm either, though – which, if you come to consider the matter, seems to be a fair epitome of Clay's character.'

'There are times when I wonder if the little worm can possibly be a son of mine!' said Penhallow, with a touch of violence.

'Oh, I should think he must be, sir!' said Eugène, with the flicker of his sweet smile. 'I mean, I don't want you to think that I'm criticizing Faith, but she always seems to me to lack the sort of enterprise that – er – characterizes our family. But do we really want Clay at Trevellin?'

'You'll put up with him,' replied Penhallow curtly.

'Oh, quite easily!' agreed Eugène. 'I shouldn't dream of letting him worry me. I don't somehow think that Ray will like it, though.'

Penhallow showed his teeth. 'Ray's not master here yet,' he said unpleasantly.

'No, thank God! I don't think I should stay if he were. I find him very dull and worthy, you know. And then there's Cliff!'

'What's the matter with him?' demanded Penhallow. 'He's a damned dull dog, if you like, but he doesn't live here.'

'Ah, I wasn't thinking of that! Merely I was wondering what weapons you had to employ to induce the poor dear fellow to take Clay on. I mean, there are limits even to Cliff's good-nature. Or aren't there?'

'Cliff,' stated Clifford's uncle, 'will do as I tell him, and that's all there is to it. He wouldn't like to have his mother thrown on his hands – or, at any rate, that stiff-necked wife of his wouldn't!'

'Yes, I thought you'd probably been more than usually devilish,' said Eugène, amused. 'Poor old Clifford!'

CHAPTER FOUR

IF she could have found Loveday Trewithian, Faith would have wept out all her troubles into that comfortably deep bosom, and would no doubt have been soothed and petted back to some semblance of calm, since she was very responsive to sympathy, and found a good deal of relief in making some kindly disposed person the recipient of her confidences. Upon leaving Penhallow's room, almost the first member of the household she encountered was Eugène, and such was her agitation, her urgent desire to unburden herself of her latest woe, that she forgot for the moment that she had never liked him, and was indeed afraid of his soft, yet disquieting tongue, and began to tell him of his father's brutality. From this infliction he very soon escaped; Vivian, who presently stalked through the hall on her way to the front door, brusquely refused to be detained, saying that she was going for a walk on the Moor, and didn't want to talk to anyone. Faith went upstairs to her room, and rang the bell. It was answered by one of the housemaids, and a demand for Loveday was met with the intelligence that she had stepped out to the village for a reel of cotton. Faith was too much absorbed in her troubles to reflect that this was a very odd errand for Loveday to run in the middle of the morning. She dismissed Jane rather pettishly, and occupied herself for the next twenty minutes in dwelling upon her wrongs, Penhallow's tyranny, and the injustice of his behaviour towards Clay. By this simple process she worked herself into a state of exaggerated desperation, in which she saw herself as one fighting with her back to the wall, and badly in need of an ally. Her nervous condition made inaction impossible to her, and after pacing about her room for some time, an abortive form of energy which exasperated far more than it relieved her, she decided to go to Liskeard, to see Clifford Hastings.

As she had never learnt to drive a car, and Liskeard was rather more than seven miles distant, this resolve necessitated the service of a chauffeur. It might have been supposed that in a household which employed a large number of servants there could be little difficulty about this, but although there were several grooms, stable-hands, gardeners, and boys employed on odd jobs, there was no official chauffeur. The Penhallows were inclined to despise motor-cars, and although Raymond often drove to outlying parts of the estate in a dilapidated runabout, and Conrad transported himself to and from his office in Bodmin in a dashing sports car, none of the family ever sat behind the wheel of a car from choice. A large landaulette of antique design and sober pace was kept for the use of the ladies, or to meet trains at Liskeard, and was driven either by one of the under-gardeners, who had a turn for mechanics, or by Jimmy the Bastard, or, if these two failed, by one of the grooms, who was willing to oblige, but always managed to stall the car when he changed gear on the uphill way home.

Fortunately for Faith, who resented Jimmy's presence in the house so much that she would rather have postponed her visit to Liskeard than have demanded his services, the under-gardener was engaged in bedding-out plants in the front of the house, and so was easily found. By slipping a raincoat on over his working clothes, and setting a peaked cap upon his head, he was able speedily to transform himself into a chauffeur; and after an agreeable passage of arms with the head-gardener, who took instant exception to his absenting himself from his work on the front beds, he went off to bring the ancient landaulette round from the garage.

Trevellin being situated above the village of Polzant, the way to Liskeard lay downhill, and eastward, into the valley of the Fowey. The landaulette crawled ponderously out of the lodge-gates, and lumbered off down the narrow lane, passing the Dower House, where Ingram Penhallow lived with his sharp-tongued wife, Myra, and his two sons, Rudolph and Bertram, whose ambitions were to resemble their twin uncles as nearly as possible, but who were at present, happily for all concerned, gracing a respectable public school some hundreds of miles away from Trevellin. The peculiar beauty of the countryside through which she was being carried was entirely unnoticed by Faith, who, besides being wholly engaged in rehearsing what she should presently say to her husband's nephew, considered that it was all too familiar to her to be worthy of having any attention bestowed upon it. So absorbed was she in her thoughts that she failed to observe the Vicar's wife, Mrs. Venngreen who was coming out of the village shop when the landaulette drove through Polzant, and who bowed to her. Mrs. Venngreen was a Churchwoman of rigid principles, and rarely crossed the unhallowed threshold of Trevellin, but she was sorry for Faith, whom she thought a poor, downtrodden little thing, and sometimes asked her to tea at the Vicarage. Her husband, an easy-going gentleman of comfortable habit of body, who liked a good glass of wine, and who was not unmindful of the benefits accruing to the Church from Penhallow's lavish, if casual, generosity, talked vaguely about the need to bear an open mind, and was not above visiting his eccentric parishioner. His curate, Simon Wells, no Cornishman, but a lean and severe Midlander, thought that his Vicar possessed to a remarkable degree the faculty of being able to shut his eyes to whatever he did not wish to see, and himself seemed more likely to curse the Penhallows, root and branch, than to accept their hospitality. As he was not a sporting parson, the Penhallows were scarcely aware of his existence, so that his deep disapproval of them troubled them not at all.

In due course, the landaulette reached the outskirts of Liskeard, and entered the town, passing between rows of Georgian houses to the establishment near the market-place which bore a modest brass plate beside its front door indicating that the premises were occupied by Messrs. Blazey, Blazey, Hastings, and Wembury. This, however, was misleading, the late Mr. Blazey senior having deceased a good many years previously, Mr. Blazey junior having become a sleeping partner, and Mr. Wembury being a valetudinarian whose activities were mostly confined to the not too arduous duties attached to the various Trusts in his care.

The resident partner was Mr. Hastings, to whose sanctum Faith, after a short period of waiting in a room inhabited by a shabby-looking clerk and a youth with a lack-lustre eye and a shock of unruly hair, was admitted.

Clifford Hastings was the same age as his cousin Raymond, but although rather stout he had a roundness of face and a freshness of complexion which made him appear the younger of the two. He was not in the least like his mother; and except that he was a good man to hounds, and was not above slipping his arm round the waist of a pretty woman, he had little in common with his Penhallow relations.

When Faith came into the room, he rose from behind a desk piled high with papers, and littered with a collection of pens, inkpots, blotters, pen-wipers, and coloured pencils, and came round the corner of it to shake hands with her. He was blessed with an uncritical, friendly disposition, and was always genuinely glad to see any of his relations. He greeted Faith with hearty good humour, saying: 'Well, Faith! This is very nice of you! How are you, my dear? How's Uncle Adam? And my mother? All well, eh? Sit down, and tell me all the news!'

Not being in the mood for an exchange of ordinary civilities,

Faith wasted no time in answering his inquiries, but plunged at once into the nature of her errand to him. 'Cliff, I've come to beg you to help me!'

He retreated again to his chair behind the desk. A look of slight uneasiness crossed his placid features, for although he was a kindly man, he shared, in common with the majority of his fellow-creatures, a dread of becoming entangled in another person's trials. However, he folded his hands on the blotter before him, and said cheerfully: 'Anything I can do to help you of course I should be only too glad to do! What is it?'

She sat bolt upright in the chair on the other side of the desk, gripping her handbag between her nervous hands. 'It's about Clay!' she said breathlessly.

The look of uneasiness on Cliff's face deepened. He carefully rearranged various small objects in front of him, and replied: 'About Clay! Oh, yes! Quite! As a matter of fact, Uncle Adam sent for me a couple of days ago to talk to me about him.'

'I know,' she interrupted. 'He told me today. Cliff, you mustn't take him! Please say you won't consent!'

He perceived that this was going to be an extremely difficult interview. 'Well, but, Faith—'

'I suppose Adam is going to pay you to take him, but I know that wouldn't weigh with you! I don't know how these things are arranged, but—'

'It simply means that he'll be articled to me,' he explained, glad of the opportunity afforded to lead her away from the main point at issue. 'I've no doubt he'll—'

'He'd hate it!' she declared vehemently. 'Adam's only doing it because he's never liked Clay, and he delights in upsetting me! Clay is going to write!'

'Well, well, I don't know any reason why he shouldn't write, if he has a bent that way. In his spare time, you know.'

She said impatiently: 'You don't understand. It would be *death* to Clay to be cooped up in a stuffy office, slaving over a lot of horrible deeds and things. He isn't cut out for it.'

He looked a little startled. He was not very well acquainted with Clay Penhallow, the boy being twenty years his junior, but he had not supposed, from the little he had seen of him, that he was made of such fiery metal as could not endure to be confined within four walls. He said feebly: 'Oh, well, you know, it's not such a bad life! Not like a London practice, you know. I mean, I see that to a lad reared as he has been it would be a bit trying for him to be obliged to live in London all the year round. But you take my life! Of course, I can't spare the time my cousins can, but I manage to hunt once a week, and sometimes twice, and I get quite a bit of fishing, besides—'

'It isn't that! Clay isn't interested in sport. He would *like* to live in London! But he's *artistic*! It would simply kill him to be tied to a desk!'

If Clifford felt that a young gentleman of this character would scarcely be an asset to the firm of Blazey, Blazey, Hastings, and Wembury, he concealed it, merely remarking: 'I see. Quite!'

'Besides, I don't want him to be a solicitor,' continued Faith. 'Or even a barrister. I mean, it isn't in the least his line for one thing, and for another I should simply hate a son of mine to spend his time defending people whom he knew to be guilty.'

This ill-informed view of the activities of barristers-at-law made Clifford blink, but since Clay was not destined for the Bar there seemed to be little point in disabusing his mother's mind of its feminine belief that every barrister spent his life defending blood-stained criminals. He did indeed wonder vaguely why a barrister should be almost invariably credited, first, with a criminal practice, and second, with a prescience which made it possible for him to feel certain of his client's guilt or innocence, but this thought he also kept to himself, He said: 'I quite understand your point of view, but it isn't really such a bad life, Faith. In any case, Uncle Adam—'

'Adam's only doing it to hurt me!' declared Faith, on a rising note which made Clifford stir uneasily in his chair, and hope that she was not going to treat him to a fit of hysterics. 'I had it out with him this morning. I can't tell you the things he said: sometimes I think he's absolutely insane! He told me he'd arranged it all with you, so I thought my only hope was to come at once to see you, and to explain that I don't want you to let Clay be articled to you, or whatever it is! After all, Adam hasn't any hold over you, Cliff! He can't *do* anything to you if you refuse, and you can easily keep out of his way, if he flies into one of his awful rages!'

Clifford went on fidgeting with the lid of the ink-pot. His face now wore an extremely thoughtful expression. Faith's artless exposition of her son's character inspired him with a strong desire to be exempt from the necessity of admitting Clay into his firm, but there were reasons which made it extremely difficult, not to say impossible, for him to refuse to oblige his uncle in the matter. It was almost equally impossible for him to explain to Faith that fond as he was of his widowed mother, he would find it very awkward indeed if she were to be ejected from Trevellin, and thus (for her private means were of the slenderest) thrown upon his hands. It was not that he was an undutiful or an unaffectionate son, but he was married to a lady who would certainly not welcome to her home anyone so eccentric as her mother-in-law. Nor, he knew, would she feel at all inclined to retrench her household expenditure so as to enable him to make Clara a suitable allowance. Indeed, he scarcely knew how he would be able to manage such a thing, considering the difficulty of the times, and the increasing demands made on his purse by his three daughters, damsels aged twelve, ten, and seven years respectively, whose careers, he was assured, would inevitably be blighted by any failure on his part to provide them with riding, dancing, and music lessons. His father having died when he had been a boy at school, and his mother having then returned to the house which was her birthplace, it had never fallen to Clifford's lot to support her. He had spent his holidays at Trevellin, and was indebted to his uncle for his present position in a respectable firm of country solicitors. This circumstance alone made him very unwilling to disoblige his uncle; when, to ordinary feelings of gratitude, a lively dread of having to add another member to his household was added, there could be no question of his doing such a thing. He wished very much that he had not admitted Faith into his office, for although she would probably understand his reluctance to take the support of his mother upon his shoulders, he really did not see how he could put such a delicate matter into plain words without appearing to her in the guise of a most unnatural, not to say callous, son.

He cleared his throat, and began to draw patterns on the blotter with one of the pencils scattered over the table. 'Well, but after all, Faith!' he said. 'Clay must do something, mustn't he? You'll have him living at home, too, if he comes to me. You'd like that, wouldn't you?'

Her eyes filled with tears. 'If everything were different! Not as things are. He hates it at home. He doesn't get on with Adam, and his stepbrothers are horrid to him. They don't understand how anyone can be more sensitive than themselves. I've suffered from their absolute unfeelingness all my life, and I'm determined Clay shan't be sacrificed as I was!'

The conversation seemed to Clifford to be soaring towards an elevated plane which he, a plain man, could not aspire to. He said in a soothing way: 'Well, if he finds he doesn't like law, after he's given it a fair trial, we shall have to think of something else.'

'If you think that Adam would ever let him leave the firm, once he'd got him into it, you don't know him!' exclaimed Faith.

'Well, well, a great many things may happen to alter circumstances, after all! Really, Faith, I don't think you need—'

'You mean Adam might die,' she said. 'He won't. I know he won't. He'll go on for years and years, making us all miserable! Look at his grandfather! He lived to be over eighty, and had all sorts of things the matter with him.'

'*Really*, Faith!' expostulated Clifford, quite shocked.

She burst into tears. 'Oh, I know I ought not to say so, even to you, but if you only knew what I have to put up with, Cliff, you wouldn't be surprised at my having reached the end of my tether! I could bear it while Clay was safe from Adam's tyranny, but if he's to be forced into doing something he doesn't want to do, and kept down here at the back of beyond, when he'd rather be in London, I simply can't go on!'

He began to feel very uncomfortable, and wondered how much of this interview was audible to the clerk and the boy in the outer office. Faith's sobs had, he thought, a peculiarly penetrative quality. He made sympathetic noises in his throat, and was glad to see her making an effort to calm herself.

'Taking him away from college, too, for no *reason*!' choked Faith, applying her handkerchief to her reddened eyes. 'It's so *unfair*!'

'Yes, well, I do feel that that is perhaps a mistake,' agreed Clifford, perceiving in this circumstance a means of pacifying, if only temporarily, his unwelcome visitor. 'I'll tell you what, Faith: I'll have a talk with Uncle Adam, and see if I can get him to let Clay finish his three years at Cambridge. You never know: something might happen between now and then to make uncle alter his mind.'

'He won't,' Faith replied wretchedly, but in quieter accents. 'I don't suppose he'll even listen to you.'

Clifford felt quite sure that he wouldn't, but he naturally did not say this. Instead, he looked at his watch, discovered, with artless surprise, that it was already one o'clock, and suggested, with a return of his usual hearty manner, that Faith should postpone her return to Trevellin until the afternoon, and should take luncheon with himself, and his wife, Rosamund. 'Rosamund,' he said mendaciously, 'would never forgive me if I let you go home without seeing her. Besides, you haven't seen the kiddies for I don't know how long! We can talk it over after lunch. It's a pity uncle won't have the telephone installed at Trevellin, but I dare say they won't worry if you don't turn up to lunch, will they?'

'No one at Trevellin would miss me if I *never* turned up again,' said Faith tragically, opening her compact, and beginning to powder her nose. 'But I don't see why I should inflict myself on Rosamund, only that it's like being let out of prison, to get away from Trevellin for a bit.'

'Now, now, now!' said Clifford, rising, and patting her clumsily on the shoulder. 'It isn't as bad as that, Faith. I'll tell you what: I've got one or two things to see to before I leave the office. You trot off to the house, and have a chat with Rosamund. I'll join you in a few minutes. Perhaps I shall have thought of something,' he added hopefully.

She was not very fond of Rosamund, whom she considered to be a cold, unsympathetic young woman, but being in that state of mind when it was imperative to her to unburden herself to as many people as possible, she accepted his invitation, and went out again to re-enter the ponderous landaulette. The under-gardener received her order to drive to the Laurels with evident gratification; and in a few moments the landaulette was again in motion.

The Laurels, a square Georgian house, was situated on the outskirts of the town, so that by the time Faith walked up its well-kept front path Clifford had been able to warn his wife by telephone of the trial in store for her. Rosamund, who thought Faith the least objectionable member of the Penhallow family, received the tidings with her usual calm, issued a few necessary orders to her domestic staff, and was ready to receive her guest when Faith set her finger to the electric bell-push.

A neat house-parlourmaid (so unlike the servants at Trevellin!)

46

admitted Faith into a square, white-painted hall, and conducted her across it to the drawing-room at the back of the house. This was a comfortable apartment overlooking the garden, and was furnished in a somewhat characterless but agreeable style, which included well-sprung chairs; a plain pile carpet of neutral hue; a low tea-table of burr-walnut; oxidized fire-irons dangling from a stand in one corner of a hearth lined with glazed tiles; a swollen floor cushion, shaped like a cottage-loaf, and covered with the same flowered cretonne which provided loose-covers for the chairs, and the sofa, and for the curtains hanging in the bay window. The pictures on the walls, which were all framed alike, were inoffensive, and gave a general air of quiet decoration to the room without attracting any particular attention to themselves. One or two illustrated papers were piled neatly on a long, cane-seated stool placed in front of the fireplace; and several books bearing the label of a local lending library stood upon a semi-circular table by the wall, maintained in an upright position by a pair of book-rests fashioned in the shape of china dogs. Everything in the room was new, and well-kept. The pictures were arranged symmetrically; no single piece of furniture had been placed in such a position that it was not balanced by another, similar, piece; nothing had been chosen to go into the room which did not match its surroundings. There was no dust anywhere to be seen; there were no thin patches on the carpet; no priceless rugs flung down with an entire disregard for jarring colours; no jumble of ornaments on the mantelpiece; no sagging springs to any of the chairs; no discordant note introduced by the juxtaposition of a Victorian chiffonier with a Chippendale ladderback chair. Rosamund had no Victorian furniture in her house. Similarly, she had no Chippendale chairs either, although her dining-room was furnished with a set of very good replicas.

Faith, to whom the queer, distorted beauty of Trevellin made no appeal, liked the room, and envied Rosamund her possession of a clean, compact house, full of labour-saving devices and seemly, unambitious suites of furniture. She considered, looking round the the room, with its nicely graduated tones of blending browns and yellows, that Rosamund had an eye for colour, and thought that if she had stood in Rosamund's shoes she could have achieved very much the same pleasing result.

Her hostess came into the room while she was still taking stock of her surroundings. Rosamund Hastings was a handsome woman with a somewhat chilly pair of blue eyes, and a quantity of fashionably waved fair hair. She was dressed suitably in a well-cut suit of grey flannel, with a canary shirt, and low-heeled shoes over very good quality silk stockings. She was five years younger than Faith, but was possessed of more assurance than Faith would ever own. She was a good, if a rather frigid wife; an excellent mother; a competent housekeeper; and an attentive hostess, who never forgot to order sherry from the wine-merchant, nor to offer her guests Indian as well as China tea.

She came forward now, with her well-manicured hand held out, and a polite word of greeting on her lips. The two ladies kissed, without conviction; Faith was placed in a chair with its back to the light; Rosamund sat down on the sofa at right-angles to her; and while she inquired civilly after all the members of the household at Trevellin, the neat house-parlourmaid quietly entered the room with a silver tray supporting a cut-glass decanter, and three sherry glasses, and set it down on the low table in front of her mistress. Faith noticed wistfully that the tray was brightly polished, and that the decanter and the glasses all matched each other.

'It seems an age since I saw you last,' remarked Rosamund. 'Now, do tell me all about youself! You'll have a glass of sherry, won't you?'

Faith accepted the sherry, remembered to ask after the three daughters of the house, and prepared to unbosom herself.

Rosamund listened to her with an air of calm interest, offering neither criticism nor advice. In reality she was not at all interested. She disliked her husband's maternal relatives, and profoundly disapproved of them. There was a raffishness about them that offended her sense of propriety. She was sorry that her husband's occupation necessitated his residing within eight miles of Trevellin; and although she never made any attempt to stop his consorting with his cousins, she herself did not visit Trevellin more frequently than she was obliged to. She was aware of the circumstances which made it desirable for Clifford to accept Clay as an articled pupil, and although she felt that it was disgraceful that his hand should have been forced in such an unscrupulous manner, she considered the entry of a young man, however unwanted, into the firm, as preferable to the entry of Clara into her well-ordered house. She never permitted herself to utter any criticism of her mother-in-law, but she privately thought her an extremely trying old lady, eccentric in her behaviour, not over-clean in her habits, and very injudicious in her spoiling of her nicely-behaved granddaughters.

It was not, then, to be expected that Rosamund would support Faith in her endeavour to keep Clay out of Clifford's office. However, she lent an indulgent ear to Faith's rather agitated history of the morning's interview with Penhallow, and agreed with perfect sincerity that he had behaved in a thoroughly illbred and over-bearing manner. She even bore with unmoved composure Faith's disparaging comments on Clifford's profession, and did not allow herself to do more than raise her plucked eyebrows slightly at Faith's assertion that Clay's intellect was of too high an order for the law.

Clifford came in a little after half-past one o'clock, but any hopes Faith might have cherished of reopening the discussion with him were blighted by the house-parlourmaid's announcement that luncheon was served. Rosamund said: 'You know the way, Faith,' and Faith preceded her across the hall to the dining-room in the front of the house. Here the three little girls, Isabel, Daphne, and

Monica, awaited them, and any private conversation had naturally to be abandoned. The children, who attended a day-school in the town, were dressed alike, and closely resembled their mother. They were very well brought up, answered politely when spoken to, and prattled, until hushed by a sign from Rosamund, about their activities at school. Clifford was very proud of them, and encouraged them to show off by asking them leading questions. It was obvious that while they were present he had no attention to spare for Faith's troubles, and as he looked at his wrist-watch when they all rose from the table, and exclaimed that he had an appointment, and must hurry off immediately, it became equally obvious that he did not intend, at least for the present, to go any further into the question of Clay's future. Saying that he knew Faith would excuse him, he bustled away. The two ladies returned to the drawing-room for coffee; Rosamund told Faith what the music-mistress at St. Margaret's School had said to her about Isabel's music; and how Monica seemed to have a real talent for dancing; and how the head-mistress believed that Daphne was going to be an influence for good in the school. Faith complimented Rosamund upon her excellent management of her children, and her household, and wondered how she contrived to get such well-trained servants in these days. In this innocuous fashion, an hour passed, at the end of which time Faith said that she must really be going. Rosamund, who was going out to a bridge-party, made no effort to detain her; the under-gardener was haled from the kitchen, where he had been regaling the cook and the house-parlourmaid and the nursery-maid with tales of the goings-on up at Trevellin; and Faith, after bidding farewell to her hostess, once more entered the landaulette, and was driven back to Trevellin.

CHAPTER FIVE

RAYMOND PENHALLOW'S day, since, in addition to the estate, he managed not only the hunting-stables, but a small stud-farm as well, began at a very early hour, for although he employed an excellent stud-groom, and Weens, the hunting-groom, had worked at Trevellin since boyhood, he was not the man to entrust the all-important business of grooming, feeding, and exercising to underlings. No groom, using a brush on a shedding coat, or seeking to impart a gloss to a coat by the administration of surreptitious doses of arsenic, could ever feel himself safe from the Master's penetrating eye. He had an uncomfortable habit of appearing in the stables when least expected, and no fault of omission or commission ever escaped him when he made his daily round of inspection. He was respected without being very much liked; and it was generally agreed that he was an extremely ill man to cheat.

His brothers Ingram and Bart were both joined with him in the management of the stud-farm and the stables, the former having been started some years previously largely on Ingram's representations to his father that something must be done to bolster up the dwindling finances of the estate, and that the upland situation of Trevellin made it particularly suitable for breeding purposes. But if Ingram was responsible for obtaining Penhallow's consent to the scheme, the original inspiration was Raymond's. It was due to Raymond's sound sense and driving-force that the ramshackle old stables, with all their abuses of hay-lofts, high-racks, and sloping stalls, had been pulled down, and modern buildings erected in the form of a quadrangle upon a more convenient site. It was due to Raymond's hardheadedness that Bart's wild plan of breeding race-horses was nipped in the bud. It was due to his unerring eye that so few unsound horses ever found their way into the Trevellin stables. Even Penhallow, who lived at loggerheads with him, grudgingly admitted his ability to judge a horse, and could never be prevailed upon to support Ingram or Bart in any disagreement with him on the questions of buying or breeding.

Only a year separated Raymond and Ingram. They resembled one another, in that both were very dark, with aquiline features, and their father's piercing grey eyes, but Ingram was half a head the taller, a circumstance which was a source of considerable annoyance to him, since it necessitated his riding only big, strong hunters. They had shared the same nursery, had gone to the same schools, possessed the same tastes and interests, and had never, all their lives, been able to agree. As boys, they had fought incessantly; as young men, neither had lost an opportunity to thrust a spoke in the other's wheel; now that they had reached middle-age they preserved an armed neutrality, each being on the alert to circumvent any attempt on the part of the other to interfere with jealously guarded rights and prerogatives. The World War of 1914–1918 had left Ingram with a permanently stiff leg. He had served with distinction in a cavalry regiment, and had won the Military Cross. Raymond, producing food for the nation under Penhallow, had been exempt from military service.

After the war, Ingram, who had married a Devonshire girl during one of his leaves, settle down on his gratuity, and the small fortune left to him by his mother, at the Dower House. He was a favourite with his father, who could always be induced to disburse money for such extraneous expenses as Myra's operation for appendicitis, Rudolph's and Bertram's schooling, the upkeep of half-a-dozen good hunters, and the building of a garage beside the Dower House. These depredations were a constant thorn in Raymond's flesh; and an added annoyance was supplied by Ingram's having inherited the whole of his mother's private fortune. Since Raymond would inherit the estate, which was entailed, this arrangement seemed fair enough to any impartial critic, but his being wholly left out of Rachel's will had always galled Raymond unbearably.

Alone amongst his brothers, he, who passionately loved every stone, every blade of grass on the estate, had not been born at Trevellin. Not even Ingram, uncannily swift to find out the joints in his armour, guessed with what irrational bitterness he resented this. His sturdy insularity made it revolting to him that he had been born abroad, but so it was. Penhallow had taken his Rachel on a prolonged honeymoon, attended by Martha, her maid, who came from Rachel's own home; and joined later by Delia, her sister, who had been with her when Raymond was born. Raymond was three months old before he saw the home of his fathers. But Ingram, Eugène, Charmian, Aubrey, the twins, and even Clay, had all first seen the light in that big, irregularly-shaped room at the head of the main staircase, which looked south to the valley of the Fowey.

He had been a peevish baby, a cross-grained little boy, and had grown into a taciturn man, who bade fair to develop, in later years, into an eccentric. He had no interest in anything beyond the bounds of Trevellin; and from never having been a favourite with either parent had early acquired a sturdy independence, and a habit of keeping whatever thoughts he cherished to himself. His younger brothers stood a little in awe of him; his father, recognizing in him a will quite as stubborn as his own, accorded him a certain amount of respect mixed with a good deal of exasperation at the pedestrian commonsense which was wholly alien to his own fantastic and extravagant character. Since Penhallow insisted on keeping his hand on the reins of government, they were obliged to see more of one another than was good for their tempers. Penhallow stigmatized Raymond as a cheeseparing hunks, with the soul of a shopkeeper; Raymond said bitterly that if some restraint were not put upon Penhallow the whole estate would be wasted before it came into his own more careful hands.

It was, however, quite impossible to put any restraint upon Penhallow. Eccentric he might be, but he was not in the least mad. His near neighbour, and oldest acquaintance, John Probus, said that he had been born into the wrong age, and reminded him of his grandfather, a hard-drinking, hard-riding, nineteenth-century squire, whom he could just remember, and who had gambled away a considerable portion of his estates, and had ended his days a martyr to gout. Penhallow did not gamble away his estates: he mortgaged them.

He had other habits, less disastrous but almost as irritating to his heir, chief amongst which was his predilection for keeping enormous sums of money locked away in a battered tin box, which he stowed in one of the cupboards of his preposterous bed. It was nothing unusual for him to hoard several hundreds of pounds in this freakish way, which he saved, or cast about with a lavish hand, just as his fancy dictated. He would bestow a casual handful of crumpled notes upon any of his children who had happened to please him; scatter coins amongst his servants; send one of his sons, or old Reuben, off with a bulging wallet to purchase some piece of furniture which he had seen advertised in the local paper as being put up for auction in a sale and which he had taken a sudden fancy to possess; bid the Vicar help himself from the open box, when that gentleman called to beg a donation for the poor of the parish, or for the renovations to the Church; and generally behave as though he were a sort of Midas to whom gold was no sort of object. It amused him to compel Raymond to keep him supplied with money, which he did by threatening to send Jimmy the Bastard to the Bank in Bodmin with his cheque, if his disapproving heir refused to perform the errand.

Raymond had one of these scrawled cheques in his pocket as he left the house after his morning's interview with his parent. These daily meetings seldom passed without friction, but this one had been stormier than most. Raymond, going straight from the breakfast-table to his father's room, had found Penhallow in a smouldering rage, shouting abuse at old Martha, who, had just finished tidying the room. His eyes had gleamed at sight of his son, and he had lost no time in trying to pick a quarrel with him. Eugène would have diverted his wrath with his nimble tongue; Ingram, or either of the twins, would have gratified him by losing their tempers, and shouting back at him with a complete lack of filial respect, or self-control; Raymond merely stood before the fire, with his feet wide-planted, the first three fingers of either square hand thrust into the slit pockets in the front of his whipcord breeches, and a heavy scowl on his face. Nothing could have annoyed Penhallow more than this invariable refusal to be goaded into fury.

'Dumb, are you?' he roared, heaving himself up in his bed. 'You sulky young hound, if you'd the spirit of a louse you'd find your tongue quick enough!'

'When you've quite finished,' Raymond had said coldly, 'you can take a look at that lot!'

He jerked his head towards the ledgers he had placed on the table beside the bed, but he did not move from his position before the fire. Penhallow sneered at him. 'I ought to have made you into a damned accountant! I don't doubt you'd have been happy to have spent your life totting up columns of figures!'

As this taunt had no visible effect upon Raymond, he passed to a wholesale criticism of his management of the estate, and ended by remarking that he had heard from Ingram that the Demon colt was likely to prove a failure. Ingram had said nothing of the sort, but the shaft served to bring a flush to Raymond's cheeks. He replied briefly: 'I've got a hit.'

Penhallow at once forgot that he wanted to enrage his son. His brows drew together. 'A hit, eh? Well! Early days yet. Got his sire's shoulders?'

'Grand shoulder-blade, and forearm. Powerful quarters; hocks well-bent; stifles high and wide,' Raymond responded.

'Back?' Penhallow shot at him. 'Out with it! I remember thinking, when I saw his dam—'

'Short above and long below,' interrupted Raymond, the corners of his mouth lifting.

Penhallow grunted. 'I'll take a look at him. Got him out yet?'

'I've had him out a couple of weeks now.'

'Where?' Penhallow demanded.

'The Upper Paddock.'

'Good! How many have you put with him?'

'Three others.'

Penhallow nodded. 'Quite right. Never have more than four yearlings to a paddock.' He looked Raymond over. 'Bred him for selling, I suppose?'

'Yes.'

'God, I don't know where you get your huckstering instinct from!'

Raymond shrugged, and was silent. Penhallow's ill-humour descended upon him again. He bethought him of a piece of news likely to find no sort of favour with his grim-faced heir. He informed him casually of his plans for Clay.

That did rouse Raymond, if not to an exhibition of Penhallow rage, at least to a considerable degree of annoyance. It seemed to him poor economy to remove Clay from college before the expiration of his three years there; it exasperated him to be obliged to stand by while his father laid down a substantial sum of money to buy Clay into a firm which he would infallibly leave the instant Penhallow was underground; and in addition to these considerations he wanted no more brothers quartered at Trevellin. When Penhallow added to these unwelcome tidings an announcement that he thought it high time young Aubrey stopped messing about in town, and came home, he shut his lips tightly, turned on his heel, and strode out of the room.

When he reached the hunting-stables, his face still wore so forbidding an expression that a stable-boy, carrying a couple of buckets across the yard, made all haste to remove himself from his sight; and a groom, who was engaged in strapping a flea-bitten grey, exchanged a significant glance with one of his mates.

Raymond paused for a moment, silently watching the busy groom. Apparently he had no fault to find, for, to the man's relief, he passed on. The upper halves of the loose-box doors stood open, and a row of beautiful heads looked out. Raymond stopped to caress one of his own hunters; parted the hair on the neck of a bay mare with his fingers; inspected the ears of a neat-headed Irish hunter; entered one of the boxes to examine the hooves of a nervous chestnut under treatment for thrush; and was joined presently by his head-groom, with whom he held a brief discussion of a highly technical nature. He still looked rather forbidding, but his scowl had lightened as it always did when he came amongst his horses. He glanced round the quadrangle, thinking how good were these stables of his designing, thinking that the new groom he had engaged shaped well, thinking that he would advise Bart to have his grey's shoes removed, thinking that when Penhallow died— But at this point his thoughts stopped abruptly, and he swung round to visit the harness-room. One of the hands was washing some dirty harness there, which hung on a double-hook suspended from the ceiling; Bart and Conrad, as well as himself, had been exercising horses earlier in the morning, and three saddles were spread over the long iron saddle-horse. Glass-fronted cupboards running round the walls contained well-polished saddles on their brackets, gleaming bits attached to neatly-hung bridles, all in demonstrably good order. A quick look over some horse-clothing, spread out for his inspection, a glance along the shelf stacked with bandages, a nod in answer to a request for more neat's foot oil and some new leathers, and he passed on to the hay-chamber, and to the granary, with its corn-bruiser, its chaff-cutter, and its many bins.

When he left the stables, he strode off to the ramshackle building which housed his runabout, and backed this battered and aged vehicle out into the yard. He decided that he had just time to pay a visit to his stud-farm before motoring into Bodmin, and drove off noisily up the rough lane which led to it.

He found Ingram there, talking to Mawgan, the stud-groom. The brothers exchanged a curt greeting. Ingram, who was sitting on his shooting-stick, said: 'I've been saying to Mawgan that we'd do well to get rid of the Flyaway mare.'

Raymond grunted.

'Guv'nor all right?' Ingram asked casually.

'Much as usual.'

'Going to take a look at the Demon colt? I'm on my way to the Upper Paddock myself.'

Raymond had meant to take a look at the colt on which his present ambitions were centred, but he had no wish to do so in Ingram's company. He replied: 'No, I haven't time. I've got to get to Bodmin.'

'Oh! Did Weens show you that quarter-piece?'

'Yes.'

'Dam' bad,' remarked Ingram, easing his game leg a little. 'If you're going in to Bodmin, you might tell Gwithian's to send me up another dozen of lager. Save me a journey.'

'All right,' Raymond said. 'Nothing wanted here?'

'Not that I know of.' Ingram eyed him shrewdly. 'Bank again?' he inquired laconically.

Raymond nodded, scowling.

'Going the pace a bit, isn't he?'

'If you think you can clap a curb on him, try!' recommended Raymond savagely. 'I'm fed-up with it!'

Ingram laughed. 'No bloody fear! Leave him alone: he'll quieten down if you don't fret him. You never had an ounce of tact, that's your trouble.'

Raymond got into his car, and started the engine. 'He's having Clay home,' he said grimly.

'Hell!' ejaculated Ingram.

'*And* Aubrey,' added Raymond, thrusting out his clutch.

'Hell and blast!' said Ingram, at the top of his voice.

'Laugh *that* one off!' recommended Raymond sardonically, and bucketed away down the lane.

It did not take him long to reach Bodmin, and his business there was soon transacted. It was when he was coming out of the bank that he encountered his Aunt Delia, fluttering scarves, veils, and ribbons, and carrying a laden shopping-basket in one hand, and a capacious leather bag in the other.

Those who had known Delia Ottery since her childhood said that she had been a very pretty girl, although cast a little into the shade by her sister Rachel. Her nephews, not having known her as a girl, were obliged to take this opinion on trust. They could none of them remember her as anything but an untidy, faded old maid, whose lustreless hair was prematurely grey, and always falling down in unsightly tails and wisps. Girlish slimness had early changed to middle-aged scragginess, and as she had never outgrown a youthful predilection for bright colours, frills, and fluffiness, this was considerably accentuated by the clothes she wore. When she accosted her nephew, becoming quite pink in the face from pleasure at seeing him, she was wearing a straw picture-hat on the back of her head, its brim weighed down by a large, salmon-coloured rose. A veil floated from this structure, getting entangled, in the breeze which was blowing down the street, with the ends of a fringed scarf which she wore loosely knotted round her neck. A frock of a peculiarly aggressive shade of blue was imperfectly concealed by a long brown coat; and since the month was May, and the weather not as summery as the picture-hat would have seemed to imply, she wore in addition a feather-boa of a style fashionable in the opening years of the century. She was of a very nervous and retiring disposition, and appeared to be almost as much frightened as pleased at walking into her nephew. She gasped: 'Oh, Raymond! Well, this *is* a surprise!' and dropped her handbag.

Raymond, whose innate neatness was invariably offended by his aunt's untidy appearance, betrayed no pleasure at the meeting. He responded briefly: 'Hallo, Aunt Delia!' and bent to pick up the handbag.

She stood there, blinking at him with her myopic grey eyes, and smiling a little foolishly. 'Well, this *is* a surprise!' she repeated.

As Raymond drove into Bodmin never less frequently than twice a week, and Miss Ottery did her marketing there every morning, there seemed to be very little reason for her to feel any surprise. However, the Penhallows had long since decided that their aunt was a trifle soft in the head, so Raymond merely said: 'I came in on business. You and Uncle Phineas both well?'

'Oh, yes, indeed, very well, thank you! And are you quite well, dear?'

He replied with a slight smile: 'Thanks, I'm always well.'

'That's right!' she said. 'And dear little Faith? It seems such ages since I saw her. I don't know how it is, but one never has time to turn round these days!'

'She's much the same as usual,' he answered.

They stood looking at one another, Miss Ottery tremulously smiling, Raymond wondering how to get away from her.

'It's so nice to see you, dear, and looking so well, too!' produced Delia, after a slight pause. 'I was only saying to Phineas the other day – actually, it was Tuesday, because I saw Myra in the town, which made me think, not but what I know you young people have your own affairs to attend to, especially *you*, Raymond dear, I'm sure – well, I was saying to Phineas that we haven't seen anything of you for ages. And now here you are!'

'Yes,' agreed Raymond. He could see no way, short of walking off, of escaping from her, and added: 'Can I give you a lift home?'

She turned pinker than ever with pleasure, and stammered: 'Well, that *is* kind of you, dear! Of course you have your car here, haven't you? I was just going into the corn-chandler's to buy some seed for my birdies, and then I thought I would catch the bus, but if you wouldn't mind waiting for me, I'm sure it would be *most* kind of you. Though I oughtn't to be keeping you, I know, for I'm sure you're very busy.'

'The car's over there,' interrupted Raymond, indicating its position with a jerk of his head. 'I'll wait for you.'

'I won't be a minute!' she promised. 'I'll just pop across the road for my seed, and be back in a trice. You remember my birdies, don't you? Such sweets!'

As it was only three weeks since Raymond had visited the grey house outside the town where Delia lived with her brother, upon which occasion it had seemed to him that as much of the drawing-room as was not filled with glass-fronted cabinets containing Phineas's collection of china was occupied by love-birds and canaries in gilt cages, all making the most infernal din, he had a very vivid recollection of the birdies, and said so, somewhat grimly.

It was fully a quarter of an hour later when Miss Ottery climbed into the runabout beside her nephew, and disposed her shopping-basket in the cramped space at her feet. She explained her dilatoriness as having been due to her desire to get the corn-chandler's advice about Dicky, one of her roller-canaries, who had been ailing for several days. 'Such a nice man!' she said. 'He always takes such an *interest*! Of course, we have dealt there all our lives, which I always think makes a difference, don't you? Only you're more interested in horses than in birds, aren't you, dear? Naturally, you would be. It would be very strange if you weren't, considering. And how are the dear horses?'

He did not feel that it was necessary to answer this question. He told her instead that he had one or two promising youngsters turned out to grass.

'Oh, how nice!' she exclaimed. 'I was always so sorry when we gave up our stables, not but what I was never such a wonderful horsewoman as dear Rachel, only I have always loved horses, as long as they aren't too skittish for me. Rachel used to ride *anything* – such a picture as she was, too! – but my dear father – your grandfather, Raymond, only you can't remember him, because he died before you were born – used to mount me on such gentle, well-mannered horses that I quite enjoyed it. But I never hunted. I never could quite bring myself to approve of it, not that I mean anything against people who do hunt, because I'm sure it would be a very dull world if we all thought alike. But I used to drive a dear little governess-cart. You remember my fat pony, Peter, don't you Raymond?'

Yes, Raymond remembered the fat pony perfectly, a circumstance which made Miss Ottery beam with delight, and recall the various occasions when the fat pony had been *so* naughty, or *so* clever, or *so* sweet. Branching away somewhat erratically from this fruitful subject, she said wistfully that she wished she could see Raymond's darling colts, because she loved all young animals, even kittens, though when you considered what they would grow into, and the perfectly dreadful way they played with poor little birds, and mice, it seemed quite terrible.

'You must come up one day, and walk round the stables,' Raymond said, safe in the knowledge that she was a great deal too nervous of Penhallow to accept the invitation.

The suggestion threw her into a twitter of embarrassment at once, and she was still faltering out excuses when the car pulled up outside Azalea Lodge.

Refusing her pressing invitation to come in for a moment to see his uncle, Raymond leaned across her to open the door of the car. By the time she had extricated herself, and had received her basket from him, Phineas, who had seen her arrival from behind the muslin curtains which shrouded the drawing-room windows, had come out of the house, and was advancing down the garden-path.

Common politeness compelled Raymond to refrain from driving off, which he would have liked to do, until he had shaken hands with his uncle. He did not, however, get out of the car, and he did not retain Phineas's soft, white hand in his a second longer than was necessary.

'Well, well, well!' uttered Phineas. 'I declare, I wondered who could be bringing you home in such style, Delia! This is indeed kind! And how are you, my boy? You have no need to answer: you look to be in splendid shape. You must come inside, and take a little refreshment. No, no, I insist!'

'Thanks, uncle, I'm afraid I haven't time. Glad to see you looking so fit.'

Phineas smoothed back a lock of his white hair, which the breeze was blowing into his eyes. There was an agate ring upon his finger, and his nails were carefully manicured. 'Not so bad, Raymond, not so bad for an old fellow! And how is your dear father?'

As Raymond was well aware that Phineas disliked Penhallow

intensely, this unctuous inquiry made his brows draw together. He replied bluntly: 'He's the same as he always was.'

'Ah!' said Phineas. 'A wonderful constitution! A remarkable man, quite remarkable!'

'Why don't you come up and see him sometime?' suggested Raymond maliciously. 'He'd like that!'

Phineas's smile did not lose a jot of its blandness. 'One of these days . . .' he said vaguely.

Raymond gave a laugh, and turned to bid farewell to his aunt. She laid a timid hand on his shoulder, and since it was plain that she intended to kiss him, he submitted, leaning sideways a little, and himself perfunctorily kissed her withered cheek. A nod to his uncle, and he drove off, leaving the portly brother and the skinny sister standing in the road, waving to him.

CHAPTER SIX

THE family did not assemble again in force until tea-time, since neither Faith nor the twins returned to Trevellin for lunch. But at five o'clock everyone but Penhallow himself foregathered in the Long Drawing-room, an apartment more akin to a gallery than a room, since it was immensely long, very narrow in proportion, and contained most of the family portraits hanging on the wall which faced the line of windows opening on to the front of the house. Some extremely valuable pieces of furniture were scattered about, amongst an almost equal number of commonplace chairs and tables; there was a small fire burning at one end, so hedged about with sofas and chairs as to give the other end of the room the appearance of a desert. Tea, which was brought in on a massive silver tray, was set out on a table in front of Clara's accustomed chair; and a quantity of food was spread over two other tables, on Crown Derby and Worcester plates, and several silver cake-baskets, which were embellished with crochet-mats of Clara's making. Ingram and Myra had walked up from the Dower House; and while Myra, a leathery woman with sharp features and an insistent voice, regaled Clara with an account of her triumph over the local butcher, Ingram straddled in front of the fire with his hands in his pockets, loudly arguing with Conrad on the merits of one of Conrad's hunters.

'He's a comfortable ride, which is more than can be said for that nappy brute you were fool enough to buy from old Saltash,' Conrad said.

'Ewe-necked!' snorted Ingram.

'A ewe neck never yet went with a sluggish gee, so who cares?' retorted Conrad, dropping four lumps of sugar into his tea-cup. 'He jumps off his hocks, too, *unlike*—'

'Oh, dry up, for God's sake!' interrupted Vivian. 'Can't you talk of anything but horses, any of you?'

Bart, who was sprawling in a deep chair with a plate of Cornish splits poised on the arm of it, grinned, and said: 'You wait till Clay comes home, Vivian, and then you'll have an ally. I say, Con, have you heard the great news? The Guv'nor's going to farm Clay out on poor old Cliff!'

'Who says so?' demanded Conrad.

'Eugène. It's true, isn't it, Faith?'

'I have no wish to discuss the matter,' said Faith stiffly.

Conrad paid not the smallest attention to her, saying in an incredulous tone: 'Go on, Bart! Cliff wouldn't have him!'

'Well, you can ask the Guv'nor, if you don't believe me,' yawned Bart, selecting another split from the plate, and consuming it in two mouthfuls.

'Good lord, he must have blackmailed old Cliff into it!' said Conrad. An unwelcome thought occurred to him; he added with foreboding: 'I say, does it mean that we shall have Clay living here, year in, year out?'

'That's the idea,' nodded Bart.

'Christ!' exclaimed his twin, in shattered accents.

Faith flushed angrily, but as she knew Conrad too well to suppose that he would attend to any remonstrances from her, she pretended to be listening to what Myra was saying to Clara.

'I must say, I should have thought that there were more than enough people living here already,' remarked Vivian, getting up to take Eugène's empty cup from him, and to carry it to Clara to be replenished.

'Thank you, my sweet,' he murmured. 'Not quite so much milk this time, please, Aunt Clara. I do wish you would move away from the fire, Ingram: I am feeling very chilly, and I got up with the suspicion of a cold in my head this morning.'

'Eugène! You never told me!' Vivian said quickly. 'Are you sure you're all right? I thought you didn't look quite so well today, but I put it down to the wretched night you had. Ingram, can't you sit down? You're screening all the warmth from Eugène!'

'Blast Eugène and his colds!' responded Ingram, without any particular ill-will. He removed himself to a chair beside Bart's, and lowered himself into it, stretching his stiff leg out before him. 'Hand over those splits, you young hog!'

'Eugène, I know you're sitting in a draught,' Vivian said anxiously.

'Yes, darling, I imagine you might,' said Eugène, 'since it is impossible to sit out of a draught in this room.'

'Somebody run and get our fragile pet a nice warm shawl,' suggested Bart. 'Perhaps he'd like a foot-warmer as well?'

'No, dear little brother, he would not,' retorted Eugène, in no way discomposed by this heavy satire. 'But I think if someone — you, for instance — were to move that screen a little, I, and possibly others as well (though that is not as important) should be much more comfortable.'

'Gosh, you have got a nerve!' ejaculated Bart. 'I fancy I see myself!'

'I'll do it!' Vivian said, setting down her cup-and-saucer, and laying hold of the screen in question, a massive, fourfold, ebony piece, with a peacock brilliantly inlaid upon it.

'Here, don't be a fool, Vivian!' Bart said, hoisting himself out of his chair, and lounging over to her assistance. 'You can't move that! What a blooming pest you are, the pair of you! Where do you want the damned thing?'

'Just behind my chair,' directed Eugène. 'Yes, that will do very well. I thought that I could make you move it, and you see that I was quite right.'

'If you weren't a lazy swine you wouldn't let Vivian haul furniture about just because you think you feel a draught!' said Bart, returning to his chair, and wresting the plate of splits away from Ingram.

'Ah, but I had an idea that your chivalry would be stirred, you see,' smiled Eugène. 'Of course, I wouldn't have risked it with Con or Ingram, but I have often observed that you have a nice nature, beloved. Now I'll reward you by divulging a piece of news which I rather fancy will make you view the prospect of Clay's arrival in our midst as a wholly minor ill. Our respected parent has taken it into his head to draw Aubrey back into the fold.'

'*What?*' demanded Bart, horrified.

'He won't come,' said Conrad confidently. 'Not enough scope for Aubrey in these parts.'

'Yes, but he's broke,' Bart pointed out. 'Oh, I say, but it's too thick! Honestly, Aubrey puts me right off my feed!'

'Bet you he doesn't come,' Conrad insisted.

'You ass, he's bound to come down for the old man's birthday!' Bart reminded him. 'Even Aubrey wouldn't miss that! Then, if he's broke, I'll lay you any odds he stays. Oh, Ray, is it true that Aubrey's coming home?'

Raymond, who had just come into the room through the door at the far end, replied harshly: 'Not if I have anything to say to it.'

'As you won't have anything to say to it—' began Ingram sarcastically.

Bart cut in on this. 'Well, say everything you can think of, will you? Damn it all, we can't have Aubrey here, corrupting our young minds! Think of Con and me!'

A shout of laughter went up from three of his brothers, but Raymond remained unsmiling. He walked over to the tea-table, and stood waiting for his aunt to fill a cup for him.

'It only remains for the old man to summon Char home for the circle to be complete,' said Eugène, in his light, bored voice. 'What a memorable day this has turned out to be!'

'One way and another,' remarked Conrad, cutting himself a large slice of seed-cake, 'there's a good deal to be said for Vivian's point of view. Too many people already in this house.'

'Don't worry!' said Raymond. 'One day there will be fewer!'

Vivian flushed hotly, but Eugène smiled with unimpaired good-humour. 'Do tell me!' he invited. 'Is that to my address?'

'Yes,' replied Raymond bluntly.

'Now you know what to expect!' said Ingram, with one of his aggressive laughs. 'Raymond was always overflowing with brotherly affection, of course.'

Raymond stood stirring the sugar in his tea. He glanced at Ingram, with a slight tightening of his mouth, but he did not speak. Bart, having eaten the last of the splits, turned his attention to a dish of saffron cakes. 'Oh, I say, Ray! Are you going to turn us all out when the old man dies?'

The frowning eyes rested on his face for an instant. 'Shan't have to turn you out,' Raymond said. 'Father will hand Trellick over to you – if you don't make a fool of yourself.'

Bart coloured up, and muttered: 'Don't know what you're driving at. I wish the old man would hurry up, that's all.'

Ingram's eyes went from him to Raymond, with quick curiosity. 'Hallo, what have you been up to, young Bart?'

'Nothing. You mind your own business!'

'Love's young dream!' murmured Eugène.

'Oh, is *that* all!' said Ingram, disappointed.

At this point, Myra, who had not been paying any attention to the interchange, appealed to her husband to corroborate her statement that Bertram's housemaster had said that that young gentleman had plenty of ability, if he would but learn to take more pains; and under cover of the animated account, which followed, of Rudolph's and Bertram's prowess in the field of athletic achievement, Bart lounged out of the room.

He found Loveday in one of the passages upstairs, curled up in a deep window-embrasure, and looking pensively down upon Clara's fern-garden. She turned her head when she heard his step, for she had been expecting him, and embraced him with her warm, slow smile. He pulled her up from the window-seat without ceremony, and into his strong young arms. 'Gosh, it's an age since I saw you last!' he said in a thickened voice.

Her body yielded for a moment; she kissed him with parted lips; but murmured, with a quiver of laughter in her voice, as he at last raised his head: 'This morning!'

'For two minutes!'

'Half-an-hour!'

'It isn't good enough. I can't go on like this! Here, come into the schoolroom!'

He thrust her into the room as he spoke, grasping her arm just above the elbow, and kicked the door to behind him. She let him kiss her again, but when he pulled her down beside him on the old horsehair sofa, she set her hands against his chest, and held him a little away from her. She was still smiling, and there was a kind of sleepy desire in her eyes, but she slightly shook her head. 'Now, Bart! Now, Bart!'

'You little devil, I don't believe you love me at all!' he said, half-laughing, half-hurt.

She leaned swiftly forward to plant a quick, firm kiss upon his mouth. 'Yes, then, I do, my dear, but you're a bad one for a poor girl to trust in. A clean-off rascal you are, love, aren't you now?'

He dragged her across his knees, so that her dark head lay on his arms. 'I swear I'll marry you! Loveday!'

She made no attempt to free herself from the rough grip upon her, but said softly: 'No.'

His hand, which had been stroking one of her thighs through the thin stuff of her dress, tightened on her firm flesh. 'You're driving me mad! I'm not going on like this.'

'We must be patient,' she said. 'Give over, Bart-love! you'll have me bruised black and blue. Let me sit up like a decent woman, now do!'

He released her, and she began to straighten her dress, and her dishevelled hair. 'You'll get me turned off without a character, my dear, that's what you'll do. We've got to be careful.'

'To hell with that! I'm my own master, and I'll do as I choose. If the Guv'nor won't give me Trellick Farm, I'll cut loose and make a living on my own! I could do it.'

'No, but you shan't then,' she said, taking one of his hands between hers and fondling it. 'There's never one as would employ you, love. You with your wildness, and your high-up airs, and the crazy notions you do be taking into your head! The poorhouse is where we'd end, and you promising to set me up in style at Trellick!'

He grinned, but said: 'I'm damned useful to Ray. He'd be willing to employ me up at the stud-farm.'

'He would not, then, and well you know it. You tell Raymond you're planning to marry Loveday Trewithian, and see what! Besides, there's nothing he could do for us, whatever he chose, while your father's alive.'

'Well, then, I'll set up as a trainer on my own.'

'Not without some money you won't, love. Leave the Master give old Penrose his notice to quit, and put you into Trellick, and you may put up the banns the first Sunday after.'

'I can't wait!'

She sighed. 'Why won't he set you up the way he said he would, Bart?'

'What's the good of asking why my father won't do a thing? I don't know – daresay he doesn't either. He talks a lot of rot about my not being ready for it, but that's not it.'

'Seeming to me,' she said thoughtfully, 'he's set on keeping you here under his thumb, my love, the same as he has Mr. Raymond. But he'll not last for ever, not the way he's carrying on, and so they all say.'

'Well, I'm sick of hanging about, meeting you in odd corners.

I'd rather have it out with the old man, and be damned to him!'

'Wait!' she counselled him. 'There's plenty of things can happen yet, and now's not the time to say anything to him that he wouldn't be pleased to hear. He put himself in a fine taking over the letter he had from Mr. Aubrey, by what my uncle told me. Wait, love!'

'I don't believe you mean to marry me,' he said sulkily.

She leaned towards him, till her arm touched his. 'Yes, I do mean. You know I do! And I will be a good wife to you, even if I'm beneath your station, my darling Barty. But there's not one of your brothers, nor your father neither, would leave you marry me, if they could stop it. We must be sensible. If it were found out you were keeping company with me before you've twopence to call your own, they'd send me packing, and manage it so that you couldn't come next or nigh me.'

That made him laugh; and he hugged her to him, and pinched her cheek. 'You don't know me if you think anyone of them could manage anything of the kind! Besides, why should my brothers care what I do?'

'Your brother Conrad would,' she insisted. 'Bart, I do be afraid of Conrad. He looks at me as though he'd like to see me dead.'

'What rot!' he scoffed. 'Con? Why, you little silly thing, Loveday, Con's my twin!'

'He's jealous,' she said.

But Bart only laughed again, because such an idea was so alien to his own nature as to be ridiculous to him. If Conrad looked darkly, he supposed him to be out of sorts, and gave the matter not another thought. When Loveday suggested that Conrad might divulge their secret to Penhallow, he replied without an instant's hesitation: 'He wouldn't. Even Eugène wouldn't do that. We don't give each other away to the Guv'nor.'

Her fingers twined themselves between his. 'Jimmy would,' she said, under her breath.

'What?' he exclaimed.

'Hush, my dear, you'll have one of the girl's overhearing you, and telling my uncle on me! Jimmy wouldn't make any bones about carrying tales to your father.'

'If I catch the little bastard's nose in my affairs, I'll twist it off!' swore Bart. 'He carry tales to my father! Let me see him snooping round us, that's all! You needn't worry, my sweet! He's a damned sight too scared of me to pry into my business.'

'He'd do you a mischief if he could,' she said in a troubled tone.

'Rot, why should he?'

She lacked the words to be able to explain her own vague intuition to him, and sat tongue-tied, twisting the corner of a little muslin apron she wore. He would not have understood her had she had the entire English vocabulary at her command, for he had a very simple mind, and such twisted thoughts as flourished in Jimmy's crafty brain he would neither have believed in nor comprehended. He sat looking at Loveday's downcast face with a puzzled frown, and presently asked: 'You haven't said anything to him, have you?'

She lied at once. She was ashamed to confess to him that her pride in her conquest had made her boast to Jimmy that she was soon to be married to a Penhallow. Besides, it was certain that he would be roused to quick wrath, and she was afraid of his anger, which, although it might be of short duration, quite possessed him while it lasted, and made him do things which afterwards he was sorry for. She said: 'Oh, no! But he's sly, Jimmy is, and there's little goes on in this house he doesn't know about. We did ought to be careful, Bart, love.'

'I want you,' he said. 'I don't care a damn for Jimmy, or anyone else. I'm going to have you.'

'Get Trellick, and there's no one can stop us marrying,' she said. 'I won't have you, love, else.'

Her caressing tone robbed her words of offence. She was passionately in love with him, but she had a native caution, born of her circumstances, which he lacked. She had the more subtle mind, too, and he was aware of it, sometimes a little puzzled by it, but on the whole respectful of it. He said: 'Well, I'll try to get the Guv'nor to see reason. But if he won't—'

'We'll think of something else,' she said quickly.

His hold round her waist tightened; he forced her head up with his free hand, and stared down into her face, a little smouldering light glowing at the back of his eyes. 'It won't make any difference! Or will it? Come on, out with it, my girl! Would you turn me down, if the old man chucked me out? I believe you would!'

Her lips invited him to kiss her. He did not, and she said: 'You silly! Don't I love you fit to die? There won't never be anyone else for me, my dear.'

He was satisfied at once. She herself could hardly have told whether she had spoken the truth or not, for she meant to have him, and to make him a good wife, too, and had not so far considered the possibilities of defeat. But without being consciously critical of him she was in no way blind to his faults, and she knew that his autocratic temper, as much as his dislike of submitting to any form of discipline, would make him a very unsatisfactory man to employ. As his own master, with his own farm, he would, she thought do very well, for he understood farming, was generally popular with his men under him, and would, besides, be largely guided by herself.

Having put him in a good humour again, she soon impressed upon him once more the need for caution, representing to him the folly of approaching his father at a moment when he was already exasperated by the extravagance of another of his sons, and coaxing him into promising to wait until Penhallow was in a mellow mood before bringing up the question of Trellick Farm again. Bart thought her a clever little puss, and laughed at her, and kissed her until she was breathless, swearing to be entirely guided by his long-headed little darling. Left to himself, he would have blundered in upon Penhallow then and there, blurting out the whole business, plunging into a noisy quarrel, and ending up very much where he was when he started. He could see that there might be something to be said for his Loveday's more roundabout methods.

She slipped away from him presently, but not without difficulty. He was daily growing harder to manage, more determined to possess her utterly, less easily held at arm's length, incapable of perceiving the need for secrecy in their dealings with each other. He could not understand her fear of being discovered in his company, and the thought that she could be afraid of her uncle and her aunt seemed to him ludicrous. One was not afraid of one's butler or of one's cook.

But under her smiling front Loveday was uneasy. She had caught Reuben looking at her narrowly once or twice, and had been obliged to listen to a crude warning from Sybilla, who told her with the utmost frankness that she need not look to her for help if she let Mr. Bart put her in the family way. She received the warning in demure silence, too shrewd to speak of Bart's promise to marry her. Sybilla and Reuben might treat the young Penhallows with the familiarity of old servants, but they would have been shocked beyond measure at the bare notion of their niece's aspiring to marry into the family.

There was a good deal of gossip amongst the other maid-servants, in more than one of whom Bart would have found an easier conquest; but since it was plain from their hints and giggles that they had no more suspicion of the true state of affairs than had the Lanners Loveday was content to suffer their whisperings, and met teasing and innuendo with unruffled placidity. She was not very popular amongst her fellows, being thought to give herself airs, and to be above her company, but as she had no intention of associating with any of the servants once she became Mrs. Bart Penhallow this in no way troubled her.

In her more hopeful moments, she was tempted to think that Penhallow would not dislike the marriage as much as her native shrewdness told her clearly that he would. It sometimes fell to her lot to wait on Penhallow, carrying in his trays when Martha could not be found, and Jimmy was otherwise engaged. Penhallow blatantly approved of this arrangement, told her she was the prettiest sight that had come his way for many a long day, pinched her cheek (and any other portion of her anatomy which she allowed to come within his reach), and told her she was a hard-hearted little bitch for refusing to give him a kiss. Sturdy common sense, however, made her admit to herself that this was scarcely behaviour to be expected of a prospective father-in-law, and she never permitted herself to indulge for long in undue optimism, but set herself instead to think out ways and means of achieving her ends with the least possible amount of unpleasantness.

It was characteristic of her that she sought no allies in the household. Her mistress had raised her to the role of confidante, but she gave no confidences in return for the many poured into her sympathetic ears. When Faith, with Vivian's words of warning nagging in her head, said awkwardly, and after a good deal of circumlocution, that she hoped Loveday was too sensible a girl to lose her head over any attentions which might be paid to her by Penhallow's sons, she was able to meet Faith's anxious gaze perfectly limpidly, and to reply in her soft way: 'You don't have to worry about me, ma'am, indeed.'

That was quite enough to allay Faith's misgivings, and when Penhallow remarked, with a chuckle, that if he knew anything of his sons she would soon be obliged to get rid of Loveday, she replied with perfect sincerity that Loveday was not at all flirtatious, and could be trusted to keep his sons at a distance.

Penhallow looked at her with undisguised contempt. 'Lord, my dear, if ever I met such a soft fool as you! Don't you know a hot-blooded wench when you see one? She's got a warm eye, that girl of yours, and there ain't a trick in the game she isn't up to, you mark my words!'

'I think you're all of you most unfair about Loveday!' Faith said, in her most complaining tone. 'It's simply because she's my maid that you say these disgusting things about her!'

'I don't trust the gal,' said Clara, who was sitting by the fire, engaged upon yards of her interminable crochet-work. 'She's sly. You'll have Bart or Con gettin' mixed up with her, if you don't take care, Adam.'

He gave a laugh. 'They've been wasting their time if one or other of them hasn't got mixed up with her already, old girl,' he remarked. 'Damn it all, the wench has been in the house close on a year!'

'It was all right before Faith took her out of the kitchen where she belongs,' said Clara. 'I don't hold with puttin' ideas into gals' heads.'

But Penhallow refused for once to condemn his wife's actions, merely saying derisively: 'Bless your silly old heart, Clara, you can't put ideas into the heads of girls like that ripe bit of goods: they grow there.'

'In any case, I don't see what it has to do with you, Clara,' said Faith tactlessly. 'I'm sure I have a perfect right to employ whom I choose for my personal maid!'

Penhallow rolled an eye in her direction. 'Who said you hadn't? Don't, for God's sake, start one of your grievances! It's coming to something if Clara can't give her opinion without having you jump down her throat!'

'Oh, well!' said Clara peaceably. 'I wasn't criticizin' you, my dear. It isn't anything to do with me, though that Bart of yours is a young rascal, Adam, and the way the gals fall for him is shockin'!'

He roared with laughter. 'Spit and image of me!' he declared. 'He's the best of the bunch, when all's said and done!'

'When are you goin' to set him up for himself at Trellick?' Clara inquired, obedient to her favourite nephew's instructions.

Penhallow grunted. 'Time enough for that. He's useful to Ray here.'

'I don't believe Ray wants him, or any of them,' said Faith.

'Oh, you don't, don't you?' said Penhallow, bending a fierce stare upon her. 'And what do you know about it, I should like to know?'

Her colour fluctuated, as it always did when he spoke roughly to her. She replied defensively: 'Oh, nothing! Only Ray never makes any secret of the fact that he thinks there are too many people in this house. And, really—'

He interrupted her brusquely. 'Ray's not master here yet, and so I'll thank him to remember! I'll have whom I choose in the house, and be damned to the lot of you!'

'Now, Adam, don't put yourself in a temper for nothin'!' his sister admonished him. 'Ray doesn't mean anythin'. He's cross-grained, but he's got a good heart, and if Faith hasn't got more sense than to believe every word he says when he's a bit put out, it's time she had. All the same, 'tisn't natural for a young fellow like Bart to be hanging about with no more to do than Ray gives him, and if I were you I'd set him up on his own. Keep him out of mischief, I daresay.'

'I don't mind his mischief,' replied Penhallow cheerfully. 'I'll hand over Trellick to him in my own good time. Won't hurt him to stay at home for a while longer, and learn what Ray can drum into his thick head. He's feckless, that lad. Ray's a dull dog, but he knows his job. I'll say that for him.'

So Clara had presently to report failure to Bart, who grimaced, and said: 'Blast!'

'I daresay he'll change his mind, give him time,' she said consolingly. She looked at him with mild curiosity. 'What's got into you all of a sudden, Bart, to make you so keen to get to work? Not thinkin' of gettin' married, are you?'

'Wouldn't you like to know?' he said, laughing, but reddening a little too. 'Who said anything about getting married? I've got to settle down sometime, haven't I?'

She shook her head dubiously. 'You're up to something: don't tell *me*! Is she a nice gal?'

'Who? The future Mrs. Bart? Oh, sure!' he said, grinning at her. 'Don't you think I've got good taste, auntie?'

'No,' she said bluntly. 'Not that it's my affair, and when you come to think of it—' She left the sentence unfinished, and rubbed the tip of her nose reflectively.

'Come to think of what?' asked Bart.

'Nice gals,' said Clara. 'Look at that daughter-in-law of mine!'

'I don't want to,' replied Bart frankly. 'Cliff's welcome to her.'

'Well, there it is,' said Clara, not very intelligibly. '*She* was a nice girl, and I daresay she's a good wife.'

'Any time I want to go to bed with a cold compress, I'll look around me for her double,' said Bart.

'That's it,' said Clara vaguely. She stood looking at him in a puzzled way for a few moments, gave her head another shake, and walked off, leaving the conversation suspended in mid-air.

CHAPTER SEVEN

CLARA'S representations to Penhallow on Bart's behalf having failed of their object, it next occurred to him to approach Raymond on the matter. Raymond's undisguised anxiety to rid Trevellin of its many inhabitants made him hopeful that he might find an ally; but his first interview with him was disappointing. Raymond said caustically that if he wished to convince Penhallow that he was fit to be entrusted with the sole management of Trellick he had better pay a little more attention to his duties on the estate and up at the stud-farm. Bart, whose resentment of his stricture was not lessened by a knowledge of having lately deserved it, replied hotly, and the interview came to an abrupt close. When his anger had had time to cool, he again opened the matter to Raymond, offering him an awkward apology for sundry errors of omission, and saying in excuse that he had been busy with affairs of his own for the past few weeks.

'Yes, I know that,' said Raymond unhelpfully. 'Loveday Trewithian.'

Bart turned scarlet, but said: 'Rot! The fact is, I'm sick of hanging about at home. I want to be on my own. Damn it, I'm twenty-five!'

'It's a pity you don't behave as though you were,' said Raymond.

Bart kept his temper with an effort. 'Look here, Ray! You've as good as said you want to get rid of me! Why can't you back me with the Guv'nor?'

'I don't want to get rid of you. You're quite useful, when you can keep your mind on the job. Eugène's the one I want to get rid of.'

'Oh, I don't know!' Bart said, momentarily diverted. 'He's so damned funny, with his ailments, and that spitfire of a wife of his. I think I should miss them if they cleared out. Mind you, I'm not in favour of Aubrey's coming home. Or Clay. But if they *are* coming, all the more reason for me to make myself scarce.'

Raymond gave him a straight look under his lowering brows. 'If you imagine I'm going to help you to Trellick so that you can make a fool of yourself over Loveday Trewithian, you've got another guess coming to you.'

'I don't know what you're talking about,' muttered Bart.

'Do you mean to marry that girl?'

'Look here, who's been talking to you about my affairs?' Bart demanded.

'I've got eyes in my head.'

'Well, keep them off my business, will you?'

'If you're thinking of marrying Loveday Trewithian, you'll find

I'm not the only one to take an interest in what you call your business. You young fool, so it is true, is it?'

'I didn't say so. What if it is? I suppose I can please myself when it comes to getting married!'

'Oh, no, you can't!' retorted Raymond grimly. 'You're a Penhallow!'

'Oh, to hell with that!' said Bart. 'That kind of snobbery's been dead for years!'

'You'll discover your little error, my lad, if you go any farther with that girl. What the devil's the matter with you? Do you see yourself calling Reuben uncle?'

Bart could not help grinning, but he replied: 'I shan't. It'll all work out quite easily: you'll see!'

'No, I'm damned if I shall! If you can't get that girl out of your system, she'll have to go.'

Bart's chin jutted dangerously. 'You try interfering with Loveday, and *watch me!*'

'Don't be a bigger ass than you can help! God, I thought you had more pride! Since when has a Penhallow gone to the kitchen for a wife?'

Bart flushed. 'That'll be all from you, Ray! Loveday's worth a dozen of Faith, or Vivian, or that stuck-up bitch Cliff landed himself with. The trouble with you is that you're eaten up with conceit. Who cares two pins for the damned family, I should like to know?'

'Go and tell Father your plans, and you'll find out who cares,' replied Raymond.

'Oh, go to hell!' Bart exploded, and turned on his heel.

The only result of this interview was that Raymond took the first opportunity that offered of warning Loveday to leave his young brother alone. She stood demurely before him, looking up at him under her lashes, and keeping her hands folded over her apron. She denied nothing, and admitted nothing, and she betrayed no hint of resentment. She said, 'Yes, sir,' and 'No, sir,' in her meekest tone. He thought her either a fool, or a dangerously clever young woman, and was tempted to speak to Reuben about her. Natural taciturnity, dislike of discussing the failings of a Penhallow with a servant, and a wary foreboding of Bart's probable reactions to any intervention of Reuben's, made him forbear. He mentioned the matter instead to Conrad, but Conrad, who had been picking quarrels with his twin for weeks, still would not allow anyone else to criticize him. 'Oh, there's nothing in it!' Conrad said. 'She isn't the first, and she won't be the last.'

'Do you know that he means to marry her?'

'Rot!' Conrad said scornfully. 'Bart wouldn't be such a fool!'

'I'll take damned good care he doesn't get the chance to be!' Raymond said. 'What's got into the kid, I should like to know??'

Conrad shrugged, and would not answer. He did not know what

had got into Bart, and his jealously possessive nature was profoundly troubled. Bart was as friendly as ever he had been; as ready to go off with him, a hand tucked in his arm; as willing, had he received the smallest encouragement, to confide in him; but in some indefinable way he seemed to Conrad to have withdrawn himself, to be living in a snug world of his own, which had no room in it for his twin. None of his earlier amatory adventures had affected him in this manner, and without pausing to consider the unreason of his own feelings, Conrad allowed hatred of Loveday to fester in his soul, until he could scarcely see her without wanting to do her an injury. When the turmoil in his own breast led him to snap Bart's head off, which it often did, and he caught Bart looking at him with a puzzled, rather hurt expression in his face, he wanted to hit Bart, or to spirit him away to some unspecified locality far beyond the reach of predatory females: he was never quite sure which.

Eugène, whom little escaped, was as well aware of his jealousy as of its cause, and lost few opportunities to plant his barbs in Conrad's flesh, impelled more by a natural love of mischief than by any real desire to wound. A spirit of considerable unrest dwelt in the house, and was not improved by a sudden recrudescence of energy upon the part of Penhallow, who, after a long spell of physical quiescence, took it into his head to arise from his bed nearly every day, and to meddle with every concern of the house, estate, and stud-farm. He sat in his wheeled chair, usually clad in his disreputable old camel-hair dressing-gown, and wrapped about in a plaid rug, and insisted upon being pushed to the various places where he was least wanted. He harried Raymond, Ingram, and Bart unmercifully, finding fault with all their activities, countermanding most of their orders, roaring abuse of them in front of stable-hands and grooms, and driving them into an uneasy alliance against him. Finding Clara triumphant at having coaxed the rare adder's tongue to show its head in her garden, amongst the more general *Osmunda regalis*, and the *Hymenophyllum Tunbridgense*, and *unilaterale* which she cherished with such anxious care, he threatened to convert the whole area into a sunk garden of Italian design, to give pleasure to his wife. As Faith's efforts at gardening were confined to the plucking of flowers for the house, and an unsuccessful but characteristic attempt to induce roses to flourish in a climate more suited to fuchsias and hydrangeas, no one was taken in by the blatant falsity of this reason for disturbing Clara's peace of mind, and the family banded together temporarily to protect her interests. In this they were ably assisted by Hayle, the head-gardener, who said that he had enough on his hands already, and couldn't get through the work of the place as it was, what with being short-handed, and Mrs. Penhallow taking Luckett, the under-gardener, off his work to drive her about the country in season and out of it. This served instantly to divert Penhallow, who, after scarifying his wife for being fool enough to require the services of a chauffeur, and ignorant enough to remove him from his proper sphere in the middle of the bedding-out season, commandeered Luckett's services himself, and spent several days in being driven up on to the Moor, down to the coast, and into the neighbouring towns of Bodmin and Liskeard, where he called upon a number of acquaintances, hailing them from their houses to stand beside the car exchanging the time of day with him, and marvelling at the robustness of his constitution. He fortified himself upon these drives from a flask of brandy, and insisted upon being accompanied by whichever member of his entourage he thought least wished to go with him. He took Jimmy with him when he went to call at the Vicarage, well knowing that Jimmy's very existence was an offence in Mrs. Venngreen's eyes; and when the Vicar, standing in a sharp wind in the road, made his wife's excuses, showed such alarming signs of preparing to descend from the car with Jimmy's and the startled Vicar's assistance, that Mrs. Venngreen was obliged to come out of the house after all, to prevent his invading it, and very likely (she thought) succumbing there to a heart-attack. She joined her husband in the road, and since she had very good manners forced herself to accept with the appearance at least of credulity Penhallow's jovial assurances that he had come to call at the Vicarage with the express purpose of discovering how she did. Her private opinion was that he was possessed of a peculiarly malignant devil. He was certainly in a riotous mood, and when she inquired politely after the health of his sons, said with a fiendish twinkle that they were all eating their heads off, including the young rascal he had with him. Under Mrs. Venngreen's outraged gaze, he indicated the regrettable Jimmy, just so that she should have no doubt of his meaning. Mrs. Venngreen's countenance became so rigid and enflamed that he drove off in high good-humour to see if he could get such interesting reactions out of Rosamund Hastings, whom he cordially disliked. Upon the whole, Rosamund's behaviour was not so satisfactory as Mrs. Venngreen's, but even her cold air of breeding could not conceal her disgust, and Penhallow thought that she would certainly have a good deal to say to poor old Cliff about it when he came home from his office later in the day. He returned to Trevellin, considerably exhausted, but still, apparently, driven by his strange fit of energy, since although he retired to bed he summoned his entire family to spend the evening in his room, in the usual way, and kept them there till an advanced hour of the night, playing backgammon with him, discussing the merits and faults of every horse in the stables, recalling extremely funny and generally improper incidents which belonged to his youth, drinking a quantity of whisky, and consuming a sort of rear-banquet consisting of all the foods most likely to ensure him a restless night.

His medical adviser, Dr. Wilfred Lifton, who had attended him for more years than either could remember, besides delivering Rachel of all her children, from Ingram down to the twins, paid him one of his periodical visits, and solemnly warned him that he was fast killing himself; but Penhallow merely laughed, and said that he didn't want any damned leech to tell him what he could do or what he could not do. He refused to allow his old friend to sound him, but recommened him to join him in a glass of sherry instead.

Dr. Lifton was neither brilliant nor modern, but since he was a sportsman, and a good man to hounds, he was popular with a certain section of the community, who in any case disliked the up-to-date methods of his partner, an earnest and severe gentleman who treated his patients with a sternness quite alien to anyone accustomed to Dr. Lifton's casual attentions.

However, Dr. Lifton was sufficiently impressed by the folly of Penhallow's present conduct to warn Faith and Raymond severally that if they wished him to survive they must put a stop to his disastrous energy, and regulate drastically his consumption of wines and spirits. Raymond, when this was propounded to him, gave a short laugh, recommended the doctor to address his advice to the patient, and walked out of the room, saying that he had something better to do than to talk about impossibilities.

Faith, when similarly admonished, faltered that Dr. Lifton knew what her husband was. He could not deny this, but said that he could not be responsible for the outcome if Penhallow continued to indulge his taste for strong drink to the extent he was now doing.

'He says – he says you told him that he might take stimulants to keep his strength up,' faltered Faith.

'Mrs. Penhallow, are you aware of the amount of liquor your husband consumes?' demanded Lifton.

'Yes – no – I mean, I've always said he drank too much, but it never seems to affect him. And really he does seem better now than he's been all the winter.'

'He has the most amazing constitution I ever met with,' said Lifton frankly. 'But he can't last at this rate. All this dashin' about the country, too! It isn't fit for him. You'll have to use your influence with him, my dear.'

Faith was incapable of admitting that she possessed no influence over Penhallow – a fact of which he was well aware – and said rather vaguely: 'Yes, of course. Only he has a – a very strong will, you know, doctor.'

'He's the most obstinate old devil in the county, and well I know it!' responded Lifton, not mincing matters.

Clara, when this conversation was reported to her, shook her head, and said that Lifton was an old woman, and knew less about Penhallow's constitution than she knew about the workings of a combustion engine. 'He's been sayin' for years that Adam will kill himself with his goin's on, but he's not dead yet, my dear, nor likely to be. It's my belief this heart-dropsy of his isn't as bad as he likes to make out. You mark my words: he'll go on for a good many years yet. As for all this dashin' around, it's the spring got into his blood. He'll quieten down again, if you don't pester him, or take any notice of his antics.'

Faith was roused to say with some indignation: 'It's impossible not to take any notice of him when he does such outrageous things! Do you know that he actually took Jimmy with him when he went to call on Rosamund the other day; and insisted on her more or less recognizing the creature?'

'He shouldn't have done that,' agreed Clara. 'But there! he was always one to enjoy his bit of fun, and nothin' ever tickles him more than to shock people. I've no patience with Rosamund for kickin' up such a song and dance about it!'

'Well, I think it was disgusting!' said Faith. 'And apart from anything else, taking Jimmy about with him in that way is simply making him more objectionable than he was before. Jimmy, I mean. He's beginning to behave as though he could do exactly as he liked, and I'm sure I'm not surprised at it!'

'I wouldn't worry about it if I were you,' said Clara. 'The boys will soon knock it out of him, if he gets above himself.'

'Knock what out of whom?' inquired Eugène, who had come into the room in time to overhear this remark.

'Faith thinks your father's makin' a fool of Jimmy.'

'Repulsive by-blow!' said Eugène, lowering himself into an easy-chair. 'He's quite beneath my notice. Of course, I see that bringing him under our roof is a truly superb gesture, but if he's a fair specimen of Father's illegitimate offspring I can only be thankful that he hasn't extended the practice of adoption to the rest of them.'

'I don't expect any of you to see the thing in an ordinarily decent light,' said Faith, 'but I regard his presence here as a direct insult to me!'

Eugène regarded her with some amusement. 'Oh, I don't think you need!' he said sweetly. 'That little episode was before your time.'

'I sometimes think you none of you have any moral sense at all!' Faith cried.

'Well, not much, anyway,' agreed Eugène. 'Except Bart, of course.'

'Bart!'

He smiled. 'It does seem odd, doesn't it? Deplorable, too, one must admit. There is something almost suburban about the respectability of his present matrimonial intentions.'

Faith coloured hotly. 'It isn't true! Loveday has never dreamt of such a thing! If it hadn't been for you starting what I can only call a malicious rumour, no one would ever have thought of it!'

Clara looked from one to the other of them, with an expression of mild dismay on her face. 'You don't mean it! Well, I thought he was up to something. But I don't like that at all, and, what's more, his father will never hear of it.'

'Clara! It's nothing but one of Eugène's scandals! I'm perfectly sure Loveday has never looked at Bart!'

Clara looked unconvinced, merely remarking gloomily that she had said all along that Loveday was a sly gal. Thoroughly incensed,

Faith left the room. Eugène yawned, and said reflectively that it was really very hard to discover what Penhallow had ever seen in her.

'Well, she's a tiresome creature, and there's no gettin' away from that,' conceded Clara. 'But you shouldn't tease her, Eugène, when you know it upsets her. I daresay she's got a lot more to put up with than any of us realize. She's worried too about Clay's havin' to come home, which isn't what she wants. You leave her alone!'

'If she doesn't want Clay to come home I can even sympathize with her,' replied Eugène. 'Though I should hardly have expected Faith to show such good taste, I must say.'

'Now, that's enough!' said Clara severely. 'The doctor's been here, and he says your father can't go on like this.'

'He's been doing it for a good many years,' said Eugène, selecting a fat Egyptian cigarette from his case, and lighting it.

Clara rubbed her nose. 'Well, that's what I say, but I'm sure I don't know what's got into the man, for I never knew him quite so wild as he is this year. He's goin' on as though someone had wound him up, and he couldn't stop.'

'Yes, I thought he seemed distinctly above himself,' said Eugène, with detached interest. 'Perhaps he'll have a stroke, or something. That ought to please a good many of our number.'

Clara ignored this rider. 'If this story you've got hold of about Bart is true, he'll very likely burst a blood-vessel,' she said. 'I don't like it at all, Eugène, and that's the truth.'

'Personally, I feel that Loveday is just the sort of wife to suit Bart down to the ground,' replied Eugène, blowing smoke-rings, and lazily watching them float upwards. 'Not, of course, that the rest of the family is likely to see it in that light. You're all so hidebound.'

'Now, don't you go backin' him up!' Clara begged him. 'There'll be trouble enough without you addin' to it. I never liked that gal.'

As Eugène showed no disposition to continue the discussion, she relapsed into silence. That she was unusually disturbed, however, was seen by her working nearly an inch of her crochet-pattern wrong, a thing no one had known her to do before.

In spite of her soothing remarks to Faith, she privately felt that Penhallow was working himself up to a crisis. His conduct had never been orthodox, but he had not until lately indulged in as many extravagances as were fast becoming commonplaces in his life. His career had been characterized by a sublime disregard for convention or public opinion; he seemed now to be taking a malignant delight in outraging his family and his acquaintance, a significant change in his mentality which made Clara feel uneasy. The robust and generally unthinking brutality of his maturity was changing to a deliberate, if irrational, cruelty, which seemed often to be as purposeless as it was ruthless. From having exercised his power over his dependants to force them to conform to that way of life which suited himself, he was now showing alarming signs of exercising an arbitrary tyranny for the sheer love of it. The wounds his rough tongue had dealt during the years of his rampant strength and health had seldom been intentional; now that his health had broken down, and his strength had failed, nothing seemed to please him more than to aim such wicked shafts at his victims as penetrated even the armour of a Penhallow. If he could upset the peace of mind of any of his household, he would lose no time in doing so, as if he were bent on revenging his physical helplessness on his family. The absence of motive for many of his wanton attacks made his sister wonder whether his brain were going. He had unblushingly boasted to her of the weapon he had used to compel Clifford to receive Clay as a pupil, and had appeared to be hugely entertained by her shocked face. She had said, with an odd dignity: 'If you want me to leave Trevelin, Adam, you've only to tell me so. There's no need to drag my boy into it that I know of. I can shift for myself.'

'Lord, _I_ don't want to get rid of you, old girl!' he had replied carelessly. 'Catch Cliff calling my bluff! Made me laugh to see him squirming, though.'

Either he was impervious to the very natural feeling of hurt which she must experience from learning her son's reluctance to receive her under his roof, or he had made the disclosure on purpose to enjoy her discomfiture. She could not be sure, and she would not gratify him by betraying a wound. A silent woman, she did not refer to the matter again; nor, in her behaviour, did she show the least sign of having taken his words seriously. But she was disturbed, filled with vague forebodings of disaster, regarding the growing indications of brewing strife in the house with a concern quite foreign to her aloof temperament.

CHAPTER EIGHT

UPON Clay's learning of the fate his father had in store for him, he lost little time in subjecting his mother to a spate of letters, which varied in tone between the darkly threatening and the wildly despairing. He informed her that death would be preferable to him than life at home; that the study of the law would kill his soul; that he had no intention of submitting to Penhallow's arbitrary commands; that he had never had a chance in life; that no one understood him; and, finally, that his mother ought to do something about it.

To all of these effusions Faith replied suitably; and although she had no idea what she could possibly do about it, she quite agreed that it was her sacred duty to protect her only son from Penhallow's tyranny. She paid a great many visits to Clifford's office, and would no doubt have paid more had he not prudently instructed his clerk to deny him; and tried successively to enlist the support of each of Clay's half-brothers. This attempt was unattended by success. Eugène and the twins, while viewing Clay's prospective sojourn at Trevellin with disfavour, were yet too little affected by it to meddle in what was admittedly a sleeveless errand; Ingram, who believed in keeping upon easy terms with everyone except Raymond, gave her a good deal of sympathy, agreed with every word she had to say, promised to do what he could, and left it at that; and Raymond replied curtly that Penhallow was already aware of his disapproval, and that to say anything more on the subject was a waste of time which he for one did not propose to indulge in. He added that since, under the terms of Penhallow's will, Faith would be in possession of an ample jointure upon his death, she had better contain her soul in patience for a year or two, at the end of which time she would no doubt be in a position to finance Clay in whatever wild-cat scheme for his advancement he had taken into his head. This brusquely delivered piece of advice so much annoyed Faith that she succumbed to one of her nervous attacks, complained of head-ache and insomnia, and sent Loveday to Bodmin to procure for her at the chemist's a quantity of drugs the free consumption of which might have been expected to have ruined any but the most resilient constitution; and bored everyone by describing the increasing number of veronal-drops now necessary to induce the bare minimum of sleep.

It might have been supposed that she would have found, if not an ally, a sympathizer in Vivian, but Vivian, besides feeling that anyone who had been fool enough to marry Penhallow deserved whatever was coming to her, was a great deal too absorbed in her own troubles to have any attention to spare for another's. Her last interview with Penhallow on the question of her enforced residence at Trevellin seemed to have stirred the fire of her resentment to a flame. Every petty inconvenience or annoyance became a major ill in her eyes; she tried in a variety of ways to inspire Eugène with a desire to break away from his family; wrung from a reluctant editor a half-promise to employ him as dramatic critic on his paper; obtained orders to view a number of desirable flats in London; and even evolved an energetic plan for earning money on her own account by conducting interested foreigners round London, and pointing out places of note to them. None of these schemes came to fruition, because it was beyond her power to goad Eugène into making the least alteration in his indolent habits. A perpetual crease dwelled between her straight brows; she developed an uncomfortable trick of pacing up and down rooms, smoking rapidly as she did so, and obviously hammering out ways and means in her impatient brain. It was the freely expressed opinion of Conrad that she would shortly blow up, and this, indeed, was very much the impression she conveyed to a disinterested onlooker. Inaction being insupportable to anyone of her restless temperament, and the natural outlet for her energy being effectively plugged by her husband's refusal to bestir himself, she took to tramping for miles over the Moor, an exercise which might have had a more beneficial effect upon the state of her mind had she not occupied it the whole time in brooding over the insufferable nature of her position at Trevellin. When in the house, she spent her time between ministering to Eugène's comfort, quarrelling with her brothers-in-law, and finding fault with the domestic arrangements.

It was she who was loudest in condemnation of Jimmy's increasing idleness, and of his dissipated habits, which were becoming daily more marked. She said that he spent all the money which Penhallow casually bestowed upon him at the nearest public-house, and complained that he had several times answered her in a most insolent manner. No one paid any heed to this charge, but none of the Penhallows was blind to the deterioration in their baseborn relative. Penhallow was becoming still more dependent upon him, and seemed to prefer his ministrations even to Martha's. As it amused him to encourage Jimmy to recount for his edification any items of news current in the house, it was not surprising that the young man should have begun to presume upon his position, which he did to such an unwise extent upon one occasion that Bart kicked him down the back-stairs, causing him to sprain his wrist, and to break a rib. He picked himself up, muttering threats of vengeance, and directing so malevolent a look upwards at Bart that that irate young gentleman started to come down the stairs to press his lesson home more indelibly still. Jimmy took himself off with more haste than dignity, fortified himself with a considerable quantity of gin, and in this pot-valiant condition went to Penhallow's room, where he made a great parade of his hurts, and said sullenly that he wasn't going to stay at Trevellin to be knocked about by them as was no better than himself. Had he received the slightest encouragement, he would have embarked upon an account of his suspicions of Bart's intentions towards Loveday, but Penhallow interrupted him, barking at him: 'Damn your impudence, who are you to say where you'll stay? You'll stay where I tell you! Broken a rib, have you? What of it? Serve you right for getting on the wrong side of that young devil of mine! I've spoilt you, that's what I've done!'

But when Penhallow discovered that the sprained wrist made it impossible for Jimmy to perform many of the duties in the sick-room which had been allotted to him, he swore, and commanded Bart to leave the lad alone.

'I'll break every bone in his body, if he gives me any of his lip!' promised Bart.

Penhallow regarded him with an irascibility not unmixed with pride. 'No, you won't,' he said mildly. 'I need him to wait on me. When I'm gone you can please yourself. Until then you'll please me!'

Bart scowled down at him, as he lay in his immense bed. 'What you want with such a dirty little tick beats me, Guv'nor!' he said. 'I wouldn't let him come within a ten-foot pole of me, if I were in your shoes!'

As this interchange took place after dinner, when the entire family had been gathered together in Penhallow's room, after the custom which he had instituted upon first taking to his bed and ever afterwards refused to modify, it seemed good to several other people to join in the conversation, each one adding his or her mite to the general condemnation of Jimmy's character and habits. Even Ingram, who had limped up from the Dower House to pass the evening in his father's room, gave it as his opinion that the air of Trevellin would be the purer for Jimmy's absence; while Conrad asserted that he had lately missed a number of small articles, and was prepared to bet that they had found their way into Jimmy's pocket.

'You're all of you jealous of poor little Jimmy,' said Penhallow, becoming maudlin. 'You're afraid of what I'll leave him in my will. He's the only one of the whole pack of you who cares tuppence about his old father.'

Everyone knew that Penhallow was under no illusions about the nature of his misbegotten offspring, and was merely trying to promote a general feeling of annoyance, but only Raymond, who contented himself with giving a contemptuous laugh, could resist the temptation of picking up the glove tossed so provocatively into the midst of the circle.

They were all present, scattered about the great room, which was lit by candles in the wall-sconces, and in massive chandeliers of Sheffield plate, which stood upon tables wherever they were needed. There was also an oil lamp upon the refectory table, brought in by Faith, who complained that she could not see by the flickering candle-light. She sat with her fair head bent over a wisp of embroidery, her workbasket open on the oak table at her elbow, the scissors in it caught by the flames of the candles on the wall, and flashing back brilliant points of light. She had chosen a straight-backed Jacobean chair, and drooped in it, seldom looking up from her work, her whole pose suggesting that she was enduring a nightly penance. Her sister-in-law occupied an arm-chair on one side of the fire, opposite to the one in which Raymond sat, glancing through the pages of the local paper. Clara was wearing a tea-gown, once black, now rusty with age; she had turned the skirt up over her knees to preserve it from the scorching heat of the leaping fire in the huge hearth, and displayed the flounces of an ancient petticoat. Her bony fingers were busy with her crochet; a pair of pince-nez perched on the high bridge of her nose, and was secured to her person by a thin gold chain, attached to a brooch, pinned askew on her flat chest. The disreputable cat, Beelzebub, lay asleep in her lap. Near to her, seated astride a spindle-legged chair with a rotting brocade seat, was Conrad. He had crossed his arms along the delicately curved back of the chair, and was resting his chin on them. Eugène, after a slight dispute with Ingram, had obtained sole possession of the chesterfield at the foot of the bed, and lay on it in an attitude of lazy grace. Vivian, wearing a dress of flaring scarlet, was a splash of colour in the open space immediately before the fire, hugging her knees on a stool between Clara's and Raymond's chairs, turning

78

her back upon the bed, staring moodily into the flames. Ingram, oddly discordant in a dinner-jacket and a stiff shirt, which Myra insisted on his wearing every evening, sat in a deep chair pulled away from the fire, with one leg stretched out before him for greater ease, his elbows on the arms of his chair, and his fingertips lightly pressed together. Bart was leaning up against the lacquer cabinet with his hands in his pockets, the light from the candles above his head, which was wavering in the draught from the windows, playing strange tricks with his face, giving it a saturnine expression, making him look, Faith thought, glancing up from her work, like a devil, which he was not. The atmosphere was heavy with the scent of the cigars Penhallow and Raymond were smoking, which overcame the thinner, more acrid fumes of the twins' cheap cigarettes. How unhealthy it was, Faith thought, to sleep in a room stale with tobacco smoke! How hot it was in here, how fantastic the candle-light, dazzling the eyes, making the red lacquer cabinet glow as though it were on fire, casting queer shadows in the corners of the room, playing over the strong, dark faces of Penhallow and his sons! She gave a little inward shudder, and bent again over her needlework, wondering how many purgatorial evenings lay ahead of her, and how she could save Clay from being drawn into a circle as alien to him as it was to her.

'Jealous of Jimmy the Bastard!' Ingram was saying. 'Oh, come now, sir, that's a bit too steep!'

'He's a good boy,' said Penhallow. 'Damme if I don't do something handsome for him!'

'If you want to do something handsome for anyone, let it be for one of your legitimate sons!' Vivian threw over her shoulder.

'Your precious husband, I suppose!' jeered Penhallow.

'Why not?' she demanded.

'Because I don't want to, that's why not, you little madam!'

'That's where you're so beastly unfair!' she said. 'You only encourage that disgusting Jimmy because you know everyone else loathes him!'

Eugène reached out a long arm, and tickled the back of her neck where the short tendrils of hair curled upwards. His fingers conveyed comfort and remonstrance both. She flushed quickly, and shifted the stool on which she sat nearer to the sofa, so that he could put his arm round her, and she lean back against his shoulder.

'Look here, Father!' said Conrad, raising his chin from his wrists. 'Nobody objects to your employing your little mistakes, if you want to, but for God's sake teach 'em to keeep their places! If Jimmy treats me to much more of his bloody impudence there'll be murder done!'

'Somebody might, at the same time, teach him to polish my shoes properly,' suggested Eugène, in a gentle voice.

'So he's been cheeking you, has he, Con?' grinned Penhallow. 'By God, he's got spirit, that lad!'

'Spirit!' exploded Bart. 'He's a sneaking little rat, trading on your blooming protection! You lie there letting him gammon you into thinking he's worth his salt, but if you saw how he behaves outside this room you'd darned soon kick him out!'

'That's right,' nodded Clara. 'Can't stand corn. You shouldn't take him round the country with you, Adam, introducing him to decent people. It stands to reason the boy must get above himself.'

'Old Mother Venngreen been complaining to you, Clara?' asked Penhallow, with a chuckle. 'That did me more good than all Lifton's drenches, I can tell you. Nearly split my sides watching the old turkey-hen gobble and ruffle up her feathers!'

The twins shouted with laughter, not having known previously of this historic encounter, but Ingram looked a trifle shocked, and said in an expostulating tone: 'No, really, sir, I say! You can't do that sort of thing! I mean, the Vicar's wife—!'

Bart gave a crow of delight. 'Ingram and the old school tie! Play up for the side – don't let the school down – stick to the done-thing, fellers!'

'White man's burden,' said Conrad. 'Example to the neighbourhood. Long live our *pukka sahib*!'

'Shut up, you young fools!' Ingram said, reddening. 'All the same, in your position, sir—'

'Blast your impudence, are you going to tell me how I ought to behave myself?' demanded Penhallow, but with more amusement than anger.

'I don't know how we are ever to look Mrs. Venngreen in the face again, any of us,' said Faith, in low voice.

'Speaking for myself,' murmured Eugène, drawing Vivian's head back so that he could smile down into her adoring eyes, 'I don't find that I have any very overpowering desire to look her in the face. None that I can't master, you know.'

'I had a horse with a face like Mrs. Venngreen's,' remarked Clara reminiscently. 'You'll remember him, Adam: a chestnut with a white blaze. He had a bad habit of jumpin' off his forehand.'

'Talking about horses,' interrupted Bart suddenly, turning his head towards Raymond, 'Weens says it's spavin, Ray.'

'What's that?' Penhallow demanded. 'If you've got a spavined horse in the stables, get rid of him!'

'That's right,' agreed Clara. 'I don't care what anyone may say: a spavined horse is an unsound horse.'

'Rubbish!' said Raymond, retiring into the newspaper again. 'You manage your own horses, and leave me to manage mine, Aunt Clara.'

'Well, what's to be done about it?' asked Bart. 'Blisters?'

'Likely to cause absorption,' Raymond responded briefly. 'I'll look him over in the morning.'

'You'll have to cool his system before you treat him,' said Ingram.

'Thanks for the tip!' Raymond retorted, throwing him a scornful glance. 'Any other obvious reminders?'

'I'd fire him,' remarked Conrad.

Eugène yawned. 'From which one gathers that he's not one of your horses. Don't you, Ray! Ruin his appearance for good and all if you do.'

'Try setons!' recommended Bart.

'Oh, shut up, the lot of you!' said Raymond. 'There's nothing but a slight exostosis! Do you think I was born yesterday?'

'Biniodide of mercury,' said Penhallow. 'Nothing like it!'

Raymond grunted, and refused thereafter to be drawn into the discussion which waxed louder and louder, Penhallow recalling cases he had known of spavined horses from his youth upwards; the twins arguing hotly on the most efficacious cure for the complaint; and Ingram and Clara putting in comments and suggestions whenever they could make their voices heard above the rest.

Faith set her teeth, and rethreaded her needle, trying to shut out the sound of boisterous voices, to wrap herself up in some world of her own that contained no horses, no aggressively assertive young men, no coarse-tongued old ones, and above all no overheated, overcrowded, fantastically furnished bedrooms where she could be compelled to sit night after night while her temples throbbed, and her eyes ached from the unguarded flames of the countless candles all round the room.

Vivian, within the circle of Eugène's arm, leaning her head back against his shoulder, had let her eyelids droop, one part of her mind irritated by the turmoil of dispute raging about her, the other dreaming of a little flat where she could be alone with Eugène, who was so very dear, whose very touch could soothe and comfort her exasperation, and whom she wanted to possess utterly, wrapping him round with her love, keeping him safe from his lusty, unappreciative brothers. While he remained at Trevellin she could never feel him to be wholly her own. He might bicker languidly with his brothers, but he was one of them, sharing many of their interests, imperceptibly changing from the man-of-the-world, the artist, she had married to one whose life was bound up in the confines of a Cornish estate which she hated.

I must get him away, she thought. Somehow, anyhow, I must manage to get him away from this dreadful place!

The discussion on the proper treatment of, and improbable cure of, bone spavin was brought to an abrupt end by Penhallow, who suddenly said: 'I want a drink! Where's that damned boy, Jimmy?' and reached out a hand to tug at the crimson bell-pull beside his bed.

No agreement had been reached, the maximum amount of abuse had been indulged in, opinions scoffed at or shouted down, and a quantity of irrelevant anecdote recited. The Penhallows, in fact, had spent a pleasant twenty minutes, giving vent to their exuberant vitality, and were now perfectly content to allow the subject to drop.

How awful they are! thought Faith. I can't go on like this! I can't, I can't! I shall go mad!

The bell was answered in a few moments by Reuben and Jimmy both, Reuben carrying in the massive silver tray with all the bottles, decanters, glasses, and sandwiches with which it was the custom of the Penhallows to refresh themselves during the evening; and Jimmy, with one arm ostentatiously in a sling, bearing the overflow on a small, tarnished salver.

'What the hell makes you so late, you old rascal?' demanded Penhallow jovially.

Reuben dumped the large tray down on the refectory table, and gave a sniff. 'If Master Bart would be so obliging as to leave this young varmint the use of both his arms, perhaps I wouldn't be late,' he said severely. A glance at the clock caused him to add: 'Which I'm not, sir, I'll thank you to notice. Ten o'clock's been the time for you to call for a drink since I don't know when, and if you're going to change your habits at your time of life we shall be all at sixes and sevens.'

'Damn your impudence!' said Penhallow cheerfully. 'What the devil are you doing with that thing round your neck, Jimmy? Take it off, and come and shake up my pillows!'

'Mr. Bart's sprained my wrist,' said Jimmy, with an air of patient endurance.

'I know that, fool! Think yourself lucky he didn't break it, and stop makin' a damned exhibition of yourself! You leave your little half-brother alone, Bart, or I'll have something to say to you!'

Raymond looked up at this, a heavy scowl on his brow, and exclaimed: 'My God, that's too much! You can get out, Jimmy!'

'Oh, no, he can't!' said Penhallow, grinning wickedly. 'I want him to shake up my pillows. Come here, Jimmy, my boy! Don't you pay any attention to them: I won't let 'em hurt you.'

Jimmy was so pleased at being told to disregard Raymond's orders that he slipped his injured arm out of the sling, and went towards the bed. Bart, straightening himself suddenly, got between him and it, and said dangerously: 'You heard Mr. Raymond: get to hell out of this before I boot you out!'

'Bart!' roared Penhallow, making Faith start nervously, and prick her finger.

'I'll shake your pillows up for you when I've seen your pet cocktail off, Dad,' replied Bart, not turning his head.

'Hark forrard, Bart!' Conrad encouraged his twin, in a ringing tone.

Jimmy retreated a few paces, casting a sidelong look at the door. Reuben went on setting out the glasses on the table, as though nothing out of the way were taking place.

'*Bart!*' thundered Penhallow.

'Now, don't let's have any vulgar brawling, I do implore you, Bart!' begged Eugène. ''Ware riot, my lad, 'ware riot! Really, a false scent! It isn't worth it.'

Bart hunched his shoulders, and turned reluctantly to confront Penhallow, who had reached for the ebony cane beside his bed, and was raising it threateningly. The fierce old eyes met and held the sullen young ones. 'By God, Bart, if you don't obey me I'll have the hide off your back!' Penhallow swore. 'Jimmy, you little rat, come here!'

Bart seemed to hesitate for an instant; then, with a laugh, and a shrug, he lounged back to his position by the lacquer cabinet. With an air of conscious virtue, Jimmy shook up the pillows, and replaced them, straightened the flaring patchwork quilt, and asked if there was anything else he could do for his master.

Penhallow gave a chuckle. 'You take yourself off, and don't you give your brothers any more of your impudence, hear me? One of these days I shan't be here to hold the pack off you, and then where will you be, eh? Off with you, now!'

'And no sneaking off on the sly either,' said Reuben, accompanying Jimmy to the door. 'Since that wrist of yours isn't too bad to let you shake up the Master's pillow, we'll see if it won't lend a hand in the pantry after all.'

The double doors closed behind them. Penhallow looked under his brows at Bart, a smile hovering round his mouth. 'You young devil! Getting the bit between your teeth, aren't you? Pour me out a drink!'

Raymond, who had risen to his feet, the local paper crushed in one hand, said with a rasp in his voice: 'Hell, do you think I'll put up with that?'

'Yes, or anything else I choose to make you put up with!' Penhallow returned contemptuously.

'Our half-brother! My God, what next?' Raymond said furiously.

'Oh, he's one of mine all right!' Penhallow said, malice twinkling in his eyes. 'Look at his nose!'

'I don't doubt it! But if you imagine I'm going to have my orders ignored by him or any other of your bastards, you'll learn your mistake!'

'Well, damn it, it was you who tried to over-ride Father's orders to him!' interrupted Ingram.

Raymond rounded on him, an ugly look on his face. 'You keep out of this! What are you doing here anyway? Haven't you got a home of your own to sprawl in – rent-free?'

Conrad gave a crack of laughter, and started to chant: 'Worry, worry, worry!' Eugène began to laugh; and Bart ranged himself on Raymond's side, loudly applauding his conduct in having ordered Jimmy out of the room. Above the tangle of angry voices, Penhallow's made itself easily audible. Vivian, realizing that the family fairly embarked upon one of its zestful quarrels, clenched her fists, and said sharply: 'Oh, my God, how I *loathe* you all! how I *loathe* you all!'

Faith folded her embroidery with trembling hands, and slipped from the room. She found that her knees were shaking, and had to stand for a moment, leaning against the wall, to recover herself.

The quarrels were becoming more frequent, she thought, or she was too worn-down to bear them as once she must have been able to. The sound of angry voices beat still upon her ears; she fled from it, down the long broad passage to the main hall, and up the shallow stairs to her room at the head of them, and sank into a chair, pressing her hands to her temples.

She found herself thinking of Clay, picturing him in the midst of such a scene as was now raging in Penhallow's room. As sensitive as she was herself, afraid of his father, and of his brothers, wincing from a raised voice, life at Trevellin, if it did not drive him out of his mind, must surely wreck his nervous system. He would be expected to do all the things his more robust half-brothers delighted in, and between his fear of their contempt if he refused his fences, and his fear of the fences themselves, his life would be a lasting misery.

His last letter to his mother had announced his intention of defying the parental mandate, and seeking employment in London, but Faith knew that this was only bluster, and not meant for other eyes than hers. He would come home at the end of the term, resentful, yet not daring to speak out boldly to Penhallow. He would pour out his troubles to his mother; he would think that somehow or other she ought to be able to protect him, unable or perhaps unwilling, to see that she was as helpless as he in Penhallow's remorseless grip. She did not blame him: she knew that she ought to help him, and thought that there was nothing she would not do to set him free from Penhallow's tyranny. But there did not seem to be anything she could do, since her entreaties had been of no avail, and she was wholly without the means of supplying Clay with money to make him independent of Penhallow.

She tried to explain this to him when he came back to Trevellin early in June, but he had inherited her dislike of facing unwelcome facts and was more inclined to descant upon what they might both have done, had almost every circumstance of their respective positions been other than they were, than to form any plan founded on the situation as it was.

She went to meet him at the station in the aged limousine. His greeting was scarcely designed to flatter her. 'Oh, Mother, this is too ghastly!' he exclaimed, hurrying towards her on the platform. 'Can't you do *anything*?'

It was not in her nature to return a baldly unpalatable answer, so a good deal of time was spent in a discussion founded on eventualities which might, but almost certainly would not, occur. 'If only Cliff would have the courage to tell your father he doesn't want you as a pupil!' Faith said. 'If only I had some relations with money! If only I could get your father to see that you'd be wasted in Cliff's office!'

'I do think you ought to have *some* influence over Father!' Clay said.

In this unprofitable fashion the drive to Trevellin was accomplished, mother and son arriving at the old grey house below the Moor in a state of considerable nervous agitation, Faith having developed a nagging headache, and Clay experiencing the familiar sinking at the pit of his stomach which always attacked him at the prospect of having to confront Penhallow.

In appearance, he was not strikingly like either parent. His colouring was nondescript, inclined to fair, but although his eyes had something of Faith's expression they were not blue, but grey. He had the aquiline cast of features of all the Penhallows, but his mother's soft mouth and indeterminate chin. He was rather above the average height, but had yet to fill out, being at present very thin and immature. He had several nervous tricks, such as smoothing his hair, and fidgeting with the knot of his tie; from having been the butt of his brothers he had acquired a defensive manner, and was often self-conscious in company, assuming an ease of manner which it was plain he did not possess. He was apt to take offence too readily; and was far too prone to adopt a belligerent tone with his half-brothers and no amount of mockery could break him of unwise attempts to impress them by recounting unconvincing tales of his strong handling of such persons as form-masters, Deans, and Proctors.

The first person he encountered on entering the house was Bart, who hailed him good-naturedly enough, saying: 'Hello, kid! I forgot you were descending on us today. Skinny as ever, I see.' He turned his head, as Eugène came out of the library, and called: 'Hi, Eugène! The budding lawyer's blown in!'

Clay bristled at once, and replied in rather too high-pitched a voice: 'You don't suppose I'm going to go into Cliff's office, do you? I can assure you that I shall have something to say to Father about that!'

Bart grinned. 'I'll bet you will! I can hear you: *Yes, Father! No Father! Just as you wish, Father!*'

Faith at once rushed to the defence of her young. 'Can't you let the poor boy set foot inside the house without starting to tease him? I should have thought that after not having seen him for three months you might have found something pleasant to say to him!'

'Kiss your little brother, Bart!' said Eugène reprovingly. 'Well, Benjamin? Will you receive our address of welcome now, or later?'

'Oh, shut up!' said Clay. 'You're not a bit funny!'

'Darling, I know you'll want a bath after that horrid journey,' Faith said, ignoring Eugène. 'I told Sybilla to be sure to see that the water was properly hot. Come upstairs, won't you?'

She took his arm, and pressed it affectionately, and he went with her up the stairs, leaving Bart to grimace expressively at Eugène, and to observe that why Penhallow should want to draw such an appalling little wet back into the fold was a matter passing his comprehension.

CHAPTER NINE

CLAY'S first meeting with his father took place that evening, after dinner, in the presence of the rest of the family. Upon setting eyes on his youngest son, Penhallow at once demanded to be told why he had not presented himself several hours earlier, shooting this question at Clay in such a fierce way that the boy changed colour, and stammered out a rather incoherent reply, which was to the effect that he hadn't known that Penhallow wanted to see him particularly. This had the effect of making Penhallow scarify him soundly for his lack of filial respect; and as he addressed most of his diatribe to him in a thunderous tone, and ended by asking him what he had to say for himself, Clay was speedily reduced to a state of pallid terror, and was only able to say, in shaken accents, that he was sorry, and hadn't meant to offend anyone. Such supine behaviour roused all the worst in Penhallow, who set about bullying him in good earnest, insisting on receiving answers to quite impossible questions, and saying everything he could to goad him into making a hot retort. Faith, perilously near tears, tried to come to Clay's support, and succeeded, inasmuch as Penhallow's ire was instantly diverted, and fell upon her luckless head. Clay slid into the background, and tried to look as though he did not mind having been roared at, and was not in the least upset by the interlude. Conrad, who had seen Bart kissing Loveday in the orchard, and was in a smouldering temper in consequence, began to bait him, with so much ill nature that Bart came to his rescue, telling his twin to lay off the kid, for God's sake! Bart was quite capable of inflicting physical hurt on anyone who roused his wrath, but he was never spiteful. But since he could not understand that his good-natured intervention increased Conrad's ill-humour, Conrad's jealous temperament being unable to brook his twin's siding with another member of the family against himself, he did Clay very little service. Raymond, who had scarcely been on speaking terms with Penhallow since their quarrel over Jimmy, took no part in the general turmoil, but sat scowling into the fire, and occasionally exchanging a brief word or two with his aunt. He glanced contemptuously at Clay, when that unfortunate young man withdrew to a chair in a secluded corner, and seemed slightly amused by Conrad's baiting of him.

Having worked off his rage, Penhallow was ready to discuss the affairs of the estate, the stables, the farm, and the neighbouring countryside with his sons. Clay, bearing as little part in this animated conversation as his mother, sat with clenched teeth, wondering with sick distaste whether it was worse to be rated by Penhallow than to be obliged to sit through an evening of such talk as this. When Reuben and Jimmy brought in the usual refreshments, he had to help the twins dispense these. He carried a glass of whisky-

and-soda to Vivian, and told her in an undertone that he couldn't stand this sort of thing.

She shrugged her shoulders. 'You say that, but you will stand it. I know you!'

He coloured, and asserted more loudly than he meant to: 'Well, I shan't. I'm not a child any longer, and the sooner everyone realizes that, the better it will be for – for them!'

Conrad overheard this, and said at once: 'Listen to this, all of you! Dear little Clay isn't a child any longer! Isn't it wonderful what a Varsity education will do for one? What did they teach you at Cambridge, Clay? *We* never managed to teach you anything – not even to throw your heart over!'

'Or to stop pulling his horse right into a fence,' said Raymond dryly. 'If you are going to stay at home, Clay, I suppose you will have to be mounted.'

Clay dared not assert that he was not going to stay at home, although every minute spent in the company of his family made him the more determined by hook or by crook to escape from Trevellin; but he showed so little interest in the question of what horses he could ride during the coming season that even Eugène roused himself to remark dispassionately that no one would take him for a Penhallow. Fortunately, Penhallow was too much absorbed in what Bart was telling him about the Demon colt to pay any heed to this interchange; and as any mention of the Demon colt had the invariable effect of drawing nearly every member of the family into the discussion, Clay was presently able to slip out of the room without attracting attention. His mother soon followed him, and they went upstairs together to her bedroom, where Clay at once unburdened his mind to her, pacing about the room as he did so, and fidgeting with whatever came in the way of his unquiet hands. Faith's attention was thus divided between what he had to say, and what he was doing, and she found herself impelled to interrupt him several times, to beg him not to twirl the lid of her powder-bowl round; to take care of that chair, because one leg was broken; and *please* not to swing the blind-cord to and fro, because it made her giddy.

'I don't believe,' said Clay gloomily, 'that you have the least idea how *desperate* it all is!'

'Oh, darling, how can you say that to me?' Faith reproached him.

'I suppose you're used to it,' pursued Clay, disregarding this interpolation. 'You simply don't realize how ghastly it is here! But I've been away from it, and you just can't imagine how it strikes one, after having lived in civilized surroundings, amongst cultured people! I couldn't bear it, Mother. It's no use expecting me to. I mean, I should simply cut my throat. There's *nothing* I wouldn't rather do!'

Correctly assuming that this sweeping assertion excepted any form of manual toil, or office drudgery, Faith said: 'Yes, but what can we do about it? I've tried my best to make your father see reason, but you know what he is. If only you'd done better in your First Part I think there might have been some hope, but—'

'Of course, anyone who imagines that one goes to the Varsity merely to swot, and pass examinations, just doesn't understand the first thing about it,' said Clay loftily. 'And, what's more, I never heard that Eugène did so damned well up at Oxford, or Aubrey either, if it comes to that!'

'I know,' she said quickly. 'That's what's so unfair! You were much too young to know anything about it at the time, but actually Eugène cost your father a great deal of money, when he was up, besides getting into the sort of scrapes I should have thought any father would have— However, that's his affair! Only, I believe the awful thing is that your father wouldn't have *minded,* if you'd disgraced yourself at Cambridge, and got entangled with dreadful girls, and been sent down for sheer hooliganism!'

Clay stared at her. 'Of course, he's mad!' he said, with conviction. 'Absolutely batty!'

She shook her head, but said, as though she feared to be overheard: 'He's got very strange lately. Not mad, but very – very eccentric. More than that, really. He has been doing some outrageous things, and he seems to me to be drinking more than he used to. I'm very worried about him.'

Clay accepted this conventional statement. He himself disliked his father, but he would have been rather shocked had Faith admitted that she too disliked him. He said: 'He looks all right. I didn't notice any change.'

'Dr. Lifton says he can't possibly go on as he is doing. You've no idea what unsuitable things he eats, and the amount he drinks, and the way he's been rushing about the country.'

'I suppose his inside is pretty well accustomed to strong drink,' said Clay, with a slight laugh.

'Yes, but, really, darling, there are limits! I don't mean that he gets drunk, actually, but I have seen him – well, in that reckless state which always means he's been drinking steadily. You saw the whisky Con measured into his glass tonight. Well, that's nothing. I mean, it isn't only what he drinks when we're all there, but I know from Loveday that Martha has orders to leave the whisky decanter beside his bed when he settles down for the night, and if you ever saw the drink bills you'd realize what an appalling amount he must dispose of.'

'Can't you stop him?' inquired Clay, without much interest.

'No. He wouldn't listen to anything I said. Reuben does what he can, by seeing to it that there's only a certain amount of whisky left in the decanter each night, but you never know when your father will put a stop to that. No one can do anything with him once he's determined on getting his own way.'

'Well,' said Clay, sticking out his chin, 'I can't say I care two hoots how much he drinks, but he's not going to get his own way as far as my affairs are concerned. I'm damned well not going to be jockeyed into Cliff's office to suit his convenience!'

'Oh, darling, I'm quite heartbroken about that, but what can you do?'

'Why can't he make me an allowance, and let me do what I want to do?' demanded Clay. 'He lets Aubrey please himself, hang it all!'

'Yes, but he says he isn't going to any longer,' sighed Faith. 'He's got a sort of mania for keeping you all at home. I'm sure I don't know why, because he doesn't do anything but quarrel with you. He even went for Bart the other night, and Bart's his favourite.'

'I shouldn't have thought,' said Clay, in an ill-used voice, 'that it was much to expect, that I should be allowed to choose my own profession!'

'If only I had the means to help you!' sighed Faith.

A gentle tap on the door was immediately followed by Loveday's entrance, bearing the hot-water bag without which Faith never, summer or winter, went to bed. She smiled warmly upon her mistress, and, as she slipped the bag between the sheets, let her eyes flicker over Clay. Clay, who had not noticed her much on his previous vacations, was conscious of a strong attraction, and was enough a Penhallow to return the glance with a kind of invitation in his own eyes. In his mother's presence he was debarred from making any further overtures, but when, next morning, he encountered Loveday in the hall, he slid an arm round her waist, and said clumsily: 'I say, Loveday, you might welcome a fellow home!'

Her smile, though it was indulgent, excited him. He wondered how it came about that he had never till now realized how beautiful she was, and said so, stammering a little.

'I expect you're growing up, Mr. Clay,' she replied demurely. 'Give over now, my dear, do!'

'Give me a kiss, Loveday!' he said, grasping her more securely.

She shook her head. 'Leave me go,' she replied. 'You're getting to be too big a boy now for these games, Mr. Clay!'

He coloured, for he hated to be laughed at, and would probably have pulled her into his arms had he not heard the door of Eugène's room open. He looked round in quick alarm; Loveday slipped away, in no way discomposed, and went gracefully down the stairs.

Eugène's face showed that he fully appreciated the situation. He said, in his light languid way: 'So the puppy's growing into a hound, is he, Benjamin? Well, I am sure that is all very edifying, but if you think my advice worth taking I can give you a piece of it which may save you from future unpleasantness.'

'Oh, shut up!' said Clay. 'I don't know what you're talking about!'

'I wonder,' said Eugène amiably, 'from where you get your instinctive love of prevarication? Keep your paws off Loveday Trewithian, little brother! She's Bart's meat.'

'Good lord, I was only fooling with her!' Clay said.

'I'm sure!' Eugène retorted. 'The point, thickhead, being that Bart isn't.'

'What on earth do you mean? You can't mean that Bart's serious about her?'

'Can't I? Well, you trespass on his preserves, and you'll find out,' said Eugène.

Clay looked very much astonished, but as Jimmy the Bastard came up the backstairs at that moment, with an armful of boots, he questioned Eugène no further.

Jimmy, whose ears were extremely sharp, had heard every word of the brief conversation. It confirmed his own suspicions, and he was pleased, seeing a way of revenge on Bart. His countenance, however, betrayed no emotion whatsoever, and he met Eugène's narrowed eyes without blanching. Clay went off, whistling, but Eugène lingered to say: 'You have quite a genius for turning up where you are least expected, haven't you, Jimmy?'

Jimmy looked sullenly at him. He recognized an intelligence superior to his own, and resented it. The other Penhallows despised him, and generally ignored him, so that he was able to spy upon their doings pretty well as he chose; but Eugène, he knew, was fully alive to his activities, and, therefore, rather dangerous. He said defensively: 'I was bringing your shoes up.'

'Kind of you,' said Eugène. 'Do you know, Jimmy, that if I were you I'd be very careful how I trod? Somehow I feel that one of these days, when your natural protector is removed, an evil fate may befall you.'

'I haven't done any of you any harm,' Jimmy muttered, turning away. But he knew that Eugène was right, and that if Penhallow were suddenly to die he would be kicked out of the house without ceremony or compunction; and he began to think that he would do well to make provision against an uncertain future. He thought he would rather like to go to America. His knowledge of that vast country having been culled solely from the more lurid films dealing with the underworld of bootleggers and racketeers, he was strongly attracted to a land where it seemed that his own buccaneering talents would find ample scope. His only day-dream consisted of an agreeable vision of himself as the chief of a gang, living in an opulent apartment with one of those glamorous blondes who apparently abounded in gangster circles. But he was a practical youth, and he knew that the achievement of his ambition depended largely on his amassing some initial capital. He wondered whether Penhallow would leave him any money in his will, but was inclined to doubt it. Penhallow, he knew quite well, encouraged him partly because it amused him to do so, and partly to annoy his family, and was not in the least likely to leave his money away from his legitimate offspring.

He placed the boots he had brought upstairs in their respective owners' rooms, and went slowly back to the kitchen, where, since Sybilla was baking, he thought he would pick up one of her saffron cakes. But before he had traversed more than half the length of the stone passage, Martha came out of the still-room, and informed him that Master was shouting for him, and he had better go to him at once, or he would learn what was what.

Penhallow was sitting up in bed, with the fat spaniel sprawling beside him, and a blotter on his knees. As Jimmy came into the room he was licking the flap of an envelope. He remarked genially that he had a job for Jimmy to do. Jimmy saw at once that one of his restless, energetic moods was upon him, and reflected coldly that if he didn't quieten down again there was no knowing when he mightn't be took off sudden.

'I shall get up today,' Penhallow announced. 'It's time I saw something of my dear family. We'll have a tea-party. I've got a fancy to see that old fool Phineas again. I've told Con to fetch him and his sister out to tea in that flibberty-gibbet of a car of his; and you can take yourself to Liskeard, you lazy young dog, and give this letter to my nevvy. I'll have him and his stuck-up wife out here too. And on your way back, stop at the Vicarage, and give my compliments to Venngreen, and tell him I find myself good and clever today, and I'll be happy to see him and his good lady to tea at five o'clock.'

'*She* won't come,' observed Jimmy dispassionately.

Penhallow gave a chuckle. 'I don't care whether she comes or not. You tell her you won't be there, and maybe she will. But Cliff will come, and what's more he'll bring his wife, because he knows better than to offend me. He can take a look at Clay while he's here, and settle when the whelp's to start work with him.'

Jimmy put the letter he had been given into his pocket, and removed the blotter and the inkstand from Penhallow's knees. 'I see Mr. Clay hugging Loveday Trewithian upstairs just now,' he said, casting a sidelong look at his parent.

'The young dog!' exclaimed Penhallow, warming towards Clay. 'So there is some red blood in him, is there? She's a damned fine girl, that one.'

'Ah! Maybe there's others as thinks as much,' said Jimmy darkly. 'There'll be trouble and to spare if Mr. Bart was to hear of it, that's all I know.'

A smile curled Penhallow's mouth; he looked across at Jimmy with a little interest and some amusement narrowing his eyes. 'One of Bart's fancies, is she? Young rascal! If I were only ten years youngeer, I'm damned if I wouldn't cut him out with the girl! All the same, I'll tell him to be careful: Reuben wouldn't like it if his niece got herself into trouble, and I don't want any fuss and nonsense from him.'

'You don't have to worry about that,' Jimmy said, with a fair assumption of innocence. 'Mr. Bart's going to marry her.'

'Going to do *what*?' demanded Penhallow, his brows beginning to lower.

'Well, that's what I heard Mr. Eugène say,' Jimmy muttered, carrying the inkstand over to the refectory table, and setting it down there.

'You're a fool!' Penhallow said irascibly. 'Marry her! That's a good one!'

'I didn't ought to have spoken of it,' Jimmy said. 'Mr. Bart would very likely murder me if he knew I'd let it out. Don't let on I told you, sir!'

Penhallow's brow was by this time as black as thunder. 'What cock-and-bull story have you got hold of?' he shot at Jimmy.

'Loveday said to me herself as how she would be Mrs. Bart Penhallow.'

'Oh, she did, did she? Well you may tell Loveday that she's flying too high when she thinks to trap one of my boys into marrying her!'

'She'd tell Mr. Bart on me if ever I said a word to her she didn't like,' Jimmy said. 'They're only waiting till you set Mr. Bart up at Trellick, Master, and that's the truth, for all nobody dares to tell it to you.'

An alarmingly high colour suffused Penhallow's cheeks, and his eyes glared at Jimmy under their beetling brows, as though they would drag the whole truth out of him, but he said nothing for some moments. Then he barked: 'Get off with you to Mr. Cliff's, you damned little mischief-maker! I don't believe a word of it. Trying to pay Mr. Bart out for having twisted your arm, eh? I'd do well to send you packing! Get out!'

Jimmy departed, satisfied with his morning's work, since he knew his father well enough to be sure that the information he had imparted would rankle.

Penhallow lay thinking it over for some time. The spaniel sat up, and began to scratch herself. He cursed her, and she sat on her haunches, lolling her tongue at him, and wagging her stump of a tail. 'Old fool!' Penhallow said, and pushed her off the bed, and tugged at the bell-pull.

Martha answered its summons, and came in scolding. 'The devil's in you, surely!' she said. 'Ring, ring, ring, and Jimmy gone off to Liskeard, as well you know! If it's whisky you want, I'll not give it to you, my dear, not at this hour of the day I won't.'

'Shut up! You cackle like a hen!' Penhallow replied roughly. 'Where's Eugène?'

'Where would un be, but keeping himself out of the draughts, and driving everyone that can be bothered to listen to un silly with his talk of neuralgia in un's head?' retorted Martha. 'There never was one of them, not even Clay, and it was not me had him to nurse, I thank my stars! that was a more troublesome child than Eugène, and un's no better, nor never will be! What do you want with un, my dear?'

He pinched the patchwork quilt between his fingers, regarding her in a brooding way for some moments. 'What's between young Bart and Loveday Trewithian?' he asked abruptly.

She gave a dry chuckle. 'Eh, you'm a nice one to ask!' she said. 'What do you expect of a son of yourn, when you put a ripe plum in his reach? Why should you worry your head?'

'Jimmy's got hold of a damned queer story,' he growled. 'He's been telling me Bart means to marry the girl.'

'Jimmy!' she ejaculated scornfully. 'I rackon Jimmy would be glad to do un a mischief if he could!'

'Maybe.' He went on pleating the quilt, still looking at her under his brows. 'Seems to me Con's none so friendly with Bart these days.'

There was a question in his voice, but she merely tossed her head, and said: 'Chuck-full of crotchets, Con be and always will! Marry Loveday Trewithian! Please the pigs, her bain't come to that!'

'What the girl like?' he asked.

She sniffed. 'As bold as yer mind to! Sech airs! I never did see!'

'You send my sister in to me!' he ordered. 'You're nothing but a doddering old idiot, Martha!'

She grinned. 'Iss, sure, but I was a fine woman in my day, maister!'

'You were that,' he agreed.

'When I was in my twenty,' she nodded. 'That Loveday warn't nothing to me, but *I* never took and thought to marry above my station, as well you knaw, my dear! I don't knaw where the world's a-going!'

'Get out of this, you old wind-bag, and send my sister to me!' he said impatiently.

She went off, chuckling to herself; and some minutes later Clara came into the room, with her hands grimed with earth-mould, a trowel in one of them and a fern in the other. She left a clod of mud from one of her shoes on the carpet, and had evidently caught her heel in the hem of her skirt again, since it sagged unevenly and showed a frayed edge.

'You're a sight, Clara,' Penhallow told her frankly. 'What's that miserable thing you've got hold of?'

'Nothin' much. One of the film-ferns,' she replied. 'You wouldn't know.'

'No, nor care. Sit down, old girl: I want to talk to you.'

She obeyed, choosing the chair nearest to her, as though she had little intention of remaining long. 'They tell me you've been settin' the house by the ears again,' she remarked.

'My house, ain't it? I'm going to get up.'

'You'll get up once too often one of these days, Adam.'

'You leave me to know what's best for me! That wasn't what I wanted you for. I've been hearing things about Bart.'

She did not speak, but he was watching her closely, and he thought that she stiffened.

'Oh!' he said dangerously. 'So you know something, do you, Clara? Didn't think to tell me, did you?'

'I don't know anythin' at all, Adam,' she replied. 'It's none of my business.'

'That girl, Loveday Trewithian!' he said, stabbing a finger at her. 'What's she up to? Come on, out with it!'

She rubbed the tip of her nose, leaving a smear on it from her grimy finger. 'I don't know, but I don't like the gal.'

93

'Bart said anything to you?'

'No.'

'I'll have to look into this,' he decided. 'Buffle-headed, that's what he is! Jimmy says Eugène spoke of Bart's wanting to marry her.'

'I don't want to hear anythin' Jimmy said, Adam,' Clara replied severely. 'And Eugène's got a wicked tongue, which he uses to make trouble with. I wouldn't set any store by what he says either.'

'By God, I believe you're all of you in league to keep me in the dark!' he swore, suddenly angry. 'I'll know the truth of this business! Think I'm helpless, do you? You'll find I can still govern this family!'

'There's no sense in losin' your temper with me,' she said.

'If you'd the sense of a flea you'd know what's apparently been going on under your long nose!'

'I don't go pokin' it into what's none of my business. Well for you I don't, and never did!' she replied, rather grimly.

'Oh, get to hell out of this!' he shouted. 'A fat lot of use you are! You and your ferns! I'll have that garden of yours dug up, damned if I won't!'

'You'll do as you please,' she said, rising. 'You always have.'

He picked up a copy of the *Field*, and hurled it after her retreating form. It struck the closing door, and fell in a flutter of crumpled pages to the floor. He was rather pleased with himself for having still enough strength to throw an unhandy missile so far and so accurately; but the effort made him pant, and for some time he lay back against the welter of pillows and cushions, raging at his infirmity. When he had recovered his breath, and his heart had ceased to thud so sickeningly in his chest, he reached out a hand for the whisky-decanter. He splashed a liberal amount into a club-tumbler, and drank it neat. He felt better after that, but bent on pursuing his inquiries into Bart's activities. He was shrewd enough to guess that he would get little satisfaction out of his sons, and presently sent for Loveday herself.

He looked her over critically when she came into the room, appreciating her graceful carriage as much as the beauty of her face. She betrayed no alarm at having been summoned unexpectedly to his room. Her dark eyes met his with a look of submissive inquiry; she came to a halt beside his bed, and folded her hands over her apron. 'Sir?'

His lips began to curl at the corners. He didn't blame Bart for making a fool of himself over this girl: he would, in fact, have thought him a poor-spirited young man to have overlooked charms so obvious. He addressed her with a suddenness calculated to throw her off her balance. 'They tell me my son Bart's been making love to you, Loveday, my girl.'

Her eyelids did not flicker; her deep bosom rose and fell easily

94

to her calm breathing; she smiled slowly, and after meeting his gaze for a limpid moment, cast down her eyes, and murmured: 'Young gentleman do be high-spirited, sir.'

He was very nearly satisfied with this answer. He let one of his short cracks of laughter, and reached out a hand to grasp her arm above the elbow. 'Damme, if I were only ten years younger—!' he said, drawing her closer. 'You're a cosy armful, Loveday, aren't you? Eh?'

She cast him a sidelong glance, provocative and alluring. 'There be them as has said so, sir. You're very good.' Her smile broadened, and became a little saucy. 'I try to give satisfaction, sir,' she said demurely.

He roared with laughter at this, slid his hand down her arm, and began to fondle one of her hands. 'You little baggage!' he said. 'I'll swear you're as sly as a sackful of monkeys! I'd do well to get rid of you.'

She raised her eyes. 'Have I done wrong, sir?'

'That's between you and Bart, my lass!' he retorted. 'You should know better than I what's between the pair of you. Well, you're no innocent! I know your kind: you're well able to take care of yourself. Have your fun: who am I to object? But don't think to inveigle my boy into marrying you, Loveday Trewithian! Understand me?'

She achieved a look of wide-eyed innocence. 'To marry me?' she repeated. 'Why, who said such a thing? It's nothing but a bit of a flirtation! I can look after myself.'

He pulled her down, so that she almost lost her balance, and took her throat in his large hand, holding her so that she was obliged to look into his face. 'I've got a strong notion you're maybe better able to take care of yourself than any of us guess,' he said. 'Answer me now! How far's it gone?'

Her heart beat a little faster, and her colour deepened to a lovely rose. 'Indeed, I'm a good girl, sir,' she said.

'You're a damned little liar!' he returned. 'I don't trust you, not an inch! What's more, I don't doubt Bart's no match for you in wits. But I am, my girl! Don't you make any mistake about that: I am! I'm warning you now! Don't you make any plans to marry a Penhallow! I'd hound you into the gutter, you and all your family with you, before I'd allow Bart to take you to church! There! Give me a kiss, and be off with you!'

She made no objection to his kissing her, and stroking her smooth throat where he had grasped it, but she said, as she disengaged herself: 'There's no call for you to take on, sir. If it's Jimmy that's been trying to set you against me, I know well he has a spite against me.'

'And why?' he demanded. 'What have you been up to to give him a spite against you, I'd like to know?'

She withdrew to the door, and bent to pick up the *Field*. She laid this down on a table, and replied with one of her saucy smiles:

'Indeed, I wouldn't know, sir, unless it might be he's jealous of me for being born right side o' the blanket.'

He slapped his thigh with a shout of laughter. 'That's one for me! You impudent hussy!'

She dropped him a mock curtsy and left him still laughing.

Outside his room, she lifted a hand to her breast, as though to feel the beating of her heart. She was profoundly disturbed, little though she had shown it; and she felt as if she had been running a great distance. She thought that she and Bart now stood in a position of danger, liable at any moment to be torn apart, for she was sure that once Penhallow suspected the truth he would be on the watch for confirmation of his suspicion. She was prepared to fight for possession of Bart; she thought that if it came to it she would fight the whole world by his side; but she had been brought up in poverty, and, unlike him, she did not minimize the hardships and the difficulties that must lie ahead of them if Penhallow disowned his son. Her most instant need was to find Bart, and to warn him not to own his intention of marrying her. She hoped she could induce him to behave prudently, but she was doubtful, knowing that he was innately honest, scornful of the tricks and shifts which were second nature to her. He did not condemn the little lies and deceits she used to protect herself: he laughed at them, believing that all women lied, and were not to be blamed for it. It was a feminine weakness, but a weakness to which he, rampantly male, was not subject. She would need all her art to persuade him to dissimulate to his father; and she became all at once frettingly anxious to find him before he could have time to go to his father's room. He had gone off to a distant part of the estate, and had taken his lunch with him. She feared that he would only reach the house again in time to join the tea-party Penhallow was arranging, and she knew she would have no chance then of speaking to him, since she would be expected to help Reuben in the drawing-room.

Her mistress came into the hall, carrying a bowl of flowers which she had been replenishing, and exclaimed at finding her there standing with her back to Penhallow's door. She took refuge instinctively in one of her lies. 'I've been making up the Master's fire, ma'am,' she said easily. 'Let me take that for you!'

'I wish you would help me to do the vases in the Long drawing-room,' Faith said, with a suggestion of complaint in her voice. 'Mr. Penhallow has invited all sorts of people to tea, and someone must attend to the flowers. I have one of my bad heads.'

'You leave it all to me, and go and have a good lay-down,' Loveday said coaxingly. ' 'Deed, you look fit to drop, ma'am!'

'I don't know what I should do without you, Loveday!' Faith sighed.

CHAPTER TEN

In spite of the fact that Penhallow's determination to hold a tea-party pleased no one, least of all the invited guests, it took place, Mrs. Venngreen being the only person to decline the invitation. It was considered unlikely that Delia Ottery would come, since she visited Trevellin rarely, but she did come, persuaded, it was believed, by Phineas, who, for all his dislike of Penhallow, was extremely inquisitive, and rarely refused an invitation to visit him. Rosamund obviously came because Clifford had begged her to; and the younger Penhallows held that the Vicar came because Sybilla's scones and cakes were very much richer than any baked under Mrs. Venngreen's auspices.

Penhallow did honour to the occasion by making Jimmy and Martha dress him, a circumstance which relieved one at least of his wife's anxieties. The apprehension that he would appear at the party in his aged dressing-gown had induced her seriously to consider the advisability of retiring to bed with an unnamed illness.

Tea was served in the Long drawing-room, and the first guests to arrive were Clifford and Rosamund, Rosamund looking cool and remote in one of her excellent tailor-made flannel suits, and Clifford overflowing with geniality, and professing the greatest satisfaction on beholding his uncle in such robust health.

Penhallow, who had been wheeled into the drawing-room, and placed near the fire, which he had insisted on being lighted, quite regardless of the sultriness of the day, saw that Rosamund was looking cool and self-possessed, and maliciously summoned her to sit beside him, where, between the heat of the fire, and the raffish nature of his remarks, she very soon began to look hot, and even a little flustered. This pleased Penhallow so much that by the time Conrad ushered the Otterys into the room he was in a state of good humour which was felt to be only less dangerous than his moods of blind rage. He looked Delia over with twinkling eyes and said as he took her nervous hand in his: 'Well, well! What a sight for sore eyes! Seeing you with pink roses in your hat takes me back to the time when I first met you, Delia, by God it does! Now, how long ago would that be? How old are you, Ray? Thirty-nine? Then it must be about forty years ago, eh, Delia?'

Miss Ottery blushed to the roots of her untidy grey hair, and stammered something almost inaudible. She was always at her worst and most incoherent in Penhallow's presence, and looked now to be so unhappy that Faith, indignant with Penhallow for jibing at the poor lady's youthful taste in dress, affectionately invited her to come and sit beside her on a sofa a little removed from his vicinity.

'No, no, you let Delia sit next to Ray!' said Penhallow. 'He's the one she really came to see, didn't you, Delia? Always have had a soft corner for him, eh?'

'Oh, I'm sure Ray doesn't want to be bothered with his old aunt!' Delia said, in a flutter of embarrassment. 'Anywhere will do for me – not too near the fire!'

'And how, my old friend,' inquired Phineas, softly rubbing his hands together, 'do you find yourself these days? It is indeed a pleasure to find you up and about!'

'I'm still pretty clever,' Penhallow boasted. 'I'll surprise the lot of you, yet, Lifton included. You're not wearing so well, Phineas: you've developed a paunch. You're flabby, that's what you are. Gone to seed. Lord, I remember when you were as thin as a rake, with all the girls after you! Sold you a horse once which wasn't up to my weight.'

'Indeed, yes!' smiled Phineas. 'A straight-shouldered grey, always throwing out a splint. I remember him well.'

'Honours,' said Eugène, 'may now be said to be even. Of course, I feel that Father would have sold you an unsound horse.'

Penhallow accepted this tribute with a grin, and upon Clay's coming into the room at that moment, at once called upon Clifford to 'run your eye over this young cub!' Clifford shook hands with his cousin, and said that he looked forward to having him in his office.

'Oh well, as to that – I mean, nothing's decided yet, is it?' Clay said with an uneasy laugh. 'I'm afraid my bent isn't in the least legal. I've always been more on the artistic side – if you know what I mean.'

'You know, even Aubrey doesn't make me feel as sick as Clay,' remarked Conrad to the room at large.

'That will do, thank you!' Faith said sharply.

'Edifying close-up of the Penhallows at home!' muttered Vivian.

'But where is the rest of the family?' asked Phineas, in a light tone plainly meant to cover an awkward breach. 'I seem to descry gaps in your ranks. Aubrey and Char I suppose we must not hope to see, but are we not to have the pleasure of meeting Ingram, and his charming wife; and this tall fellow's counterpart?' He laid an affectionate hand on Conrad's arm as he spoke, and smiled winningly round the circle.

'Ingram's coming up to tea, but there's nothing charming about his wife,' said Penhallow, with brutal frankness. 'She's as rangy as old Clara here, and not so good-looking. The best thing I know of Myra is that she's bred a couple of lusty sons, and that with no more fuss and to-do than my Rachel would have made.'

This shaft impaled two victims, as it was intended to do. Faith flushed painfully, and Rosamund, the mother of three daughters, stiffened. The entrance of Ingram and Myra was felt to create a welcome diversion.

Ingram, who was rather gregarious, greeted everyone with loud-voiced heartiness; and as Myra was both shrill and voluble, Bart, who had entered the room in their wake, was able to pause for an instant by the table which Loveday was quietly spreading with one of Clara's crochet-edged cloths, and to exchange a low word with her. She shot him a warning glance, and whispered that she must see him presently. He said tersely: 'Schoolroom, as soon as this mob has cleared off.'

She saw that Penhallow's eyes were upon them, and said clearly: 'You'll find them in your room, sir.'

'What?' said Bart, unused to such subtleties. Then he too saw that his father was watching them, and added: 'Oh, I see! All right!'

'Ah, here he is!' Phineas exclaimed, coming towards him, with his white hand outstretched. 'My dear fellow, what a giant you have become, to be sure!'

'It would, I suppose, be tactless to remind Uncle Phineas that the twins attained their present stature six years ago,' remarked Eugène softly to his Aunty Clara.

'For goodness' sake, don't you go makin' bad worse!' she replied. 'You'd better let me pour out, Faith. You'll only go askin' everyone whether they take milk or cream, and upsettin' the conversation, if you do it. There's no need to wait for the Vicar. I daresay he won't come.'

'I'm afraid,' said Faith to Delia, with a slight laugh, 'that I'm one of those hopelessly unpractical people who never can remember who takes cream, and who doesn't.'

'I'm not at all surprised, not at all!' Delia assured her. 'Such a big family as you have to pour out for! I'm sure I should always forget, for I have a head like a sieve. So unlike dear Rachel! Now, Rachel never forgot anything. I often used to say that she ought to have been a man. Not that I meant to speak of— But I'm sure you don't mind— Always so sensible!'

'Talking of Rachel?' said Penhallow, suddenly propelling his chair towards them. 'What a woman! What a grand lass she was! By God, she'd drive the lot of us the way she wanted to go, whether we wanted to or not, eh, Delia?'

'She was always so good – so kind!' Delia stammered. 'Such a strong character – there was no one like her.'

'No, nor there ever will be. No offence to you, my dear,' he added, turning to his second wife.

Delia began nervously to fidget with the clasp of her handbag. 'I'm sure dear Faith— Not that anyone could take Rachel's place, but it takes all sorts to make a world, doesn't it? Oh, Conrad, thank you, is this my tea? So wonderful of Clara to remember just how I like it!'

At this moment, Ingram suddenly became aware of his half-brother's presence. He broke off in the middle of what he was saying to Phineas to exclaim: 'Good lord, the kid's back! Hallo, how are you?'

'I'm all right,' Clay answered.

Ingram looked him over critically, remarking with the paralysing candour of his family that it was time he started to furnish a bit. He grasped Clay's arm above the elbow, feeling his muscle, and expressed himself as profoundly dissatisfied. 'Why, my young rascal, Rudolph, could give you a stone!' he said. 'Bertie's got more muscle than you! Hi, Ray! you'll have to do something about the kid! He's growing up a positive weed!'

The fact that Ingram's elder son was only two years junior to him always had the effect of making Clay feel that Ingram was even farther removed from him in age than Raymond. He stood more in awe of him, hated his loud, cheerful voice, and lost no time in escaping from his clutch. Phineas engaged Ingram's attention once more by inquiring after the health and progress of Rudolph and Bertram, and Ingram was still descanting upon this theme when Reuben Lanner ushered the Vicar into the room.

The Reverend John Venngreen, a stout cleric with a wide, bland smile, and a gift for overlooking the obvious which amounted to genius, came in exuding good-will. Finding one member of the household, Ingram, boring the circle by the fire with an account of his sons' exploits; another, Penhallow himself, reducing his wife and sister-in-law to a condition of acute discomfort; a third, Eugène, apparently suffering from acute spiritual nausea; and a fourth, Clay, trying to make himself as inconspicuous as possible at his Aunt Clara's elbow, he was prompted to exclaim: 'Ah, this is a pleasure indeed! And may I be allowed to join this happy family party? Penhallow, my dear fellow! Mrs. Penhallow! Mrs. Hastings! Mrs. Ingram, my indefatigable helper! I am more fortunate than I knew! Mrs. Eugène, too, as bright and blooming as ever! Well, well, well!'

'Where's your wife?' demanded Penhallow, wheeling his chair round, and shaking hands.

'Alas!' The Vicar's smile widened, and he made a deprecating gesture. 'She sent me to be the bearer of her excuses. This east wind has awakened her old enemy, I fear, and she would not venture out.'

'There!' said Penhallow, with an air of chagrin. 'And I particularly arranged for poor little Jimmy to be kept out of the way!'

The Vicar managed, by suddenly affecting to perceive Rosamund for the first time, to remain deaf to this outrageous speech. He said: 'If it is not Mrs. Clifford! How *do* you do? And you dear little girls? Your nosegay of bright blossoms!'

'Now, don't talk nonsense!' said Penhallow. 'There's nothing wrong with the kids, but one of 'em's got teeth that stick out. You ought to do something about it, Rosamund. You don't want her growing up rabbit-faced.'

'That's right,' agreed Clara. 'She ought to have a plate made for her, poor little soul! I remember we had to have one made for Char, and look at her now!'

Ingram was at once reminded of all the improper uses to which

Charmian had put her plate, and Rosamund, ignoring the whole family, made room for the Vicar to sit down on the sofa beside her, and engaged him in a rather conventional conversation about gardening. Clifford went over to the tea-table, and after exchanging a few words with his mother, smiled in a friendly way at Clay, and asked him when he thought of starting work with him.

'I told you, nothing is settled yet,' Clay replied desperately. 'I may as well tell you that I was never consulted about this, and it's absolutely the last thing in the world I want to do! I don't mean that I'm not very grateful to you, and all that, for being willing to take me, but I shouldn't be the least use to you, and I do wish to God you'd say something to Father!'

'Well, well, you never know what you can do till you try!' said Clifford bracingly. Feeling himself to be standing on the brink of deep waters, he sought to escape by hailing Raymond, who was coming towards the table with Delia's cup-and-saucer. 'Hallo, Ray, old boy! Donkey's years since I laid eyes on you! How's the young stock?'

Raymond set the cup-and-saucer down before Clara, saying briefly: 'Aunt Delia,' and turned to his cousin. 'I've got one hit, and several promising colts.'

'Yes, Ingram told me about your Demon colt. I'd like to have a look at him. Got anything likely to suit me?'

'I might have. Come up to the stables presently, and you can cast your eye over what I've got.'

'If he weren't a bit short of bone, that liver-chestnut would do nicely for Cliff, Ray,' remarked Clara, replenishing Delia's cup.

'Cliff likes a lot in front of him,' put in Bart. 'Tell you what, Cliff, I'll sell you my Thunderbolt!'

'Why, what's wrong with him?' retorted Clifford.

'I don't like a sorrel,' said Clara, with a decisive shake of her head.

'A good horse,' said Bart sententiously, 'can't be a bad colour. There's nothing wrong with him.'

'Barring his being at least three inches too long behind the saddle,' interpolated Raymond dryly.

Realizing that Clifford was now embarked fairly upon a discussion of horseflesh which would in all probability last for the rest of his stay, Clay relieved his feelings by saying, 'O God!' under his breath, and sighing audibly.

As might have been expected, the conversation gradually extended to nearly everyone else in the room; and after arguing loudly over the merits and demerits of quite half the horses at present in the stables or out to grass, the Penhallows surged out, under Penhallow's direction, to conduct the guests to the stud-farm. As this lay at a considerable distance from the house, the services of all the available cars were requisitioned, Penhallow himself being hoisted into the dilapidated limousine, which Bart had had to fetch from the garage to accommodate him, the Vicar, Faith, Clara, and Phineas.

Delia, after fluttering about in an aimless fashion for a few minutes, got into Raymond's two-seater, reminding him that he had promised to show her his dear little colts. The only people to abstain from the expedition were Eugène and Vivian. The rest of the party drove off towards the uplands, taking in the hunting-stables on the way, and having most of the horses there paraded before them. Faith, who had developed a nagging headache, leaned back in the corner of the car with closed eyes, trying to shut her ears to the sound of insistent voices tossing scraps of hunting jargon to and fro; and Clay, standing in the yard amongst, yet apart from, his brothers, watched a succession of horses pass him, and, with a sick feeling in the pit of his stomach, imagined the most restive apportioned to him. Raymond said, as Weens led out a bay whose chosen mode of progression was a sort of restless dance: 'He might suit you, Clay.'

'Quite a good frontispiece,' Clay said judicially, thinking that the brute had a vicious eye. He could imagine how he would hump his back under a cold saddle; and could almost hear, in advance, his half-brothers' adjurations to himself to keep him walking, for God's sake to keep his heels away from his sides! He knew he would soon part company with a horse like that, but he dared not say it.

Bart put him out of his agony. 'Too nappy for Clay,' Bart said. 'What about that half-bred mare Con picked up at Tavistock?'

'Oh, she's a terrible brute!' Conrad said. 'I'm frightened to death of her. Clay could never hold her, except on a twisted snaffle.'

Clay thought resentfully that if ever he should say that he was frightened, which he had never possessed the moral courage to do, they would all mock at him unkindly. But his brothers often swore to their terror of some horse, or some jump, and not even Penhallow did more than laugh at such confessions.

'Now, why shouldn't Clay have my Ajax?' Clara said. 'I'm sure he's a comfortable, safe ride.'

'Oh, Clara darling, you old coper!' Bart crowed. 'He rides green, and well you know it! I'll mount young Clay. I've got a nice little horse: no, really, a *nice* little horse, that'll suit him down to the ground!'

A fantastic thought crossed Clay's mind. He tried to picture the scene there would be if he were to say all that was in his head: that he hated horses, hated hunting, never took any but the easiest fence without expecting to be thrown, could not see a bullfinch without imagining himself lying beyond it with a broken neck. He knew that he would never have the moral courage to say any of these things, and indeed felt quite sick as his fancy played with the idea of what would happen if he did.

Of the rest of the party, Phineas stood beside Ingram, passing quite shrewd judgments on the various animals shown him; Clifford pointed out the excellence of the new stables to his politely uninterested wife; the Vicar stood near the limousine, exchanging hunting reminiscences with Penhallow; and Delia, holding her unsuitable hat on with one hand, and clutching her feather boa with the other, remained at Raymond's elbow, exclaiming continually, asking foolish questions, and receiving rather curt replies to them. Occasionally Penhallow shouted criticism, or demanded enlightenment of either Raymond or Ingram. There were few better judges of a horse, but he was in a perverse mood by this time, and stigmatized a favourite mare belonging to Raymond as short of a rib; told Ingram that a brown gelding of his breeding was tied in below the knee; and bestowed haphazard amongst the rest of the horses shown him such belittling terms as flat-sided, goose-rumped, sickle-hocked, peacocky, and roach-backed. His sons exchanged significant glances. Ingram tried to argue with him, but Raymond contemptuously ignored his strictures.

When the stables had been exhausted, the company got into the various cars again, and drove up the rough track to the stud-farm. The paddock in which the Demon colt had been placed abutted on this track, and they all stopped to observe this promising youngster. Penhallow's keen eyes picked him out unerringly, and as he merely grunted, offering no immediate disparagement, it was considered that he privately considered that his eldest son had bred a winner. Everyone except Faith had some remark to make, or praise to bestow. Miss Ottery said the darling thing had such a pretty head. No one replied to this until the Vicar said, Indeed, indeed, if he had to choose a horse on one point alone it would be on the head. Clay then stupefied everyone by suggesting that the colt was surely a bit straight-shouldered, a criticism which provoked a storm of condemnation and mockery only exceeded in violence by that which followed the discovery that he had been looking at the wrong colt. Even the Vicar gave an indulgent laugh, and said, Tut, tut, it was not like a Penhallow to make such a mistake. Red to the ears, Clay played first with the idea of murdering all his half-brothers, and then with that of committing suicide; while Penhallow made the Vicar sheer off from his side in a hurry by once more stating his doubts of Clay's parentage.

By the time the stud-farm had been inspected, and Penhallow had offended the sensibilities of his wife by indulging in a very obstetric conversation with Mawgan, the groom, on the mares at present in use, most of the guests discovered that it was time to be going home. They all drove back to the house, and while the Vicar announced his intention of walking, and Penhallow commanded Clifford to attend him to his room, where he proposed instantly to go to bed, the under-gardener was summoned to drive the Otterys back to Bodmin in the limousine. Faith went upstairs to bathe her throbbing brow with eau-de-Cologne; Bart slid away to meet Loveday in the schoolroom; and Ingram, after telling Raymond that in his opinion the old man was breaking up, took Myra back to the Dower House.

Penhallow, as might have been expected, was considerably exhausted by his exertions, and consequently in a very bad temper. Nothing, however, would make him postpone his discussion with Clifford on Clay's future. As soon as he had been undressed and got into bed, and revived with whisky-and-soda, he sent Jimmy to summon Clay to his presence, and then and there made such ruthless and sweeping plans for his immediate study of the law, that that unfortunate youth felt that he was being borne along on a flood tide it was useless to battle with. After that, Penhallow dismissed both him and Clifford, and might have enjoyed a much-needed period of repose had he not suddenly bethought himself of Bart's possible entanglement, and decided to have it out with the young fool then and there. Once more his bell pealed violently in the kitchen, and Jimmy was dispatched on this new errand. Since Bart was shut up with Loveday in the disused schoolroom, he had to report failure to find him. In his present mood, any opposition made Penhallow the more determined to get his way, and nothing would now do for him but to set the entire staff searching for Bart, regardless of what other and more important duties any of them might have to perform. By the time that Reuben, Sybilla, Martha, Jimmy, four housemaids, the kitchenmaid, and a woman who came in from the village to help with the rough work, had all been sent to different parts of the house and stables, and had most of them shouted 'Mr. Bart!' in varying keys until they were hoarse, and such members of the family as were resting before dinner driven to the verge of desperation, Bart had emerged from the schoolroom, choosing a moment when the coast was temporarily clear, and had gone down the backstairs to his father's room. As he omitted to inform those searching for him that he was now found, the hunt continued long after he had entered Penhallow's room, and dinner was set back three-quarters of an hour in consequence.

Bart knew why he was being shouted for, and went to his father with the intention of obeying Loveday's directions. But Penhallow, enraged by having been kept waiting, greeted him with an accusing stab of his finger, and the announcement that he knew very well where he had been, and that that was in a hiding-place with that bitch of a girl.

Bart was not prepared to allow even Penhallow to refer to Loveday in such terms, and his colour deepened at once, and his obstinate chin began to jut dangerously. 'Who the devil are you talking about?' he demanded.

'To hell with your insolence, you young cub!' thundered Penhallow. 'I'm talking about Loveday Trewithian, and well you know it! I say you've just come from her!'

'What of it?' Bart shot at him. 'Supposing I have? So what?'

Penhallow looked him over sardonically, and replied in a quieter tone: 'That depends on what you've been hatching, the pair of you. There's a damned queer story running around the house that you've offered the girl marriage.'

Bart turned away, and kicked a smouldering log in the hearth so that it broke, and the flames leaped up the chimney. 'Yes, I know all about that,' he said. 'Jimmy the Bastard. I should have thought you'd have known better than to listen to what the little skunk tells you.'

'Maybe I do,' Penhallow said. 'Now, look here, my boy! I don't blame you for giving that girl a tumble: I'd do the same myself in your shoes. But don't let's have any nonsense about marrying her! She's a handsome bit of goods, she moves well, and she doesn't speak so badly, but don't you be misled into thinking she's your equal! She's my butler's niece, and if half Sybilla told me was true, her mother was as common as a barber's chair before she got Trewithian to make an honest woman of her. There's damned bad blood there, Bart, make no mistake about that!'

'At that rate there must be some damned bad blood in me too!' retorted Bart.

Penhallow grinned. 'Now, don't you give me any of your impudence! There may be wild blood in you, but there's nothing in your breeding to give you the kind of genteel respectability that can't let you look at a pretty girl without making you think of marriage. If she's trying to blackmail you, make a clean breast of the whole affair, and no nonsense about it, and I'll soon settle with her.'

'She's not,' said Bart shortly, keeping a tight hold on his temper. He added: 'She's not that kind of a girl. What's more, I've done nothing to be blackmailed about.'

Penhallow's eyes narrowed. 'You haven't, eh? That's what you say!'

'It's true.'

Penhallow brought his fist down upon the table beside him with such force that the glass and the decanter standing on it rang. 'Then if it's true, what the devil are you playing at?'

'Nothing.'

'Don't you stand there lying to me!' roared Penhallow. 'Do you think I was born yesterday?'

'All right, I won't!' said Bart, wheeling to face him. 'I am going to marry her, and be damned to you!'

Penhallow looked for a moment as though he would heave himself out of bed, but after glaring at Bart in hard-breathing silence, he relaxed against his pillows again, and drank what remained of the whisky in his glass. He set the glass down then, and said slowly: 'Going to marry her, are you? We'll see!'

'You can't stop me.'

This seemed to amuse Penhallow for he smiled. 'There's a lot of things I can do, my lad, which you don't know yet. Now, don't let's have any more of this tomfoolery! You can't marry my butler's niece, and if you don't know it you ought to! I see what's happened: the girl's been playing you on the end of her line, and she's made you think you'll only get her by putting a ring on her finger. Don't you believe it! There's no need to tie yourself up for the sake of a little love-making. If she's so high in her notions, there are plenty of other fish in the sea. Come to that, I'd as soon you left her alone. Reuben won't like it if you mess about with her, and I don't want to upset the old fellow. Damn it, we were boys together!'

'I'm going to marry her,' Bart repeated.

The obstinacy in his face, and the dogged note in his voice infuriated Penhallow, and made him lose his temper again. He began to curse his son, and the whole room seemed to shudder with the repercussions of his fury. A torrent of invective, mingled with bitter jeering, poured from him; he shouted threats; broke into fierce, mocking laughter at Bart's greenness; and very soon goaded Bart into losing control of himself, and giving him back threat for threat.

Suddenly Penhallow stopped. He was panting, and his face was dangerously suffused with colour. Bart, staring at him with hot, angry eyes, and his underlip out-thrust pugnaciously, wondered if he was going to go off in a fit. But the colour gradually receded from his cheeks, and his breathing grew more easy. He was no fool, and he knew that to rail at Bart was no way of bending him to his will. The boy was too like himself, and one half of his mind delighted in the mulishness which exacerbated the other half of it. 'There, that's enough!' he said a little thickly. 'Young devil! Come here!'

'What for?' Bart asked sullenly.

'Because I tell you to!' Penhallow said, anger flaring up again momentarily.

Bart hesitated for an instant, and then, with a shrug of his shoulders, walked up to the bed. Penhallow put out a hand, and grasped his arm, pulling him down to sit on the edge of the bed. He transferred his grasp to Bart's knee, and gripped it through the whipcord breeches. Bart looked defensively at him. 'Well?' he said.

'Damn it, you're the best of the bunch!' Penhallow said. 'You've got no sense, and you're an impudent young dog, but there's more of me in you than in any of your brothers. Now, Bart lad, there's no point in quarrelling with me! I'm not going to last much longer, by what Lifton tells me.'

Bart's simplicity was moved by this. He said in a slightly mollified tone: 'I don't want to quarrel with you, Guv'nor. Only I'm not going to be dictated to about this. I'm not a kid. I know what'll suit me, and that's Loveday.'

'If I hand Trellick over to you,' Penhallow said dryly. 'What if I don't?'

'I'll manage somehow.'

'Talk sense! Who do you suppose is going to employ you? You don't run well in harness, Bart. You're too headstrong.'

'I'll start a training stables of my own.'

'Where's the money coming from? You'll get none from me.'

'I don't know, but you needn't think you can force me to give Loveday up by cutting off supplies. I'm young, and strong, and I know enough about farming to get a job any day of the week.'

'And what does Miss Loveday say to all this?' inquired Penhallow the corners of his mouth beginning to lift.

He knew from Bart's silence that he had set his finger on the weak link in his armour, and was satisfied. He tightened his grip on Bart's knee. 'Come on, my lad! Let's have it from the shoulder! What are you going to do? Walk out on me? *I* can't stop you!'

'Hell, why can't you hand over Trellick, and let me please myself?' Bart exploded. 'I'm not your heir. It doesn't matter a tinker's curse what I do! All that tosh about birth and breeding! It's out of date – dead as mutton!'

'Well, I'm out of date,' said Penhallow. 'Daresay I'll be dead as mutton too before very long. Wait till I'm gone before you take that girl to church!'

Bart said awkwardly: 'You're all right, Guv'nor. See us all out.'

'Oh, no, I shan't! I'm done, my boy. Drinking myself into my grave. I'll be bound that old woman, Lifton, has told you so! Damned fool!'

Bart looked at him with a little concern in his face. 'You're good for years yet. Why don't you ease up on the whisky a bit?'

'God damn it, do you suppose I want to add a few miserable years to my life?' Penhallow demanded. 'Lying here, a useless hulk, gasping like a landed trout every time I so much as heave myself over in bed! I, who could throw any man to my inches, and better! No, by God! The sooner I'm laid underground the better I'll be pleased!' He released Bart's knee, giving it a little push, as though to drive him away. 'Go and be damned to you! Marry the girl! I've taken some knocks in my time, and I can take this last one.'

'I say, Father, don't!' Bart begged uncomfortably. 'I don't want to clear out, honestly I don't! But I don't see why you should be so cut up about it. I'm not going to be a ruddy literary bloke, like Eugène or Aubrey: I'm a farmer, and I want a wife who'll be some use to me, not a blamed little fool like Vivian, or a cold poultice like Rosamund!'

Penhallow bit back an appreciative chuckle at this, and said: 'I'm too old to change my way of thinking. It'll be a bitter day to me when you tie yourself up to a wench out of my kitchen. I'm fond of you, Bart. I shall miss you like hell if you leave Trevellin. Wait till I'm gone, boy! When I'm in my grave I shan't care what kind of a fool you make of yourself. You'll get Trellick: I've left it to you in my will.'

Bart grinned at him. 'Any strings tied to it, Guv'nor?'

Penhallow shook his head. 'No. It's not entailed. I bought it with you in my eye. I want you to have it.'

'I know it's unentailed. That wasn't what I meant.'

'I know what you meant. No strings.'

Bart flushed. 'Jolly good of you, Guv'nor!' he said gruffly. 'Puts me in a filthy position, though. I'm not going to give Loveday up.'

'I've told you, I don't care a damn what you do when I'm gone. All I'm asking is that you have a bit of patience, Bart.'

A vague, half-formed suspicion crossed Bart's mind. He said: 'I shan't change, you know.'

Penhallow's full lips curled a little. 'No harm done, then. If you do change, I shall be glad; if you don't, it won't have done either of you any harm to wait a while. You're young yet.'

Bart got up. 'I'll think about it,' he said reluctantly.

'That's right: you think about it,' said his father, with the utmost cordiality.

CHAPTER ELEVEN

WHEN Bart had left the room, Penhallow settled himself, with a chuckle, more comfortably amongst his pillows. He thought he had Bart's measure, and was fairly confident that he had averted the disaster of his marriage. It amused him to reflect how easy it was to disarm this most hot-headed of his sons. Bart had a tender heart; Penhallow did not think that Loveday would find it a simple matter to induce him to darken what he had been led to believe were his father's last weeks on earth.

She made no such attempt. When Bart came out of Penhallow's room she was awaiting him by the door into Clara's garden. She saw at once that he was looking troubled, and directed an inquiring glance up at him. He took her by the wrist, and briefly said that he must talk to her. She went with him into the garden, without demur, though she should have been in her mistress's room by the time, and let him lead her through it to the gate in the crumbling grey wall which led to the orchard. Here they sat down in their favourite place, out of sight of any window; and Bart, with his arm about her waist, told her what had passed between him and his father.

She was quick to see, and in a measure to appreciate, Penhallow's cleverness. She thought that his appeal to Bart's affection was pure artifice, but she did not say so, because she saw that Bart really did think that his father was nearing the close of his life, and was inclined to be distressed about it. For herself, she believed that Penhallow expected to live for many more years; and she felt certain that now that he was in possession of their secret he would never make Bart independent of him by handing Trellick over to him. She ventured to suggest this to Bart. He wrinkled his brow, considering it, and finally replied: 'Well, if he doesn't die, and won't give me Trellick, we shall just have to cut loose. I'm not afraid if you're not. I shall get Trellick in the end. He meant that all right. You know, Loveday, he's an old devil sure enough, but it's quite true that I've always been more or less his favourite. He's been rather decent to me, one way and another, and it does seem a bit low-down not to agree to wait a bit before I marry. He knows I won't give you up. And naturally I don't mean to hang about for ever.' His arm tightened round her; he turned her face up to his, and kissed her, and fondled her cheek. 'All the same, my girl, if you're willing to take a risk with me I'm ready to burn my boats, and marry you tomorrow – today, if I could!'

She said: 'No.' She was thinking, slowly, but acutely, realizing more completely the hold Penhallow had established over them both. She discounted his assurance to Bart that no matter whom he married he should have Trellick in the end. He had known how to disarm his son, and would not, she thought, abide by his word an instant longer than it suited him to do. She was filled with resentment, but she concealed it. She tilted her head, which rested on Bart's shoulder, so that she could watch his face, and asked timidly: 'Am I to be turned off?'

'No! Good lord, no!'

She twined her fingers in his. 'Did he say so, Bart-love?'

'No, he didn't say so, but he knows damned well I'd walk out of the house tonight, if he sent you away!'

She was silent, turning it over in her mind. After a few moments she made him tell it all to her again, how his father had first stormed at him, and then softened towards him; how he had said that he did not care what Bart did once he was dead. At this point she interrupted, to say: 'That's queer, seeming to me.'

'Well, as a matter of fact I think the old man's breaking up,' Bart said.

She was again silent. She was beginning to perceive the purpose behind Penhallow's apparent unreason. Pondering it, she did not doubt that she was to be kept on at Trevellin, for that would suit Penhallow's plan admirably. He knew Bart: he was banking on one of two things happening, either fatal to her hopes of becoming Bart's wife. She guessed, without precisely formulating the thought, that Penhallow expected his son's impatience to get the better of him. For that reason, then, he would keep her hovering in Bart's sight. She had been brought up too close to the soil to be trammelled with sentimentality, and her experience taught her to know that if she allowed Bart to enjoy her body outside the bond of wedlock it was unlikely that he would afterwards think it necessary to marry her. If, on the other hand, she denied him, he would soon or late look elsewhere for a woman, for he was a healthy and a lusty young man, with a passionate, and certainly not very profound nature. She did not suppose for a moment that he would be always faithful to her when they were married, but she was quite sure that she could handle him, that whatever favours he might bestow elsewhere he would return to his wife, just as his father had returned to Rachel Penhallow. But that he would accord as much fidelity as that to a woman who was his neither in name nor in deed was beyond the bounds of her expectation.

Hatred of Penhallow surged up in her, for she now perceived that he was fighting her with diabolical cunning. She was tempted to urge Bart to run off with her, and so to be sure of him, but even in her anger she did not quite lose sight of prudence, and when Bart, feeling her tremble in his arms, asked her what was the matter, she said: 'Nothing.'

Holding her in his arms made Bart feel that he could not wait to possess her. He said: 'Damn the Guv'nor! Let's take a chance, my little love!'

She shook her head. She wanted him, and loved him with a depth of feeling perhaps exceeding his for her, but she did not believe that he would succeed in making a living if his father's support were to be withdrawn. Poverty was too real to her to be regarded lightly; she dreaded it, and even more, the effect she dimly felt that it would have on one of Bart's temperament and upbringing. 'We must wait,' she said. 'A little while longer. Something may happen.'

'Seems pretty steep to be looking forward to the poor old Guv'-nor's death,' he said, grimacing. 'That's about what it amounts to.'

She did not answer. She had no compassion to waste on Penhallow, and would count his death a blessing.

'At the same time,' continued Bart, 'I don't see why he shouldn't come round to the idea. He really doesn't know anything about you, my bird.'

She was sure that Penhallow would remain obdurate, but she did not say so. She wanted time to think the matter over, and so agreed with Bart.

In this state of indecision the matter was allowed to rest, the only person to be satisfied being Penhallow, who was so satisfied that his mood was unusually mellow for several days.

Bart told the whole to his twin, and while Conrad agreed that someone ought to break Jimmy's neck, he was so antagonistic to the idea of Bart's marrying Loveday that a breach was created between them, a circumstance which confirmed the suspicions of the rest of the family of what Bart's intentions were. Penhallow mentioned the affair to no one except Faith. He told her about it in a fit of temper, and for the purpose of laying the blame of it on her shoulders. It was just like her, he said, to raise Loveday out of her proper sphere, to throw her in Bart's way, and to encourage her to develop ideas above her station. Faith was at first incredulous, but when she heard that the story did not rest upon Eugène's unsupported testimony, but had in fact been admitted by Bart himself, she was so much upset that she burst into tears, thereby exasperating Penhallow into throwing a book at her. She was not physically hurt, but any form of violence was so nauseating to her that she looked for a moment as if she were going to faint. Penhallow recommended her roughly to have a drink of whisky. She shuddered, and her lips formed the word No.

'Well, don't sit there staring at me like a ghost!' said Penhallow. 'Why the devil will you be such a damned little fool? You ought to know by now that I hate snivelling women!'

'You *struck* me!' she said, as though the hurling of the book had wounded her more than his bitter tongue had done over and over again. It had certainly shocked her profoundly, for he had never raised his hand against her before, and she still cherished the belief that only a brute sunk beyond recall in depravity could offer violence to a woman, and that woman his wife.

'No, I didn't,' he contradicted her. 'I threw a book at you, and damme, you asked for it! Don't put on those tragedy-queen airs, as though I'd been knocking you about for the past twenty years! Serve you right if I had knocked you about a bit! What have you ever done but whine, and complain, and pity yourself, and treat me to enough airs and graces to give any honest man a belly-ache? Oh, I'm forgetting one thing, aren't I? You presented me with a fine son! My God, *what* a son! A weedy young good-for-nothing, who mistakes a commoner for a blood-horse, and has to fill himself up with jumping-powder before he dare so much as look at a three-foot fence! If I weren't a soft fool, I'd wash my hands of him, and turn him loose to find his own way in the world!'

She forgot her own injuries as soon as he mentioned Clay, and now said quickly: 'Then do it! Nothing could be worse for him than to be kept here, in this house where everyone despises him!'

'What, and have him masquerading as a Penhallow, and bringing my name into contempt?' he said jeeringly. 'No, by God! He'll stay at home, under my eye, and he'll do what a Penhallow should do, or I'll know the reason why! If Ray won't school him, Bart shall. He hasn't got quite Ray's seat, or hands, but he may be able to put a bit of courage into the boy. Head free and loins free: that's what I taught my sons! and every one but that brat of yours learned it as soon as he could throw a leg over a horse!'

'Adam!' she said desperately, 'can't you understand that there's more in life than horses?'

'Precious little, for one of my blood!' he said, adding caustically: 'There's women, of course, but he doesn't seem to show much of a turn in that direction either.'

'He's my son as well as yours!' she said, clasping her hands nervously. 'You don't understand him! You've never tried to understand him! He's like me: he can't bear being bullied and shouted at, and that's all you do, or ever have done! If I hadn't persuaded you to let him go to school you'd have broken his spirit years ago!'

'Bosh!' he retorted. 'He hasn't got any spirit to be broken.'

'Yes, he has!' she cried vehemently. 'But he's a delicate, highly-strung boy, and your treatment of him is enough to drive him out of his mind! You encourage the others to bully him, and mock at him! You force him to do the sort of things he loathes! You don't see what sort of an effect you're having on his nerves!'

'So that's the modern youth, is it?' he sneered. 'The best cure I know for his kind of nerves is to be made to face up to your fences.'

'Adam, I beg of you, let Clay continue at Cambridge, and choose his own profession!'

'Now, don't let's have all that over again!' he said. 'The whole thing's settled. He can have a bit of a holiday before he starts work with Cliff, but start work with him he shall, make no mistake about that! If there's anything in the boy at all, he'll thank me for it one day. What the devil are we talking about Clay at all for? He's provided for. It's Bart, and that wench you took out of the kitchen, who's on my mind just now.'

She got up jerkily, and said in an unsteady voice: 'You care nothing for Clay, Adam. Well, I care nothing for Bart, and his affairs, except that I consider Loveday far too good for him!'

She went towards the door, but he thundered at her to stop. She paused, her fingers already grasping the handle, and looked back at him with an expression on her face half of fear, half of defiance.

'Come back here, my girl!' he commanded grimly. 'I've got something to say to you!'

'No!' she said, in a faint voice. 'I can't bear any more. I *can't*!'

She made as if to open the door, but he said very distinctly: 'If you leave this room till I say you may, I give you fair warning, my dear, I'll have you brought back to me. I'll send Jimmy for you, and tell him to see that you come.'

A sound like a whimper escaped her; she looked at him with strained, fearful eyes. 'I think you're mad!' she whispered.

'Oh, no, I'm not! Come here!'

She approached reluctantly, and perceptibly winced when he grasped her wrist. He pulled her down on to the bed, and she sat stiffly there, almost shivering under his hand. 'Now, look you here, Faith, my girl!' he said. 'A damned fool you've made of Loveday Trewithian, but what's done can't be undone. But if I find that you've been encouraging the girl to marry my son Bart I'll make you sorry you were ever born! Do you understand?'

'Yes,' she said. 'I don't want her to marry Bart. Why should I encourage her?'

'Because you're a sentimental little fool! There, that'll do! You needn't sit there looking as though you were a rabbit, and I was a boa-constrictor. I haven't been such a bad husband to you.'

'I sometimes think that you have killed my soul!' she said in a trembling voice.

He almost threw her hand from him. 'Oh, for God's sake get out, and stay out!' he shouted. 'Killed your soul indeed! What trashy book did you pick that up from? Get to hell out of this! Do you hear me? *Get out!*'

She got up from the bed with shaky haste, and left the room, conscious of having failed again to help Clay. When she reached the hall, and stood under the portrait of Rachel, she looked up at it, thinking that Rachel would not have failed in her place. The hard, painted eyes mocked her. 'Fool!' Rachel seemed to say. 'Haven't you learnt yet how to handle Penhallow?'

She averted her gaze from the portrait, and thought of the new disaster which had fallen on the house. Although she had said that she considered Loveday to be too good for Bart, she was conventional enough to be shocked by the idea of his marrying her. It was one thing to raise the girl to the position of confidential maid: quite another to be obliged to receive her on equal terms, as a stepdaughter-in-law. Then she realized that when Loveday married Bart she would go away from Trevellin, leaving her old mistress without any other comforter than Clay, who was too miserable himself to have any sympathy to spare for his mother. She began already to feel herself deserted, and stood there, in the middle of the hall, with slow tears welling up in her eyes, and rolling down her cheeks. She wiped them away, but still they continued to fall. She knew that the whole family would blame her for Bart's entanglement; and she felt that Loveday had acted treacherously towards her, abusing her trust, and perhaps only pretending to sympathize with her as a move in the deep game she had been playing.

But this was a minor evil compared with the terrible thing which had happened in Penhallow's room. By dint of dwelling upon it, adding to it all her previous cruelties (though these had not included physical hurt), and recalling her own dutiful behaviour during the twenty years of their marriage, she very soon persuaded herself into believing that she was a deeply-wronged woman. The habit of self-deception being engrained in her, she had always been incapable of perceiving that there were faults in her own character. Starting her married life on a misplaced belief that a husband, unless he were a brute, must think his wife perfect in all respects, a being to be ceaselessly cherished and indulged, she had never since been able to readjust her ideas; and as Penhallow from the outset fell lamentably short of her ideal, she early began to regard herself as a martyr. She belonged to that order of women who require a husband to combine the attributes of a lover and a father. This instinct had led her to feel a stronger attraction towards men many years her senior, and had finally betrayed her into marrying Penhallow. He had failed her; her temperament, as much as her lack of mental capacity, made it impossible for her to discern her own failures.

She heard footsteps approaching, and went out of the open front door into the garden. Here she was presently joined by Clay, who had been wandering about in an aimless fashion, awaiting the result of her interview with his father. One glance at her face was sufficient to inform him that she had not succeeded in her mission. He said: 'O God!' and slumped down upon a rustic seat, and gazed moodily at a hedge of fuschsia.

Faith sat down beside him, and, after blowing her nose, and dabbing at her reddened eyes, said: 'I did my best. He just won't listen.'

He was silent for a moment, kneading his hands together between his knees. His mouth worked; he said after a slight pause: 'Mother!'

'Yes, dearest?'

'I can't stick it.'

With a vague idea of consoling him, she said: 'I know, but perhaps you may not mind the work as much as you think. One thing is that Clifford's nice. I mean, he's kind, and I'm sure he—'

'It isn't that – though that's bad enough! It's having to go on living here. I – I simply can't!'

'You'll have me, darling. And it may not be for very long, perhaps. I mean, one never knows what may turn up.'

He paid no attention to this. 'Mother, I – I hate Father!' he said,
as though the words were wrenched out of him.

'Oh, dearest, you mustn't say that!'

'It's true. What's more, he hates me. He'll make my life a hell
on earth. He and the twins between them. It isn't so bad now,
but you wait till the hunting-season starts! I know just what'll
happen: I've been through it before. They'll expect me to master
all the most raw-mouthed brutes in the stable, and they'll go for
me day and night, pulling my style to bits, telling me that all I need
is a little jumping-powder when I don't happen to feel like hunting.
You heard Ray, the other day! You'd think it was a worse crime to
pull your horse right into a fence than to embezzle a bank! I loathe
horses! I loathe hunting! But what do you suppose would happen
if I said that I don't approve of blood-sports? Actually, I think
they're absolutely wrong, but that's a detail.'

'I know so well how you feel,' Faith sighed, with more sympathy
than tact. 'I was always terrified of riding.'

He reddened, and replied rather loftily: 'It isn't that, so much as
that I simply disapprove of the whole business. Of course, the
others are utterly incapable of understanding that. All they think
about is hunting! If you're unlucky enough to be born a Penhallow
you've *got* to be a good man across country, and God help you if
you're not! Yes, and if you refuse to take a drop fence, which
nobody likes, hang it all! you're told you've got no heart! Actually,
I've always had a sort of premonition about jumping, but it isn't
the sort of thing one talks about, and I've never said anything about
it.'

'Oh, darling, whatever do you mean?' exclaimed Faith.

'Oh, nothing!' Clay said. 'Merely that I have a sort of feeling –
some people would call it an intuition, I expect – that that's how I
shall meet my end.'

His mother responded in the most gratifying way to this dark
pronouncement, expressing so much horror at the grim thought
thus conjured up before her that he was soon obliged to try to calm
her fears and even to admit that he had not so far experienced any
definite vision of his own lifeless form stretched beside an oxer. He
made her promise not to mention the matter to his half-brothers. He
said that they would only laugh, or put up jumps in one of the
paddocks and school him over them until he went mad. Having,
in this artless fashion, added a considerable weight of anxiety to
the load already bowing Faith's shoulders down, he said that as far
as he could see he might just as well be dead for all the good he was
ever likely to do now that his career had been blighted, and walked
off to throw pebbles moodily into a pond below the south lawn.

Matters were in this unsatisfactory state when the two remaining
members of the family, Charmian and Aubrey, arrived at Trevellin to
spend a week there in honour of Penhallow's sixty-second birthday.

They journeyed down together, and were met at Liskeard by Jimmy the Bastard, driving the limousine. Only two years separated them in age, Charmian being thirty, and Aubrey twenty-eight; but although both lived in London they rarely met, and only discovered a sort of affinity between themselves when forced to return to the parental roof. Here, by tacit consent, they formed a defensive alliance against the barbarity of the rest of the family.

In appearance, both were dark, with aquiline features, but Charmian was stockily built, and did her best, by cutting her strong, wiry hair short and wearing the most masculine garments she could find, to look as much like a man as possible; while Aubrey, a slender young man with an exotic taste in pullovers and socks, affected a great many feminine weaknesses, such as a horror of mice, and revolted his more robust brothers by assuming a decidedly *fin-de-siècle* manner. He was generally held to be the cleverest of the Penhallows; had published two novels, both of which had enjoyed a moderate success; a quantity of verse conceived in so modern a medium as to baffle the comprehension of the greater part of the reading world; and was at present working in collaboration with one of his artistic friends on the libretto for a satirical revue. He inhabited a set of chambers near St. James's Street, which were at the moment furnished in the Turkish style; rode a showy hack in the Park; contrived to hunt at least once a week with the Grafton; and divided his time between his artistic and his sporting friends. Occasionally, it amused him to bring both together at one of his evening parties, as a result of which the intellectuals went away saying that Aubrey was too adorably whimsical for words, and probably a case of split personality, which was what one found so intriguing in him; and the sportsmen agreed amongst themselves that if Penhallow weren't such a damned good man to hounds, really, one wouldn't quite know what to think.

Charmian, rendered independent of Penhallow by the timely demise of a godmother who had left her a sum of money sufficient to provide her with a small income, shared a flat with a very feminine blonde, who resembled nothing so much as a pink fondant. The Penhallows had only once been gratified by a sight of this object of their masterful sister's passionate solicitude, Charmian having on one occasion brought her down to spend the week-end at Trevellin. The visit had not been repeated. Leila Morpeth and the Penhallows had not found themselves with anything in common; and the younger Penhallows had been so transfixed with amazement at the spectacle of Charmian hovering protectively over an opulent female of generous proportions, who had a habit of referring to herself as 'poor little me' in accents suggestive of extreme childhood, that they were struck dumb, and mercifully only recovered full power of self-expression when the visitor had departed with Charmian on Monday morning.

The brother and sister, meeting at Paddington Station, occupied themselves for the first part of the journey in exchanging poisoned shafts, Charmian shooting hers with a ruthlessness worthy of her father, and Aubrey planting his darts with precision and sweetness; but when they approached the end of their journey they entered upon a temporary truce, which developed into a positive alliance as soon as they discovered that Jimmy had been sent to meet them.

'Darling,' said Aubrey, in flute-like accents, 'how it does bring the horror of it all back to one, to see that face! Oh, I do think it is quite too low and dreadful of Father, don't you?'

'I shouldn't mind it,' said Charmian fairly, 'if the little beast weren't so obviously a wrong 'un.'

'Wouldn't you, sweet? You're so strong-minded and wonderful. Do you suppose the twins will be dreadfully hearty? It was quite too awful the last time I was here. Con was always slipping away to cuddle a most deplorable female in the village. So disgusting!'

Unlike her brother, who lounged gracefully in one corner of the car, Charmian sat bolt upright, keenly scrutinizing the countryside, and conveying the impression that it was distasteful to her to be obliged to sit still and idle. She said: 'I never pay any attention to what the twins do. I consider them quite beneath contempt. I doubt whether either of them has ever read a book in his life.'

'Oh, darling, are you sure? There's a kind of distinction about that. I do feel you're wrong, somehow. Don't you think they read Stonehenge On the Horse?'

'I dare say. I meant a real book. I can't think how Vivian stands it here. I love Trevellin, and I always shall, but the absence of any form of culture in the house, and the paucity of ideas of everybody in it would drive me to desperation if I had to live here!'

'Darling, you don't mean to imply, do you, that that afflictive woman you live with exudes culture as well as Attar of Roses?'

She darted a kindling look at him, and replied stiffly: 'Leila has extremely advanced ideas, and is a most interesting woman. In any case, I don't propose to discuss her.'

'You're always so right, precious. Bricks without straw.'

She ignored this remark, and the silence remained unbroken for some time. At length, she said abruptly: 'If Father hadn't married again, I expect I should have stayed here all my life.'

'Do you say that in a complaining spirit, or are you acknowledging your indebtedness to Faith?' he inquired.

'I could never play second fiddle to anyone,' she said. 'Oh, I wouldn't choose to come back, now that I have experienced a fuller life!'

He looked amused, but refrained from making any reply. She was looking out of the window, and presently remarked in her urgent way: 'All the same, this country has a hold over one! I shall tramp up to Rough Tor, and Brown Gilly. Oh, the smell of the peat!'

'Do you find scents nostalgic?' he asked languidly. 'They don't have that effect on me at all.'

'The peat-stacks on the Moor, and the wild blocks of granite, and the still pools!' she said, disregarding him. 'The white bedstraw under one's feet, and the sharp scent of the thyme! Oh, there is no place on earth quite the same!'

'Darling, ought you to be quite so sentimental?' he asked solicitously. 'I mean, it makes one feel slightly ill-at-ease. Besides, one has such a different conception of you.'

She gave a reluctant laugh. 'You needn't worry!'

'I do hope you are right, but I have the gravest misgivings. Oh, not about you, sweetie! Eugène wrote that Father has developed a most oppressive desire to gather us all together under the parental roof, and to keep us there.'

'Thank God I'm independent of Father!' Charmian said.

'Yes, darling, I am sure that is a most gratifying reflection, but it fails entirely to bring any relief to me,' said Aubrey somewhat acidly. 'In fact, I find it a most corroding thought that you, who are *so* unworthy (being uncreative, my pet, which is the most degrading thing to be), should find yourself divorced from monetary cares, while I, who have created such lovely things, am obliged to come into these wilds for the express purpose of cajoling Father into paying the more urgent of my debts.'

'Well, why don't you write a book that will sell?'

'Darling, really you ought to abandon the fuller life, and take up residence at Trevellin again!' Aubrey told her. 'I'm saying it for your good: that remark could only be appreciated by the Philistines.'

'Oh, I've never pretended to be anything but practical!' she replied. 'If you don't want to prostitute your art – is that how you would put it? – you'd better sell your hunters, and give up racing.'

'No, darling, that is not how I should put it,' said Aubrey gently. 'You may have noticed that I have quite a horror of the *cliché*. What an arid type you are, dear one! Do not let us talk any more! It is dreadfully bad for my nerves, and I find that I have stupidly left my vinaigrette behind.'

Charmian gave a snort of contempt. The rest of the journey was accomplished in silence, the limousine setting them down at Trevellin in time for them to join the family at tea, which had been spread in the Yellow drawing-room.

Neither of the twins was present, but Ingram had walked up from the Dower House, Eugène reclined on a brocade sofa, and Raymond had just come in from the stables. Clara was pouring out, as usual; Faith and Clay were sitting together by the window; and Vivian was perched on the arm of Eugène's sofa.

The Penhallows expressed themselves characteristically on beholding two of their number, Ingram ejaculating in accents of strong disgust: 'Oh lord, I'd forgotten you were turning up today!' Raymond giving the returned couple a brief Hallo; and Eugène waving a languid hand at them. Clara said she was glad to see them; but it was left to Faith to rise from her seat, and to make them welcome.

Charmian shook hands in a very strong-minded way, pulled the severe felt hat from her head, and threw it on to a chair, giving her head a little toss. She then dug her hands into the pockets of her flannel jacket, took up a stance by the table, with her feet widely planted, and said briskly: 'Well! How are you all? I see you're down already, Clay. I suppose Eugène's still fancying himself a hopeless invalid. How's Father?'

'I'm afraid he hasn't been quite so well lately,' Faith answered. 'At least – well, you'll see for yourself. He's had one of his restless moods on him.'

'Drinking, I suppose,' said Charmian. 'If that's Indian tea Aunt Clara, none for me. I brought a packet of Lapsang down with me, and handed it to Reuben as I came in, with instructions to Sybilla to make it in a china pot, and not in a metal one.'

'Heaven bless you, darling!' said Aubrey. 'I forgot the tea-question. Oh, just look at Eugène, ruining his digestion with that dreadful stuff! Eugène, how imprudent of you!'

'If you imagine that Sybilla's likely to make two separate lots of tea, you've probably got another guess coming to you,' observed Raymond. 'You'd better forget that kind of affectation while you're here. We've always had Indian tea, and we're not likely to change.'

'I have no patience with people who allow themselves to be tyrannized over by old servants,' Charmian said forcefully. 'This house has been crying out for someone to manage it for years. Faith of course, is hopelessly inefficient; and Clara isn't the housewifely type; but I must say, Vivian, I did hope that you might have pulled things together. You can't have anything else to do. That rug needs darning, and I should say no one has polished the fender since I was last here.'

'It is not my house, and I've no interest in it whatsoever,' said Vivian coldly.

'In saying that I fervently trust that your visit is not to be of long duration, dear Char, I feel that I speak as the mouthpiece of us all,' said Eugène, giving his cup-and-saucer to Vivian. 'No, not any more, darling: my appetite – such as it ever was – has been destroyed. But I must add, in fairness to Char, that Aubrey's socks had as much to do with that as her east-wind personality.'

Aubrey gave a little shriek. 'Cruel wretch! My lovely socks! Poems in silk, no less! How can you, Eugène?'

'They – and you—' said Eugène, closing his eyes, 'make me feel as though perhaps I should go to bed before dinner.'

'My dear, how too interesting!' Aubrey said, quite unruffled. 'Antipathies and inhibitions! They say antipathies are always reciprocated, but I don't think they can be, because I haven't the least antipathy towards you. I adore being with you. There's a fundamental likeness between us which always makes me say to myself: "There, but for the grace of God, goes Aubrey Penhallow."'

'Damned young puppy!' growled Ingram. 'You want kicking more than anyone I ever met!'

'Oh, no, really not!' Aubrey assured him earnesly. 'I've got a perfectly charming nature. It's just my manner that you object to. I do *so* sympathize with you! I find all of you more than a little trying, so I know *exactly* how you feel!'

Ingram immediately became alarmingly red in the face, and began to say that Aubrey had better be careful. Clara recommended them all not to quarrel; and Clay wondered bitterly why he was wholly unable to hold his own against his family as Aubrey so triumphantly could, and did.

CHAPTER TWELVE

By the time Aubrey had been twenty-four hours at Trevillin, the family, with the single exception of his father, heartily wished him otherwise. The twins took one look at the effeminate length of his wavy hair, another at his tie, a third at his socks, and gave realistic impressions of persons taken suddenly unwell. When he appeared at dinner in a soft silk shirt and a maroon velvet smoking-jacket, each expressed his firm conviction that nothing short of debagging would meet the case. Had it not been for the presence of females in their midst, they would undoubtedly have put the efficacy of this cure to the test; as it was, Aubrey smiled sweetly upon them both, and told them not to be nasty, rough brutes. When they showed a tendency to make the stables the chief topic of conversation, he flickered a glance at Charmian, and began to tell them about the revue upon which he was at work. After dinner, he lit a Russian cigarette, in a very long holder, and said that the cigars which those dreadful strong men, his brothers, smoked made him feel too terribly ill. 'And what do we do now?' he asked. 'If the piano were in tune, which I am sure it is not, I would play to you. Or do we still congregate in Father's room in the repellent fashion reigning when I was last here?'

'Yes, we do,' replied Raymond. 'And I don't advise you to talk in that style to Father!'

'No, no, I wouldn't annoy him for the world!' Aubrey said. 'I do think he was quite pleased to see his little Aubrey, don't you? I have always regarded myself as the feminine influence in the family, and definitely beneficent. Oh, Char my sweet, would you let me have a teeny-weeny share of your lovely China tea for my early-morning tray? So dear and generous of you!'

'Before you go to Father I want a word with you!' said Raymond curtly. 'Come into my office!'

'Oh, must I?' Aubrey said, in an appealing voice. 'I do so admire you, Ray, but I can never think of anything to say to you. I always feel – but I expect it's just my foolish fancy – that you don't really like me, and that's terribly daunting to anyone with a very, very sensitive nature, like mine.'

Raymond deigned no reply to this speech, but strode off in the direction of the room at the end of the house which he used as an office. Aubrey said falteringly: 'Oh dear, do you think I've offended him? I do hope not!' and followed him meekly.

Once inside the office, which was a severely-furnished apartment largely given over to the transaction of all business connected with the estate, Raymond wasted no words on preliminaries, but gave his younger brother an abrupt and unvarnished account of the financial position of the family. Aubrey said plaintively that he knew he was dreadfully stupid about money-matters, but all these rents and things meant nothing – but definitely *nothing*! – to him.

'Don't pretend to be a bigger fool than you are!' said Raymond. 'There's only one point you've got to grasp, and that is that the estate won't stand the demands you've been making upon it. I don't know what your prospects are, but I hope for your sake they're good. When Father dies, you'll come into a small amount of capital, and I give you fair warning that you'll get not a penny out of me after that. For the immediate present, Father may or may not pay your debts. If he listens to me, he won't.'

'Oh, I do hope he won't listen to you!' interrupted Aubrey. 'I don't want to hurt your feelings, Ray dear, but he never does, does he?'

'If he goes on at his present rate, it will become a question of taking the entire conduct of the estate out of his hands,' replied Raymond grimly. 'One of these days he'll go a step too far, and do something crazy enough to convince even a damned old fool like Lifton that he's incapable of dealing with his affairs. When that day dawns, you and Eugène and Ingram will find yourselves without the sort of support you've been getting whenever you asked for it. You can damned well get down to a job of work, the lot of you!'

'I *knew* I wasn't going to enjoy talking to you!' Aubrey said. 'You're so rough, and unkind! I don't wonder poor Father wants me to live at home. I expect he feels the need of a softening influence about the house.'

Raymond looked at him under his brows. 'He's told you he wants you to stay here, has he?'

'Oh, yes, definitely! And if he won't pay my debts unless I do it's going to be very awkward. Because I don't really think I could stand it here.'

'You'll have to sell your horses,' Raymond said.

'And you a Penhallow!' Aubrey said, in a shocked tone.

'I know for a certainty that you've got one three-hundred-guinea hunter. From what I know of you I should say your other hunter cost you as much, if not more. I don't know what your debts amount to—'

'Oh, the merest nothing, Ray! It's marvellous how I manage. I've no head for figures, but I feel sure a couple of hundred would put me in the clear.'

'You're living far beyond your means, and it's got to stop,' Raymond said uncompromisingly. 'Nobody wants you to come and live here, but if I've either got to watch Father squandering hundreds on you every year, or put up with you under my nose all day and every day, I'll put up with you! It'll be less expensive in the long run.'

'How noble and sacrificing of you! No, really, I do feel for you very much, Ray! I mean, it must be so shocking to have Eugène here – and I shouldn't think he'd ever go, would you? – and now you're facing up to the thought of having me too in the most heroic way. Only I'm not a bit like that. I just couldn't bear it. I find I am definitely allergic to this household.'

'Then I advise you to get yourself out of debt, and to draw your horns in!' Raymond said. 'The old man's breaking up a bit, and you're likely to find him a damned sight more pig-headed than you're prepared for. He's taken it into his fool-head to keep you at home – God knows why! – and if you're banking on being able to talk him into paying your debts and letting you go, you'll lose. There's only one way for you to get away, and that is to do what I tell you: get rid of your hunters, cut your expenses down, and make yourself independent of Father. That's a friendly bit of advice, and you'd be wise to take it.'

'But I don't think it's friendly at all,' objected Aubrey. 'You're simply trying to get rid of me. Mind you, I'm perfectly willing to be got rid of, but you can't expect me to sell my lovely gees, and live in squalor! I'm sure Father would be shocked.'

Raymond strode over to the door, and opened it. 'You'd better think over what I've said,' he replied.

They joined the rest of the family in Penhallow's room.

Since eight persons, besides Penhallow, were already assembled there, it might have been supposed that even his patriarchal instinct would have been satisfied. The room seemed overcrowded, and as several different conversations were being held, anyone wishing to make himself heard above the prevailing babel was obliged to shout. This did not worry the Penhallows in the least, but Faith looked exhausted, and Vivian was trying to read a book, with her elbows on her knees, and her hands over her ears to shut out the hubbub. Penhallow, who seemed to draw renewed vitality from his children, easily dominated the stage, contributing his share to every conversation in progress, and loudly deploring the absence of Ingram from the circle. When Raymond and Aubrey came in, his eyes glinted satisfaction, but since he addressed no word to Raymond, and promptly began to jeer at Aubrey, it was hard to understand why he was so pleased to have them in his room. Charmian, who had escaped from his sphere of influence, was the one of his children in whom he had the least interest, and beyond making a few ribald references to her appearance, and to her friendship with Leila Morpeth, he paid very little heed to her. To Faith, spiritually outside the circle, this seemed strange, for she thought that Charmian was the most like him of them all. Charmian too desired to dominate the company, and although her energy was not as fantastically directed as his, there was a strong suggestion of his driving-force in her trenchant voice and in the belligerent tilt of her chin. Charmian, who had compelled Sybilla to make China tea, and had harried one of the housemaids into polishing the fender in the Yellow drawing-room, was like a strong and slightly unpleasant wind sweeping through the house. She criticized everyone and everything in it, and would, if she remained there long enough, set them all by the ears, Faith thought. She was still the scornful little girl who had rescued her step-mother from a field full of bullocks, and Faith both resented her interference, and feared her ruthless tongue.

As might have been expected, there was a good deal of loud-voiced dispute in Penhallow's room that evening, developing every now and then into a sudden quarrel, which flared up between any two of the family, attracted the others to take sides, raged for a little while, and as suddenly died down. Penhallow enjoyed it all immensely, and did not seem to be in the least exhausted by the noise and the strife. He was looking forward to his birthday, boasting of his vitality, promising to surprise them all yet. He drank a quantity of whisky during the evening, and when they left him had reached a reckless, elated condition, in which he laughed boisterously flew into quick rages, recalled tangled anecdotes of his youth, and was by turns bawdy and maudlin.

Charmian, exclaiming that the room smelled like a pot-house, strode out of it as soon as her father's recollections became raffish. Faith longed for the courage to follow her example, and glanced at Vivian, wondering what she was thinking. Vivian's face showed only indifference. Faith supposed that she had become inured to these evenings, or perhaps had never been very squeamish.

'One would imagine,' Aubrey said, later, picking up his candle from the table in the hall, 'that Father will be very, very unwell in the morning.'

'No, he won't,' Vivian replied curtly. 'Merely bad-tempered. He's been going on like this for weeks.'

'What, every night?' asked Aubrey, horrified. 'Oh, I am glad I don't live at home!'

'You may well be!' she said, with such suppressed passion that he blinked at her. 'It's hell here! The worst hell you ever dreamed of! He's like a giant squid, lying there, sucking you all in!'

He giggled, and, with a glance of contempt, she went past him up the stairs.

The morning found Penhallow in a brittle, dangerous mood. He had apparently passed a considerable portion of the night in weaving fuddled plans for the future activities of his numerous offspring. These were in general too extravagant to be taken seriously, but the recital of them exasperated Raymond, who had been summoned at an early hour to learn his father's pleasure, and to receive a quantity of arbitrary orders, not the least maddening of which was one to cash another of Penhallow's lavish cheques.

'What the devil have you done with the money you drew out

only a week or so ago?' demanded Raymond, his straight brows beginning to lower.

'What the hell has that got to do with you?' retorted Penhallow, kindling at once. 'By God, it's coming to something when you cubs start questioning my doings! I don't want any comments from you, my lad! You'll do as you're told.'

'I'm damned if I will!' Raymond said forcibly. 'Do you know the extent to which your personal account is already overdrawn?'

'I know all I want to know – and I've heard more than I want to from you! You'll take my cheque into Bodmin, and keep your comments to yourself!'

Raymond drove his hands deep into the pockets of his breeches, and stood facing the bed, with his feet widely planted and his head a little thrust forward, in a belligerent attitude, which added to Penhallow's anger. 'You'll have my comments whether you want them or not,' he said. 'I'll cash no more of these senseless cheques.'

'No?' said Penhallow, his eyes narrowing. 'You'd rather I sent Jimmy, would you?'

'You can send whom you please. You won't do it often. I've already had an interview with the manager. It may interest you to know that he wanted to know if I considered you fit to be trusted with a cheque-book. I don't, but I haven't said so – yet.'

There was silence for a few hard-breathing seconds. Penhallow had heaved himself forward from his supporting pillows, as though in an attempt to reach his son. His face had become suffused with dull colour, and his eyes blazed with an expression of naked hatred. 'You hound, Raymond!' he said thickly, panting. 'You ill-conditioned mongrel-cur! So that's it, is it? You'd like to get a couple of doctors to declare me incapable, would you?'

'No,' Raymond answered coldly. 'I prefer to wash our dirty linen at home. But I won't stand by idly while you waste the estate, so don't think it! If you drive me to it, I will have you declared incapable – God knows it's the truth!'

Penhallow raised his clenched fists in an impotent, raging gesture. He let them fall again, and began to rock himself from side to side. 'Have me declared incapable!' he said. 'By God, I've been too easy with you! Think yourself master here already, don't you? You're not! Not by a long chalk, Raymond! I've been watching you; I've seen you beginning to think you own Trevellin, grudging every penny I've spent on my other sons. You didn't like it when I had Eugène and his wife give up that damned London folly. You didn't want Clay here. You're like a bear with a sore head because I mean to keep Aubrey under my eye. That doesn't matter to me. I get a laugh out of seeing you play the Squire. But my hand's still on the reins, my fine son, and there was never a horse could unseat me, no, nor get the better of me! There's been no love lost between you and me, but I've made use of you because it suited me to. You were always a surly, cross-grained boy. I should have known that you wouldn't stand corn!'

Raymond shrugged his shoulders, indifferent to this flood of abuse. 'You should know better than to waste your breath telling me what you think of me,' he said. 'I've never cared what you thought, and I'm not likely to start now. All I care for is the place, which you're doing your best to ruin. But you'll not do it! You've been behaving for the past weeks as though you were out of your mind: it wouldn't be so difficult to get all the business out of your hands.' A grim little smile curled his mouth; he said with a note of mockery in his voice: 'You're not certifiable, but it isn't necessary that you should be. I've been into all that.'

'Have you?' Penhallow said. 'Have you indeed, Ray? Maybe you think it's you who are in the saddle now?'

'It's I who am going to hold the purse-strings,' Raymond replied uncompromisingly. 'Better make up your mind to that. You can yield gracefully, or you can wait to be forced into it.'

'Yield!' Penhallow ejaculated. He flung back his head, and broke into a roar of laughter. The spaniel lying at his feet sat up on her haunches, flattening her ears, and lolling her tongue at him. He kicked at her, and she jumped down from the bed, and waddled over to a patch of sunlight, and lay down in it. 'Yield!' Penhallow said again. 'And what would you like me to do, Master Ray? Turn Eugène out, I suppose, for a start! Ask you politely for a little pocket-money every week! You're riding for a fall, Ray!'

'Turn Eugène out for a start,' Raymond agreed. 'Leave Aubrey to settle his own debts, and Ingram to pay for his brats' schooling! And stop squandering money on your dirty little bastard!'

Penhallow's eyes glinted suddenly. He began to rock himself about again, chuckling with a kind of fiendish amusement. 'Don't like Jimmy, do you, Ray? God, that's given me the best laugh of my life! It was always you who objected to him the most. Like me to turn him off, wouldn't you?'

'Keep him to wait on you, if you want him,' Raymond said contemptuously. 'But teach him his place!'

'I'll teach you yours, you misbegotten young swine!' Penhallow said, an ugly sneer disfiguring his countenance. 'He has as much right to be here as you, let me tell you!'

Raymond gave a short laugh. 'Has he, by God? He'll learn his mistake when I'm master here!'

'When you're master here!' Penhallow repeated. 'So sure of yourself, aren't you? So damned sure of yourself! You'll never be master here except by my consent!'

Raymond glanced scornfully at him. 'I shall be master here as soon as you're dead, and nothing you can do can alter that. I'm as familiar with the terms of the entail as you are yourself, so you may as well reserve that kind of bluster for someone it'll impress. It cuts no ice with me.'

Penhallow leaned right forward, supporting himself on one fist, and clenching and unclenching the other. 'You cocksure fool, the estate goes to my eldest legitimate son!'

'I am your eldest son,' Raymond said impatiently.

'Not by a long chalk you're not!' Penhallow replied, with a hiccough of a laugh. 'I had at least a couple of sons before I begot you. Bastards, of course. Like you, Ray! Like you, and poor little Jimmy!'

There was a moment's stunned silence. The colour draining from his face, Raymond stared into his father's wickedly twinkling eyes. He seemed for an instant to cease to breathe; then he shattered the silence with a rasping laugh. 'I don't believe it!'

Penhallow jerked his thumb over his shoulder at the painted cupboards set in the bed-head. 'I've got papers to prove it.'

The old grandfather clock in the corner gave a whirring sound, and began tinnily to strike the hour. Raymond found that the palms of his hands were sweating and cold. Wisps of thought jostled one another in his brain; he was unable to seize any one of them, but the wild improbability of his father's words prompted him to say again: 'I don't believe it! You old fool, you must be in your dotage to put up such a tale as that to frighten me with! It couldn't be true!'

Penhallow leaned back against his pillows once more. The rage had faded from his face, leaving it gloating and grinning. 'I thought that 'ud make you sing a different tune,' he said, with diabolical satisfaction. 'It's done me good too. Damme, it's gone against the grain with me to keep that secret from you during all the years that you've been giving yourself enough airs to make a cat sick!'

Raymond drew one hand from his pocket, found that it was shaking, and put it back again. He passed his tongue between his lips, and said carefully: 'I think you're more insane than any of us suspected. How could I possibly have been brought up here— Oh, don't talk such damned rubbish!'

'Ah, that was Rachel's doing!' Penhallow said amiably. 'I wasn't in favour of it, but she would have it so. She was a grand lass, my Rachel!'

'*Mother?*' Raymond said incredulously. 'My God, you *are* mad!'

'She wasn't your mother,' Penhallow replied, heaving himself on to his elbow, and picking up the decanter of claret from the table by the bed. He poured himself out a glass, and relaxed again, sipping the wine, and grinning at Raymond. 'Haven't you ever wondered why you were born abroad? Lord, I made sure you'd smell a rat! Especially when Rachel left her money to Ingram.'

The overfurnished room seemed to close in on Raymond, although he saw it through a blur. He felt as though he were hot and cold at once, and became aware presently of the spaniel, which had got up, and was whining and scraching at the door to be let out. This trivial circumstance, intruding upon a moment heavy with a sense of impending disaster, recalled him from the whirling nightmare which had caught him up and threatened, for an instant, to overpower him. The dog's insistence was not to be borne; he moved to the door, and let her out, feeling this mundane action to have in it some quality of unreality. He went back to the huge fireplace, and took up his former position before it. He was extremely pale, but he thought he had himself under rigid control. Yet his voice, when he spoke, sounded unfamiliar in his ears. 'If what you say is true, why did my – why did your wife bring me up as her son?'

'She was proud, was Rachel,' Penhallow responded reminiscently. 'She didn't want a breath of scandal about the business. Damned nearly murdered me, when she found out about it! But she loved me, she did, through it all. A grand lass! There was never any need to explain to Rachel: she knew what I was! Knew it didn't mean a thing. She took me as I came: never dripping forgiveness over me, bless her!'

'I don't want to hear about your relations with Mother!' Raymond interrupted roughly. 'I should have thought you'd created plenty of scandal! She never paid any heed to what you did, that I can remember!'

'Ah, but this was different!' Penhallow said, pouring out more wine. 'Touched her more nearly. She didn't mind a village affair or two.'

There was something else in the room besides Penhallow's malice, some dark shadow of horror creeping towards Raymond. He laid his hands on the back of the Gothic chair, and gripped it hard. 'Why did it touch her more nearly?' he forced himself to ask. 'Who was my mother?'

Penhallow gave a chuckle. 'Delia,' he replied.

To Raymond's shocked senses, his father's swollen figure, lying in the bed in the middle of the room, had become inseparable from the ivory god, Ho-Ti, leering at him from the top of the red lacquer cabinet. Everything in the room assumed nightmarish proportions; the warring colours in curtains, carpet, and table-cloths almost seemed to shout at him; the bright hexagons of the patchwork quilt danced before him, dazzling him. He lifted his hand instinctively to his eyes, saying hoarsely: '*No!* It's a lie!'

'Oh, no, it isn't!' retorted Penhallow. 'You mightn't think it to look at her now, but when she first came home from some finishing school or other in Switzerland Delia was as pretty as a picture.'

Raymond gripped the chairback again. He stared into his father's face, unable either to believe a tale so fantastic, or to think himself in his right senses. 'But I was born – Are you telling me you seduced a girl just out of school? The sister of the woman you were engaged to? It isn't possible! Damn you, you're making all this up!'

'Ho-ho!' jeered Penhallow. 'Precious little seduction about it! She was head over ears in love with me. She thought she knew what she was about. I believed she did. The trouble was, I didn't know as much about women in those days as I do now. You'd have thought I'd have had sense enough to realize that Delia was just the sort of romantic little fool who'd talk a lot of highfalutin balderdash about no one's being the worse for our precious affair, and then lose her nerve, and run bleating to her sister as soon as she found that she hadn't been quite so damned clever as she thought. But I was only a bit over twenty-one myself, and I'd a lot to learn.'

'But Mother – Rachel!' Raymond uttered numbly. 'How can such a thing have happened, under her very nose?'

'Lord bless you, it didn't!' Penhallow said cheerfully. 'Dare say it wouldn't have happened at all if she hadn't been away at the time. By the time she got back, the mischief was done, and that damned fool, Delia, was spending her time shuddering at the sight of me – a fat lot of right she had to do that! – and trying to put an end to herself by drinking disinfectant, or some such tomfoolery. The wonder is that she hadn't blurted out the whole story to her father!'

Raymond lifted one hand from the chairback, and brought it down again. 'No!' he jerked out. 'It's preposterous! grotesque! It couldn't have happened! Why, you must have married her, if there were a word of truth in any of this!'

'Marry her! I was sick to death of the sight of her!' exclaimed Penhallow callously. '*She* didn't want to marry me, don't make any mistake about that! I gave her the horrors, that's what I did.' A laugh shook him; he drank some of his wine. 'I've met her type often and often since. Don't you ever be taken in by a girl who tells you she's got advanced ideas! She'll be the first to talk about being betrayed. Marry her, by God! No, there was never any question of that.'

'But Mother—!' Raymond said, the words sticking in his throat. 'Are you telling me that she *knew* this, and married you yourself?'

'Put the date forward,' said Penhallow, chuckling at the memory. 'Oh, she scratched my face for me all right! But she was a remarkable woman, was Rachel. She hadn't got a pack of sentimental ideas, like that whey-faced bitch I took for my second wife, God help me! Queer, the way I've never been able to steer clear of baby-faced women who think you're a sort of hero to start with, and shudder at you the instant they find their mistake. But Rachel wasn't like that. Not she! She knew what I was like. She knew it was herself I really cared for. She never set a bit of store by any of my little side-shows. But she was proud, and she was determined no one should ever know the fool Delia had made of herself. She fixed it so that no one ever did – no one in this country, barring Martha. Unless old Phineas guessed, which he may have done, for all I can tell.'

A wave of nausea swept over Raymond. 'Martha! Oh, my God, no! no!'

Penhallow regarded him with a satirical twist to his full lips. 'You fool, you don't suppose we could have worked the trick without her, or another like her, do you?' he said. 'Rachel and I were married at once. She gave it out that I was impatient to put the date forward. True enough: I was. Lord, and she made Delia be chief bridesmaid, just as it had been arranged at the outset!' He began to laugh again, his great bulk shaking. 'What a woman! What a woman! No half-measures about my Rachel! We went off on our honeymoon. She'd fixed it all up that Delia was to join us, with

Martha, before it got to be obvious that she was big with child. She'd thought up a whole lot of cast-iron reasons for remaining abroad beyond the time we'd arranged. I had nothing to say to any of it: she'd drive the lot of us the way she meant to go, and never even see how damned comical it was, the three of us living under one roof in some God-forsaken Austrian village or other – forgot its name for the moment. As a matter of fact, you're a couple of months older than we gave out. That was all right: you were a backward, undersized brat. I never thought you'd turn out as well as you have. I didn't want Rachel to palm you off as one of her own, but I'm bound to admit there's precious little of your mother in you.' He set his empty glass down, and surveyed Raymond, triumph gleaming in his eyes. 'But you're only another of my bastards, Ray, and don't you forget it! Maybe I'll let you succeed me, and maybe I won't! But whichever way I decide, *that's* where you are, my boy!' He jabbed his thumb down hard upon the table as he spoke, and grinned malevolently at his son's ashen face.

The gesture seemed to release Raymond from the spell of horror which had held him rooted to the ground, gripping the Gothic chair, and listening with only half-comprehending ears to the story so casually recounted. The blood rushed suddenly to his head; an uncontrollable shudder ran through him; he flung the heavy chair out of his way; and with a sound between a groan and a curse launched himself upon Penhallow, seizing him by the throat, trying with all his strength to choke the breath out of him.

'Devil! Devil!' he panted, his lips drawn back from his teeth in a snarling grimace. 'I'll kill you for this, do you hear me? I'll *kill* you, you fiend, you devil!'

Penhallow grabbed at his wrists, trying to wrench them from his throat. They struggled together, Penhallow heaving his bulk half across the bed, and dragging Raymond with it, still pressing on his windpipe with his desperate thumbs, and cursing him in a dreadful whisper.

He was sprawling on top of Penhallow, one knee up on the bed, when the door opened, and Jimmy ran into the room, shouting at him. Jimmy leaped on him from behind, yelling to Reuben to come to his assistance, and managed to jerk back his head. In that instant Penhallow tore the hands from his throat, choking and gasping amongst his tumbled pillows. The table by the bed had been over-turned, the papers and fruit on it spilled all over the floor, the glasses smashed, and the decanter rolling over the carpet, leaving a trail of claret in its wake.

Reuben came hurrying in as Raymond threw Jimmy violently off, and, taking in the scene in one glance from his quick, shrewd eyes, attached himself to Raymond's right arm like a limpet. 'Give over, Master Ray, give over now! You should knaw better than to do like this, and you in your forty! Set down a crum! Lor' jimmery, what's got into un all on a sudden?'

'He were trying to choke the life out of the Master!' Jimmy said, picking himself up from the floor. 'If it hadn't ha' been for me he'd ha' done it, surely!'

'You keep a still tongue in your head, and get the whisky out of the cupboard, quick!' Reuben commanded, his concerned gaze on Penhallow. He gave Raymond a push towards a chair, and thrust him down into it, repeating: 'Set down a crum! Please the pigs you haven't done for him!'

Raymond sank down and dropped his head between his clenched fists. 'I hope I have!' he said savagely.

Reuben, finding that his mad rage was waning, paid no more heed to him, but snatched the whisky from Jimmy, and bade him help him to straighten Penhallow. The laboured breath rattled alarmingly and Penhallow's colour was very bad, but when they had laid him back on his pillows, and revived him with neat spirit, he began to recover, and even to be able to speak. 'Murderous dog!' he gasped, his lips twisting into a rueful grin. 'Hot-blooded ruffians, my sons, Reuben!'

'You lay quiet, Master! As for you, Jimmy, get along out of this! You'm not wanted here!'

'Happen I might be needed yet,' Jimmy said, looking at Raymond.

Penhallow waved him away with one hand, feeling his bruised throat with the other. His gaze travelled to Raymond, who had risen, and walked over to the fireplace, and was staring down at the smouldering logs in the hearth. He smiled rather unpleasantly, and transferred his attention to Reuben, directing him to pick up the table, and the scattered papers. 'And clear that mess of glass away before my poor little bitch can cut her paws on it!' he said huskily. 'Go and get a dustpan, you old fool! There's nothing the matter with me. Heave me up a bit first!'

The effort of struggling into a more upright position made him pant again, and drag a hand across his brow to wipe away the sweat, but he nodded dismissal to Reuben, who, after looking undecidedly from him to Raymond for a moment, reluctantly left the room.

Penhallow lay recovering his breath, allowing his over-driven heart to steady down. Its wild flurry made him feel sick; he pressed his hand to his side, and swallowed once or twice, and licked his lips. Raymond raised his head, and, turning it watched him sombrely and in silence.

'A nice, dutiful son you are!' Penhallow said presently. 'Oh, I don't blame you! Tickled you up a bit, didn't I? Well, you asked for it, and, by God, you got it! I shouldn't wonder but what we'll get along better now.'

'Was it true?' Raymond said, in a low voice.

'Lord, yes! Truest thing you know!'

'Then God damn your soul to hell!' Raymond said, with suppressed violence, and, striding to the door, wrenched it open, and plunged out of the room.

CHAPTER THIRTEEN

WHEN he left his father's room, Raymond was in the grip of an overmastering instinct to get out of the house, and away from the curious eyes of its various inmates. He had no clear notion of where he was going, or what to do. He felt as a man might who, half-stunned, had survived an earthquake only to find his home and his life-work in ruins. He would have gone out of the house by one of the garden-doors but for Reuben, who met him, and checked him, by saying dryly: 'If you've done trying to be the death of the Master, happen you'll 'tend to Tideford. He's been waiting this twenty minutes in your office.'

Raymond stopped, with his hand already on the door, grasping the iron ring that lifted its latch. He stared stupidly at Reuben, feeling himself so remote from the ordinary cares of the estate that a visit from one of Penhallow's tenants had no meaning for him. He repeated, in a blank tone: 'Tideford.'

Reuben pulled down the corners of his mouth, and gave one of his disapproving sniffs. 'What do you want to go a-losing your temper for?' he asked severely. 'Fine doings! If Master was to go off sudden, we'll knaw whose door to lay it at.'

Raymond passed his hand across his eyes, as though to clear away the red mist that still obscured his vision. 'That's enough from you!' he said roughly. 'Tideford, did you say? All right: I'd forgotten.'

He released the iron ring, and went on down the broad passage towards his office at the other end of the house. He remembered now that Tideford had come up to see him by appointment; and realized that whatever cataclysm had over-turned his life, the mundane occurrences of the everyday world had not stopped in sympathy with him, and would have to be attended to. He paused for a few minutes outside his office, attempting at once to thrust to the back of his mind the horror numbing his faculties, and to recall the business upon which Tideford wanted to see him. He was surprised, when he presently confronted Tideford across his desk, to find how calm he was, how steady both his voice and his hands. The interview helped to bring his faculties under his control again; when he saw Tideford off the premises half an hour later, he had recollected various duties waiting to be performed, and was able to attend to them in his usual methodical way. He was still conscious of a sensation of numbness, as though one half of his brain were clogged and weighted, unable to comprehend or to grapple the hideous secret which had been disclosed to him; and he was still bent on escaping from the house, and carrying his trouble out into the open, as far from human sight as he could contrive. When he had finished such office-work as lay upon his desk, he left the house, and strode off to the stables, and briefly ordered a favourite hack to be saddled. While he was waiting, he listened to some complaint Weens had for him, about one of the stable-hands, and dealt with it rather summarily. Bart came into the yard as his horse was led out, and would have detained him on some question of a strained fetlock, but he cut him short, and, swinging himself into the saddle, rode out of the yard in the direction of the stud-farm.

He did not pause there, however, but rode past it, up the hill towards the Moor, keeping to the west of the upper reaches of the Fowey, and heading for Browngelly Downs, and Dozmary Pool, beyond.

The day was very fine, with a light easterly wind making the air bright and clear. Fleecy white clouds were sailing high overhead; it had been sultry in the valley, but upon the Moor the wind was cool. To the north, Brown Willy reared up its rugged head, with the wild rocks piled on the summit of Rough Tor plainly visible to the north-west of it. Leaving the track, Raymond let his horse break into a canter, skirting some old peat-borings, and crossing one of the streams with which the Moor was intersected. Two or three miles farther on, the still expanse of Dozmary Pool came into sight, its flat, wind-swept banks lying deserted in the sunlight. It had been a favourite haunt of Raymond's since the days of his boyhood, and he had made for it instinctively, meaning to sit on the thyme-scented ground beside its mysterious waters, and to force his brain calmly to confront and to consider the intelligence which had so stunned it. But when he had hobbled the grey, he found himself unable to sit still, and began to pace up and down, jerking at his whip-lash, and fancying that he could hear some echo of his father's jeering voice in the vast solitude around him. It was long before he could achieve any coherence of thought. His mind, at first refusing to credit Penhallow's words, presently began to flit backwards and forwards across the past, recalling incidents and half-forgotten circumstances, meaningless pieces in a puzzle, which, if fitted together, might show him a picture he shrank from seeing.

Although, in the first moment of revelation, a blinding kaleido-scope, composed of all the various implications attached to his illegitimacy, had flashed across his mind's eye, this had swiftly faded into a general feeling of shock, and of nausea. It was not until he had been walking up and down beside the Pool for some time that the particular significance of Penhallow's words began clearly to present itself to him. If the story were true – and his brain still clung to the hope that it might not be true – he would never be Penhallow of Trevellin, for although Penhallow's unpredictable caprice might lead him to carry the secret into the grave, he, who was mostly nearly concerned, knew it, and would never, all his life long, be able to forget it. His stiff pride in his name, even his passionate love for Trevellin, seemed in an instant to have become empty things. There was not one of his brothers who had not a better right to call himself Penhallow of Trevellin than he; there could never in the uncertain future be a day unclouded by the fear that someone by some unforeseen chance, might discover the imposture, and arise to denounce him. It was, he thought, unlikely that Penhallow, having once broken his long silence, would refrain from dislodging him, in the end, from his position as heir to Trevellin. He would no doubt keep the secret for as long as it suited him, using it to compel obedience to his will. He needed a manager for the estate, but a manager who, besides performing his duties conscientiously, would yet permit him to commit whatsoever depredations he chose; and not one of his more favoured sons would fill his requirements as well as the only one amongst them all who, besides having a business head on his shoulders, dared not oppose him in the smallest particular. But Raymond could not doubt that he would see to it that it was Ingram who stepped finally into his shoes.

The thought of Ingram at Trevellin struck Raymond like a blow over the heart. He found that he was uttering a stream of obscene curses aloud, and stopped himself quickly, frightened of his own lack of self-control. He knew an impulse to cast himself down on the sweet-smelling turf, and to writhe there, digging his nails into the earth, as though in such physical abandonment he might find relief from the mental anguish he was suffering. For a time, coherent thought became impossible again, and he foundered in a nightmare of his imaginings, seeing Ingram in his place, enjoying the fruits of his careful husbandry, seeing himself, for a distorted moment, as Ingram's pensioner. So incalculable are the twists of the human brain that the very abhorrence with which he regarded this image jerked him out of his fog of sick fantasy. He began to laugh, softly at first, and then in lunatic gusts which made his quietly grazing horse raise his head, momentarily startled by this wild sound breaking the stillness.

His laughter was uncontrollable, and largely hysterical, but it did him good. When he at last stopped, and wiped his streaming eyes, he felt exhausted, but relieved of the iron restriction in his chest which had made him feel as though his heart were trying to burst from his body. He could think more reasonably, and could face the future without succumbing to the condition of mindless horror which made sober reflection an impossibility. He began to weigh what his father had recounted against his own memories, trying in these to find some refutation of Penhallow's monstrous story. After a time it occurred to him that one person only could deny or confirm the story, and without questioning the wisdom of acting upon his sudden impulse he caught and unhobbled his horse, and rode off at a gallop in the direction of Bodmin.

When he reached Azalea Lodge, he called to the gardener who was clipping the borders of the front path to walk his horse up and down, and strode up to the front door, and set his finger on the electric bell-push. The door was opened to him by an elderly parlourmaid, who ushered him into the drawing-room, and said that she would fetch Miss Ottery.

In the shock of first learning that he was not Rachel Penhallow's son, he had not until this moment had any thought to spare for the woman who might prove to be his mother; but as he stood in the middle of the stuffy, over furnished room, surrounded, as it seemed to him, by cats and canaries and cabinets crowded with china, the idea that Delia, whom he, in common with his brothers, had all his life made the subject of contemptuous jests, might claim him as her son, swept over him, and filled him with such repugnance that he was seized by an instinct to rush from the house before she could confront him. He mastered it, and picked his way between floor-cushions, spindle-legged tables, and cat-baskets to the bay window, and stood there staring out into the neat garden.

He presently heard the door open behind him, and Delia's voice utter a welcome. 'Dear Raymond! *Such* a pleasure! So unexpected, too, not that I mean – because you know that we're always so delighted to see you, dear! I was just helping Phineas to wash some of his china. Quite an honour, I call it, for he will let no one else touch it! You must excuse my overall – but I daresay you men never notice such things!'

A shudder ran through his frame; he turned to face her, his strained eyes taking in, as perhaps never before, every detail of her appearance. It was not prepossessing. Her hair, escaping from its falling pins, showed a number of straggling ends, a fact of which she seemed to be conscious, since she made several ineffectual attempts to secure them. She was wearing an overall fashioned out of a flowered material eminently unsuited to her years and her faded looks; and one of the irritating scraps of lace with which she was in the habit of embellishing her dresses had worked its way over the collar of the overall. There was such an indefinable air of desiccated spinsterhood about her that Raymond could have shouted aloud his disbelief that she could be his mother.

She advanced towards him in a little flutter of shy excitement. She did not immediately perceive, since he was standing with his back to the light, how pale he was. She kept up a gentle flow of chatter, exclaiming at one naughty pussy for having curled up on one of the chairs, apostrophizing a canary, which was indefatigably singing in a gilded cage, as her precious Timmy, and directing Raymond's attention to a pair of budgerigars at his elbow. When she reached him, it was plain from the timid way she raised her face that she expected him to kiss her cheek. He could not do it; it was with an effort of will that he refrained from thrusting her away from his immediate vicinity. He found a difficulty in speaking, but managed, after an uncomfortable moment of struggle, to say: 'I came to speak to you.'

Still no inkling of his state of mind penetrated to her understanding; he had always had an abrupt manner, and she noticed nothing amiss. She said: 'I'm *so* glad to see you! It seems such a long time since you were here! Because I don't count that time you so kindly motored me back from the town, you know, because you wouldn't come in, would you? Not that I didn't perfectly understand, for of course I know what a lot you always have to do, and how little time you have to spare. But I must tell you about Dicky! You remember that I asked the corn-chandler – such an obliging man! – about poor little Dicky, who wasn't quite well?'

He interrupted her. 'I've come to speak to you,' he said again. His underlip quivered. 'I don't know how to do it!' he said desperately, looking round the room, at the cats, and the birdcages. 'Now that I'm here – No, it isn't possible!'

The chatter was stilled on her lips. She peered at him short-sightedly, sudden alarm in her face. She saw how haggard he looked, and retreated a step involuntarily. Her voice shook as she faltered: 'Of course, dear! of course! Though I can't imagine what – You must let me fetch you some refreshment! A glass of sherry, and a biscuit. Phineas will be so pleased to see you! He was only saying the other day – But what am I doing, not asking you to sit down?'

'I don't want anything. I came to you because of something Father told me. I don't trust him: he'd say anything! But I've got to know the truth, and you're the only person – Oh no, my God, there's Martha!'

There was no more colour in her face than in his. She uttered a little moan, and shrank back from him, terror in her eyes. 'I don't know what you mean! I don't know what you mean!' she cried, her voice rising to a shrill note. 'Ray dear, you – you aren't quite well! You're not yourself! Do – do sit down! I'll fetch Phineas. I expect you've been doing too much. A glass of sherry!'

He stood perfectly still, looking at her, noticing that her nose was shining, and a hairpin drooping on to her shoulder. He felt as though this were all happening to someone else, not to him, Raymond Penhallow! No more confirmation was needed than that which he read in Delia's frightened countenance. He would have gone away, but the situation was so strange that he did not know what to do in it, and so stood there, incongruous amongst the feminine knick-knacks with which the room was crammed. The muscles of his throat felt so rigid that he was obliged to swallow once or twice before he could speak. Then he said in a heavy tone which gave little indication of the turmoil in his breast: 'It is true. You are my—' He found that he could not utter the word, and changed the phrase – 'You aren't my aunt.'

She began to cry, in a gasping way, dabbing all the time at her eyes. 'Oh, Raymond! Oh, Raymond!'

He regarded her stonily. It seemed to him that she had little cause to cry. It was his life which had been ruined; he could not appreciate that she might be crying for this reason. In his own overwhelming chagrin there was no room for compassion either for her present distress, or for the misery she must have endured forty years ago, and perhaps through the intervening years. He was conscious only of loathing her, and that so profoundly that it made him feel actually sick.

She had stumbled blindly to a chair, and was crouched in it, gulping and sniffing, and still dabbing at her eyes. They were already a little swollen. She raised them fleetingly to his face, and at once they overflowed again. 'I'm so sorry! I'm so sorry, dear!' she sobbed.

The hopeless inadequacy of her words irritated him. 'Sorry!' he ejaculated. 'A trifle late in the day for you to be sorry!'

'I didn't know — I never meant — I've always loved you so!' she said piteously.

His hands clenched on the whip he was still holding; a rush of bitter, molten words crowded in his throat; he managed to choke them down. All he said, but that in a voice which made her flinch, was one word: 'Don't!'

Her sobs grew louder, more gasping. 'If you knew — I did my best—'

'No, you didn't,' he interrupted. He gave an ugly laugh. 'Don't women manage to dispose of their unwanted infants? Lie on them, or something? Couldn't you have got rid of me?'

Her horrified eyes started at him. 'Oh, Raymond, don't, don't! You don't know what you're saying! Oh, how *wicked* — Oh, you mustn't talk like that!'

'Wicked!' he repeated. 'Wasn't it wicked to palm me off as your sister's child? To let me grow up in utter ignorance — Oh my God, can't you see what you've done?'

'Rachel promised!' she said desperately. 'It wasn't my fault — Rachel arranged everything! She promised no one should ever know! Adam had no right to tell you!' A terrible thought occurred to her; she gave a whimper of fright, and cowered into the corner of her chair. 'What did he do it for? Raymond, why did he do it?'

'Does it matter?' he asked.

'But, Raymond!' Her voice was rising again, on a note of panic. 'What's he going to do?'

'I don't know.'

She sprang up, catching her foot in the fringe of the rug on the floor, and stumbling over it. 'But he can't say anything! He mustn't! Not after all these years! He *promised*! He couldn't be so dreadful!'

She was advancing towards him, with her shaking hands held out. He deliberately put a table loaded with bibelots between them, not with the intention of hurting her, for he was not thinking of her at all, but because his flesh crept at the thought of being touched by her. 'I'll tell you I don't know what he means to do. I don't know that it matters much. The mere fact — now that I know it's true — It's no use talking. I only came to find out — and I have. So that's all.'

He turned towards the door. She called after him in a distracted voice: 'Oh, don't go like that! I can't *think*!'

'No,' he said hardly. 'I can't think either. I daresay I shall be able to, when – when I've got more used to the idea of being just another of Father's bastards.'

'Oh, no, no!' she whispered foolishly, and again stretched out her hand to him.

But he went away without looking back, and a minute later she heard the clatter of his horse's hooves diminishing in the distance.

CHAPTER FOURTEEN

THE morning had not passed pleasantly for many members of the Penhallow family. Whatever gossip might be rife in the kitchen on the subject of Raymond's quarrel with his father, no echo of this reached the family, no one, in fact, having the least idea that a quarrel had taken place; but there were troubles enough besides that to agitate the household. Vivian, who had come down late to breakfast, when only Clara, Conrad, Aubrey, and Charmian still sat round the table, had rather unaccountably created a scene, during the course of which she had not only favoured those of the Penhallows who were present with her full and frank opinion of their manners, morals, and habits, but had launched forth into a diatribe against Penhallow himself, and had ended by declaring hysterically that if she did not soon escape from Trevellin she would go mad. After that, she had slapped Conrad's face, because he laughed at her, and rushed out of the room, leaving her breakfast untouched. She was later heard, wildly sobbing, in the library, to which apartment it was conjectured that she had fled in the well-founded belief that few of the Penhallows would be likely to enter it.

She left the dining-room party labouring under a strong feeling of surprise, for although she was known to be moody, she had never before been seen to lose all control over herself. The immediate cause of her outbreak seemed too trivial to warrant such a display of emotion. She had exploded with wrath at finding that Conrad had carelessly put a used plate (his own) in her place at the table, instead of removing it to the sideboard.

'And who shall blame her?' said Aubrey. 'I do think that egg-stains are quite too alienating, don't you? The twins simply have no sensibility at all.'

'But what's she want to kick up such a shindy about?' demanded Conrad. 'She'd only got to move it, hang it all! Anyone would think I'd put a live toad in her place!'

'I wouldn't pay any attention to Vivian's tantrums, if I were you,' Clara said. 'I daresay she has her troubles.'

'She's got Eugène, if that's what you mean!'

'Is she starting a baby by any chance?' inquired Charmian, who was sitting with both elbows on the table, and her coffee-cup held between her hands.

Clara rubbed her nose. 'Well, she hasn't said anythin' about it to me,' she said doubtfully. 'Of course, that isn't to say she isn't, and it would account for her comin' over squeamish, I daresay.'

'Oh, no!' said Aubrey imploringly. 'Oh, Char darling, you don't really think so, do you? I mean, what with Father being quite too gross for words, and the twins so terribly, terribly hearty, I don't think I can *bear* any more! Shall you stay here for a whole week? I'm nearly sure I shan't. It's all so primitive, and vulgar, and I find that I definitely lack the herd-instinct, without which I quite see that it's practically impossible to feel at home here.'

'Well, that's something, anyway!' retorted Conrad, getting up from the table. 'Considering that you affect the rest of us like a pain in the neck, the sooner you clear out the better!'

'Now, that's enough!' Clara said mildly. 'What with your father on the rampage, and now Vivian, we can't do with any more nonsense.'

Conrad grimaced at her, and went away, but any hopes she or others might have entertained of spending the eve of Penhallow's birthday in comparative peace were effectually put an end to, first by the discovery that Vivian was prolonging her attack of hysteria in the library; and next by the antics of Penhallow, who, as soon as he had recovered in some measure from the effects of Raymond's assault upon him, proceeded to make his presence more than usually felt in the house. Knowing nothing of his father's unpropitious mood, Clay was inspired to address an appeal to him, having nerved himself to take this desperate step by walking about the gardens for several hours, and rehearsing a convincing speech. Filial respect and manly determination were the predominant notes in the speech, as rehearsed, but since he was destined never to utter more than the opening phrases all his trouble was wasted. The very sight of his pallid countenance, nervously bobbing Adam's apple, and unquiet hands exasperated Penhallow. He had always done what lay in his power to inspire his sons with dread of him, and had heartily despised any one of them who seemed to show that he had succeeded. Confronted by Clay, obviously terrified of him, and as obviously preparing to recite a set speech, he gave the fullest rein to his ill-humour, speedily reducing that unfortunate youth to a condition of stammering imbecility, tearing his character to shreds, trampling brutally over the tenderest spots in his sensibility, and dismissing him finally with a promise to take such steps as were requisite to turn him into a worthy member of the Penhallow family.

Emerging from his father's room in a much shaken state, Clay fell into the arms of his half-sister, whom he encountered in the hall, and who promptly walked him out into the garden, and endeavoured, with the best possible motives, to instil resolution and self-reliance into him. But as he was of the type that responds only to encouragement mingled with a good deal of flattery, her methods, which were at once bracing and scornful, inspired him with nothing more than a desires to escape from her, coupled with a strong conviction that she did not understand him. He fled to his mother, and unburdened himself to her with so little reserve that it was not long before he had plunged her into a state of even greater desperation than his own.

Having passed one of her restless nights, Faith was late in coming downstairs. The hour which Clay had spent in her room had left her with a throbbing head; she felt her chief need to be quiet, and was well aware that such a commodity was not to be found under existing circumstances at Trevellin. The house seemed to teem with persons all more or less inimical to her; and as though it were not enough to find Eugène toying with an idea for an essay in the Yellow drawing-room, his wife viciously smoking cigarettes in the library, Clara mending stockings in the morning-room, and Charmian conducting an argumentative literary discussion with Aubrey in the hall, Myra had walked up from the Dower House to discover what plans had been made for Penhallow's birthday party on the morrow. Myra had been in to see Penhallow, and gave it as her opinion that he was looking wonderful. As she had very little interest in anything beyond the walls of her own home, she hardly ever came into collision with her father-in-law, a circumstance which enabled her to face the thought of his amazing vitality with perfect equanimity. 'I always say,' she remarked brightly, 'that he'll see us all out! Of course, all the Penhallows are long-lived, aren't they? I'm sure everyone thought his grandfather would die years and years before he did. He had everything in the world the matter with him, too. Of course, his father died young, but that was only because of a hunting accident.'

Faith barely repressed a shudder. Her sister-in-law replied placidly that she for one had never believed in half Penhallow's ailments. She added that Dr. Lifton might say what he liked, but that she knew her brother better than he did, and expected him to live for a good many years yet.

Faith could not listen to such a prognostication in silence. 'If he did not drink so much!' she said. 'Dr. Lifton told me himself that no constitution could stand it!'

'Ah!' said Clara, rethreading her needle. 'Time will show.'

Faith went out into the garden, murmuring that her head ached. The thought of perhaps having to endure years of the sort of purgatory she had been going through for months now was so appalling to her that she looked quite hunted, and indeed felt as though her reason were tottering. Since Aubrey's return to the fold, the noise and the strife in the family seemed to have become augmented, not one of his brothers being able, apparently, to see him without making some belittling remark to which he promptly responded in kind. Such bickering had no effect upon Clara, who largely ignored it, but it preyed on Faith's nerves to an extent that would have been quite incomprehensible to the Penhallows, had they had the least idea of it. More than ever, now that Aubrey had come and Loveday had betrayed her confidence, she found herself dreaming of the prettily furnished flat in London which she hoped to share one day with Clay. It had become her escape from the turmoil of actuality, but sometimes it seemed to her that she would never realize her ambition until she had grown too old and weary to enjoy it.

Seated in the shade of a big tree on the lawn, she glanced towards the sprawling grey house, with its graceful Dutch gables, its chamfered windows, and high chimney-stacks, and rememembered with a feeling almost of incredulity that she had once, long ago, exclaimed at its beauty, and thought herself fortunate to be its mistress.

The truth was, of course, that she had never been its mistress. No spirit ruled at Trevellin other than Penhallow's, and the tyranny he exercised was so complete that it left no member of the household untouched. Brooding over it, she realized, with a little start (for she was so much in the habit of thinking her own sufferings unique that she had never considered whether the rest of the family might not suffer too, in their degrees), that it would not only be herself and Clay who would be released by Penhallow's death from an intolerable bondage. There was Raymond, always at silent loggerheads with his father, and striving against the odds to husband the estate; there was Vivian, tied to a house and an existence she loathed, cheated of her right to her own home; there was Bart, baulked of a marriage which, however distasteful to his family, would probably turn out successfully; there was Aubrey, escaping for a little while only to be caught back again into his father's toils. Perhaps, in the end, Charmian too would be forced to abandon the peculiar life she had chosen for herself. It did not seem likely, but anything, Faith thought, was possible when Penhallow jerked on the reins. But if he were to die, as the doctor had hinted that he would, every trouble would vanish, and they would be free, all of them: free to disperse, to follow their own inclinations; free from the fear of Penhallow's wrath; free from their degrading dependence upon him for their livelihood. Bart would marry his Loveday, and take her to live at Trellick; Vivian would at last have Eugène to herself, to worship and to protect; Aubrey might pursue his exotic course undisturbed; and Raymond, coming after impatient years into his inheritance, would govern Trevellin without let or hindrance. And Clay, who was so much more important than any of them, would be saved from the grim future planned for him by Penhallow, for even if Penhallow left him nothing, there would be her own jointure, and on that he and she could live in peace and tolerable comfort while he made a name for himself with his pen.

She saw clearly that Penhallow's death would be a universal panacea, and at once it seemed to her monstrous that he should lie there, in that fantastic room, year upon year, as no doubt he would, growing steadily more outrageous, wasting the estate, spoiling so many people's lives, breeding dissension and misery amongst them, while they all, in their several ways, ate their hearts out. If only he would fulfil his doctor's expectations, and drink himself to death! If only his unwise exertions might suddenly prove fatal! It would be, she thought dreamily, as though the house had been exorcised of an evil spirit. But he would not succumb to his follies, because nothing in this world ever happened as one prayed it might. He would go on, as his grandfather had before him, triumphantly overcoming the weakness of his diseased body, wearing them all out, until, in the end, when at last he died, they would not care for their freedom any more, because it had come to them too late.

She gave a little sob, and buried her face in her hands, but raised it again quickly as she heard footsteps approaching.

Aubrey was wandering across the lawn in her direction, a lock of his overlong hair flopping across his forehead. He wore a pair of very beautifully cut biscuit-coloured trousers, a pale green sports-short with short sleeves, suède shoes and a large silk handkerchief which he had knotted loosely round his neck in an extremely artless fashion, calculated to offend his brothers. A cameo ring adorned the hand which he waved airily at Faith, and there was just the suggestion of an expensive scent about him. He paused by the seat under the tree, and said in his light, high-pitched voice: 'My dear, why did no one warn me that Father had gone gaga? Too unkind of you all! But *definitely* unhinged, darling!'

'What has he done now?' she asked wearily.

'It isn't so much what he has done as what he would *like* to do. I've just sustained half-an-hour's quite paralysing conversation – if you can call it that, for I'm sure I barely uttered – with him, in that grotesque room of his. Sweetie, *why* the Japanese screen of unparalleled meretriciousness, and *why* the tropical vegetation?'

I don't know. He takes fancies to things, and then he has them moved into his room.'

'But, precious, no one could take a fancy to an aspidistra!' Aubrey objected. 'It's like pampas grass – too dreadfully apocryphal! And is it *absolutely* necessary to his comfort to place crimson and scarlet side by side? I thought it was a trick of the candle-light last night, but it hit me the rudest blow when I *most* reluctantly entered the room this morning. Do you suppose that disgusting dog of his has eczema, or just fleas?'

She made a gesture of distaste. 'Oh, don't, Aubrey! I'd rather not talk about it, if you don't mind.'

'My dear, I do so agree with you! Quite too quelling. But you would never guess the insensate plane he has conceived for my future career! Would you believe it? – I'm to study afforestation!'

'Afforestation!' she repeated blankly.

'Oh, deforestation too! I mean, it's definitely vertiginous! Couldn't you have him certified?'

'But are you going to?' she asked.

'Sweet, is it likely? At my time of life, and with my sacred art to consider!'

'Did you tell him so?'

'No, darling, certainly not. I wouldn't be so tactless. Besides, I'm terrified of Father. I was unequivocally assuaging. But I do see that I shall be compelled to do something wholly desperate. So vulgar! I do hate active persons, don't you? Just think of poor dear Char – oh, I am being nice to Char! You must forget I said that. Let us instantly talk of something else! Don't you think there's a weird fascination about Father? He always makes me think of Henry VIII, an entrancing creature, and hardly more intimidating. There's a Tudor lavishness about him, and a general air of recklessness quite anachronous to the sordid times we live in. I've got to go and cash a cheque for three hundred pounds for him in Bodmin. I mean, just like that! Something really awe-inspiring about that, don't you think? Like lighting a cigarette with a five-pound note, which I have never been able to nerve myself to do, though I've tried, often. What can he possible want with three hundred pounds, do you suppose?'

'He will squander it on things like that dreadful bed of his, or give it away, to people like Jimmy,' she replied bitterly.

'Of course I should have known that,' he agreed. 'I don't know how you feel about it, darling, but I do rather grudge it to Jimmy. One begins to appreciate the probable feelings of the legitimate offspring of such persons as Louis XIV, which somehow had never come home to one before.'

'If he has told you to cash the cheque, it must be because Raymond wouldn't,' she warned him. 'Raymond will be very angry if you do it.'

'Yes, lovely, I'm sure he will, but Father would be very angry if I didn't, and of the two I prefer to face Ray,' he answered. 'If you don't see me again, it will either be because I have absconded with the money, or because I have failed to control that dreadful limousine. Good-bye, darling: do cheer up!'

He walked away from her with another wave of his hand. She remained under the shadow of the big tree for a long time, thinking that it was easy for him, here only on a visit and with no intention of remaining, to recommend her to be cheerful. If Penhallow succeeded in forcing him to live at Trevellin, he would speedily lose his insouciance. She wondered what he meant, if he meant anything, by his talk of doing something desperate. She wished with all her heart that he would do something desperate, desperate enough to enrage Penhallow into bursting a blood-vessel. No one could think it a crime to put an end to a life so baleful; indeed, if Penhallow's brain were going, it would be almost a kindness. She leaned her head back against the rough tree-trunk, closing her eyes, and letting her imagination stray into that halcyon world which lay beyond Penhallow's grave. It was so real to her, down to the smallest detail of that little flat in London, that when she was roused, much later, by the sound of the gong, lustily beaten by Reuben in the hall, she felt as though she had really escaped for a happy hour from Trevellin, and had been wrenched back with a sickening jolt.

Raymond did not come in to lunch, but Bart was present, and said that he did not know why Ray should not have returned, since, as far as he knew, he had not had much to do that morning. Bart was out of spirits; ever since his interview with his father he had been restless, alternating between spurts of energy, and a moody listlessness until now foreign to his cheerful temperament. He hardly spoke until Aubrey entered the room, midway through the meal, and he for the first time beheld his attire. That did rouse him, and he expressed himself with brutal freedom. Eugène added his less brutal but more deadly mite, and as Charmian considered herself in honour bound to come to Aubrey's support, the usual state of warfare soon reigned over the dining-room. Clay, who should have known better, joined in the condemnation of Aubrey's sartorial taste and effeminate habits, and was promptly told by Bart that he was a cheeky young hound, and bidden to shut up. It was at this point that Faith began to cry, quite silently, but so uncontrollably that after a moment of biting her lips, and twisting her hands together under the table, she got up, and hurried out of the room, leaving her pudding untouched on her plate.

'I suppose,' said Vivian viciously, 'that you'll all of you be satisfied when you've driven Faith into a lunatic asylum!'

Bart looked a good deal surprised. 'But what's the matter with her? No one said anything to her!'

'You shouldn't have set on Clay,' said his aunt. 'You know she doesn't like it. Not but what he shouldn't criticize his elders.'

'Good lord, I only told him to shut up! Here, Clay, you'd better go after her, and tell her it's all right! I didn't mean to upset her.'

'Tell her you've kissed, with tears,' recommended Eugène, drawing a dish of strawberries towards him.

Charmian waited until Clay had left the room before delivering herself of her opinion. Then she said, leaning back in her chair, and driving one hand into the pocket of the slacks she was wearing: 'It's amazing to me that you none of you have the wit to see what's happening under your noses. It's my belief that Faith is heading for a nervous breakdown. I never saw her so much on edge in my life. She looks as though she hadn't had a proper night's rest for months.'

Eugène, who could not bear anyone to encroach on his prerogative, said with light contempt: 'My dear Char, we have all been sufficiently bored by the recital of Faith's so-called insomnia already. If she had ever been called upon to suffer one tenth of what I go through nightly, she might have some cause to complain!'

'There's nothing whatsoever the matter with you, Eugène,' retorted his sister. 'You are fast turning into a hypochondriac, and Vivian can apparently find nothing better to do than to encourage you. Don't bother to rush to his defence, Vivian! I haven't the slightest interest in either of you. But unless I'm much mistaken Faith has reached a breaking-point, and will probably have a complete collapse one of these days. When I look at her, I am reminded of the terrible time I went through with poor Leila once, when she had been living on her nerves for months, and they gave way under the strain.'

Bart broke into a roar of laughter. 'Oh, gosh! I should think they damned well might! Anything would give way under the strain of having that lump of Turkish Delight living on it!'

Aubrey intervened before Charmian could blister Bart for this irreverence. 'Of course, I don't suppose any of you will be at all interested, but I must inform you that Faith is not the only person in this house threatened with a nervous breakdown. And I do hope that when I so far forget myself as to render this board untenable by bursting into tears at it, you will remember that I am not accountable for my actions.'

'I expect,' said Clara wisely, 'that she needs a change of air.'

Clay came back into the room, with the news that his mother was lying down, so no more was said. Faith reappeared at tea-time, but from the look of dismay which came into her face when she paused on the threshold of the Long drawing-room it was plain that she would not have done so had she been informed that Penhallow intended to make one of the tea-party.

He was wrapped in his aged dressing-gown, and it was evident that it had cost him an effort to get up at all. His eyes held a look of strain; his colour was bad; and he eased himself in his wheeled chair from time to time, as though he were suffering a considerable degree of discomfort. He was quick to see Faith's instinctive recoil. He said in his roughest, most derisive voice: 'No, you wouldn't have come down if you'd known you were going to find me here, would you? A fine wife you are! I might be dead for all the notice you ever take of me! Why haven't you been near me all day? Eh? Why haven't you?'

She could never accustom herself to being rated in public, and the colour rushed to her face as she answered in a low tone: 'I have not been very well, Adam.'

He gave a sardonic bark of laughter at this. 'Oh, you've not been very well!' he said, mimicking her. 'That's always your bleat!'

Bart crossed the room with a plate of sandwiches, which he offered to Penhallow. 'Hit one of your own size, Guv'nor!' he said briefly.

Penhallow looked up at him under his brows. 'You, for instance?'

Bart grinned. 'Sure! Go ahead!'

Penhallow put up a hand, and pulled his ear. 'Coming out as a champion, are you?' His glance swept the room, and alighted on Clay for an instant. He took a sandwich, and addressed his wife again. 'I notice it isn't your own brat who stands up for you, my dear,' he remarked.

Clay turned scarlet, and tried to look as though he had not heard this sally. It was at this moment that Raymond entered the room.

Penhallow forgot about his wife. He seemed to straighten himself in his chair when he saw Raymond. 'Didn't expect to find me up, did you?' he demanded challengingly.

Raymond's face was always impassive; it showed no change of expression now. 'I don't know that I thought much about it either

143

way,' he replied. He walked over to the table, and waited to receive his tea-cup from Clara's hands.

'You're lookin' tired, Ray,' she remarked.

'I'm all right,' he responded shortly. Conscious of his father's gaze, he looked up, and met it squarely, his jaw hardening a little. Penhallow grinned at him, but whether in mockery, or in appreciation of his self-command it would have been difficult to say.

Penhallow began to stir his tea, in a way which made Aubrey exchange a pained glance with Charmian. 'I shall sit up to dinner,' he announced.

This piece of intelligence was greeted with such a marked lack of enthusiasm that Aubrey felt in incumbent on him to say: 'How lovely for us, Father dear!'

'I don't know which of you gives me the worst belly-ache, you or Clay!' said Penhallow, with a look of disgust. 'I don't want you slobbering over me!' His fiery glance again swept the room; his lip curled. 'A nice, affectionate lot of children I've got!' he said scathingly.

'One hates to criticize Father,' murmured Eugène in his sister's ear, 'but one cannot but feel that to be a most unreasonable remark.'

'Considering you mean to sit up to dinner tomorrow, you'd be better in bed today, I should have thought,' said Clara.

'You keep your thoughts to yourself, old lady!' retorted Penhallow. 'I daresay there's a lot of you would like to see me keep my bed, but you're going to be disappointed. By God, I've let you get so out of hand, the whole pack of you, it's time I showed you who's master at Trevellin!' He stabbed a finger at his wife. 'And that goes for you too!' he said unnecessarily. 'Don't think you're going to take to your bed with a headache, or any other such tomfoolery, because you're not! And as for you,' he added, directing the accusing finger at Charmian, 'you can make what kind of a guy of yourself you please in London, but you won't do it here! You let me see you in those trousers again, and I'll lay my stick across your bottom!'

'Oh, no, you won't!' said Charmian, with a look quite as fierce as his. 'You've no sort of control over me, so don't you think it! I'm not dependent on you! I shan't burst into tears because you choose to shout at me! You'll get as good as you give if you go for me!'

'Oh, don't! please don't!' Faith gasped, shrinking back in her chair involuntarily.

Neither of the combatants paid the slightest heed to her. Battle was fairly joined, and had anyone wished to speak it would have been quite impossible to have done so above the thunder of Penhallow's voice and the fury of Charmian's more strident accents. Eugène, lounging on a sofa, lay laughing at them both; Clara went on drinking her tea in perfect unconcern; Clay found that his hand was trembling so much that he was obliged to set his cup and saucer down on the table beside him; and Conrad, entering the room when the quarrel was at its height, promptly encouraged his sister by calling out: 'Loo in, Char! Loo in, good bitch!'

Reuben Lanner, who had come in behind Conrad, crossed the room to his master's chair, and shook his arm to attract his attention. 'Shet your noise, Master, do!' he shouted in his ear.

Penhallow broke off in the middle of an extremely coarse description of his daughter's character to say: 'What do you want, you old fool?'

'It's Mr. Ottery wants to see you, Master. I've put un in the Yellow drawing-room.'

The rage died out of Penhallow's enflamed countenance quite suddenly. An interested gleam came into his eyes; he turned them towards Raymond in a speculative glance; a slow grin dispersed the remnants of his scowl. 'Phineas, eh?' he said. His great frame shook with a soundless laugh. 'Well, that's very interesting, damme if it isn't! Show him in! What do you want to put him in the Yellow room for?'

'Because he wants to see you, private, Master, that's what for.'

'Why on earth?' demanded Conrad, staring at him.

Raymond, who had heard the message delivered with an imperceptible stiffening of his face, laid down his cup and saucer, and said: 'I'll see him.'

'You're a damned fool, Ray,' said his father, but with more amusement than annoyance in his tone. 'So old Phineas wants to see me! Well, well, and why shouldn't he? Push me into the Yellow room, Reuben!'

Raymond said not more. As Reuben pushed the wheeled chair forward, Penhallow put out a hand and grasped Charmian by the arm. There, my girl! give me a kiss! Damned if you don't make me think of your mother when you fly into your tantrums, though God knows the messy way you live is enough to make her turn in her grave! But you're a high-couraged filly, and that's something!' He pulled her down as he spoke, gave her a noisy kiss, and a resounding spank, and let her go.

As soon as he had been pushed out of the room, speculation on the cause of Phineas's visit broke out, his brothers looking inquiringly at Raymond, who said, however, that he had no more idea than they.

'Why, particularly, are you a "damned fool", Ray?' asked Eugène, a little curiosity in his eyes.

Raymond shrugged. 'I don't know. Did you order those buckets, Bart?'

'No, of course I didn't. You said you'd attend to it yourself,' Bart replied, surprised.

'Oh!' Raymond coloured slightly. 'All right: slipped my memory.'

'Good God, how are the mighty fallen!' exclaimed Conrad, folding a slice of bread-and-butter, and putting it into his mouth. 'Chalk it up, somebody! The Great, the Methodical Ray has at last forgotten something he ought to have remembered! Keep it up, Ray: you'll become quite human in time!'

Raymond smiled in a rather perfunctory way, and soon after left the room. Aubrey sighed audibly. 'There is something more than oppressive about this house,' he said. 'I expect you're all quite used to it, but coming as I do from the beautiful peace of my own chambers it strikes me quite too dreadfully forcibly.' He described a vague gesture with his delicate hands. 'I shan't say that an evil influence appears to me to brood over the place, because I do think esoteric remarks of that nature are terribly embarrassing, don't you? But you all seem to me to be a trifle more than life-size, and *definitely* febrile!'

'You're perfectly right!' Charmian said. 'But can you wonder at it?'

'No, my sweet. At least, I don't mean to waste my time in trying. I'm just profoundly repelled. Something so deplorably indecorous about an uninhibited display of the more violent emotions, don't you agree? Ah, no! How unremembering of me! You have just demonstrated to us, haven't you, darling, that you don't agree at all?'

As Eugène, who was as jealous of Aubrey's clever tongue as he was of his success in the field of literature, began to engage him in a wordy duel, Faith got up, and quietly left the room.

CHAPTER FIFTEEN

A HIRED car, which had presumably brought Phineas from Bodmin, was drawn up outside the front door. Faith saw it, as she crossed the hall towards the staircase, but beyond thinking fleetingly that it was strange that Phineas should have come so unexpectedly to call upon Penhallow she wasted no speculation on his visit. The throbbing in her temples had developed into a dull ache which seemed to emanate from a point midway between her brows. The skin across her forehead felt tight and unyielding; she smoothed it once or twice with her hand as she mounted the stairs. When she reached her room, she sat down in a chair by the window, not leaning back in it, but holding herself rigid, with her hands clasped in her lap, the fingers working a little. While she had cowered in the depths of the big chair in the Long drawing-room, wincing at the strident voices of Penhallow and Charmian, she had caught sight of Clay's white face, and had read the sick terror in it. She had seen how his hand shook when he set down his cup and saucer, and it had come to her quite suddenly that he and she must escape from Trevellin. He had cast her an imploring look which had recalled to her mind the way he used to run to her for protection when he was a little boy. She realized that for all his lofty talk, and his desperate pretences, he was still near enough to his childhood to cherish the shreds of that old, unreasoning trust in her ability to keep him safe from any hurt or any danger. Her love for him had nerved her in the past, to fight his battles for him, against her step sons, and even against Penhallow himself; it flamed high in her heart now: she could not fail Clay.

She began to think of what she must do. She supposed it would be easily possible for them both to leave Trevellin, and for an idle minute considered how such a flight could best be accomplished. Then she remembered that she had too little money to make it feasible; and that Clay was under age. She did not know whether Penhallow could lay legal claim to him, but she thought it very likely. They would never be able to hide from him; he would hunt them down for the sheer sport of it.

Her gaze was fixed and unseeing; she remained motionless, except for the working of her fingers. She thought and thought, trying to find the certain way of escape which must surely exist if she had but the wit to perceive it. But every path she explored seemed to lead, in her overwrought brain, only to a huge painted bedstead, in which Penhallow lay roaring with laughter at her attempts to evade him.

So real was this image that she gradually became convinced that there was no scheme she could evolve that he would not be able easily to frustrate. She had always been afraid of him: he was beginning now to assume grotesque proportions in her mind, so that she felt herself to be as powerless, while he lived, as some fairy-tale creature under an evil spell.

She wished that her head would stop aching. She was tired, too; she had not slept naturally for several nights, and had been obliged lately to increase the veronal she took from twenty to thirty drops. She had sent Loveday into Liskeard the day before, to have the prescription made up again at the chemist's, and Loveday had protested diffidently, telling her that it was not right that she should drug herself, that she ought to see Dr. Rame about her insomnia, because he was younger than Dr. Lifton, his partner, and was said to be a clever man, and very up-to-date. She had not listened to Loveday, partly because she had drawn away from the girl since her discovery that she meant to marry Bart, and partly because she did not like Dr. Rame, and had come to think that she could not do without her sleeping-draught. The new bottle, as yet unopened, stood beside the old on the shelf above her wash-stand. She turned her eyes towards it, thinking that it was as well she had sent Loveday for it, since she would be obliged to broach it tonight, if her head-ache continued. If it were not for Clay, she thought she might be tempted to empty the bottle into her glass, and drink it all at a gulp, thus putting a painless end to herself.

It seemed to her that her brain, which had not seriously con-templated such an action as this, became suddenly suspended above the thought that had so casually occurred to her. She sat with her eyes riveted to the little bottle, and her heart beating so hard that it thudded against her ribs.

No one would ever know. That was the thought which leaped to her mind, and stayed there, behind all the others which swiftly followed it. Dr. Lifton had told her that not even Penhallow's constitution could stand the strain he was imposing on it. He would feel no surprise if Penhallow were to die suddenly; he would say that he had warned them of what must happen if they could not persuade him to change his way of life. Everyone knew that so · far from modifying his eating and his drinking and his crazy spurts of energy he had been going from bad to worse during the past weeks; and although Clara, and perhaps others of his family as well, might be confident that he would survive his excesses, they would only think, when he died, that they had been mistaken after all, and had paid too little heed to the doctor's warning.

With fatal clarity, the very means by which she could hasten Penhallow's end (for it was no more than that, she told herself) showed themselves to her, so that it almost seemed as though she were meant to take this course. It was so easy that it seemed strange that she had never thought of it before. He would not suffer; he would not even know that he had swallowed the drug, for when he was already a little fuddled, as he had been for many nights, he had a way of tossing off his whisky at a gulp. It appeared to her that if he felt no pain she could not be thought to have committed so great a crime. She was sure that she had many times heard him inveigh against the life he was forced to lead, saying that the sooner he died the better pleased he would be, and if her brain could not quite accept this declaration at its face-value, at least it was ready to receive it as a half-excuse for what she meant to do.

The more she thought of it, the more clearly she perceived that every trivial circumstance militated so strangely in her favour that her task began to assume the colour of a predestined act.

When they left Penhallow every evening, and the trays of refreshments had been removed from his room, Reuben was compelled to get out the decanter of whisky from the corner-cupboard, and to place it on the table beside the bed. Reuben had a trick of reducing the quantity of liquor in the decanter to a bare minimum, so that there should be a check on the amount his master could consume when he was left alone for the night. There was never anything left in the decanter in the morning, so that there could be no fear that others besides Penhallow might drink the drugged whisky; nor was it ever produced during the course of the evening for the refreshment of those who foregathered in his room. Penhallow would not touch his private store of whisky, she thought, until he had been made ready for sleep, and left alone in his huge, over-heated room.

The fancy had seized him to get up today; he meant to take the head of his table at dinner, when he would no doubt eat and drink too much, grow boisterous, and exhaust himself, as he always did on such occasions. Surely it would seem the most natural thing in the world if he should be found to have died in his sleep after a day of most unwise exertion!

Martha, she knew, had seized the opportunity to turn out his room that afternoon. It was done now, all the sweeping and the dusting, and the great bed stood ready for its occupant. There could be nothing to take anyone to the room again until Penhallow re-entered it; all she had to do was to go down to it at a moment when it was unlikely that she would encounter any of the household in that part of the house. That was as easy as the rest. Before dinner, when the family was gathered in the Yellow drawing-room, drinking sherry; and Reuben with Jimmy to help him, was busy laying the table in the dining-room, she could pass with little fear of meeting anyone on the way down the narrow stairway at the far end of the house into the small hall on to which Penhallow's room opened. All she had to do then to win freedom for herself, and for Clay, for Raymond, for Vivian, for Bart, even for Aubrey, was to cross the wide floor to the corner-cupboard, to open it, to lift the stopper from the decanter in it, and to empty in the contents of one small bottle. It seemed such a little thing to do to achieve so much that was good that it scarcely bore the appearance to her of a crime. All the troubles which now beset the Penhallows would be settled by this one act; there would be peace at Trevellin, and happiness: a release for more persons than herself and Clay from an intolerable bondage.

A long sigh heaved her breast. The thudding of her heart had abated; she felt calm, and clear-sighted; even the ache in her head was less, although it had left her, as it so often did, with a feeling of narcosis, as though the pain had been merely blanketed by a strong anodyne. She glanced at the clock on the mantelpiece, and, getting up from her chair, began to change her dress for dinner.

She thought that if she met anyone on her way to Penhallow's room, or heard someone in the room when she came to it, it would be a sign to her that she was not, after all, meant to carry out her intention; but she felt so sure that she was meant to that it would have been a shock to her to have encountered even so small a hindrance as a housemaid upon the landing.

When she came out of her room, there was no one in sight. She could hear the twins' voices raised in the hall below, and Charmian singing, rather unmelodiously, behind the shut bath-room door. The broad corridor at the back of the house, with its deep window embrasures, was deserted too. The doors into the twins' rooms stood open on to it; Conrad had put his shoes outside; she caught a glimpse, as she passed, of Bart's clothes tossed carelessly on to the floor of his room. The corridor led into a smaller hall, the counterpart of the one below it. Here was Eugène's and Vivian's bedroom, with its dressing-room beyond, and Aubrey's room opposite. Aubrey had gone downstairs, but a murmur of voices sounded in Eugène's room. Faith went softly down the narrow, worn stairs, meeting no one, holding the phial in her handkerchief. A scent of lavender drifted into the hall at the foot of the stairs from the door which stood open on to the garden; and one of Bart's dogs, an old setter, lay on the mat with his head on his paws. He cocked his ears, and followed Faith with his eyes, but he did not lift his head, because he was uninterested in anyone but Bart. The double doors into Penhallow's room stood wide, as though to invite her to enter. From the hall she could see the patchwork quilt upon the bed shimmering and glowing in a shaft of late sunlight striking into the room slantways through one of the windows. She went in, quite unafraid, and crossed the room to the corner-cupboard. The decanter stood there, with a glass beside it, and a siphon, upon a silver tray. As she had expected, there was only a little whisky in it. She removed the heavy cut-glass stopper, and poured in the veronal. A tiny sound behind her made her start, and look over her shoulder. But it was only Penhallow's cat, Beelzebub, which had awakened, and was stretching luxuriously. She replaced the stopper, and closed the cupboard door. The cat sat on its haunches, and began to wash one foreleg. As she moved away from the cupboard, it paused to regard her fixedly, holding its paw suspended. She did not like cats; she thought that this one looked malevolently at her, as though it knew what she had done. She left the room; and the setter's eyes followed her again as she went towards the staircase.

Eugène and Vivian were still talking in their room; Charmian was whistling an air from *La Bohème* in the bathroom. Faith went into her room, and put the empty veronal phial back on the shelf beside the other bottles and pots that stood there. She felt strangely calm, as though she had not done anything at all out of the ordinary, but she thought that her headache would be sure to return before she had spent many minutes amongst the Penhallows, so she swallowed a couple of aspirin tablets before going downstairs to join the party in the Yellow drawing-room.

No one paid much attention to her when she entered the room, and she went to sit down by the open window. Bart, who was standing by the pie-crust table upon which Reuben had set the tray with the sherry, had the decanter in his hand, and did indeed acknowledge his stepmother's presence by lifting it suggestively, and saying: 'Faith?'

She shook her head. There was a motley collection of glasses in the room for it seemed that nothing broke quite so readily as a sherry glass, or was so hard to replace. Penhallow held one of an old set in his hand, and Clara had another; but Conrad was drinking from a tinted glass of thin Czecho-Slovakian ware, obtained from Woolworth's; and Bart had a miniature club-tumbler. Faith thought dreamily that when she and Clay lived together in their London flat everything should match.

Phineas's call had left Penhallow in high good-humour. Not even the appearance of Aubrey in his maroon velvet jacket provoked him to more than a sardonic crack of laughter. He said a little boastfully, that he had not felt so well for years. Then he saw Bart look at him with narrowed, frowning eyes, and he added that he was going to die on his feet, or at any rate in his chair. When the time came to go in to dinner, he had his chair wheeled to the head of the table, remarking agreeably to Raymond that he was not going to be deposed yet. Raymond returned no answer to this jibe, but took his place between Charmian and Eugène. His brothers thought that the set look on his face betokened annoyance at Penhallow's presence, and were amused at seeing him put out of countenance. But Penhallow's resumption of the place which he had not sat in for so long affected him not at all. He was thinking of the strange interview which had taken place in the Yellow drawing-room after tea.

Hardly knowing what good, if any good at all, he hoped to do, he had joined his father and his uncle there, encountering, as he had entered the room, so bleak a look of hatred from Phineas that it had surprised a laugh out of him. In her dread of having her youthful indiscretion exposed by Penhallow, it appeared that Delia had cast herself upon her brother's protection, openly acknowledging what Phineas had known, or perhaps only guessed, for forty years, but had shrunk fastidiously from facing. It was evident that he was furious at having the discreet veil in which he lived torn down by rude, Penhallow hands; and from the expression of distaste on his countenance it seemed that he blamed Raymond as much as Penhallow himself for the disturbance created in his ordered life.

'Hallo, Ray!' had said Penhallow genially. 'Here's your uncle been playing ostrich for forty years! You've upset his apple-cart nicely! What did you go running off to Delia for, you fool?'

'To learn the truth!' Raymond replied.

Penhallow had chuckled. 'There's an undutiful son for you! Mistrusting your own father! Didn't I tell you that Delia was the sort of little fool who couldn't keep a still tongue in her head? You might have known she'd scuttle off to blurt the whole thing out to Phineas, who didn't want to hear it.' He directed his attention to his visitor, scanning him appreciatively. 'Knew it all along, didn't you, Phin? Old pussy-cat Phin! I thought you did. Lacked the plain guts to tackle me! Lord, there was never more than one man in your family, and that was my Rachel!'

Phineas had passed his tongue between his lips. The hostility he had been at pains to disguise for so many years was naked in his eyes, but his dread of scandal was more powerful than his dislike of Penhallow, and he had not allowed himself to be goaded into any intemperate rejoinder. He had said smoothly, picking his words with care: 'I conceive it to be useless, my dear Penhallow, to indulge in idle recriminations. I have come here today to learn from you what your object was in making this unsavoury disclosure to the — er — unfortunate outcome of an interlude in your past on which I prefer not to dwell.'

'That's you, Ray,' remarked Penhallow.

'He wants an answer,' Raymond had replied. 'So do I.'

One of his soundless laughs had shaken Penhallow. 'Damme if

I ever thought I was going to get so much amusement out of it when I told you!' he had said. 'Maybe I hadn't got an object.'

Phineas had set his slightly trembling finger-tips together. 'I require your assurance, Penhallow, that this affair will go no farther.'

'You won't get it,' Penhallow answered genially.

Phineas's voice had become a little shrill. 'Have you considered what my sister's position must be if any word of this disgraceful story again passes your lips?'

'*Your* position is what you mean, Phin!' Penhallow had retorted. 'A fat lot you ever cared for Delia's troubles! All you want is to be able to live snug and soft in your damned respectability! Well, you won't live quite so snug in future. Time some of the lard was sweated off you!'

'What about me?' Raymond had demanded, his words falling heavily between the two older men.

His father's eyes had glinted at him mockingly. 'You'll learn to sing small, Ray. Maybe if you behave yourself I'll hold my tongue.'

Raymond had been silent, bitterly envisaging his future at Penhallow's hands.

'I apprehend,' had said Phineas, 'that a woman who was once in my father's employ, and later became nursemaid to your children, is also privy to this affair. I must insist that adequate steps be taken to ensure her silence.'

'Oh you must insist, must you?' had retorted Penhallow, kindling to quick wrath. 'By God, Phineas, I'd like to know where you think you are! This is *my* stamping ground, let me tell you, and the only man to do any insisting at Trevellin is Penhallow! Perhaps you'd like to offer old Martha a fat bribe? Or perhaps you're going to *insist* that I should? That 'ud be more like you, wouldn't it, so careful as you are with your money? Well, I shan't do it, but I've no objection to your trying it on! Lord, I'd like to see your smug face well-scratched!'

'If you are satisfied that the woman's loyalty may be trusted,' had replied Phineas, with what dignity he could muster, 'I must of course bow to you superior knowledge of her character, but I would point out to you—'

'You'll bow to more than my superior knowledge of Martha's character!' Penhallow had interrupted brutally.

Phineas had been obliged to swallow that. For how long the interview had been prolonged Raymond did not know. He had left the room, perceiving that neither he nor Phineas was serving any other purpose in remaining than that of providing Penhallow with a sport after his own heart. From the exultant joviality of Penhallow's present mood, he inferred that he had succeeded in thoroughly discomfiting Phineas. He was obviously enjoying an extension of his power, and had as obviously begun to exercise it in a fashion as fiendish as it was capricious, since he announced, with a good deal of relish, that the Otterys were going to join his birthday party on the morrow.

'Well, it's your party, sir,' said Eugène, in a tone that left no one in any doubt of his own sentiments.

'Who's coming?' asked Conrad. 'Have old Ma Venngreen, and make it a real riot of clean fun!'

'Damned if I don't!' said Penhallow gleefully. 'Faith, my girl, you'll attend to that!'

She was quietly eating her dinner, safe in the citadel of her knowledge that there would be no nightmare of a party to be endured. She raised her eyes, and said: 'Very well, Adam.' The length of the table separated them, but she had an odd fancy that he was farther removed from her than that.

Reuben, who had watched with patient disapproval his master's zestful attack upon a lobster, interposed at this point, remarking severely that since shell-fish were fatal to Penhallow's digestion the chances were that the party would have to be put off, anyway.

The only result of this was to make Penhallow curse him cheerfully for being a meddling old buzzard, and demand the other half of his lobster. He next bethought himself of a piece of information likely to infuriate Raymond, and let it be widely known that he had sent Aubrey to cash a cheque for him in Bodmin that morning.

'Going the pace a bit, aren't you, Guv'nor?' said Bart. 'Thought you drew out a tidy bit not so long ago?'

'What's it go to do with you how much I choose to keep by me?' demanded Penhallow. 'If I have any damned criticism from any of you, I'll give the whole three hundred to Aubrey to pay his debts with!'

'Good lord!' ejaculated Conrad. 'You didn't draw out three hundred at one blow, did you?'

'Yes,' said Aubrey, 'and I do hope that you will all of you criticize him a great deal, because if Father were to give it to me it would be a very lovely gesture, I feel.'

'We shouldn't!' Conrad retorted.

'Well, I hope you're as rich as you think you are, Father,' said Charmian. 'Though personally I should doubt it.'

Penhallow signed imperatively to Reuben to refill his wine-glass, and turned his head to look at Raymond. 'Well? well?' he said. 'You're not usually backward in giving me your opinion of my actions! Lost your tongue all of a sudden?'

'You know very well what my opinion is,' Raymond replied curtly.

'To think I was forgetting that I'd already had the benefit of your criticism!' Penhallow exclaimed. 'Held a pistol to my head, didn't you? Well, well, it's been a fullish day one way and another! Clara, old lady, here's to you!'

Raymond chanced to look up, as Penhallow was drinking his sister's health. He found that Jimmy, who was helping Reuben to wait upon them all, was watching him covertly, an expression of mingled curiosity and gloating on his dark face. He stiffened, remembering what had seemed of little importance in the first shock of his discovery, that it had been Jimmy who had rushed in to pull him off his father's throat that morning, and that with a promptitude which suggested that he had all the time been listening at the door. As he stared into Jimmy's spiteful eyes, so deadly a look came into his own that Jimmy changed colour.

The blood seemed to Raymond to drum in his head. He lowered his gaze to his plate, thinking, *He knows!*

There were too many animated conversations in progress round the table for anyone to have leisure to observe this tiny interlude; nor did Raymond's silence occasion any remark. It was supposed that one of his moody, taciturn fits had descended upon him. By the time that Bart addressed an inquiry to him across the table he had regained command over his faculties, and was able to answer with a calm that surprised himself.

Having disposed of several glasses of burgundy, Penhallow was inspired, when he was left alone with his sons at the table, to order Reuben to go down to the cellars to fetch up a couple of bottles of the '96 port.

'Anyone would think,' said Reuben dampingly, 'that it was your birthday today, which it isn't.'

'I shan't waste the '96 port on Venngreen and Phin Ottery,' declared Penhallow. 'You be off with you, and fetch it up! A glass of port will do me a power of good.'

'It won't do your gout any good,' grumbled Reuben, but he went off to obey the order.

When he had drunk as much port as he wanted to, and had reached that stage of boisterous elation which his wife so much dreaded, Penhallow had himself wheeled into the Long drawing-room to join the ladies. His intellect was just sufficiently clouded to prevent his keeping his usual strict tally on the various members of his family, so that both Clay and Bart were able to slip away unperceived; Clay to spend an unmolested evening morosely knocking the balls about in the billiard-room, and Bart to keep an assignation with Loveday in the schoolroom. However, when Penhallow decided at last to go to bed, and it was discovered that Jimmy had taken French leave, and was nowhere to be found, he insisted on having Bart to help Reuben to undress him, and get him into his bed, and for the first time noticed his absence from the room. Conrad, who, for all his jealousy of Loveday, would have been torn in pieces before betraying his twin to their father, at once said that Bart was working on some accounts in Ray's office, and went off to find him; while Reuben diverted Penhallow's rising anger by announcing that he had had enough of Jimmy's habit of sneaking off to the village as soon as his back was turned. Penhallow promptly forgot about Bart, and said that they all grudged poor little Jimmy his bit of fun, but that he was the only one amongst the whole pack who cared two pins for his old father.

'A more unjust observation,' murmured Eugène, 'in face of the Bastard's practice of deserting his post whenever he hears the call of the flesh, I have yet to listen to.'

'Ah, you're all jealous of Jimmy!' said Penhallow, shaking his head. 'You're afraid of his cutting you out.'

An expression of acute nausea came into Eugène's face, but as Conrad and Bart came back into the room at that moment, his reply was lost.

Bart was looking heated, Conrad having walked without warning into the schoolroom, where he had been sprawling in a deep chair, with Loveday on his knee, and interrupted this idyll by saying caustically that if he could think of something besides wenching for a few minutes Penhallow wanted him to assist him into bed. Bart had leaped to his feet in quick wrath, and there would undoubtedly have been a minor brawl had not Loveday represented to him the folly of keeeping his father waiting, and so arousing his suspicions.

'And where the devil have you been?' demanded Penhallow. 'Don't give me any of your lies, because I know damned well what you've been up to!'

'All right, then why ask me?' Bart retorted. 'What do you want me for, anyway? Where's Jimmy?'

'Need you ask?' said Eugène. 'He seeks his pleasures in the village. Unlike some others one might mention.'

'Shut up, you swine!' said Conrad, under his breath.

Eugène smiled sweetly at him. 'What a touching picture of loyalty you do present, to be sure, Con!'

Bart looked dangerous, and took a step towards Eugène's chair. He was arrested by Raymond, who caught his eye, and jerked his chin imperatively in the direction of the door. After hesitating for an instant, he shrugged, and turned to lay hold of Penhallow's chair. He pushed it out of the room, Reuben following him.

'And to think,' said Aubrey, stretching himself out at full length on the sofa, 'that this evening has been but a foretaste of what we shall be called upon to undergo tomorrow! Oh, I do think, don't you, that Father is becoming quite too dreadfully oppressive?'

CHAPTER SIXTEEN

RAYMOND was long in falling asleep that night. Unable to lie still in his bed, but continually tossing and turning, he got up after an hour, and, putting on his trousers and a tweed jacket over his pyjamas, and thrusting his feet into a pair of brogues, went downstairs, and let himself softly out of the house into the moonlit garden. Here he walked up and down with his pipe gripped between his teeth, and his head filled with hard, tangled thoughts, until the chill of the night, and his own physical and mental fatigue finally drove him in again. The broad stairs creaked under his feet as he went up them, and as he crossed the upper hall the door into his sister's room opened, and Charmian came out with an electric torch in her hand.

'Who's that?' she said sharply.

The moonlight, streaming in through the great uncurtained window above the stairs, made the torch superflous. She switched it off as she saw Raymond, with his hand already upon his bedroom door-handle.

'It's all right,' he said. 'Sorry I woke you.'

She had cast a severe, masculine dressing-gown over her shoulders, and now slid her arms into it, and tied its cord round her waist. 'Anything wrong?' she asked, observing his attire.

'No, nothing. I couldn't sleep, that's all.'

'I thought you looked a bit off-colour at dinner. Have you been out?'

'Yes. Couldn't get to sleep.'

She glanced shrewdly at him. 'Getting on your nerves?'

'Is what getting on my nerves?'

'Oh—! This place.'

'No,' he replied.

'No, of course you've always been ridiculous about Trevellin. Father, then.'

'I haven't got any nerves.'

'Don't be too sure of that! How long has Father been like this?'

He looked at her under his brows. 'Like what?'

'Oh, don't be a fool!' she said impatiently. 'You know what I mean! He wasn't as bad as this when I was last here. Is he breaking up?'

He shrugged. 'Lifton thinks so.'

'I never had the least opinion of that old idiot. What do you think?'

'I'm not a doctor: I don't know. I should say he'd last a good few years yet.'

'Well, I think he's going mad!' Charmian said roundly.

'He's not mad.'

'He may not be technically mad, but he seems to me to be per-fectly irresponsible. Do you know that he told Aubrey today that he was to come home and study forestry, or some such nonsense? Aubrey! And why has he suddenly removed Clay from college?'

'Thought he was wasting his time there. So he was. Clay's a waster.'

'He won't cure him of that by encouraging him to chop and change about. What was the sense of sending him to Cambridge at all if he meant to take him away before he'd got a degree?'

'There was never any sense in sending him there, except that it got rid of him. You'd better get back to bed: you'll catch cold if you stand about much longer.'

He opened his own door as he spoke, but she detained him for a moment, saying: 'Well, I'm not worrying my head about Clay, but I wish you'd tell me if Father's in the habit of drawing out vast sums of money by way of petty cash?'

'Why? What's it got to do with you?' he asked.

She disregarded this question. 'Why the hell don't you put a stop to it?' she asked.

'I have no power to stop Father doing anything he wants to do,' he replied roughly. 'Good night!'

He went into his room and shut the door. When he got into bed again he still could not sleep, and lay for a long time flogging his brain over and over the events of what had surely been the longest day of his life.

It seemed to him that he had been to sleep for only a few minutes when he was awakened by a hand shaking his shoulder, and Reuben's voice insistently speaking his name in his ear; but when he opened his eyes he found that the sunlight was flooding the room, and that the hands of the clock beside his bed pointed to eight o'clock. He raised himself on his elbow, yawning, and passing a hand across his sleep-drenched eyes. He realized that Reuben's voice sounded unusually urgent, and said: 'What's the matter?' Then he saw that tears were running down Reuben's lined cheeks, and this extraordinary sight fully awoke him, and he sat up with a jerk. 'What the devil's up with you?' he demanded.

'Master!' Reuben said, his lower lip trembling grotesquely. 'He's gone, Mr. Ray!'

'*Gone?*' Raymond repeated. 'What do you mean, Gone? Gone where?'

'He's dead!' Reuben said. 'He's dead, Mr. Ray! Cold-dead!'

'*What?*' Raymond ejaculated incredulously. He flung back the bed-clothes, and got up quickly, snatching up his dressing-gown. 'When? How?'

'I don't know when. He must have gone in the night. *You* should know how, Mr. Ray!'

Raymond tied his dressing-gown cord, and groped for his slippers. 'What the devil do you mean?' he said.

Reuben drew his sleeve across his eyes. 'It was you setting on him the way you did, trying to choke the life out of him, and him as good as bedridden! I told you then we'd knaw whose door to set it to if he was to go off sudden! Iss, sure, I told you!'

'Don't be such a blithering old fool!' Raymond said roughly. 'He was perfectly well last night! I had nothing whatsoever to do with his dying! More likely what he ate and drank at dinner. Who knows about this? Who found him?'

Reuben followed him to the door. 'Martha found him, poor soul! Stiff, he is. He must have gone in his sleep. And today his birthday! I *told* him how it would be if he ate that lobster! I *told* him!'

'Shut up! There's no need to rouse the whole house yet!' Raymond said, turning into the corridor at the back of the house, and going swiftly along it to the narrow stair down which Faith had passed the day before.

As he approached the small hall at the head of these stairs, the sound of wailing reached his ears. Martha was lamenting over Penhallow's body, and it was plain that this noise had already wakened those who slept at that end of the house. Eugène's door stood open; and even as Raymond set his foot on the top step of the stair, Aubrey came out of his room, in a very exotic-looking pair of black pyjamas piped with silver, and asked plaintively what new horror had come upon the house.

'Reuben says Father's dead,' Raymond replied over his shoulder.

He did not wait to see how this news was received, but as he ran down the stairs he heard Aubrey exclaim: 'Oh, no, not really? I simply *can't* believe it! You're not *serious*, Ray?'

In Penhallow's room, Martha was rocking herself to and fro on a chair beside the vast bed, and Vivian, with a kimono caught hurriedly round her, and clutched together with one hand, was standing in the middle of the room staring as though she could not believe her eyes, first at Martha, and then at Penhallow's still form. When she heard Raymond's footsteps, she turned, and said in a queer, hushed voice: 'He's *dead*!'

'So I've heard,' Raymond replied, brushing past her, and bending over the bed. He straightened himself after a moment. He looked a little pale under his tan, and he did not at once say anything. He was indeed so much shaken by this unexpected turn which events had taken that he was unable immediately to marshal his wits into any sort of order. Through the medley of thoughts racing past one another in his brain, one more persistent than the rest kept on recurring: that Penhallow's death was of immense importance to him, since he could never now betray the secret of his birth. He remembered that Penhallow had spoke of papers to prove his story; the picture of him jerking his thumb over his shoulder at the cupboards in the head of his bed flashed vividly across his mind. He glanced from one to the other of the three persons gathered about the bed, a coldly calculating light in his frowning eyes. He addressed Vivian. 'You'd better go and get dressed.'

She pushed her hair away from her brow. 'Yes,' she agreed mechanically. 'I – I don't seem able to take it in. He's really dead! I shan't have to live here any more! We're *free*!'

Martha lifted her head. 'You shameless malkin! There un lays, gone dead, and you stannin' there as bold and as heartless as yer mind to! Eh, my dear, my dear, the praper man that you was! Out of this, you wicked hussy! You shanna' stand staring at un! You shanna', I tell you!'

Vivian coloured slightly, and seemed as though she would have retorted. Raymond said, before she could speak: 'Go on! You had better let Eugène know what's happened. Reuben, get Martha out of this! We can't have this row going on. And send Jimmy down to Lifton's house at once, do you hear?'

'That young runagate!' Reuben said bitterly. 'For anything any of us knaws he's laying abed still!'

'Kick him out, then! Martha! I say, Martha, it's no good crying like that! You go and lie down, or something. Where's Sybilla, Reuben?'

The tears started to run down Reuben's cheeks again. 'She was cooking his breakfast. She's got him some thick-back beauties, just the way he liked them, and he won't never eat them now!'

'Well, take Martha to her!' Raymond said. 'If that little swine, Jimmy, isn't dressed, send one of the girls down to Lifton's on her cycle, and ask him to come up as soon as he can. Get a move on, man!'

'I won't leave un!' Martha moaned. 'You shanna' make me leave un! There's never another soul shall touch him! It's me and Sybilla will lay him out decent, the way he'd wish for us to do!'

'Oh, all right!' he said, trying not to let his impatience to be rid of her get the better of him. 'You can do that, but not until Lifton has seen him.'

Reuben looked at him with hostility in his reddened eyes. 'It's little you care, Mr. Ray!' he muttered; but he seemed to feel that Martha could not be permitted to continue wailing over Penhallow's body, for after a moment's indecision he bent over her, and coaxed and bullied her into going with him to the servants' hall.

As soon as they had left the room, Raymond quickly closed the double doors, and returned to the bed. He did not waste a glance on the inanimate figure in it, but began with feverish haste to pull open the cupboards and the little drawers above it.

A magpie collection was disclosed, ranging from receipted bills, most of them for trivial sums, and many of ancient date, to such irrelevant objects as a champagne cork with a tarnished silver top; a tattered copy of *Handley Cross*; an old hunting-crop; the stubs of countless cheque-books; several boxes full of paper-clips and rubber-bands; a repeating-watch with a broken face; bunches of keys bearing the rusty appearance of having been unused for decades; numerous bottles of iodine and embrocation, jumbled amongst boxes of canine worm-pills, mange-cures, and alternative powders; and a tangle of gold chains, fobs, and seals huddled into a screw of tissue paper. One of a cluster of shallow drawers was so full of old letters and papers that it could only with difficulty be opened. Without the smallest hesitation, Raymond pulled out the sheaf. At any moment Reuben might come back into the room, or some member of the family enter to put an end to his search. He had no time to do more than glance hurriedly through the papers, casting back into the drawer such immaterial items as old advertisements torn from periodicals, a collection of faded snapshots and picture post-cards, some of his and Ingram's school-reports, and a miscellaneous assortment of letters which he saw, from their superscriptions, could have no bearing on the secret of his false birth. The rest he stuffed into the pockets of his dressing-gown, his ears straining all the time to catch the sound of an approaching footfall. Drawer after drawer he opened, without discovering either a birth certificate or any other document relating to his birth. There were the pedigrees of dogs and horses, a copy of Rachel's marriage-lines, old account-books and Bank pass-books, an expired passport, and some old diaries which seemed to contain nothing but the records of day-to-day engagements, but which he also pocketed.

He felt a clammy sweat on his brow, and wiped it away with the back of one slightly trembling hand. Unless it lay hidden in one of the envelopes he had abstracted to inspect at his leisure, there was no document that in any way concerned his birth. So intent was he upon the one object of his search, so hard-pressed for time, that he never even noticed that the little tin box in which Penhallow kept his money was missing from its usual place in the central cupboard. His mind veered towards the other cupboards in the room. He looked about him irresolutely, trying to recall what his father kept in them. He strode over to the marquetry chest, and began to pull open its drawers. They contained, as far as he had time to see, nothing but clothing. He crossed to the lacquer cabinet, and opened its doors, disclosing Penhallow's ivory-backed hairbrushes, clothes-brushes, combs, and a variety of stud-boxes, corn-razors, and nail-scissors. He closed the doors again. He did not believe that Penhallow would have stowed such a document, if it existed, away out of his reach, and he began to think that Penhallow had invented it to alarm him. He walked to the door, and stepped out into the hall, shutting the door behind him. As he did so, Reuben came round the corner of the corridor, blowing his nose. He looked at Raymond over the edge of his damp handkerchief, and said rather huskily: 'I've sent the gardener's boy down to the village, but there's nothing Lifton nor any other can do for the Master.'

'I know that. Somebody had better tell Mrs. Penhallow. I'm going upstairs to put some clothes on. Send one of the maids up with my shaving-water. And keep everyone out of that room until Lifton's been!'

'I shall stay with un, Mr. Ray,' Reuben replied, a touch of belligerence in his tone. 'It's little you or Mrs. Penhallow cares, but I won't leave un laying there alone, and that's straight! I knawed un when he was not so high as that chest there, and the daringest young rascal from here to Land's End! I never left un, never, and I won't leave un now, when un's stiff and cold!'

'You can do as you like. Have you kicked that young swine out of bed? Where is he?'

'Jimmy!' Reuben said, with one of his contemptuous sniffs. 'He never come in last night, and he's not back yet, the dirty loose fish that he is! And not the first time, not by a dozen times it isn'!'

'Well, that's one of the abuses in this house that's going to stop more quickly than the little bastard thinks for!' Raymond said grimly.

Then he remembered the look he had surprised on Jimmy's face the previous evening, and his eyelids flickered, and he turned away abruptly, and went up the stairs, feeling as though an icy hand had closed upon the pit of his stomach. His mind, at one moment lightened of its fear, plunged again into an abyss of uncertainty and dread. If Jimmy knew the truth, there could never be any security for him while he lived. Buy him off? Send him out to the colonies? He thought bitterly that he would do better to strangle the little beast. He could visualize, though as yet only vaguely, years of being bled white by Jimmy, of living for ever in the fear that Jimmy's malice, or perhaps his own inability to satisfy a blackmailer's greed, would prompt him to carry his story to Ingram. In an instant, his father's death, which had seemed in the first shock of discovery to be no less than a direct intervention of providence in his favour, became fraught with lurking danger. There was Martha, too. He would have to do something about her, though what he hardly knew. He fancied that her devotion to Penhallow would lead her to pursue the course she supposed him to have wished her to; her silence, then, would depend not upon bribery but upon what Penhallow might have said to her.

He went into his bedroom, and shut the door. He was in his shirt-sleeves when a gentle tap fell on one of the oaken panels, and Loveday Trewithian came in with a jug of boiling water. He looked at her frowningly, realizing that she was one of those most nearly affected by Penhallow's death. She was a little pale, but her face was quite calm, and her dark eyes met his with no other discernible expression in them than one of timid respect.

'I've brought your shaving-water, sir,' she said, in her gentle way. 'Things is a little at sixes and sevens.'

'Thanks,' he said briefly. 'Doctor arrived yet?'

'No, sir,' she replied, setting the jug down on the old-fashioned, marble-topped washstand, and covering it with a folded towel. 'Not yet.'

'Tell Reuben to let me know as soon as he does. Does your mistress know what's happened?'

'She's sleeping, Mr. Ray. Leave me tell her when I take her tea in to her!'

'You'd better do so at once. Mrs. Hastings, too.'

'Mrs. Hastings went out early. She's up at the stables.' Loveday moved towards the door, adding as she reached it: 'Bart, too.'

He noticed that she had omitted a prefix to this last name. It annoyed him, but he said nothing. She went away, and he began to shave himself. His face was still half-covered with lather when Eugène walked in without ceremony. He met Eugène's eyes in the mirror, and could almost have laughed at the look of chagrin so clearly depicted in them. Whoever else might regard Penhallow's death in the light of a blessing, Eugène was one who saw in it a disturbance to his own indolent peace. He was still in his pyjamas and dressing-gown, and since he had not yet shaved, and was as dark-complexioned as his brothers, his chin had a blue appearance detrimental to his good-looks.

'Ray, is this really true?' he asked.

'Good lord, you must know it's true!' Raymond answered.

'Yes. That is, Vivian told me, but really I find it hard to take it in! It doesn't seem at all possible. When did it happen? Have you any idea?'

'None at all. He's cold, that's all I can tell you.'

Eugène gave a slight shudder. 'You may spare me any further details.' He looked Raymond over, his lips twisting into a wry smile. 'Well, you've got what you've been waiting for, haven't you? I congratulate you!'

Raymond wiped the soap off his razor. 'Thanks.'

'It must be a great day in your life,' Eugène remarked. He pushed his hands into the pockets of his dressing-gown, and hunched his shoulders in the semblance of a shrug. 'I suppose there isn't anything I'm wanted to do, is there?'

'What should there be?'

'Nothing, I hope. I don't propose to come down to breakfast. This has been a shock to me. I slept very badly, too.'

'You didn't hear anything?'

'If I had heard anything I should have gone down,' Eugène replied, turning to leave the room.

He was intercepted in the doorway by Bart, who came impetuously in, his whip still in his hands, and all the healthy colour drained from his cheeks. '*Ray!*' he blurted out, thrusting rudely past Eugène. 'Loveday says – the *Guv'nor*!'

'Yes, that's right,' Raymond answered, putting on his collar. 'Looks as though he went in his sleep. I'm waiting for Lifton.'

'Rame's car is standing outside. When – who found – Was anyone with him?'

Raymond had quickly knotted his tie, and was putting on his coat. 'No, no one. Martha found him dead when she went in this morning. Sorry, I must go down. Did you say Rame's car?'

Loveday tapped on the half-open door at that moment. 'The doctor's here, Mr. Ray. Dr. Lifton has the influenza: it's Dr. Rame that's come. I was thinking it might be well he should see the mistress when he's finished downstairs. It will be a shock to her nerves, surely, when she knows what's happened.'

'If she wants him, she can send a message down,' Raymond replied unsympathetically, and went out of the room.

Loveday glanced towards Bart, standing rigidly by the window, and jerking at his whip-lash. 'I'll get you a cup of tea, my dear,' she said, pity and love warming her rich voice.

He gave his head a little shake. 'No, I don't want it.' His stubborn mouth quivered. 'I cursed him last night. I – Oh, *Guv'nor*!'

She went towards him, ignoring Eugène, who stood by the door, somewhat cynically regarding her. 'Don't you take on, my dear!' she said. 'It's little he'd care for a curse or two. You were a good son to him, and he knew it.'

'No, I wasn't. I thought – I didn't even believe – But he *was* ill! I didn't want him to die! I – oh, hell, I was damned fond of him, the grand old devil that he was! and I wish to *God* he were alive now to – to bawl the lot of us out!' His voice broke on something between a laugh and a sob; he brushed his hand across his brimming eyes, and pushed his way past Eugène out of the room.

'I am afraid, my dear Loveday,' said Eugène maliciously, 'that you will find my brother Bart more upset by this event than perhaps you expected.'

'It's natural he should be,' she responded, picking up Raymond's dressing-gown, and putting it away in the wardrobe. 'If you please, sir!'

He stood aside to allow her to pass, a little nettled by her self-possession, and she went away towards the back of the house to fetch her mistress's early tea-tray up from the pantry.

Faith had fallen asleep on the previous evening without the aid of narcotics. She had gone up to her room soon after Penhallow had been wheeled out of the Long drawing-room, and, as Loveday assisted her to undress, she had noticed with vague surprise that the nightly headache which she had come to regard as inevitable was for once absent. She supposed that the aspirin she had swallowed before going down to dinner must still be operating on her system, and she had told Loveday, with a little sigh, that she felt as though she could sleep naturally. A feeling of deep peace hung over her, undisturbed by any twinge of remorse for what she had done. She was very tired, but not with the nervous fatigue which made it impossible for her to relax her limbs and to lie still in her bed. Almost as soon as she had laid her head upon the pillow, her eyelids had begun to sink over her eyes; and as she thought, not of Penhallow, but of the little flat in London, she drifted into a deep peaceful sleep from which she did not arouse until Loveday drew back the curtains next morning.

She seemed then to herself to be rising to the surface of a vast ocean of sleep, and as she stirred, and opened her eyes, she murmured: 'Oh, I have had such a lovely sleep!'

Loveday came towards the bed with her mistress's bed-jacket in her hand. Faith stretched herself, and yawned, not immediately remembering the events of the previous day. She asked what the time was, and when Loveday told her, half past eight, she said, sitting up, and putting her arms into the sleeves of the jacket: 'Why, how late! You shouldn't have let me sleep on, Loveday.'

Loveday turned to the table beside the bed, and poured out a cup of tea. 'No, ma'am, I know. But you were sleeping so sound I didn't care to wake you. There's some bad news you have to hear, ma'am.'

As she spoke these words, remembrance of what she had done came flooding back to Faith, and she gave a stifled exclamation. After so good a night's rest, with its soothing effect upon her overwrought nerves, it now seemed to her that she must have been mad, and she could almost have believed that she had dreamt the whole. She recalled quite clearly her every action, and even her thoughts, which, appearing reasonable to her at the time, seemed in the light of morning to partake of the nature of insanity. The wish that

Penhallow might die was still present; but the resolution to bring about his death had departed from her mind as suddenly as it had entered it. So unreal did her action seem to her that she felt as divorced from it as though she had performed it in a trance.

She raised her eyes to Loveday's face. 'Bad news?' she faltered, clasping her hands tightly together.

'It's the Master, ma-am.'

Then she had done it. She had succeeded. She swallowed, but found herself unable to speak. She waited, her gaze fixed on Loveday's face with an expression on it of wonder and of dread.

'The Master's dead, ma'am.'

A sound that was hardly a cry broke from her; she buried her face in her hands. 'Oh, Loveday! oh, Loveday! Oh, no, no!'

Loveday put her arms round her, drawing her to lie against her deep, warm breasts. 'There, my dear, there! don't you take on, now! He went in his sleep, the way anyone would wish for him.'

Faith wept, but not for sorrow, nor yet for pity. She wept for her own madness, which had turned her into a murderess, and for relief that her long purgatory was ended. Loveday rocked her, and murmured to her, and after a little while she stopped, and groped for her handkerchief. Loveday found it for her, and when she had dried her eyes, she coaxed her to drink her tea. She was leaning back against her banked-up pillows, sipping the tea between spasmodic sobs when Vivian came into the room. When she saw Vivian, she thought how she had set her free too, and her eyes filled with weak tears again. She said: 'Oh, Vivian!'

Vivian's uncompromising honesty made it impossible for her to understand how anyone could weep for what she was glad of. She said bluntly: 'I don't see what you've got to cry for. We all know that you've been miserable for years.'

'Oh, don't!' Faith begged, the tears brimming over. 'Don't talk like that, *please!*'

'Well, I'm sorry, but I can't pretend that I care. It would be sheer hypocrisy. As far as I'm concerned, it's the best thing that has ever happened in this house!'

Faith was really shocked by this speech, for although she had been able to do what perhaps Vivian had never contemplated doing, she was incapable of facing an unvarnished truth, and was already seeing her action, not as a crime, but as a deed undertaken as much for the good of others as for her own peace. Loveday, whispering comfort, had spoken of Penhallow's death as a release from suffering, and she realized without effort that this was true, and had begun to believe that she had been at least to some extent actuated by this thought when she had determined to poison Penhallow. But not even to herself did she use that harsh word. There were plenty of euphemisms for the ugly terms, Murder and Poison, and they came more naturally to her brain, so that she had no need consciously to evade the cruder words.

'It's been a shock to her,' Loveday said, in a reproving tone. 'Indeed, Mrs. Eugène, you didn't ought to speak like that, with the poor gentleman lying there dead.' She paid no heed to the angry flush that stained Vivian's cheeks, but turned from her to her mistress, asking whether she should prepare the bath for her.

'Oh, I don't know!' Faith said undecidedly. 'I feel so upset, and queer, Loveday!'

'Well, you aren't going to stop washing just because there has been a death in the house, are you?' inquired Vivian caustically.

Put in such blunt terms as this, it did seem absurd, but Faith felt vaguely that in the performance of every day actions at such a moment there was something bordering on the indecent. She ignored Vivian. 'I suppose I – Yes, of course I shall have my bath just as I always do. Please get it ready for me, Loveday!'

'That's right, my dear,' Loveday said, patting her hand. 'Then you'll get back into bed, and I'll bring your breakfast up to you, and you'll be better.'

'Oh, no, I couldn't!' Faith said. 'I couldn't swallow anything! Please don't ask me to! I ought to get up. Do you think I should go down at once? I – I feel so absolutely bowled over I don't seem able to think!'

'You lay quiet awhile,' Loveday counselled her. 'There's nothing you can do, my dear. The doctor's below at this moment, and I was thinking you would like to have him come up to you, and give you something for your poor nerves.'

'No. No, I shall be all right!' Faith said, pressing her finger-tips to her temples. 'I don't want a doctor. Unless I ought to see him about – about Adam. Must I? I don't feel that I can bear it! But of course if I ought to – I don't know what one does when – when a thing like this happens!'

'If you don't want to see him, there's no particular reason why you should,' said Vivian. 'Raymond's there, and I don't see that you can tell him anything he doesn't know already. I mean, it isn't as though this was unexpected. Lifton warned you, didn't he?'

'Yes, oh yes! 'And he had been getting worse lately, hadn't he? Charmian saw a great change in him. She told me so.'

'It's Dr. Rame,' Loveday said. 'Dr. Lifton has the influenza.'

'Dr. Rame!' Faith repeated nervously. 'Oh, I would rather not see him if I needn't! I never liked him. He's so hard, and unsympathetic!'

'I'll go and turn the bath on,' Loveday said, picking up the early tea-tray. 'Mr. Ray said if you wanted to see the doctor to send down a message.'

'Only if I must! But if he wants to speak to me of course I'll see him! Tell Mr. Ray that, Loveday!'

'You've no call to worry, my dear,' Loveday said soothingly.

Vivian would have remained, after she had left the room, to discuss Penhallow's death with Faith, but Faith stopped her, saying that she could not bear to talk about it. She shrugged contemptuously, therefore, and went away.

In the dining-room, several members of the family were gathered round the table, partaking of breakfast in a desultory and ill-at-ease fashion. Clara was seated as usual at the foot of the table, dispensing coffee and tea in the intervals of sniffing into a screwed-up handkerchief, with which she from time to time wiped the corners of her eyes. Conrad was somewhat defiantly consuming a plateful of bacon and eggs; Aubrey, not noticeably affected by the general depression, was spreading a thin slice of toast with marmalade; and Bart, having pushed away his plate, almost untouched, was mechanically stirring his coffee, his rather reddened eyes lowered. Neither Raymond nor Charmian was present. In response to Vivian's inquiry, Clara replied huskily that they were both in Penhallow's room still, with the doctor.

Vivian sat down, having helped herself to some fish from the dish on the sideboard. After a short silence, Conrad cleared his throat, and said: 'I shan't go to work today, of course.'

Nobody made any answer to this observation. Vivian said: 'What on earth are they taking so long for? I saw the doctor's car drive up ages ago! What do you suppose they can be doing?'

Aubrey, who had dignified the occasion by discarding his colourful sports-wear for a lounge suit which he wore with a lavender shirt, replied: 'Darling, must we go into that? You're so marvellous, with your self-possession and all that, I expect you don't mind a bit what you talk about at breakfast, but I haven't got anything like your strength of character, and I do wish you wouldn't, sweetie. Besides, some of our number are quite upset about it.'

'Not you,' Bart said, momentarily raising his eyes from his coffee-cup.

'My dear, the only thing which upset me – and you simply can't imagine how frightful it was! – was the perfectly ghoulish noise which Martha made. I mean, talk about the purely primitive! No, I'm not going to pretend that I am shattered by Father's death. You wouldn't any of you believe it if I did. He was showing the most alarming signs of being about to interfere with my lovely, ordered existence, and I regard his death as an unmixed blessing.'

'Well, I'm glad one of you has the moral courage to say what you really think!' said Vivian.

'Your approval, darling, might have been expressed more grammatically, but I can't tell you how much it has encouraged me,' said Aubrey dulcetly. 'After all, it is the spirit which counts, isn't it?'

'Anyway, you can bloody well keep what you think to yourself!' Bart said, addressing his sister-in-law. 'We all know what you thought of the Guv'nor!'

'Now, Bart, don't, there's a good boy!' Clara said. 'We don't want any quarrelin'. I daresay he was a wicked old man, but I don't know what we're any of us goin' to do now he's gone. It won't seem like Trevellin without him goin' on the rampage, and upsettin' everybody right and left.' She applied her handkerchief to her eyes again. 'I'm sure I don't know why I'm cryin', for very uncomfortable he's made me, time and again, but there it is! Has anyone been up to Faith?'

'I've seen her,' Vivian answered. 'She's having a bath at the moment.'

'Is she cut-up about it?' asked Conrad.

Vivian gave a short laugh. 'She thinks she is, anyway. I'm afraid I've got no time for these conventionally-minded women who think it incumbent upon them to shed tears just because someone whom they detested has died!'

'Here, I say, that's coming it a bit thick!' protested Conrad. 'I don't say Father didn't treat her to rather a rough passage, but you've got no right to say that she detested him! I should have thought that she'd be bound to be cut-up about it.'

'Then you won't be disappointed,' said Vivian acidly. 'She'll gratify all your ideas of how a bereaved person should behave, I'm sure!'

Clay came into the room at that moment, looking scared and bewildered. 'I say, is it true?' he asked. 'I've just heard – I overslept this morning – I didn't know a thing! But one of the maids told me – only I simply couldn't *believe* it!'

'If you mean, is it true that Father's dead, yes, it is!' said Conrad. 'So you can go upstairs again, and take off that bloody-awful pull-over, and put on something decent!'

'Of course I wouldn't have put on a coloured thing if I'd known!' Clay said. 'I'll change it after breakfast, naturally. Good lord, though! I – I can't get over it! How did it happen? When did he die?'

The barely-veiled excitement in his voice roused Bart to a flash of anger. 'What the devil does it matter to you how he died, or when he died? A fat lot you care! God damn your eyes, you're *glad* he's dead!'

'How dare you s-say such a th-thing?' Clay stammered, flushing to the roots of his hair. 'Of course I'm not!'

'Liar!' said Conrad.

Aubrey intervened, saying in his most mannered style: 'Sit down, little brother, and try to carry off this very difficult situation with as much grace as you can muster. You really could hardly do better than to model yourself on me. Now, I'm not bewailing Father's death in the least, but neither am I permitting an indecent elation to appear in my demeanour. As my raiment, so my conduct: subdued but not funereal.'

'Shut up, you ass!' said Conrad.

'Listen!' Vivian interrupted, lifting her head. 'That sounds like the doctor going!'

In another minute the door opened, and Charmian came in. She looked rather pale, as though she had sustained a severe shock, and she did not at first say anything.

'Is that Rame going?' Vivian asked. 'What on earth has he been doing all this time?'

'Where's Ray?' Conrad demanded.

'Seeing Rame off.' Charmian dug her hands into her coat-pockets, and took up her favourite position on the hearth-rug, with her feet widely planted. 'Well, you may as well know at once what has happened. Rame won't sign the certificate.'

CHAPTER SEVENTEEN

HER words were received in uncomprehending silence. Conrad broke it. 'What do you mean, he won't sign the certificate? Why not?'

'He thinks Father didn't die a natural death,' responded Charmian bluntly.

They all stared at her. 'Didn't die a natural death?' Conrad repeated. 'What on earth are you driving at, Char?'

'Oh dear, I do *wish* I hadn't come home!' said Aubrey. 'I can see, because I am very quick-witted and sensitive to atmosphere, that everything is going to become too morbid and repellent for words. Char, my precious, do put us out of this frightful suspense! I can't bear it!'

'If you want it in plain words, Rame thinks Father was murdered,' said Charmian.

Clara dropped her teaspoon with a clatter into her saucer. Bart half-started from his chair, and sank back again, his eyes fixed incredulously on his sister's face. Clay turned chalk-white, and moved his lips stickily.

'*Rot!*' said Conrad loudly and scornfully.

'Yes, that's what I said, but apparently I was wrong,' Charmian replied, drawing her cigarette-case from her pocket, and taking a cigarette from it. She shut the case with a snap, and turned to feel for a matchbox on the mantelpiece behind her.

'But what – how——?' Bart demanded.

She struck a match, and lit her cigarette. 'Poison, of course.'

'Rubbish!' said Clara strongly. 'I never heard of such a thing! Poison, indeed! He ate and drank a lot of foolish things last night, as anyone could have told Rame! What next!'

'There was a sort of blue look about him,' Charmian said. 'I noticed it myself, though it didn't, of course, convey anything in particular to my mind. Rame asked if Father was in the habit of taking sleeping-draughts. Reuben and Martha both swore that he wasn't. There was a drain of whisky left in the decanter beside the bed, and he tasted it. He has taken both the glass and the decanter away with him, and I suppose you know what that means.'

'Do you mean – do you mean that there'll have to be an inquest?' Conrad said, in a stupefied tone. 'On *Father*?'

'Of course.'

Clara, who had been staring at Charmian with dropped jaw and slowly mounting colour, found her voice to say: 'Inquest? We've never had such a thing in our family! I never did in all my life!'

Why, whatever next, I should like to know? Your father would be furious at the idea of anythin' like that happenin'! It'll have to be put a stop to: I won't have it!'

'I wish it could be stopped,' returned Charmian. 'Unfortunately, it can't. This is where the police take over. Jolly, isn't it?'

'Police?' Clay gasped. 'Oh, I say, how awful! Rame *must* have made a mistake!'

'Of course he's made a mistake!' said Clara, more moved than anyone could remember to have seen her. 'This is what comes of callin' in one of these newfangled doctors! I've no patience with it! Your father died because he ate and drank too much last night, and that's all there is to it!'

No one paid any heed to this. Bart go up suddenly, thrusting back his chair. 'But, my God, this is ghastly!' he exclaimed. 'Are you saying that somebody put poison in the Guv'nor's whisky? One of *us*?'

Charmian shrugged. Clay was inspired to say: 'It's utter piffle! I mean, who *would*?'

'Little brother, do you think you could keep your ill-omened mouth shut?' asked Aubrey plaintively. 'I am beginning to feel quite too terribly unwell, and that remark has conjured up such a number of daunting reflections that I wish more than ever that I hadn't stupidly forgotten to bring my vinaigrette with me. I don't know who *would* – at least, not yet – but when I think of all who *might* – well, I needn't go on, need I?'

'You figure on the list yourself, don't you?' suggested Conrad, not very nicely.

'Yes, beloved, I should think I am destined to occupy a prominent position on the list, and that is what is upsetting me. Fancy being so unfeeling as to point it out to me in that horrid way! Oh, I *do* wish I weren't here!'

'Do you mean to tell me,' demanded Clara, 'that we're goin' to have police at Trevellin?'

'I suppose so,' replied Charmian.

'And it's no use your saying that you've never heard of such a thing, Clara love, because they were practically never out of the house when the twins were innocent boys,' said Aubrey. 'Not to mention the various occasions when Ray and Ingram and Eugène—'

'That was nothin'!' interrupted Clara. 'A bit of boyish devilry, and your father always settled it without any fuss. But this—! Well, I shall never get over it!'

Vivian, who had been sitting in silence for some minutes, now said defiantly: 'If he really was poisoned, I quite see, of course, that *I* might have been the person to have done it.'

'Yes, darling,' agreed Aubrey, 'but there's nothing to be so grand about in that. It would be far more distinguished not to be a suspect. I mean, it's so obvious, isn't it, that it's going to be too dreadfully commonplace to be one of those who might well have murdered Father?'

Bart turned his eyes towards him. 'Not one of us – not *one* of us! – would have done such a thing!' he said fiercely.

'How sweet of you to say so, Bart! I shouldn't think it's in the least true, but I do appreciate the thoroughly nice spirit that inspired you to utter such noble words. I quite thought you would instantly assume that I was the guilty party.'

'I wouldn't put it beyond you,' interpolated Conrad.

'No, I'm sure you wouldn't, but that's only because I wear a maroon velvet jacket and a silk shirt, and you can't help feeling that such a man would be capable of committing almost any crime.'

'Well, all I know is that Father had made up his mind to make you live at home, which is about the last thing on earth that would suit your book!'

'Mustn't it be lovely to be Conrad?' said Aubrey, looking round the table. 'Sitting there in a perfectly unassailable position, making spiteful remarks to me! I can't help entertaining what I admit to be a very ignoble hope that we shall discover that he had a motive for killing Father after all.'

Conrad looked rather taken aback. 'Look here, who do you consider might have had a motive?'

'It would be so much easier to tell you who hadn't,' replied Aubrey. 'I shouldn't think even a policeman could suspect darling Aunt Clara. Unless you're cherishing a hideous secret, you would appear to be out of the running – but do try not to look so smug about it! It goes against the grain, but I'm bound to say I don't see what Eugène would have had to gain. Char and Ingram seem to be out of it too. I can't think of anyone else.'

'You'd much better not talk about it at all,' said Clara severely. 'Depend upon it, it won't lead to any good.'

'I don't know about anyone else, but if you mean to say that you think Bart would have laid a finger on Father—'

Aubrey sighed. 'I simply can't bear it when you start on your oppressive Damon and Pythias act, Con dear. I daresay Bart didn't do it, but the meanest intelligence – yes, that's my polite way of saying yours, so that angry flush isn't wasted – must perceive that he has a perfectly beautiful motive. Of course, if Ray is the murderer, the whole thing is most sordid, because he must have done it for filthy lucre, which one can't help feeling lets the whole family down; but if Bart did it, his motive, however little it may appeal to me personally, lifts the crime on to a much higher plane. All for Love, in fact. Darling Clara, please pour me out another cup of coffee!'

'I consider it in the highest degree unlikely that Bart had anything at all to do with it,' said Charmian, before Bart could speak.

'Yes, precious, so do I, but if half what one reads is true love has a most peculiar effect, even upon people like Bart. I wouldn't know. Of course, the thing that would afford one a really subtle gratification would be to find that Faith had atoned for years of almost complete ineffectiveness by – Oh dear, there's Clay! To think I had nearly committed a social solecism! I didn't quite though did I?'

'If you imagine I'm going to sit here while you cast your rotten aspersions on my mother, you're jolly well mistaken!' said Clay, growing very red in the face, and assuming the blustering tone he was too prone to use when talking to his brothers.

'Why don't you knock him down?' mocked Conrad. 'Go on! What are you waiting for?'

'Oh, shut up!' said Charmian impatiently. 'Of all the futile suggestions, Aubrey, that surely takes the cake!'

'I know, but you must admit it was a very lovely thought. Oh, look! here's Ray, looking exactly as though he'd been stuffed!'

Except for glancing scornfully at him, Raymond paid no attention to him. He took his place at the head of the table, and looked down the length of it at Clara. 'Coffee, please. I take it Char's told you all what Rame said?'

'It isn't true, Ray!' Bart had been staring out of the window, but he wheeled round to fling these words at his elder brother. 'It couldn't be true! Not the Guv'nor!'

'Oh, isn't Bart sweet?' Aubrey said, addressing the company generally. 'Or don't you like guilelessness above the age of consent? I think it's rather touching.'

'If you don't keep your damned mouth shut, I'll knock hell out of you!' Bart threatened, clenching his fists.

'The wish is father to the thought, dearie. You wouldn't believe the number of dirty Japanese tricks I've got up my sleeve.'

'You can both of you keep your mouths shut!' Raymond said. 'What good do you imagine you're doing, bickering like a couple of school kids? We're in the bloodiest mess possible, let me tell you! By midday it'll be all over the county that Father's been murdered! We're going to be dragged through the mud, all of us! We shall have reporters trying to photograph the scene of the crime, and our name splashed all over the cheaper press!'

'Will we by God!' said Conrad. 'I'd like to see a reporter trying to poke his nose into Trevellin! He'd get something he wasn't expecting!'

'You'll make a fool of yourself if you come to blows with the Press,' observed Charmian dryly. 'What happens next, Ray?'

'The body will be removed for a post-mortem examination. Rame will arrange that with the police.'

'*No!*' Clara arose in her wrath. 'That's too much! Ray, I don't know what you're thinkin' about to allow such a thing! It's not decent!'

'I've no power to stop it. You don't suppose I want any of this to happen, do you? For God's sake, don't you start kicking up a fuss! I've had a bad enough time with Martha already.'

'O *God!*' Bart said, in a breaking voice, and plunged out of the room.

Conrad rose from his chair. 'If it's found to be true that Father was murdered, I'll bet I know who did it!' he said savagely. 'It 'ud be just about what she would do, the damned slut that she is!' He looked down at Aubrey. 'As for you, you keep your tongue off Bart!'

Aubrey waited until he had slammed his way out of the room before remarking: 'Yes, that was always one of the possibilities. They say poison is a woman's weapon, don't they?'

'I never liked that gal,' said Clara, shaking her head, 'but I don't hold with tryin' to put things on people like that.'

'I know nothing about Loveday Trewithian,' said Charmian. 'What seems to me to be of more importance is the fact that Jimmy the Bastard was out all night, and isn't yet back.'

'You don't mean it!' exclaimed Clara.

'I'll bet he did it!' Clay said.

'He's disgusting enough to do anything,' said Vivian. 'But why should he? I don't see what he had to gain.'

'Robbery, or something like that.'

Raymond looked up quickly, his lips slightly parted, as though he were about to speak. Then he closed them again, and lowered his gaze. He had remembered suddenly that there had been no battered tin box in the cupboard above Penhallow's bed. At least, he thought there had not been, but in his haste he might, he supposed, have overlooked it.

'It only remains for us to discover that the three hundred pounds I fetched Father from the Bank yesterday is missing,' said Aubrey. 'An unexciting finish to the episode, but I confess I should welcome it.'

'You're right!' Charmian said. 'Now I come to think of it, Jimmy was in the room when Father spoke of it at dinner last night! Ray, was Father in the habit of drawing so much at a time?'

'No, not as much as that.'

'Well, then! Where ought the money to be?'

'In the cupboard over his head,' Vivian replied eagerly. 'I had to get it out for him once, so I know. Of course Jimmy stole it! It's as plain as a pikestaff! Don't you think so, Ray?'

'I don't know.'

'Well, can't someone go and look in the cupboard?'

'Not at the moment. The room has been locked up. There's no hurry.'

'Oh, isn't Ray just too wonderful?' said Aubrey, awed. 'So un-moved-and-all! I can't think how you preserve your exquisite calm, Ray, really I can't! *My* nervous system is definitely shattered.'

'Then it's just as well mine isn't,' Raymond replied, getting up from the table, and moving towards the door. 'One of you had better go down to the Dower House to tell Ingram what has happened. I must go into Liskeard, to have a word with Cliff.'

He opened the door as he spoke, just in time to admit Ingram himself, who came limping into the room, rather out of breath, and with a countenance expressive both of surprise and indignation.

'I suppose it didn't occur to you that I might like to be informed of Father's death!' he said hotly, glaring at Raymond. 'I might have expected you to leave me to hear of it through a servant! A fair sample of what we may expect to have to put up with now that you're mounted in the saddle!'

'I've had no time so far to think about you,' Raymond answered, his voice as cold as Ingram's was heated. 'If it comforts you at all, I've just this instant told the others to let you know.'

'Damned kind of you! How did it happen, When was it?'

'You can get the details from Char: I've got something more important to attend to,' Raymond responded briefly, and left the room, shutting the door behind him.

'Yes, it's going to be jolly with him in the seat!' Ingram said, with a short laugh. 'By Jove, though, the old man! I never was more surprised in my life, never! Thought he'd go on for years yet! Frightful shock to me!'

'Ah, and that's not the worst of it!' Clara said. 'They're sayin' your father was poisoned, Ingram!'

He stared at her. 'Why, what did he eat? I always thought there was dam' little the old man couldn't digest!'

'When Clara said poisoned,' explained Aubrey, in the kindly tone of one instructing a child, 'she meant murdered.'

'Good God!' Ingram gasped, sitting down plump in Raymond's vacated chair.

Vivian left the room as Charmian began to tell Ingram about Dr. Rame's visit, and went upstairs to put Eugène in possession of the new facts. She was overtaken on the stairs by Clay, on his way to his mother's room. He said to her with a sort of suppressed eagerness: 'I shouldn't think there could be a doubt it was Jimmy, should you? I mean, it's obvious!'

'I don't know. I suppose we most of us had pretty good reasons for wanting Penhallow dead.'

He uttered an unconvincing laugh. 'I say, I wish you'd speak for yourself! I'm sure I never had such an idea in my head!'

'Hadn't you?' she said, looking at him rather oddly.

'Of course not! Good lord, what a question!'

'It's one you're likely to be asked,' she said.

He was so disconcerted by this answer that he found nothing to say. She walked past Faith's door towards the corridor at the back of the house, and after watching her uncertainly until she had disappeared from his sight, Clay knocked for admittance into Faith's room.

She was seated at her dressing-table, fully dressed, her hands clasped in her lap. She smiled faintly when she saw Clay, and said: 'Darling!'

'Mother, have you heard?'

'Your father? Yes, dear, of course.'

'Not that! I thought perhaps Loveday might have told you, for I suppose all the servants know by this time.'

She fixed her eyes on his face with an expression in them of painful intensity. 'I sent Loveday downstairs to have her breakfast a little while ago. What is it?'

'Rame wouldn't sign the death certificate!'

It seemed to her that her pulses stopped beating with her heart. She knew quite well what Clay meant, but her instinct screamed to her to be careful, and she said, to gain time: 'I don't understand.'

'Well, it means that Rame thinks he didn't die a natural death. Frightful situation, isn't it?'

She moistened her lips. 'Why should he think that? Lifton warned me that your father couldn't go on as he was doing! Did no one tell him what your father ate and drank last night?'

'I don't know what they told him. I wasn't there. Apparently, Rame suspected poison straight away. Asked if Father were in the habit of taking sleeping-draughts. Martha and Reuben said he wasn't, and the end of it was that Rame walked off with the whisky decanter from beside Father's bed, and Father's body is going to be taken away by the police for a post-mortem examination. Pretty ghastly, isn't it?'

She said, with a catch in her voice: 'It's absurd! I don't believe it! Everyone knew how foolishly Adam had been behaving lately!'

'I know, that's what Aunt Clara said. She's fearfully upset. But the thing is that that little swab Jimmy seems to have disappeared.'

'Jimmy?'

'Stayed out all night, and hasn't turned up yet. When you remember the sum of money Father made Aubrey fetch him from the Bank yesterday – well, pretty obvious, isn't it?'

Her eyes started at him; she said faintly: 'Oh, no, no!'

'Yes, but, Mother, think! I know it sounds ghastly, Father being killed by that filthy little beast, just for three hundred pounds, but if it wasn't Jimmy – not that I think there's the least doubt that it was, mind you! – it's going to be absolutely *dire* for the rest of us! I mean, already Aubrey's been saying the most poisonous things, and you can bet your life—'

'What has Aubrey been saying?' she interrupted.

'Oh, about so many of us having motives! Actually, I shut him up pretty quickly, because he had the cheek to start on you, and naturally I wasn't going to stand that.'

Her colour fluctuated; she leaned forward in her chair. 'On me? Why? What did he say about me?'

'Oh, well, I don't think he really meant anything: it was a sort of joke – you know what Aubrey is!'

'Did Aubrey suggest that *I* had anything to do with your father's death?' she demanded.

She sounded indignant, as indeed she was, for although she had killed Penhallow she still felt her action to have been so alien to her nature that it was with a sense of the deepest injury that she learned that one who should surely have known her better could believe her to be capable of committing murder.

Not having any desire to figure as a tale-bearer before his half-brothers, Clay made haste to palliate his original statement. 'Oh, he wasn't serious, Mother! There's nothing to get hot-up about. I shut him up at once, and, anyway, nobody paid the slightest attention to him. In fact, Char said it was the most fatuous thing she'd ever heard.'

'I should hope so!' she said sharply. She picked up her handkerchief from the dressing-table, and pressed it to her lips for a moment. 'What – what has to happen now, Clay?' she asked.

'Well, I suppose Rame will do a post-mortem. We shan't know much till after that. If he does find that Father was poisoned, it will be a case for the police, of course.'

She shuddered. 'Oh, no! Oh, how dreadful!'

'I know, that's what Aunt Clara says, but it can't be helped. Mind you, I daresay Rame won't find any poison at all! It's all very well for that ass, Aubrey, to say that we've all got motives, but personally I agree with Bart, that none of *us* would dream of doing such a thing. If he was poisoned, then it's obvious that Jimmy did it.'

She swallowed convulsively. 'Clay dear, go downstairs now! I – I really feel so upset about this that I must be alone for a little while. It's so appalling – I never dreamed—! I think I'll lie down for a time.'

But when he had left the room she remained seated in her chair, clasping and unclasping her hands in her lap, her eyes travelling round the room as though in search of some way of escape. They alighted presently upon the two bottles of veronal, standing side by side upon the shelf above the washstand, and she began at once to consider how she could best dispose of the empty one which should have been full. An impulse to conceal it in one of her drawers made her start from her chair, only to sink back again as she reflected that nothing could be more fatal than for the bottle to be found in such a place. She knew very little about police procedure, but she believed that they might search the house very strictly. Then she thought that she would be better advised to leave the bottle where it was, since everyone knew that she alone amongst the household was in the habit of taking drops of veronal when she could not sleep. In the few detective novels which she had read, efforts at concealment had almost invariably proved the criminal's undoing. It would be wiser to do nothing; to leave the bottle in full view would even appear, perhaps, to the police as a strong reason for believing her innocent. And if they did suspect her, and made inquiries about her relations with Penhallow, although it would be found that Penhallow had frequently been unkind to her, it must also be found that she had borne his unkindness for twenty years, and had never in all that time quarrelled with him. Her stepchildren might despise her, but they knew that she was not the kind of woman who would murder her husband. They knew nothing of the brief madness which had possessed her on the previous evening; apparently they regarded the very possibility that she might be the guilty person in the light of a joke. No one had seen her enter Penhallow's room: of that she was certain. Without considering who might become implicated in her place, she began to reflect that anyone could have poisoned Penhallow's whisky, and with the veronal prescribed for her, since she kept it in full view in her room, and had never made any secret of her possession of it.

She remembered Jimmy suddenly, and stirred uneasily in her chair, for although she disliked Jimmy she would have thought his arrest for a crime which he had not committed a more dreadful thing than the murder itself. Then she gave herself a mental shake, realizing that since he had had nothing to do with Penhallow's death the probability was that he had merely taken French leave for a day, and would reappear in due course.

She thought that perhaps she ought to go downstairs, that it would appear more natural in her than to remain in her bedroom while such momentous events were in progress. She glanced at her reflection in the mirror, tidied a strand of her faded hair, and got up.

The house seemed strangely quiet, although why it should have done so, at an hour when she might have expected, in the ordinary run of things, to have found it deserted by most of its inhabitants she did not know. A housemaid, encountered on the upper hall, threw her an awed look. She ignored the girl, and went down the stairs to the morning-room.

Myra had followed Ingram up from the Dower House some time previously, and was now seated on the sofa beside Clara, discussing Penhallow's death in the hushed voice which she apparently considered suitable to the occasion. Ingram was standing on the hearth-rug with his hands in his pockets, talking to Charmian, who was leaning against the window-frame, a cigarette in one hand, and a cup of tea in the other. All three ladies were partaking of this stimulating beverage, but Ingram seemed to feel the need of a more invigorating tonic, since a glass half-full of whisky-and-soda stood on the mantel-piece behind him. When Faith entered the room, they all looked round quickly, and Myra at once rose from the sofa, and came towards her, exclaiming: 'You poor dear! I'm so terribly sorry for you! If there was only anything one could do!'

Faith submitted to having her cheek kissed, saying in a subdued tone: 'Thank you. It has been such a shock – I don't seem able to realize it.'

Clara blew her nose. 'I never thought I should live to see the day when my poor brother's body was carried off by the police,' she said.

Faith shivered. 'Oh, don't!' she begged. 'Has – have they—?'

'An hour ago,' replied Ingram, clearing his throat. 'A beastly business! Can't get over it. The old Guv'nor, you know! I always said he'd rue the day he brought that little swine into the house. Never would listen to reason! And this is what has come of it! Mind you, I blame Ray for allowing him to keep a sum like that in his bed! Asking for trouble!'

She raised her eyes nervously to his face. 'I don't quite— What do you mean?'

'It was that Jimmy, my dear,' Clara said. 'The strong-box is missing, with three hundred pounds in it.'

She uttered an inarticulate sound, turning so pale that Myra put an arm round her.

'Poor dear! I don't wonder you're shocked. That's what I said: it seems so dreadful to think of his having been murdered just for three hundred pounds! Come and sit down! Ingram, pull the bell, and tell them to bring another cup and saucer! A cup of tea will do her good.'

'No, please!' Faith managed to say. 'I couldn't swallow it! Have they – have they arrested Jimmy?'

'Not yet,' Ingram replied. 'He's done a bunk, of course, but they'll find him all right, don't you worry!'

She allowed Myra to lead her to a chair, and sat down, tightly grasping her handkerchief in one hand. She glanced round the room in a rather blank way. 'The others – Ray?'

'Ray said he must go into Liskeard to see Cliff, my dear,' answered Clara. 'I expect it's about Adam's will, and that sort of thing. He's not back yet.'

Ingram laughed shortly. 'Ray's not losing any time. Didn't turn a hair, as far as I could see!'

'Now, you oughtn't to say that,' Clara reproved him mildly. 'Ray's never been one to show his feelin's, but that isn't to say he hasn't got any.'

Charmian flicked the ash off the end of her cigarette. 'Queer cuss, Ray. He's always been a bit of a skirter, when you come to think of it. I don't think I ever knew him to run with the rest of the pack, even when we were kids.'

Faith turned her eyes towards her stepdaughter. 'Can't he do anything? Can't he *stop* it? Oh, don't you see how *awful*—?'

'No one can stop it,' Charmian said bluntly. 'We're in it up to our necks. Of course we see how awful it is! But we shan't make it any better by getting hysterical about it.'

'No, Char, don't be so hard and unsympathetic!' said Myra, pressing Faith's hand in a very feeling way. 'Naturally poor Faith is dreadfully upset! I mean, we all know that Mr. Penhallow was often very trying, but what I say is, you can't live with anyone for years without feeling it very much when they die. Why, I feel it myself! I'm sure the house seems different already! I noticed it the moment I set foot in it.'

'It'll seem still more different when we get Ray firmly seated in the saddle,' observed Ingram grimly. 'You mark my words: there are going to be a good few changes at Trevellin!'

'A few changes wouldn't come amiss,' said Charmian. 'I hope Ray does make them. I'd like to see Eugène doing an honest day's work; and I consider it's high time the twins learned to fend for themselves.'

Clara said forlornly: 'It won't seem like Trevellin, with all the boys gone. I don't know if he'll want me to go, I'm sure.'

'Oh, no, no! Why should he?' Faith cried.

'I suppose you won't stay here?' Charmian asked her.

'No – that is, I haven't thought. It's too soon! I don't know what I shall do.'

'Of course not!' said Myra, with a reproving glance cast at Charmian. 'Besides, it isn't as if Ray's married.'

'Well, I think there's a good deal to be said for the old man's way of keeping the family together!' announced Ingram. 'I don't say he didn't carry it to excess, but if Ray turns the twins out it'll be a damned shame!'

Clara shook her head. 'I'm afraid Bart will marry that gal,' she said. 'I don't see what's to stop him, now his father's gone.'

'What girl?' demanded Ingram, pricking up his ears.

'Loveday Trewithian. He had a set-to with his father about it only the other day.'

'Loveday Trewithian! Reuben's niece?' exclaimed Ingram. 'Good God, the young fool! He can't do that!'

'No, and of course your father wouldn't hear of it.'

'Why shouldn't he marry her, if he wants to?' asked Charmian. 'She isn't my style but I should think she'd suit Bart down to the ground.'

'Good lord, Char, he can't marry Reuben's niece!'

She shrugged. 'I don't see why not. He's going to have Trellick, isn't he? She'll make a good farmer's wife.'

'But, Char, you can't have thought of what *our* position would be!' cried Myra. 'How could one possibly call on a person like that? What would people say?'

'Don't worry!' Charmian replied, with true Penhallow brutality. 'After what's happened today, no one will be surprised at anything the Penhallows take it into their heads to do! A little scandal more or less won't make any odds.'

A tear trickled down Clara's weather-beaten cheek. She wiped it away. 'I wish I'd been taken first!' she said. 'I've lived too long: I shall never get used to havin' our name dragged through the mud, and bein' pointed at, and talked about. I'm too old: it's no good expectin' me to change my ideas at my time of life.'

Faith looked at her with wide, frightened eyes. 'No one will point at you, Clara! It hasn't anything to do with you!'

'No, my dear, but I know what people are. It isn't only that, either. I know he was a wicked old man, but I can't bear to think of him bein' murdered like that, and all for a paltry bit of money!'

Charmian lit a second cigarette, and blew a cloud of smoke down her nostrils. 'Well, I'm not so sure that he was murdered for money,' she said, frowning. 'I've been thinking it over, and I can't see why Jimmy had to poison Father to get hold of that three hundred pounds. Father was out of his room all the afternoon yesterday. It seems to me Jimmy could have taken the cash, and made his getaway without the slightest difficulty. In fact, the more you look at it the more senseless it seems to be that he should have murdered Father.'

Ingram stared at her. 'Well, but damn it all, Char, isn't it obvious? He was afraid of getting caught and jugged!'

'Be your age!' besought his sister. 'For one thing, it's extremely unlikely that Father would have prosecuted him; and for another, we all knew that that three hundred was in Father's tin box, so he can't possibly have hoped to have got away with it. Why on earth should he have tied a noose round his own neck?'

'The fact remains that he's missing, and the money too, my dear girl.'

'It wouldn't surprise me to find that Jimmy's disappearance with the money hasn't got anything whatsoever to do with Father's death,' Charmian said deliberately.

Ingram took a minute to assimilate this. 'Yes, but – I say, Char, that's a bit grim! If Jimmy didn't poison the old man, it means that somebody else did, and – Hell, that points to its having been one of *us*!'

'No, no!' Faith said imploringly.

No one heeded her. 'Not entirely,' Charmian said. 'I don't say I think it, but what Con suggested might be true, particularly if Father had nipped Bart's marriage-plans in the bud. Loveday might have done it.'

'She didn't! I know she didn't!' Faith cried. 'You mustn't say such wicked things, Char! It isn't true!'

'My dear Faith, I know you're fond of the girl, but what do you know about her after all? However, she isn't the only one who might have done it.' She regarded the end of her cigarette for a moment. 'I don't know what any of the rest of the family feels about it, but I could bear to know what brought Uncle Phin up here yesterday to see Father.'

'Uncle Phin? I never knew he had come up!' said Ingram. 'What on earth did he want?'

'That's what I should like to know. He came up after tea, and insisted on seeing Father in private.'

'But what an extraordinary thing!' Myra exclaimed. 'I thought he hardly ever came to Trevellin!'

'Did he have a row with Father?' asked Ingram.

'I don't know. Father was shut up with him in the Yellow room for nearly an hour. I didn't see him at all. As far as I know, none of us did.'

'Damned odd!' Ingram commented. 'All the same, I don't quite see what he could have had to do with it. Father never had any truck with him that I knew of.'

Charmian pitched her cigarette out of the window. 'Do you think we knew everything Father was up to? I'm damned sure we didn't! Why, we never even knew about Jimmy till he was suddenly pitch-forked into our midst! I've got a hunch that there's a darned sight more in all this than meets the eye, and – I repeat – I'd like to know what brought Uncle Phin to Trevellin!'

'By Jove!' Ingram said slowly, picking up his glass from the mantelpiece. 'By – Jove, though!'

Myra gave a nervous little laugh. 'Like a detective story!

Mysteries, and suspects, and things. If it wasn't happening to ourselves, I mean! Ought the police to know about Uncle Phin's visit?'

The walls of the nightmare seemed to Faith to be closing in on her. She got up jerkily, saying with a labouring breath: 'I can't bear it! It's too terrible! Phineas couldn't have — There was no *reason*! Oh, please don't go on! I *know* you're wrong!'

'There, Char! I knew you'd upset her!' Myra cried. 'You never have the least consideration for people's feelings! Let me take you up to your room, dear! You ought to lie down.'

'No. I'm all right. It's only that — I can't bear you to keep on talking about it like this!'

Charmian glanced contemptuously across at her. 'Always the escapist, Faith! Never looked a fact in the face in your life, have you? All right! have it your own way! But you won't be able to escape this situation, you'll find!'

CHAPTER EIGHTEEN

RAYMOND'S object in immediately seeking out his cousin Clifford was to discover, if he could, what papers Penhallow might have deposited with him. That Penhallow's will had been drawn up by the firm of Blazey, Blazey, Hastings, and Wembury he knew; and also that the various Deeds of Settlement were in Clifford's charge. He was uninterested in these, since he knew their provisions. His fear was that some document referring to himself, even, perhaps, a birth certificate, might have been placed by his father in such a place of safety as his solicitor's office. He was too level-headed to suppose that Clifford would hand over any of Penhallow's papers to him, nor had he formed any very definite plan of abstracting them; but in the torment of his brain it seemed to him of paramount importance to discover whether any dangerous document did in fact exist. The letters he had taken from Penhallow's room had revealed nothing. He had read and destroyed them, but the relief to his overstretched nerves had lasted only until he had remembered that Penhallow might have deposited such a document either at his Bank, or with Clifford. As far as he was aware, Penhallow had kept no papers at the Bank: he would ascertain that presently, for as one of the executors of the will he could inspect whatever documents existed without exciting any suspicion.

The problem of his father's death was worrying him hardly at all; he had scarcely wasted a thought on the identity of his murderer, although he was aware that Reuben, from the moment of its being made known to him that his master had not died a natural death, had been regarding him with doubt and mistrust. There had been marks of bruising upon Penhallow's throat which Rame had at once discovered. Raymond had said with an indifference which had taken the doctor palpably aback: 'Yes, I know about that. I did it yesterday morning. That didn't kill him!'

The doctor, although not intimately acquainted with the family, had practised in the neighbourhood long enough to know that the Penhallows were characterized by a wild violence shocking to persons of more temperate habits, but this cool avowal came as a jolt to his professional calm. He had said: 'This bears all the appearance of an attempt at strangulation!'

'Yes,' replied Raymond.

'A man in your father's condition, Mr. Penhallow?'

Raymond had shrugged his shoulders. 'I lost my temper with him, that's all.'

After a moment, the doctor had bent over Penhallow's body again, his lips rather tightly compressed. Reuben, who had been present, had not spoken a word, but after regarding Raymond fixedly for an instant or two, had lowered his eyes. Then Charmian had come into the room; and Rame, looking up, had asked them if Penhallow had been in the habit of taking sleeping-draughts. The additional pallor, taken in combination with slight cyanosis, had not escaped the doctor's eye, and upon Charmian's asking him what it was that he suspected, he had replied bluntly that he detected signs of possible barbitone poisoning. Glancing about him, he had perceived the whisky decanter on the bedside table, and had tasted the small amount of liquid that remained in it.

Martha, fetched by Reuben to corroborate his statement, had positively declared that Penhallow had never taken narcotics; and it had become immediately obvious that his death must be a matter for police investigation.

Of the four people standing before Rame, Raymond had shown the least trace of dismay, his expression having been one rather of annoyance. In the midst of his own overmastering preoccupation, the fact that his father had been murdered seemed to him nothing more than a needless complication. He soon became aware of the equivocal position in which he himself stood, but it scarcely worried him at all. He supposed, without devoting much thought to the question, that since Jimmy was unaccountably missing from Trevellin, the murder might be laid at his door; and as any interrogation of Jimmy by the police seemed bound to lead to the disclosure of the cause of his own quarrel with his father he was conscious only of a desperate hope that Jimmy would elude capture. If Jimmy, having murdered Penhallow, contrived to escape from the country, it was certain that he would never dare to return again to trouble the peace of Trevellin's new master.

As he drove himself to Liskeard, Raymond had leisure to consider the question a little more fully. The same aspect of the situation which had presented itself to Charmian most forcibly struck him: he could discover no motive for murder, and began to think that Jimmy would reappear, having committed no worse crime than that of absenting himself from his post without leave, to pursue his own unsavoury pleasures in the neighbourhood. If it were found that Penhallow's strong-box had disappeared, Raymond considered, weighing the matter coldly, that Aubrey was the most likely thief; and since he held the poorest opinion of his younger brother's morals, and disliked him rather more than he disliked Jimmy, he experienced no difficulty in believing him to be capable of murdering his father. In fact, the more he thought about it, the more probable it appeared to him that Aubrey, first disarming future suspicion by delivering the three hundred pounds into his father's hands, should later have abstracted it. If there was in this solution no better motive for murder than in the case of Jimmy's being the thief, the motive was to be found, Raymond believed, in Penhallow's declared intention of compelling Aubrey to take up his residence at Trevellin. No doubt Aubrey's affairs were in worse shape than he had admitted, not to be settled permanently by a mere three hundred pounds, although that might serve to pay the more urgent of his debts.

When he arrived at Clifford's office, he was ushered at once into his cousin's presence. Clifford, who had only just himself arrived at the office, greeted him cheerfully, but as soon as he learned the news of his uncle's death he looked very much shocked, and the jovial smile was wiped from his face. He ejaculated 'Good God!' a great number of times, and said more than once that he couldn't get over it. When he was made aware of the imminent entry of the police into the affair, he turned quite pale, and could only sit staring at Raymond with a dropped jaw, and the most ludicrous expression of dismay upon his rubicund countenance.

'But who——?' he gasped at length. 'God bless my soul, Ray, *who*——?'

'I haven't the slightest idea,' Raymond replied. 'Not much point in discussing that. We shall have enough discussion about it as soon as the police get going. I came here partly to notify you, and partly to look over the papers Father deposited with you. I want to know just how things stand, and just what there is here.'

'Well, of course, you're one of the executors, and you've got a perfect right to look into the papers, if you want to, but you know, old man, if the police think it was murder——'

'I don't want to take anything away,' Raymond interrupted. 'I want to know exactly what documents you've got of Father's.'

'Oh, if that's all!' Clifford said. 'Not that I've got a great deal here that you don't know about, if anything. I'll send for the keys to Uncle's deed-box. Sit down, old man! Shan't be a minute.'

While he was absent from the room, Raymond sat tapping one foot on the ground, and looking up at the shelf at a tin box that bore in white letters on its side the inscription, *Penhallow Estate*. Clifford soon reappeared with his clerk, who lifted the box down from the shelf, and set it on the broad desk, and carefully dusted it, before retiring again to the outer office.

'Do you want to take a look at the will?' asked Clifford, fitting the key into the lock. 'You and I are the sole executors, you know.

That's about all uncle left with me, except for the various Deeds of Settlement, of course. Fairly straightforward, as far as I remember. There was a codicil added some time ago, in respect of Trellick Farm: you knew about that, I expect?'

Raymond nodded, watching his cousin turn the key, and lift up the lid. Clifford took the papers out of the box, and picked the will out from amongst them. 'The estate was resettled in Joshua Penhallow's time, of course,' he said, spreading open the will. 'The eldest son succeeds to the entailed property – well, you know all about that! Four thousand pounds to each of the younger sons; two thousand to Char; one or two smaller legacies – here you are, you'd better take a look at it for yourself!'

Raymond had been quickly glancing through the remaining documents, none of which contained the slightest reference to himself. He drew a breath, and turned mechanically to take his father's will from Clifford, saying as he did so: 'Four thousand only? Well, thank God for that! I thought it would be more.'

'Well, so it was up till about five years ago,' said Clifford confidentially. 'This is the second of your father's wills.' He coughed, and began to play with one of the pencils on his desk. 'Nothing to do with me, of course, Ray old man, but I'm afraid the settlements, even as they now stand, are going to be a bit of a charge on the estate?'

'The devil of a charge!' Raymond replied.

Clifford made a sympathetic noise in his throat. 'I thought uncle had been living a bit above his means,' he said, tactfully understating the case.

'Playing ducks and drakes with his means would be nearer the mark. God knows what sort of a mess I'm going to find!'

Clifford shook his head. 'Of course, times are very bad. The estate—'

'The estate brings in about four thousand a year. It's not that. I know very well he's been selling out his invested capital for years. That's where the pinch is going to come. What's that you've got hold of?'

'Faith's marriage settlement.'

Raymond took it out of his hand, and ran his eye down its provisions. He gave one of his short laughs. 'Quite a nice little jointure! A thousand a year, most of which will be squandered on Clay!' He got up, tossing the settlement deed back into the tin box. 'All right: it seems fairly simple. You'd better bring the will up to Trevellin, and read it to the family. Usually done after the funeral, isn't it? Well, God knows when that'll be, but if I know anything about Ingram and Eugène and Aubrey, there'll be no peace until they know how much they're going to get – and precious little when they do know!'

Clifford accompanied him out to his car, expressing in an embarrassed tone the conventional wish that there were something he could do to assist the Penhallows in their affliction. As he added the conviction that Rosamund would be as anxious as he was himself to bring aid and comfort to the family, the wish sounded more than usually insincere, and drew nothing more than a grunt from Raymond. Clifford then said that if Raymond did not think that his presence in the house would be a nuisance he felt that he ought to motor out to Trevellin to see his mother. Raymond replied that he might do as he pleased, got into his battered runabout, and drove off towards Bodmin.

By the time he returned to Trevellin, the morning was considerably advanced, and not only the Vicar and Penhallow's old friend, John Probus, had called to condole, but the house was invaded by Detective-Inspector Logan, supported by Sergeant Plymstock, at present engaged in pursuing investigations which, however quietly proceeded with, had had the effect of casting at least half the household into a flutter.

The Inspector, who was a sensible-looking man of about forty-five, knew the Penhallows well by reputation, but he had not previously come into contact with them, nor had he until this morning penetrated into what must, he privately considered, be surely the most extraordinary house in the county. He had an impression of innumerable rooms of all shapes and sizes all crammed with furniture, many leading one out of the other; of long stone corridors; of irrelevant staircases; of rambling cellars; of huge fireplaces; and of odd doors which gave unexpectedly on to hitherto unsuspected halls, or passages. He had not uttered a word on first being led to Penhallow's bedroom, but he admitted to his dazed Sergeant, later, that he really did think he'd got by mistake into a sort of Aladdin's cave.

Ingram, who, in Raymond's absence, had constituted himself as head of the establishment, took him there, and was struck at once with a sense of loss. The great bed stood empty, the blazing quilt stretched neatly across it; the mountain of ash had been cleared out of the hearth; and the litter of miscellaneous objects on the refectory table had been removed. The silence of the room brought home his father's death to Ingram as nothing else had done, yet Penhallow's spirit seemed to hang over it, so that Ingram almost expected to hear that loud, jovial voice hail him. He was rather shaken, and said: 'By Jove! The poor old Guv'nor! Brings it home to one!'

From Ingram, the Inspector learned the names and relationships of those living in the house. He was obliged to write these down, and to refer to them frequently during the course of his inquiries. Sergeant Plymstock said frankly that it would be a month of Sundays before he got any of them sorted out. He had always understood Penhallow to have been a proper tyrant, but by the time his superior had elicited from Ingram various admissions which showed the extent and nature of Penhallow's despotism he began to feel that his previous impressions of the deceased had been milk-and-water bowdlerizings of the truth.

It had not taken Logan long to discover the almost certain means by which Penhallow's death had been brought about. In response to his preliminary inquiries, Faith had said: 'But I'm the only person in the house who take sleeping-draughts. Unless you do, Eugène? Only it isn't exactly a sleeping-draught. I've taken it for years. Dr. Lifton prescribed it for me. It's veronal. But I always keep it in my own room!'

'Is it kept under lock and key, madam?' Logan asked her.

She fixed her strained, startled eyes on his face. 'No. No, not under lock and key. But no one has ever—'

'Don't be an ass, Faith!' Charmian interrupted. 'Obviously some one *has*! Where is the stuff?'

'It's always kept on the shelf, with my other medicines and things. But there's only a very little left in the old bottle, and I haven't opened the new one yet! I really don't think—'

'May I see it, madam?'

'Yes, of course! Shall I fetch it, or would you like to see for yourself where it is?'

'If you please,' said Logan.

She led the way up the main staircase to her room at the head of it. 'There it is, Inspector. Those two bottles at the end of the shelf. You'll see that the new one hasn't been opened even. I'm sure—'

The Inspector, who had picked one of the bottles up in his handkerchief, said: 'This is empty, madam.'

'Empty? Oh, you must have got the old one! But I quite thought there was a little left in the bottle!'

He picked up the other bottle, and tilted it. 'In this one, madam, there is.'

She put a hand to her head, faltering: 'But I never even opened it! You must be mistaken! Oh, no, of course I know you can't be, but – but I don't understand! Do you mean he was poisoned with *my* drops? Oh, no, no, it's too awful! I won't believe it!'

He wrapped the bottle up in his handkerchief. 'You said, I think, that you have been in the habit for some years of taking veronal? Was anyone in the household aware of this?'

She sank down into a chair. She looked very white, and a little dazed. 'Oh, yes! Everyone knew I had to take drops to help me to sleep.'

'Does the bottle always stand on that shelf?'

'Yes – at least, I do sometimes have it on the table by my bed, but generally – Oh, I ought to have kept it locked away, only I never thought – Besides, who could possibly—? And they wouldn't have put it back in my room! You don't think I did it? Inspector, you can't thing I would do such a thing?'

'It's too early for me to think anything, madam. On the face of it, it seems that anyone in the house could have had access to the bottle at any time.'

'Yes, but – Oh, does it mean that I'm actually responsible? For leaving the bottle about? But I never dreamed – it didn't even occur to me that anyone would—'

'No, madam, I'm sure. Was anyone aware, to your knowledge, that you had recently had this prescription made up again?'

'I don't know. I don't think – that is, my maid knew, and of course the housemaids must have seen it, when they dusted the room.'

'How long have you had the second bottle in your possession, madam?'

She pressed her hand to her brow again. 'Let me think! Everything's such a nightmare that I find it hard to – Was it yesterday? No, I think it must have been the day before. My maid was going in to Liskeard, and I asked her to get the prescription made up again. Yes, I'm nearly sure that was when it was.'

The Inspector referred to his notes. 'That would be Loveday Trewithian?'

'Yes. She is our butler's niece. But she couldn't have had anything to do with it, Inspector!'

He raised his eyes from his notebook. 'She is engaged to be married to Mr. Bartholomew Penhallow, I believe, madam?'

She gave a gasp, and clutched the arms of her chair. 'No! There's no engagement! Who told you? Who can possibly have said anything about that to you?'

The Inspector did not feel it to be incumbent upon him to enlighten this nervous, and rather simple creature on the extent of the knowledge of the family's more private affairs which was enjoyed by Loveday's fellow-servants. He merely said: 'That is the information I have, madam.'

She thought that Bart must have avowed his intention to marry Loveday. 'It's nothing but a passing fancy. I know my stepson did – did fall in love with her, but of course marriage is out of the question, and I'm quite sure Loveday knows it, because she's a thoroughly nice girl, whatever you may have been told to the contrary!'

'Did Mr. Penhallow know of his son's intention to marry this girl?'

'Yes. That is—'

'Was he willing for the marriage to take place?'

'No. No, of course not! But I'm sure he didn't take it seriously, because he didn't wish me to dismiss Loveday, or anything like that.'

'Is it a fact that Mr. Bartholomew Penhallow expected his father to set him up at Trellick Farm?'

'Yes. But my – my husband hadn't said anything definite about it. It was always understood, but—'

'Was there any quarrel between Mr. Penhallow and his son on this subject?'

'I don't know. That is – You see, Inspector, my husband and his sons were always quarrelling, so it didn't mean anything, and in any case Bart – Mr. Bartholomew Penhallow – was very fond of his father, and I *know* he wouldn't have even thought of – of doing anything to him!'

He pursued the matter no further with her, but by the time that he left Trevellin, at the end of the morning, he had acquired enough startling and contradictory information to make him inform the Chief Constable that the case was not going to be an easy one to solve. He saw no reason for bringing Scotland Yard into it, but admitted that he had not been prepared to find quite so many people at Trevellin with motives for murdering its master.

'Well, I was never personally acquainted with Penhallow,' said Major Warbstow, 'but, speaking as a plain individual, the only wonder is that someone didn't murder him years ago, from all I've ever heard about him. The doctor's report isn't in yet, but I don't suppose there's much doubt he was murdered?'

'None at all, I should say, sir,' responded Logan. 'I've brought away a bottle of veronal which ought to have been full, and which I found empty.'

'Good lord! Where did you find it?'

'In Mrs. Penhallow's room, sir, on a shelf in full view of anyone who happened to come in.'

'Mrs. Penhallow!'

'Yes, but I don't make a lot of that, sir. She seems to have been taking the stuff for years, and though she does seem a silly creature, I shouldn't think she'd be silly enough to leave the bottle about, if she'd used the stuff to poison her husband with.'

'The use of poison often points to a woman, Logan.'

'Yes, sir. I didn't mean that I was ruling her out. But she isn't the only woman to be mixed up in this case. And really I should doubt whether she'd have had the nerve to poison anyone from the way she carries on! Of course, she's upset by the whole thing, as is natural she should be. But let alone her getting a bit hysterical at my finding the bottle empty, she goes up in the air as soon as ever I ask any questions about anyone else in the house, and keeps on telling me that she knows none of them could possibly have done it, till I could pretty well have brained her. It's plain the rest of them don't think much of her. What's more, it's plain they don't any of them think she had anything to do with the crime. And that's significant, sir, because they don't give me the impression they like her.'

The Major nodded. 'All right: go on. What about this boy who has absconded?'

'Well, we haven't managed to catch up with him yet, sir, but there doesn't seem to be much doubt that he made off with three hundred pounds in cash, which he took from Mr. Penhallow's bed.'

'From his bed!'

'Yes, sir. Oh, I don't mean he kept it under his pillow, but pretty near as bad! I've never seen such a bed in my life. It has got a whole lot of cupboards and drawers in the head of it. But there doesn't seem to have been any need for this Jimmy to have murdered Penhallow. He was his father, too.'

'What?'

'Oh, yes, sir!' said Logan matter-of-factly. 'The rest of them call him Jimmy the Bastard, making no bones about it!'

'Good God! What a set!'

'I believe you, sir. I've only spent one morning in the place, but I give you my word nothing would surprise me which I found out about them. I mean, there's no end to it. But though there's a good few of them would like to bring the murder home to this Jimmy there's two of them with enough common sense to see that he could have got away with the money without adding to the risks he was taking by killing the old man. That's Miss Penhallow, and Mr. Raymond Penhallow. *She's* one of these masterful women who make you want to run a mile to get away from them; *he's* a surly sort of chap: doesn't say much.'

'I know Ray Penhallow slightly. Always thought him the best of the bunch.'

'Yes, sir? Well, he had a shot at strangling the old man yesterday morning,' said the Inspector calmly.

The Major stared at him. 'You don't say so! Good heavens!'

'Yes, sir. No deception about it: all clean and above board, just as though a little thing like that was nothing out of the way. Which I dare say it wasn't. Interrogated, he said he had lost his temper with his father on account of the old man's interference in the business of the estate. Jimmy and the butler – chap called Lanner – pulled him off his father's throat. Lanner's been with the family since he was a lad, and his father before him, and the way I see it is that he's torn between his loyalty to the Penhallows as a whole, and his affection for the old man, which I should say was pretty considerable. He wasn't keen to talk, but I did get out of him that he'd never known Mr. Raymond to do a thing like that before.'

The Major pursed his lips. 'They're a wild lot. At the same time, I shouldn't expect a man who'd tried to strangle his father in the morning, and been prevented from doing it, to poison him in the evening.'

'No, sir. But I'm bound to say that he does look, on the face of it, to be the one with the biggest motive. A couple of his brothers gave me some interesting sidelights on the way things have been at Trevellin, and it does seem as though Mr. Raymond, being the heir, might have had very good cause to want his father dead. I got it out of the second brother—' He consulted his notes – 'Big chap, with a stiff leg – Ingram! – Well, he told me that the old man had taken to throwing his money about in a way likely to ruin the estate, and that he and Raymond were always at loggerheads about it. Said he never had got on with his father. However, I got the impression that there wasn't much love lost between himself and Raymond. Then there's the third brother – chap with a foreign name. I can't make out what he's doing in the house at all, for he's got a wife, and you'd think anyone would be glad to get away from such a place. I must say, I didn't take to him. Smooth-tongued fellow, with a nasty little way of making insinuations about the rest of the gang – family! But, then, his wife's mixed up in it, so I dare say he has his reasons. Anyway, he'd like the murderer to turn out to be Jimmy. Failing Jimmy, he favours Raymond, with Loveday Trewithian as a close second. Also ran, Aubrey, and Clay. That's the second Mrs. Penhallow's boy – and not such an unlikely candidate either, if you were to ask me, sir.'

'What about the third son's wife?' interrupted the Major. 'Why should she have done it?'

'To get away from the place. Stormy little thing: one of the kind who tells you she's going to be perfectly frank with you, and then shoots off a lot of damaging information about herself, as though she dared you to think she'd have done so if she'd had anything to do with the murder. Said she hated her father-in-law, and didn't care who heard her say so.'

'Yes, but surely that isn't a reason for murdering him!' protested Warbstow. 'She needn't have stayed at Trevellin if she hated him so much!'

'That's just it, sir. If you don't mind my saying so, you don't properly understand the lay-out. It took me a bit to grasp the hold old Penhallow must have had over the lot of them. Couldn't call their souls their own, from what I can make out. I never set eyes on him myself, but you can take it from me that he wasn't an ordinary sort of a man at all. Seems he had a passion for keeping the family hanging round his bedside. The description Mrs. – What was that name? Oh, I've got it! – Mrs. Eugène gave me of what used to go on fairly made my hair stand on end. I mean, if you'd only seen that room of old Penhallow's sir. Mrs. Eugène said they used to have to sit in it, every blessed night, watching the old man drink himself boisterous, while the rest of the family quarrelled, and shouted each other down. Enough to get on anyone's nerves, if you ask me!'

'All the same,' began Warbstow dubiously, 'I don't think I'd expect anyone to murder Penhallow for a reason like that.'

'No, sir. I'm only giving you the possibilities. Then we have this Loveday Trewithian. I don't more than half like the look of her. She's going to marry Mr. Bartholomew – the one they all call Bart. Tough young devil with a temper. She's maid to Mrs. Penhallow, and it was she got the prescription for the veronal made up the day before the murder. Not that I want to make a lot of that, because anyone could have got at that veronal at any time. She's like a good many of the people about here: sooner tell a lie than not. She denied that there was any fixed understanding between herself and Mr. Bart; said old Mr. Penhallow had never said a word to her about it. She was frightened all right. But Mr. Bart blurted out the whole thing. Said he was going to marry the girl; that his father had found it out, and they'd had a row about it, which ended though in his agreeing to do nothing about it for a bit. Told me his father said he could please himself once he was dead, and that he hadn't wanted to upset the old man, if he really was going to die.'

'Frank!' ejaculated the Major. 'I think I've seen the young fellow once or twice: generally rather well liked about here.'

'Well, I rather liked him myself,' admitted Logan, caressing his chin. 'Compared with the rest of them, that is. I'd say he isn't the sort to use poison. Violent young chap: half-killed his twin brother when I was questioning him this morning. It took Plymstock and me quite a time to drag 'em apart. That was because his brother, as soon as he saw I was taking notice of this Loveday Trewithian business, said he hadn't a doubt she'd poisoned the old man. Seems Mr. Bart told him how the old man had said he'd get Trellick Farm when he died, whatever he did. As I see it, sir, he's mad with jealousy – you do get that sort of thing in twins, I believe – and nothing would please him more than to get Loveday Trewithian removed out of his brother's path. Hates her like the devil. Told me the old man knew very well the thing would die a natural death, given time enough, and that the girl knew it too, which was why she didn't dare risk waiting for Penhallow to die in his own good time. I dare say he'd have told me a lot more, but that was where Mr. Bart walked into the room. Before I properly knew what was happening, there was one chair broken, and a table with a lot of knick-knacks on it sent flying, and this Conrad Penhallow flat on his back, with his brother on top of him, trying to choke the life out of him. However, they're much of a size, and Mr. Bart didn't have it all his own way by any means. It took us quite a time to get them separated.'

'You take it very calmly!' exclaimed the Major.

The Inspector's rather grave face relaxed into a smile. 'Well, sir, that's the way everyone else took it. The noise they made brought the old lady – Mr. Penhallow's sister, that is – into the room, with Mr. Ingram and his good lady, and all the old lady had to say about it was, "Now, boys!" while Mr. Ingram just told them to shut up. Seemed to me there wasn't anything what you might call out of the way about that little scrap, Mr. Bart being given to using his hands a bit quicker than most people.'

'Good lord! Do you mean to say he's in the habit of attacking people in that homicidal fashion?'

'Well, he threw Jimmy the Bastard down the backstairs not so long ago,' replied Logan. 'No one seemed to think much of it, and I'm bound to say that kind of high-spirited behaviour doesn't go with poisoning: not to my mind it doesn't.'

'I never heard of such a thing in my life! He sounds to be a most dangerous young ruffian! What about the other two you mentioned? Are they cut after the same pattern?'

'No, sir, not by a long chalk. Between you and me, I don't know when I've seen a nastier bit of work than Aubrey Penhallow. He's one of these writing-blokes, who wears his hair long, and goes about in fancy clothes, and smells of scent.'

'God bless my soul!' said the Major, properly disgusted.

'Yes, sir. He thinks he's got to be funny, too, and I'm not fond of humorists. Not his kind. Regular smart alec. By what I could see of it, he spends his time annoying the rest of them.'

'In face of what you've just told me, I wonder he dares!'

'Yes, so did I, sir, but he very kindly explained to me when a couple of his brothers looked like getting rough with him that they'd like to kick him into the middle of next week, but didn't dare to, on account of his knowing Jujitsu.'

'A pleasant lot, upon my word!'

'Well, they're not the kind of people you meet every day of the week, sir, and that's a fact. But this Aubrey! Well, he doesn't care who gets pinched for the murder as long as he doesn't.'

'Is he implicated in any way?'

'That's what I haven't yet satisfied myself about, sir. Mr. Eugène took care to let me know that Mr. Penhallow had suddenly taken it into his head to keep young Aubrey at home, and that that wouldn't suit Aubrey's book at all. I gather he's in debt, but I haven't yet discovered to what extent, nor how serious this living at home business was. I wouldn't put it beyond him to slip a drop of poison into a man's drink, but whether he'd poison his father is another matter. You can't spend long in that house, sir, without coming up against the feeling that however much they quarrelled with the old man, and whatever way he treated them, they all of them, barring, perhaps, Mr. Raymond, were proud of him, and even rather liked him. Young Bart, and Mrs. Hastings, the old lady, and Mrs. Penhallow are definitely upset at him dying. Well, I should think they'd miss him, I must say.'

'A darned good miss, I should imagine! Is that the full list of the people you suspect?'

'No, sir, I've got one more suspect, and one man I'll have to look into this afternoon. There's Mrs. Penhallow's son, this one they call Clay. Nervous boy, scared stiff of me, and trying to carry the whole thing off in a breezy kind of way. Seems his father had just taken him away from college, and meant to article him to his cousin – Hastings, of Blazey, Blazey, Hastings, and Wembury. I had all this from Eugène and Conrad and Aubrey. Apparently Master Clay never has got on with the rest of the family – well, it isn't likely he would: he's the soft kind, and I should think a chap like that would have a pretty thin time in that household. He's been going about talking in a wild way about how he'd go mad if he had to live at Trevellin for the rest of his life, and how he'd sooner be anything than a solicitor. What's more, he tried to hatch up some sort of an alibi for himself, which didn't exist; and altogether he struck me as a chap worth watching.'

'H'm! And the other man you mentioned?'

'Well, I don't know that there's much in that, sir, but I'll have to investigate it. Miss Penhallow – who seems to have got an idea that it's she and not me who's conducting this case – tells me that a Mr. Phineas Ottery, who was the first Mrs. Penhallow's brother, went up to Trevellin to call on Mr. Penhallow yesterday afternoon, and insisted on seeing him privately.'

'I don't see much in that.'

'No, sir, no more did I, but it's obvious the Penhallows do. They all say it was highly unusual of Mr. Ottery to come to Trevellin uninvited, and there isn't one of them that has any idea of what he could possibly have wanted with their father. None of them saw him, except the old man himself, and they all seem to think there's something fishy about the visit. All except Mr. Raymond, that is. When I spoke to him about it, he said there was nothing odd in it at all, and that his father probably had a bit of business with him. I shouldn't think much of it if it weren't for the fact that none of the servants showed Mr. Ottery out of the house, and no one can tell me whether Mr. Penhallow went with him to the door or not.'

'Penhallow? I thought he was bedridden, or next door to it?'

'No, not entirely he wasn't sir. He had a wheeled chair which he used whenever he got out of that extraordinary bed of his. He was up yesterday. Got up after lunch, and didn't go back to bed until late in the evening. That's the factor that makes this case a bit of a teaser. By what I could get out of Martha Bugle – she's the old woman that used to be nurse to the sons, and has looked after Penhallow ever since he first took ill – the room was turned out during the afternoon, but finished, and left ready for Penhallow, by five o'clock. Except for this Jimmy we're hunting for going in just before dinner to make up the fire, and draw the curtains, which they say he did, I can't discover that anyone went near the room until Penhallow was put to bed again, which would have been some-where around eleven o'clock at night. In fact, sir, from five till eleven the coast was perfectly clear for anyone to go into the room, and do what they liked there. As far as the family's concerned, you can rule out the dinner-hour, when they were all present and correct, but after dinner two of them left the room where the rest were sitting: Mr. Bart, who says he was with Loveday Trewithian, and is borne out by her and by his twin brother, who had to fetch him to help get their father to bed; and Master Clay who says he spent the evening knocking the balls about in the billiard-room. But in be-tween five and eight, when dinner was served, there was nothing to stop any of them tampering with the old man's whisky, which was kept in a cupboard in his room, and there's not one of them has an alibi for the whole of that period. Several can prove they were somewhere else for part of the time, but that's all. The room's right at the end of the house: you can get to it down a broad sort of passage on the ground floor, or through a garden-door leading into the small hall it opens into, or by way of a staircase leading down into that hall. It's at the opposite end of the house to the kitchen premises, and the chances are that at that hour of the day you wouldn't stand much chance of meeting anyone in that wing.'

The Major's face began to lengthen. 'This doesn't sound promis-ing, Inspector.'

'No, sir, it isn't promising, and that's a fact. Talk about murder made easy! Why, even the butler played into the murderer's hands, by having made it a rule never to leave more than a couple of drinks in the whisky-decanter in his master's room! And as for finger-prints, we can rule them out, because the only ones on the decanter that aren't hopelessly confused are Penhallow's own; and the only one on the veronal phial belongs to the housemaid who admits she moved all the bottles when she dusted the shelf this morning.'

'It boils down to this, that you've got nothing to go on, then, unless something unexpected transpires?'

'That's about the size of it, sir. Still, we've not caught Jimmy the Bastard yet, and you never know how people will give themselves away once they get a bit scared. I think I've rattled one or two of them already, and I don't despair, not by any means. After all, they don't know how little I've got to go on.'

The Major shook his head. 'It looks nasty to me, very nasty, Logan.'

'You're right, sir: it is nasty, or I'm much mistaken. I got the feeling I'm only on the fringe of the truth of all that's been happen-ing in that house lately. Every now and then it came over me that I was standing on the edge of a regular volcano. And I'm not what you'd call fanciful, either. Plymstock felt it too. He passed the remark to me as we came away that it wouldn't surprise him if something was to break at any moment.'

'Well, we'll hope it may,' said the Major.

'Yes,' agreed Logan slowly. 'We'll hope it may, sir.'

CHAPTER NINETEEN

INSPECTOR LOGAN, although he might suspect that his investiga-tions had alarmed some members of the household, had as yet little conception of the extent of the turmoil into which Penhallow's death, coupled with his own activities, had plunged Trevellin. Faith, watching with growing terror the unforeseen results of her crime, felt as though she had loosed a relentless tide which would soon engulf them all. When the Inspector's suspicions seemed to draw first this innocent person into his net, and then that, her horror caused the danger in which she herself stood to occupy a secondary place in her mind. It had never occurred to her that any suspicion at all would attach itself to Penhallow's death; far less that the death of the one person from whom every ill had seemed to her to emanate, should, instead of solving all difficulties, have been as a match set to a train of gunpowder.

Bart's open avowal of his intention to marry Loveday had pre-cipitated a storm whose repercussions were felt even in the kitchen, where Reuben, thunderstruck at a development quite unsuspected by him, solemnly cast off his niece; and Martha, shocked out of her abandonment to grief, declared that in her day no girl who had caught the Master's fancy would so far have forgotten her station as to dream of marriage. 'Look at me, you malkin!' Martha said. 'I did things decent! I knawed my place! I never prated to un of marriage, nor there wasn't no one troubled by the bit of pleasure I had with un!'

Sybilla, having loudly congratulated herself on being no blood relation of such a shameless hussy, penetrated into the front of the house, and confronted Raymond there, laying it upon him that he owed it to the family, to poor deluded Bart, and to the blessed memory of his father to put a swift end to so unnatural an alliance. When he told her impatiently that he had no control over Bart's actions, she sought out Bart himself, reminded him of the innumerable occasions when she had spanked him across her knee, expressed her fervent desire to perform this office for him again, and would have favoured him with a most unflattering reading of Loveday's character had he not first shouted her down, and then, when her shriller tones mastered his, slammed out of her presence.

Bart was at bay, only his sister supporting him in his resolve to marry Loveday. He, whose quick rages so soon blew over, had an uglier look in his eyes than Faith had ever seen there. His quarrel with Conrad was so bitter that all attempts at peace-making between them failed at the outset. The alliance which had weathered every storm seemed to be broken past repair. When Bart had entered the room in time to hear Conrad casting the blame of Penhallow's death on to Loveday, he had flung himself on to his twin with murder in his heart. It had taken all Logan's and the Sergeant's combined strength to hold him, when they had dragged him off Conrad's throat; and such terrible words had been spoken then as would not easily be forgotten.

Clara shook her head sadly over it, and said that there seemed to be no end to the troubles besetting the house.

'They'll make it up,' Faith said uneasily. 'They always make it up, Clara!'

'I never knew them quarrel like that before,' Clara replied. 'You see, my dear, they aren't easy to handle, the Penhallows, and there's no one to hold them now Adam's gone. I never knew anyone to drive a difficult team better than he did. Well, he's dropped the reins, poor soul, and it's a runaway team now, that'll very likely overturn us all into the ditch.'

'Raymond – Raymond will take his father's place!'

'Raymond doesn't want to take his father's place, my dear. Raymond's a skirter, just as Char said. He wants to be rid of them, that's all.'

'Clara,' Faith said desperately, 'wouldn't it be better for them to be free? To make their own lives?'

'It's no good askin' me, my dear. I'm a Penhallow, and it's a bitter day to me that sees the family breakin' up. I don't say they haven't had their quarrels, but they've always stuck together.'

When the family met at lunch-time, an uneasy tension seemed to hang over them. Bart sat silent, his eyes lowered and his brow thunderous; Conrad's sore spirit found relief in the utterance of bitter jibes at the expense of anyone who offered him the smallest opening. This had the effect of arousing Eugène's animosity, and led to several passages of arms between them. Eugène, aggrieved by the disturbance to his peace, sensitive to any fancied aspersion cast at Vivian, and deeply chagrined by the news, clumsily conveyed to him by Clifford, that his portion amounted only to four thousand pounds, was in a querulous, spiteful mood, ready to pick a quarrel with anyone. Vivian looked white, and strained, and, choosing to read covert accusations into quite innocent remarks, had adopted a defiant attitude calculated to provoke hostilities. Clay afforded his brothers an opportunity of venting their feelings on his head by pointing out, with wearisome insistence, why it was absurd to suppose that he could have had anything to do with his father's death. Charmian, ignoring the bickering and the sudden spurts of temper, held forth in an argumentative tone on the various aspects of Penhallow's murder until Raymond, who until then had maintained his usual taciturnity, rounded on her, and bade her hold her tongue. As he enforced this command by bringing his fist down on the table with considerable force, all the glasses jumped, and Faith gave one of her nervous starts.

'Naughty temper!' said Aubrey. 'Is it getting on your nerves, Ray dear? Personally, I adore listening to Char laying down the law, and telling us how the deed was done, because she's almost certainly wrong, and I do like people to make fools of themselves, don't you?'

'You're probably in a position to know!' Raymond said.

'I'm glad somebody has put that into words,' observed Eugène unpleasantly.

'Oh, how too dreadfully unkind of you!' Aubrey said. 'Oh, I do think you oughtn't to have said that, Ray! After all, I *am* your little brother!'

'One cannot help feeling that the Bastard's disappearance was providential – with, or perhaps without three hundred pounds in cash,' said Eugène.

Aubrey smiled sweetly upon him. 'Oh, no Eugène! No, really, I wouldn't commit a murder for three hundred! So paltry!'

'I maintain,' struck in Charmian, 'that there was something extremely fishy about Uncle Phin's visit, and it ought to be investigated.'

Raymond turned towards her. 'For God's sake, can't you shut up about that? Your views are of no possible interest or value to anyone! Uncle Phin had nothing whatsoever to do with Father's death!'

'How do *you* know?' Conrad put in swiftly.

'Oh, I was longing to ask that question!' said Aubrey. 'I didn't quite like to, but Con's so wonderfully uninhibited!'

'Far be it from me to make groundless accusations,' began Eugène.

'Oh, shut up!' Charmian interrupted.

'No, do let him go on, Char!' begged Aubrey. 'Whenever anyone says far be it from him to do something it means he's going to do it, and I should simply love to hear who it is Eugène's going to accuse!'

'All I wish to point out,' said Eugène, 'is that if we are to ask ourselves who stands to gain the most out of Father's death there can be only one answer.'

'But how beautifully put!' Aubrey said admiringly. 'You couldn't call it actually offensive, could you?'

Raymond looked grimly at Eugène. 'If you and your wife hadn't sponged for years on Father, you'd have been a bigger gainer today than you are! You can put that in your pipe and smoke it!'

This remark made Vivian flare up at once. She demanded to be told in what way Eugène could be considered to be any more to blame for the wasting of Penhallow's fortune than any of his brothers; and added that for her part she had always hated Penhallow, and would rather have gone out charring than have subsisted on his generosity.

'Let me advise you,' said Charmian, 'not to be quite so lavish with your abuse of Father, my good young woman! Your position is not so unassailable that you can afford to make it worse.'

'I know very well you think I poisoned your father, and I don't care what you think, any of you!' declared Vivian, shaking with indignation. 'If I'd thought of it, I would have!'

'Now, that'll do!' said Clara. 'It was Jimmy killed Adam, whatever Char and Ray may say, and so we shall find, you mark my words!'

By tea-time it had been established that Penhallow had died from swallowing an overdose of veronal; and Inspector Logan had learnt from Phineas Ottery that he had visited Trevellin to consult Penhallow on a small matter of business connected with house-property. 'My nephew, Raymond Penhallow, will bear me out that my errand to Mr. Penhallow was of the most trifling nature,' had said Phineas, with a wave of his hand. 'He was present during a considerable part of the interview, so you may see for yourself, Inspector, that there was nothing particularly secret about it. Merely, I did not wish to admit the whole family into my confidence.'

However plausible in itself, this explanation could not fail, coming as it did after Raymond's assertion that he had not seen his uncle, to arouse the Inspector's suspicions. He said nothing about this to Phineas, but returned to Trevellin, to request an explanation of Raymond.

Raymond reddened angrily, and said something under his breath. Mentally he cursed Phineas for dragging him into an episode which neither of them could satisfactorily explain; and if he had not been afraid that panic might betray his uncle into making some admission that would lead the police to discover the truth, he would flatly have denied his statement. As it was, he took time to think out his answer, and said at last: 'Very well, then, I did see him. I know nothing about his business with my father, however.'

'Why did you inform me that you had not seen him, sir?'

Raymond shrugged. 'Did I say that? I don't remember: I probably wasn't attending to you very closely. To all intents and purposes, I didn't see my uncle, since I know nothing of what his business may have been with my father, which is what you want to find out, isn't it?'

'I can't be satisfied with that answer, Mr. Penhallow.'

'Then perhaps you'll be satisfied with this instead!' Raymond retorted. 'You're chasing a red herring! My father's dealings with my uncle were entirely trivial, and can have nothing whatsoever to do with this case!'

As this brief interchange took place in the morning-room, with the door communicating with the Yellow drawing-room, where Eugène was reclining upon a sofa, standing ajar, it was not surprising that by tea-time the news that Raymond, for reasons best known to himself, had been giving false information to the police should have spread round the family. Curiosity of the most morbid nature was immediately roused, and when a hired car presently brought both Phineas and Delia to Trevellin, it was generally felt that there was more in Charmian's theory than had at first been supposed. To Faith, it appeared so fantastic that the Otterys should be caught up in the meshes of the appalling net which she had woven that she could almost have believed herself to be struggling in the toils of a nightmare.

Ostensibly, the Otterys had come to offer their condolences to the bereaved family, but although the scared look on Delia's face, and the horror and dismay to be detected in Phineas's manner might ordinarily have been considered to be the natural results of hearing of an old friend's murder, they were taken, under existing circumstances, to denote a personal concern in the affair, as intriguing as it was incomprehensible.

Phineas, holding Faith's hand between both of his, told her that even at the risk of finding themselves in the way neither he nor his sister could forbear motoring over to see how she did, and to inquire further into the very shocking nature of Penhallow's death. Delia, more than usually incoherent, opened and shut the clasp of her handbag a great many times, scattered her sympathy amongst the family, and timidly asked after Raymond. This gave Phineas an opportunity to interrupt Ingram's account of his father's death, and say with that unctuous intonation which never failed to annoy his nephews: 'Ah, the dear good fellow! This must be at once a sad and a solemn day for him! So much rests upon his shoulders! All the responsibilities of a not inconsiderable estate, the cares of a large family! I must seek him out, and place my services, such as they are, at his disposal.'

'I simply *must* know!' Aubrey said, in an anguished voice. 'I shan't be able to bear it if I don't, and we all know what repressions do to one! *What* are they, Uncle Phineas?'

'Ah, my boy!' said Phineas, reflecting that Aubrey had always been an objectionable young detrimental. 'There are many questions upon which an older head came come to the help of a young one.'

'Uncle's mixed his dates,' remarked Conrad. 'Ray's going on for forty. Incidentally, he's been managing the estate for the past ten years.

'Try again, uncle,' recommended Eugène, with drawling insolence. 'We wouldn't know why you want to see Ray, of course.'

Charmian fixed her uncle with a penetrating gaze. 'Come now!' she said briskly. 'I don't believe in beating about the bush! Just what brought you up here yesterday to see Father, uncle? That's a question which is interesting us a good deal.'

Delia made an inarticulate sound, and looked imploringly towards her brother. He pressed his finger-tips together, perhaps to control their slight unsteadiness, and replied smilingly: 'I am afraid my errand to your dear father was sadly unexciting. Tut, tut! You silly child, have you been picturing a mystery? The influence of the modern crime novel!'

'I never read them.'

He passed his tongue between his lips. 'Well, well! And so you want to know why I came to see my old friend! My dear, if it interests you so much, of course you may know: I came to seek his advice in the matter of a little land deal which I have in contemplation. Now you will all say how dull!'

'I wasn't going to,' said Aubrey. 'I mean, dull isn't the word that actually leaped to my tongue. But perhaps I'd better not say what that was.'

'Mendacious,' suggested Eugène.

'No, adroit.'

Phineas decided to remain deaf to this. Still smiling, he said: 'And did you foolish young people really think that *I* might have had something to do with your father's death? I ought to be cross with you, but I know so well what tricks overwrought nerves can play with one that I can forgive you.'

'That's all very well,' said Ingram bluntly, 'but if your visit to Father was so damned innocent, why did Raymond deny that he'd seen you here?'

Phineas's eyes snapped, and a muscle quivered in his cheek. 'The foolish fellow! Now, why should he do that, I wonder? Can he have thought that I didn't want my little project to leak out? No doubt that would be it!'

'You know, I do feel that we've all under-rated Uncle Phin!' said Aubrey, looking round appealingly.

Happily for Phineas, Raymond chose this moment to walk into the room. He checked at sight of the visitors, and his brow began to lower. 'What the devil—?' he demanded, in anything but a welcoming tone.

Delia got up, dropping her handbag, and moved towards him, her eyes suffused suddenly with tears, and her lower lip quivering. 'Ray, dear! I – we had to come to tell you how sorry – see if there is anything – I mean, if we could be of the least help in this sad time—'

'Very kind of you, but there's nothing you can do, thanks. You'd have done better to have stayed away.'

She whitened, and her hand fell from his sleeve. Aubrey said brightly: 'Isn't it strange, Eugène dear, how often quite unintelligent persons, like Ray, manage to put into clear, concise language what others, like you and me, who are much cleverer, don't you agree, feel to be the inexpressible?'

'That'll be all from you, thanks!' said Raymond harshly.

'Ray, dear old fellow!' said Phineas, rising from his chair, and advancing towards his nephew. 'I have just been learning from your brothers of your absurdly quixotic behaviour in regard to my stupid affairs! Did I say that I was anxious my little deal should not be noised abroad? I did not mean by requesting your silence to embroil you with the police, my boy!'

'Oh!' said Raymond, glancing round the room. 'Pity some of you can't think of something better to do than to poke your noses into my affairs! I'll have a word with you about that little deal of yours, uncle, if you've no objection.'

'Just what is this so-called deal?' demanded Ingram.

'You'd better tell him, uncle,' recommended Raymond sardonically.

'My dear boy, I've already told you that all I wanted was your father's advice on a certain piece of land.'

'Well, it seems a damned queer business to me!' Ingram said.

Raymond shrugged, and held the door for his uncle to pass out of the room. He conducted him to his office, remarking that since the house appeared to be full of busybodies there only could they be sure of any privacy. Once in that austere apartment he shut the door, and turned to confront Phineas. 'What the devil did you mean by dragging me into yesterday's business?' he asked fiercely.

'My dear Raymond, I could hardly be expected to guess that you had been foolish enough to deny having seen me when I was here,' Phineas returned. 'Really, I can't imagine what possessed you!'

'God's teeth, don't you suppose I've got enough to contend with without getting embroiled in that? What's this cock-and-bull story you've hatched up about a land-deal? If you're going to tell the police I can corroborate your stories I'll thank you to let me know first what they are!'

'There is no point in losing our tempers, my boy,' Phineas said smoothly. 'We shall say that I have it in mind to buy up Leason Pastures.'

'You can say what you dam' well please, but you won't lug me into it. I've told Logan I know nothing about your business with Father, and I'm sticking to that.'

Phineas sat down in a chair by the desk, and began to drum his soft white fingers on the arm of it. 'In view of the – er – very equivocal position in which you stand, Ray, do you feel that you are wise to take up this unhelpful attitude?' he inquired.

Raymond looked contemptuously down at him. 'You must think I'm a fool if you imagine I don't know that you're quite as anxious to keep my secret as I am myself!' he said. 'You'd have to leave the neighbourhood, if that got out, wouldn't you?'

Phineas went on smiling, but the expression in his eyes was hardly in keeping with the benevolent curl of his lips. 'We won't go into that. A most unfortunate affair, which we must, I agree, do our utmost to conceal. It was for that reason that I came up to see you today. I must know how matters now stand.'

'They don't stand in any better shape for this precious visit! Already the others are beginning to smell a rat.'

'Then you must have been singularly clumsy, my dear Ray. I thought I could rely on you to present my call upon your father in satisfactory colours. However, there is no profit in repining now that the mischief is done. I have no intention of inquiring into the circumstances of your father's untimely death, and I beg you will not seek to take me into your confidence. What is done cannot be undone—'

'It wasn't done by me,' interrupted Raymond.

Phineas bowed his head in polite acceptance of this statement. 'That, as I have said, is a matter in which I do not propose to interest myself. My sole concern is to keep my sister's name unsullied. To this end I must request you to tell me what steps you have taken in regard to the woman, Martha Bugle?'

Raymond answered curtly: 'None.'

Phineas raised his brows. 'Indeed! Then may I suggest that you give your serious attention to this question?'

Raymond strode over to the window, and stood staring out, his hands thrust into his pockets. After a short pause, he said: 'I gather that you believe I murdered Father. I didn't, but it's quite likely others will share your belief. If Martha thought it, there's no bribe I could offer her that would induce her to keep her mouth shut.' He paused. A bleak look came into his face; his mouth twitched as though from a twinge of pain. 'You're wasting your time. I don't know what I'm going to do yet. Martha isn't the only one who knows.'

Phineas stopped his gentle drumming. 'What? Who else?'

'Jimmy the Bastard.'

'This lad who has absconded with the money from your father's strong-box? His mouth must be shut at once! I consider him far more dangerous than the woman!'

'You're right,' Raymond said evenly. 'I should think he'd demand a high price for giving up the chance of being able to call me – Raymond the Bastard.'

Phineas winced, and glanced at his nephew's broad back with an expression of distaste. 'Really, Raymond, *must* you—?'

Raymond laughed mirthlessly. 'Don't you like the sound of it? Well, if you don't, what do you think I feel about it?'

'Properly managed, there is no reason why anyone should—'

Raymond wheeled about. 'God, can't you *see*? Even if I could shut Jimmy's and Martha's mouths, *I* know the truth, don't I? I'm not Penhallow of Trevellin! I'm just another of Father's bastards! I've no more right here than Jimmy! Do you think I can take that thought to bed with me every night, get up with it every morning, carry it with me all through every day? No, you don't understand! Why should you? You weren't brought up to believe yourself Penhallow of Trevellin: it doesn't mean a thing to you! But it means something to me! You and your land-deals! What have you ever cared for the land? what have you ever known about it? I've never cared for anything else. Trevellin, and my name! Well, I haven't got a name, and if I hold Trevellin it'll be by the courtesy of my nurse, and my fellow-bastard! I can't stand it, I tell you!'

'My dear fellow, you're – you're overwrought!' Phineas said, looking frightened. 'You don't know what you're saying! No doubt the whole affair has been too much for you. Naturally I understand how you feel, but really there is no reason for these – well, really, I must say these heroics! If you do not care to approach your nurse, I am perfectly willing to act for you, but I do feel—'

'You'll keep your nose out of it!' Raymond said savagely. 'That was one thing Father told you that was true! You'd get your damned smug face scratched open if you approached Martha, as you call it! If Father told her to keep her mouth shut, she will; if he didn't, there's nothing you or I can do about it, and – hell, I won't buy my place here!'

'Of course, if you believe that your father's wishes would influence the woman to such a great extent—'

'She was his mistress for years. Didn't you know? Cared for him, too. I never knew why: he wasn't any more faithful to her than to any of the rest of them.'

'Need we go into that?' said Phineas disgustedly. 'I was certainly unaware of this – this extremely unsavoury relationship, and I should prefer not to discuss it. But I must point out to you that matters are very precariously poised, and you have need to behave with the greatest circumspection. If anything should – er – leak out, I felt sure I can rely on your sense of delicacy to keep my sister's name out of it. There is really no reason why it should ever be known who your mother was, even if—'

He broke off, shrinking back instinctively in his chair, for Raymond had taken a hasty step towards him with such a look of fury in his face that he thought for a moment that he was going to be assaulted.

But Raymond did not touch him 'Get out!' he said, his voice grating unpleasantly. 'Get out, and take your sister with you! If you cross this threshold again, you fat hypocrite, I'll throw you out myself!'

Phineas rose with more haste than was consonant with his dignity. 'I realize that you are not yourself, Raymond, so I shall leave you. It was not my wish that my sister should have accompanied me. I was, in fact, very much against it, but her very natural feelings towards you were such that she could not rest until she had seen you.'

'I don't want to see her! Can't you grasp that the very sight of her makes me sick? O God, it makes me *sick* to think—' He stopped, and covered his eyes with a shaking hand. 'You'd better go.'

Phineas retreated to the door. 'I can assure you I have no desire – But I must insist on being told what you mean to do.'

'I don't know.'

'I appreciate the painful position—'

'Get – out!'

Phineas withdrew, gathering the rags of his dignity about him.

CHAPTER TWENTY

HER worst enemy could not have accused Loveday Trewithian of possessing a rancorous disposition. She bore her aunt and uncle no malice for the denunciation of her behaviour, but listened meekly enough to all they had to say, standing with her lovely head a little bowed, and a corner of her muslin apron held between her hands. Martha's more violent attack upon her she met with a like calm. She was sorry for the old woman, and looked at her with pity in her dark eyes, and presently slipped away from her without returning any retort to her taunts. She had expected to have to run the gauntlet of backstairs condemnation; it did not worry her, nor did it rouse any feeling of resentment in her breast.

Her instinct was to serve, and she was kept so fully occupied in attending to her mistress, and in stepping into the various breaches in the household caused by Sybilla's collapse on first hearing of Penhallow's death, and the hysterics into which the upper-housemaid thought it proper to fall, that she had very little time at her disposal to speculate on the manner of Penhallow's death. When she had been sent for by the Inspector, she had been so frightened that she had lied instinctively. She felt the police to be her natural enemies; and no sooner did she learn that Penhallow had in all probability been poisoned with Faith's veronal than she at once perceived the dangerous position in which she might stand, and denied her engagement to Bart. Bart scolded her for this afterwards, and told her what a silly girl she had been, and swore to protect her from Inspector Logan and a dozen like him. With Bart's strong arms round her, she regained control over herself; but it was not long before she bethought herself of Conrad. She faltered out her fear that he would try to get rid of her by putting the blame of the murder on to her. Bart had laughed such an idea to scorn, cherishing such confidence in his twin's loyalty that the shock of finding it had been misplaced came like a blow to the solar plexus. Prevented from choking the life out of Conrad, he had stormed away in search of Loveday, who no sooner saw the condition of rage and grief which he was in than she forgot her own troubles, and put her arms round him, and drew his head down on to her breast, and soothed and petted him into some sort of calm. When he was beside himself, she felt as though she might have been his mother. Her flesh ached with the love a mother has for her first-born, and she would cheerfully, at such a moment, have gone to the scaffold in his stead. She disliked and feared Conrad, but since Bart loved him she was willing, even anxious, to propitiate him, and made up her mind to do it just as soon as his first wild jealousy had had time to wear off. Stroking Bart's short, crisp locks, she told him that he mustn't mind so, for his brother would come round when he saw what a good wife she meant to be.

'He doesn't darken my doorstep!' Bart said, his eyes smouldering. 'Con! *Con* to say such a thing!'

'Yes, but, Bart-love, it's because he don't like to think of losing you the way he thinks he must if you marry me. He don't think me good enough for you, besides, and indeed I'm not! I don't know that I blame him so much as all that. Now, you won't quarrel with him, my dear, will you? For if you do, they'll say it was me turned you against him.'

He turned his head, as it lay on her shoulder, and mumbled her neck. 'O God, Loveday, my poor old Gov'nor!' he said in a broken voice. 'If I knew — if I only knew who did it, I'd kill him with my own hands, whoever it was! Loveday, who *could* have done such a thing?'

Provided that neither she nor he were implicated in the murder, her private feeling was that the unknown murderer had done her a good turn, but since such a point of view would plainly shock Bart, she replied suitably, assuring him that indeed she had liked his father very well, and wished him alive at that moment. She experienced not the slightest difficulty in uttering these sentiments. If she had considered the matter ethically, which she did not, she would have considered her insincerity justified by the comfort it evidently brought to Bart.

In a similar fashion, later in the day, she listened sympathetically to the jerky outpouring of poor Clara's over-charged heart. At sundown, with the approach of the dinner-hour, it had occurred to Clara that it was Penhallow's birthday, and that he had been going to give a party. It was too much for her: she had gone away to her own room, and had given way there to a burst of weeping which was none the less violent for being very unusual in one of her reserved temperament. Loveday had heard her strangled sobs as she had passed the door, and without pausing to consider whether her presence would be welcome, had softly entered the room. The sight of Clara, crumpled up in a chair, draggled and damp, and convulsed by her grief, woke all that was best in her. She coaxed and persuaded Clara on to her bed, tucked her up with a hot-water-bag, and fondled and petted her, as though she had been Faith, until she at last fell into an exhausted sleep. When she emerged from the room it was to find that Faith had been ringing for her for twenty minutes, and was in a state of mind quite as overwrought as Clara's.

'I can't bear it!' Faith said wildly, lifting both hands to her head, and thrusting the hair back from her brow. 'It's hideous, hideous! No one's safe from their suspicions! I never dreamed – Even the Otterys! Oh, do they ever convict innocent people, Loveday? Do they?'

'Of course they don't, my dear! There, now, leave me bathe your face with lavender-water! It's been too much for you, and no wonder! You'll have your dinner quietly in your bed, and give over worrying your poor head any more about it today.'

'I ought to go down,' Faith said wretchedly. 'They'll think it strange of me if I don't.'

'No, they won't, They'll think it natural that you, that was his wife, should be upset.'

Faith gave a shiver. 'Oh, don't! I tried to be a good wife! I did, Loveday, I did!'

'And so you were, my dear, never fret!'

Faith's eyes crept to her face. 'Loveday, you don't think they could suspect me?'

The girl gave a rich little laugh. 'No, that I don't!'

'Or Clay? Loveday, has anyone said anything to you about my boy? Loveday, tell me the truth! Do they – do they think he could have done it?'

Loveday patted her hand. 'Now, will you be easy, my dear? There's no call for you to work yourself into a state on Mr. Clay's account, nor on anyone's. Seeming to me, there's nothing to show who did it. You let me get you to bed, with one of those aspirins of yours, and you'll be better.'

'Don't leave me!' Faith begged.

'Yes, but, dearie, I must, for a little, for my uncle's that upset that I'll have to give a hand in the dining-room, or no one won't get a bite of food this night. I'll come back to you, surely. Now let me get the clothes off you, and some water to wash your face with, and I'll soon have you comfortable, my poor dear.'

The appearance of Loveday in the dining-room, waiting on the family in Reuben's place, though it excited no remark from the greater part of the company, made Clara say grudgingly that she was bound to admit that the gal had a good heart. Clara, restored by her short nap, had reappeared with rather swollen eyes, but all her accustomed self-possession. 'I'll say one thing for her, it hasn't gone to her head, all this nonsense of Bart's,' she observed. 'I shouldn't have been surprised if she'd started takin' advantage. If it weren't for her bein' Reuben's niece, I wouldn't mind it so much, for I'm sure I don't know what we should have done without her this day.'

Conrad compressed his lips, and kept his eyes fixed on his plate. Charmian said: 'Well, I don't believe in class distinctions, and I consider she's rather an exceptional girl. I haven't the slightest objection to having her for a sister-in-law, and I hope you'll invite me to Trellick when you're married, Bart!'

He threw her a glowing look of gratitude. 'By God, I will, Char!'

'Pile it on thick enough, and he'll invite the Pink Fondant too,' drawled Eugène.

'Well, I'm sure I don't mind whom Bart marries,' said Aubrey. 'But I do think it's frightfully anomalous and shy-making to have his intended waiting on one at meals. I feel I ought to leap from my seat, and say Allow me! or something like that.'

Loveday came back into the room just then, with the sweets, and Charmian instantly said: 'I've just been telling Bart that I hope you'll both of you invite me to Trellick one of these days, Loveday.'

Everybody but Bart looked slightly outraged. Loveday blushed, and stammered: 'You're very good, miss, I'm sure.'

'You'd better get used to calling me Charmian, my dear girl, if you're going to be my sister-in-law,' said Charmian, by way of demonstrating her freedom from class consciousness.

Conrad got up, violently thrusting back his chair. 'I don't want any pudding!' he said. 'All I need is a basin to be sick into!'

He slammed his way out of the room, and Bart, who had started up, was pressed down again into his chair by Loveday's hand on his shoulder. She said in her gentle way: 'It wouldn't be seemly, miss, not as things are. It's better we should go on the same for the present.'

This speech, while it rather discomfited Charmian, still further predisposed Clara in Loveday's favour. She said, a little later, when the family repaired to the Yellow drawing-room, that it showed a good disposition. Since Bart was not present, she was able to add that nothing would ever make her like the gal, but that things might have been worse.

The nightly gathering in Penhallow's room had never been popular with any member of the family, but a melancholy feeling of loss and of aimlessness descended upon the company when the lamps were brought in, and the curtains drawn. The sense of that empty, darkened room at the end of the house lay heavily upon the minds of the family; and the absence from the gathering not only of Faith, but of Raymond, Clay, and the twins as well, brought home Penhallow's death more poignantly to his children than anything else during that interminable day had done.

Ingram, walking up after dinner from the Dower House, was

instantly struck by the change, and blew his nose loudly, and said that the old place would never be the same again. Gregarious by nature, he had enjoyed the evenings spent in his father's room, and he had enough of Penhallow's patriarchal instinct to wish to herd as many of his family together (always excepting Aubrey and Clay) as he could. He would have gone to look for the twins, had he not been dissuaded by Clara, who said gloomily that it would be better to leave both of them alone; and although he had very little interest in his stepmother, he inquired after her as well, and seemed disappointed to hear that she had gone to bed.

'She's upset, poor gal,' said Clara. 'It's been a tryin' day for everyone.'

'It may have been trying,' remarked Vivian, in her intolerant way, 'but why Faith should think it necessary to weep over Mr. Penhallow's death, I fail to see. In fact, I've no patience with it. She's behaving as though she'd cared for him, and we all of us know she was absolutely miserable, and hated the sight of him! I can't stand that kind of hypocrisy.'

'Here, I say!' expostulated Ingram. 'You've got no right to talk like that, Vivian! You don't know how she may feel!'

Vivian hunched her shoulder. 'If she had a grain of honesty she wouldn't pretend to be heartbroken at what she must be glad of.'

'That,' said Charmian, preparing to hold the stage, 'is rank bad psychology. Faith's behaviour is perfectly consistent with her whole mental make-up, and outlook on life. I know the type well. I haven't the smallest doubt that she is quite sincere in her present grief, just as I am sure that she was equally sincere when she thought herself unhappy with Father. Her nature is shallow; she is easily swayed, and extremely impressionable. She is the sort of woman who, having complained of her wrongs for God knows how many years, will now spend the rest of her life telling herself that she was always a perfect wife to Father. Just at the moment, she's had a severe shock, which has jolted her out of her normal rut. I dare say she's suffering from a good deal of remorse, wishing she'd made more allowances for Father, and that sort of thing, and remembering the days when she was in love with him. It won't last, but it's all perfectly sincere while it does.'

'You may be right, my dear Char,' said Eugène languidly, 'but in justice to Vivian I must observe that Faith has given us all the impression, for longer than I care to reckon up, that she would regard Father's death as an unmixed blessing.'

'My good Eugène, can't you realize that there are a great many people in the world, of whom Faith is one, who talk vaguely about what they want to happen, and not only are horrified when it does happen, but find as well that they didn't really want it at all?' said Charmian scornfully. 'It is typical of Faith that she must always have a grievance. She's the kind of woman who *enjoys* a grievance! She'd rather keep it than lift a finger to set it right, as often and often she might have done, merely by exerting herself a little. What is more, she dramatizes herself incessantly. Oh, quite unconsciously! It has been my experience that many ineffectual and supine people do. It's their only form of mental exertion – if you can call it mental! At the moment, she is seeing herself as the sorrowing widow. *Really* seeing herself! You can call it hypocrisy if you like: I don't, because I understand her perfectly, and I know that she believes so thoroughly in her own poses that they cease to be poses, and become an integral part of her character.'

'Thank you very much,' said Eugène, in an extinguished voice. 'I'm sure we're all most grateful to you for your masterly exposition of Faith's character. And now may we talk about something interesting?'

'As a matter of fact,' interposed Ingram, before Charmian could wither Eugène, 'I came up to have a word with you, Char. Something I want to talk to you about.'

'I'm at your disposal,' replied Charmian briskly. 'Come into the library!'

'Oh, Char darling, don't say you're going to talk secrets with Ingram!' begged Aubrey, looking up from the embroidery, which he had brought down from his room, and was working on under the light thrown by one of the lamps. 'I was just going to ask your advice about this spray I'm about to start on. Do you think a blending of russet-tones would be *rather* lovely?'

No one supposed for a moment that Aubrey felt the faintest interest in Charmian's opinion of his work; but although Eugène refused to be drawn, Ingram rendered the gambit an outstanding success but turning to glare at Aubrey with a mixture of loathing and astonishment in his face. He had not previously noticed his deplorable young brother's occupation, for which reason Aubrey, who had hoped to infuriate the twins, and was feeling defrauded by their tiresome absence, took care to call his attention to it. He at once delivered himself of a scathing denunciation of Aubrey's character and habits, employing so many well-worn phrases, and looking so extremely like the military man of any farce, that even Eugène's lips twitched, and he said: 'An officer and a gentleman, sir!' while Aubrey himself was so entranced that he forgot to add fuel to this promising blaze, and only recovered his presence of mind when Charmian began to drag Ingram out of the room.

'Don't be such a fool, Ingram!' Charmian said impatiently. 'Can't you see he's trying to get a rise out of you?'

'Puppy!' said Ingram.

'Char, my precious, don't, *don't* take him away! Not before he's said he'd have liked to have had me under him in the regiment! Oh, I do think you're mean, I do, really!'

Charmian, however, was unmoved by this plea, and marched Ingram off to the library. As she lit the central lamp in this rather dismal apartment, she said severely: 'You simply make him more outrageous by taking any notice of him. He does it to annoy you.'

'He's a namby-pamby, effeminate – well, I won't say!'

'Good lord, I know all about Aubrey! As a matter of fact, he isn't such a wet as you might think. I never saw anyone ride straighter to hounds.'

'That makes it worse!' said Ingram, not very intelligibly, but with immense conviction. 'But I didn't come here to talk about that young so-and-so! Now, look here, Char, you've got a head on your shoulders! What's your frank opinion about Father's death?'

'I don't know. What's yours?'

'Well, I've been having a long pow-wow with Myra about it, and we both of us feel the same. Of course, it isn't for me to say anything – damned awkward position, and all that! – but taking one thing with another, and looking at it all round – perfectly dispassionately, mind you! – everything points in the same direction.'

'You mean you think Ray did it.'

'Well, what do you think?'

'I've told you: I don't know. I shouldn't have thought he was the sort to poison anyone, but as I said this morning, he takes his own line. I've never got to the bottom of Ray, and I don't suppose I ever shall.'

'Never did hit it off with the old man, you know. It has struck me lately that things were worse between them than usual. And then there's this extraordinary business about his trying to strangle Father! Upon my word, Char, I could hardly believe it! I don't hold any brief for Ray, but I honestly didn't think he was as bad as that! Seems to me a perfectly astonishing affair.'

'Yes,' Charmian agreed thoughtfully. 'I wonder what Father did to make him lose his temper to that extent?'

'Oh, some row about money! They've had any number.'

'I know that. But they never ended in that kind of a scene before. I can't help feeling that there's something very odd behind it.'

'Connected with Uncle Phin?'

'That I can't make up my mind about.'

'Frightful thing if it was Ray,' Ingram remarked, in rather an unconvincing tone.

Charmian disliked blatant insincerity, and said at once: 'It would suit your book all right, wouldn't it?'

'Now, look here, Char!' expostulated Ingram, reddening. 'That's a poisonous thing to say! I don't pretend that I've ever got on with Ray, but I call it a bit thick to insinuate—'

'I wasn't insinuating. You can't stand Ray at any price, and he can't stand you. You probably think you'd make a better head of the family than he will, and you know darned well that life won't be nearly so easy for you now he's holding the purse-strings.'

Ingram looked disconcerted by this forthright speech, and muttered: 'Never thought of such things! All the same, *I* shouldn't want to get rid of the rest of the family if I were the heir!'

'Well, my opinion is that it may be the saving of the family to be obliged to fend for themselves.'

As Ingram chose to take this as a reflection upon himself, the interview came to an abrupt end. Charmian went away to write her nightly letter to Leila Morpeth; and Ingram returned to the Yellow drawing-room to propound his views to Eugène.

Eugène, who was more worried than he cared to admit, would have subscribed to any theory which exonerated Vivian; and although he privately considered it unlikely that Raymond would have descended to such a weapon as poison, he did not like Raymond, knew very well that he would receive little, if any, pecuniary assistance from him in the future, and so experienced no difficulty in suppressing his inner scepticism, and discovering a number of good reasons for believing him to be guilty. Clara was distressed, and made several attempts to put an end to the discussion, maintaining stoutly her conviction that it was Jimmy who had killed Penhallow; but Vivian, who for all her brazen attitude, was haunted by dread, supported Ingram, rather in the manner of one catching at a straw. Clay, who had come back into the room, also added his mite, with more eagerness than was seemly; but he was speedily reduced to silence by Aubrey, who looked up from his needlework to say kindly: 'Dear little fellow, we all feel sure you believe Ray did it, but you must learn to be seen and not heard. Besides, it's very dangerous to draw attention to yourself. What with one thing and another – well, you see my point, don't you?'

This had the effect, first of shutting Clay up, and then of making him leave the room to seek reassurance of his mother.

Faith, coaxed by Loveday to eat some dinner, was feeling better, and had begun to argue herself into the belief that the police would never discover the authorship of the crime; but a very little of her son's companionship sufficed to throw her back into a condition of extreme terror. Clay's account of the discussion at present in progress downstairs made her eyes dilate. She said faintly: 'No, no! Of course it wasn't Ray! How can they say such a thing?'

'Well, but Mother, you must admit it does look fishy. I mean, we know he went for Father yesterday morning: he didn't deny it. And, on top of that, we know he had rows with Father about his spending so much. Then, too, he's the heir. What's more, he's behaving damned queerly, you know. Of course, I know he's always a surly sort of a chap, but honestly, Mother, ever since Father was killed—'

'Stop!' Faith exclaimed, sitting bolt upright in bed. 'You mustn't say such things, Clay! I – I forbid you! It's wicked! I *know* Ray didn't do it!'

'It's all very well to say that, but you can't *know* it,' objected Clay. 'It's obvious the police have got their eyes on him. He's the one who stands to gain the most. And what about all that business with Uncle Phin? It stood out a mile that there was something up between the pair of them. Why was Ray so anxious to squash the idea that Uncle Phin could have had anything to do with it? For he was: no getting away from that! What did Uncle Phin come up here for today? I'll bet it wasn't just to inquire after you! No: he and Ray have got some kind of an understanding.'

She broke in on this to say in a desperate tone: 'What can Phineas Ottery possibly have had to gain through your father's death? They scarcely ever met! It's the most absurd, the most far-fetched—'

'Well, what did he want with Father yesterday, Mother? And why did Ray say he hadn't seen him, when he had?'

'I don't know – I can't imagine! There's probably some perfectly simple explanation!'

'Of course, I quite see that it'll be a shocking affair, if it does turn out to be Ray, but, after all, Mother, it'll be just as bad if it was Aubrey, or Bart.'

'Aubrey or Bart!'

'Well, Con thinks it was Loveday, but I can't see why it mightn't just as well have been Bart. Apparently, Father had put a complete spoke in his wheel, and you have to bear in mind that in all probability he was afraid Father meant to cut him out of his will. Or it might have been Bart and Loveday between them. In fact—'

'Clay, I tell you I can't bear this! How dare you talk like that? I won't permit it! What would you feel if they spoke about *you* in this dreadful way?'

He gave an uneasy laugh. 'As a matter of fact, Aubrey as good as told me he believed I'd done it. I know very well they all think I might have. Of course, it merely amuses me, because it's so utterly absurd, but all the same—'

She turned so white that he was startled. 'Aubrey – no, no, they wouldn't pay any attention to him! He always says spiteful things. The police don't think you had anything to do with it!'

'Oh, lord, no! Well, I mean to say, why should they?' said Clay, with an assumption of carelessness.

The prospect he had conjured up, however, was terrible enough to keep his mother awake long into the night; and when, during the following day, it became apparent that the police were pursuing their investigations very strictly, and were fast bringing to light every circumstance which the family would have wished to bury in decent oblivion, she began to look so hag-ridden that Charmian observed dispassionately that she would probably end up in a Home for Nervous Breakdown Cases.

It was amazing how easily the police seemed to be able to ferret out information. A chance word led them to question first this member of the household, and then that; one discovered, to one's dismay, how little had ever taken place in the family of which the servants had not had the fullest cognizance. The between-maid had heard Clay say that he would go mad if his father forced him to work in his cousin's office; all the housemaids remembered perfectly being sent to find Mr. Bart, and send him to his father's room, and recounted with zest the rage Penhallow had been in at the time; Martha disclosed that Penhallow had, previously to that occasion, summoned Loveday Trewithian to his presence, and had also questioned her on the relationship between Loveday and Bart. Martha, who had no love for Faith, told too of the occasion when Penhallow had rung for her to remove his weeping wife from his sight. Encouraged by Inspector Logan, she dilated upon this theme, with the result that the Inspector formed the opinion that her stories were greatly exaggerated. As he had by that time reached an understanding of the peculiar position she had held in the house ever since the first Mrs. Penhallow's death, he had no difficulty in concluding that she was actuated largely by jealousy of Faith. That Penhallow had often reduced his meek, faded wife he did not doubt: he had already had evidence of the astonishing ease with which Faith shed tears. He did not exclude her from his list of possibles, but he did not consider it likely that, having borne patiently with Penhallow for twenty years, she should suddenly have taken it into her head to murder him. That she might have done it on her son's behalf did not appear to him to be a tenable theory. The fate Penhallow had had in store for Clay did not strike Inspector Logan as being at all terrible. He could appreciate that a young gentleman might object strenuously to being removed from college (where he had obviously been wasting his time), but he set very little store by the various accounts he heard of his hysterical pronouncements. Young gentlemen of Clay's type were much given, in the Inspector's experience, to talking a lot of wild nonsense, and behaving as though the end of the world had come when they had to do things they didn't fancy doing. To be articled to his own cousin, well known to be a very nice and sporting gentleman, and to be kept at home, with nothing to pay for his board, and every agreeable luxury of horses and cars and such-like at his disposal, could hardly be expected to impress the Inspector as being anything but a very pleasant life; and even if he had been able to believe that Clay, who seemed to him a silly, spoilt sort of a young man, might not have liked the career planned for him, it would have been quite incomprehensible to him that his mother should not have perceived the advantages of having him so well provided for, and, moreover, kept at home under her fond eye.

Inspector Logan had heard a great deal about Penhallow's tyranny, but from never having encountered him, nor experienced life at Trevellin under his rule, he did not arrive at any real understanding of the circumstances which had driven Faith and Vivian to distraction. From all he was told, he formed a picture of a jovial old ruffian, of autocratic temperament, casual morals, quick rages, and apparently boundless generosity. The very fact that so many of his children lived under the parental roof seemed to him to show that Penhallow could not have oppressed them very badly. It even appeared that he condoned the wild exploits of their riotous youth, and had always been ready to rescue them from the consequences of their lawlessness. His despotism seemed, in fact, to have been a benevolent one; and although the Inspector could readily imagine that his rages and his excesses might make him at times an awkward man to deal with, he could not perceive that there had been anything in his behaviour to drive even two such highly-strung women as Faith and Vivian to poison him.

His suspicions, then, pending the apprehension of Jimmy the Bastard, began to centre upon Raymond, and upon Loveday Trewithian, who, alone amongst the suspects, seemed to him to have had adequate motives for committing murder. The possibility that Bart might have had some hand in the affair he kept at the back of his mind, but did not consider very probable. He thought Bart's grief at his father's death was real enough, and hardly believed him to be the type of man who would murder anyone in cold blood, and by such means as poison. Loveday, on the other hand, had she decided to get rid of the only barrier to her marriage, might naturally have been expected to choose poison as her weapon, particularly since poison was ready to her hand. On the face of it, she seemed to be the most likely suspect, and might have absorbed all the Inspector's attention had not Phineas Ottery paid a call on Penhallow on the day of his death, and had not Raymond denied having seen him upon that occasion.

It did not take the Inspector long to discover what had been the main cause of the quarrels which he knew had constantly cropped up between Raymond and his father. To one who was heir to the estate. Penhallow's crazy extravagance must have been more than galling. Had Raymond not committed a violent assault upon his father on the very morning of the date of his death, the Inspector would have considered him the most obvious man to suspect of having poisoned Penhallow. But the two circumstances did not, in his experience, dovetail together. To start with, he thought, men who blatantly attempted to choke their victims did not resort to poison; to go on with, to poison a man, having been prevented earlier in the day, from strangling him, would have been the act of a lunatic, and Raymond, so far from being a lunatic, bore all the appearance of being a level-headed man, long past the age of youthful folly. It might be that the explanation given him of Phineas Ottery's visit, and of Raymond's denial of having seen him, was the true one. But every time the Inspector reached this point in his cogitations, his intuition stirred uneasily, and he could not rid himself of the feeling that there was something behind that episode which he had not so far discovered.

'I'm not one to talk a lot of hot air about my instinct,' he told Sergeant Plymstock, 'but the further I go into this case, the more certain I am that there's something being hidden from me that I can't get hold of. What's more, I've got a hunch it's got something to do with Mr. Ottery's visit.'

'Well, I don't know, sir,' said the Sergeant dubiously. 'It don' seem likely Mr. Ottery could have had anything to do with the case not on the evidence.'

'What I'm telling you is that I haven't got all the evidence.

wish I knew what it was that set Raymond Penhallow on to his father's throat!'

'They all seem to think it was the old trouble about the money Mr. Penhallow got away with, don't they, sir? That's what he said himself.'

'Oh, yes! He wouldn't cash his father's cheque, and all the rest of it! It might be true; I don't say it wasn't, but I do say I'm not satisfied.'

His conviction that a possibly vital clue was eluding him led him to interrogate still more closely the various members of the household, amongst them being Faith, who was, by that time, so obsessed by the fear that Clay, or Loveday, or one of her stepsons, or even Vivian, might be arrested for her crime, that she almost lost sight of her own danger, and consequently answered Logan's questions in a manner far more calculated to allay any suspicions of her which he might have nourished than the most studied defence could have done. She perceived that the two persons whose activities most interested the Inspector were Raymond and Loveday, and she did her best to paint their characters in such colours as must convince him that neither would have so much as contemplated murdering Penhallow. She had never liked any of her stepchildren very much, but of them all Raymond and Bart had been the least inimical to her, Bart's good-nature having precluded his treating her with anything but careless kindness; and Raymond having generally refrained from criticizing or condemning either her actions or her opinions. His attitude was largely one of indifference, but whereas the rest of the family more often than not behaved as though she did not exist, he had always accorded her a curt civility, and had more than once sternly checked attempts on the parts of Eugène, Conrad, and Aubrey to exercise their wits at her expense. Nor did he bully Clay; and while his habit of almost entirely ignoring his half-brother scarcely indicated any liking for him, Faith was grateful to him for not reducing Clay to that state of stammering nervousness which was usually the result of any intercourse with the rest of the family.

As soon as she realized that she had unwittingly placed Raymond in a position of considerable danger, Faith began insensibly to exaggerate these somewhat negative qualities, and to see in him the only one of her stepsons who had ever been kind to her, or had sympathized (tacitly, of course) with her misfortunes. She saw that he was looking more than ordinarily grim, and her conscience reproached her painfully. She had never meant to place him – nor indeed anyone else – in so dreadful a situation; she had thought that in hastening Penhallow's end she would be bringing peace to his whole family. Instead of this, and by what she could not but believe to have been the mischance of Doctor Lifton's indisposition, the consequences of her action were as appalling as they had been unforeseen. When she saw the frown in Raymond's eyes, and knew that he was being harried by the Inspector; when she became aware of Ingram's barely disguised hope; when she realized that Clara

213

and Bart had loved Penhallow, and bitterly mourned him; and most of all when she saw the growing suspicion of one another in the faces of her stepsons, she regretted her mad deed as she had never thought it possible that she could. If she could have called Penhallow back to life, she would have done it. He had epitomized for her all that she most hated at Trevellin, but without him chaos, uneasy tension, and dissensions far more serious than the cheerful quarrels which had flared up under his auspices made the house gloomy as it had never been in his lifetime. She had loathed the noisy gatherings in his bedroom, but the silence that now reigned in the room seemed to her more unendurable than the noisiest gathering had been, and she could almost have wished to hear his loud, bullying voice accost her from the great bed.

She clung desperately to the hope that the police would not succeed in finding Jimmy the Bastard, that they would be forced through lack of evidence to abandon the case; for it seemed to her that if only the menace of their presence could be removed from Trevellin some part at least of the horror now lurking in every corner of the old house would vanish. But on the third day the police found Jimmy the Bastard.

CHAPTER TWENTY-ONE

JIMMY had been arrested in Bristol, whither he had made his way, with the intention of working his passage out to America. Upon reading the news of Penhallow's death in one of the cheaper newspapers, panic had not unnaturally seized him. He had abandoned his plan of signing on as one of a ship's crew, and had made up his mind to stow away instead.

The paths down which this information travelled to Trevellin were varied and circuitous, but the Penhallows had heard several versions of it by the time they were formally told it by Inspector Logan, who came up to Trevellin to report to the head of the family that most of the stolen money had been discovered upon Jimmy's person.

There were present at this brief interview not only Raymond, but Faith, and Charmian, and Ingram as well. Having already heard the news, none of them betrayed any emotion when the Inspector made his announcement. Faith, the only member of the family to go into mourning, sat by the window, looking like a ghost in her unrelieved black dress. One of her thin hands grasped the arm of her chair, the other fidgeted incessantly the folds of her skirt; her overlarge eyes fixed themselves with an expression in them of painful anxiety on the face of whichever of the four other persons in the room happened to be speaking. Charmian straddled as usual in front of the empty hearth, a cigarette between her lips. Ingram, whose stiff leg had been troubling him, sat with it stretched out before him. Raymond, to whom the Inspector addressed himself, stood in the middle of the room, one hand in the pocket of his breeches, the other resting on the back of a Hepplewhite chair. He merely nodded when the Inspector reported the finding of the three hundred pounds in Jimmy's possession. It was Charmian who at once took command of the situation. Removing the cigarette from between her lips, and flicking the ash on to the carpet, she said: 'Yes, we've already heard various accounts of Jimmy's arrest. Very nice work, Inspector. What I should like to know is whether it's true that he told the men who took him in custody that he had a most important statement to make?'

Raymond stood like a graven image, his countenance impassive. The ground beneath his feet was cracking; he could see the whole structure of his life beginning to totter; and knew himself powerless to prevent it crashing to earth, and leaving him stripped of everything he had worked and lived for amongst the ruins. He could scarcely have moved, for he felt as though animation had been suspended in his body. He was aware with some dispassionate portion of his brain that Ingram was watching him covertly, but he lacked the volition to move and hardly cared if he should betray himself.

The Inspector looked annoyed. He said repressively that he did not know how such tales got about, to which Charmian replied that if that were so he was strangely ignorant of the peculiarities of English town and country life.

'I have no information to give you on that subject, miss,' said the Inspector, taking refuge in officialdom.

'Come, my good man, you needn't be so damned discreet!' said Ingram impatiently. 'We've already had it from more than one source that Jimmy said when he was arrested that he could tell the police something that would change the whole complexion of the case, or words to that effect.'

'Indeed, sir? No doubt I shall have more information on what the young man has to say for himself when I have seen him. My object in coming here today was merely to apprise you of the missing notes having been found.' He glanced at Raymond. 'The question of prosecution arises, sir. In the circumstances—'

'I shan't proceed against him.'

The words, uttered in a heavy tone, at once roused a small storm of condemnation. The Inspector, finding that his measured explanation of the intricacies of the situation was rendered inaudible by Ingram's and Charmian's far more penetrating voices, relapsed into attentive silence, his keen gaze intent upon Raymond's face.

'The hell you won't!' Ingram exploded. 'I suppose he's to be allowed to get away with three hundred pounds with your blessing?'

'Plus the hundred Father left him in his will!' added Charmian. 'If you're thinking of the scandal, you needn't. We're chest-deep in scandal already. Of course, I don't pretend that it will be pleasant

215

to have Jimmy's relationship to us blazoned all over the county, which I expect is what will happen, but—'

'Good lord, Char, everyone knows it!' exclaimed Ingram scornfully. 'Who cares a damn for it, anyway? Father's bastards fairly litter the place! It's something new for you to be so nice all of a sudden, Ray! Why shouldn't you prosecute the little beast? Developed a liking for him? Bit of a change, isn't it? *I* was under the impression that you hated his guts!'

'Of course, we're assuming that the creature isn't facing a charge of murder,' said Charmian, her voice over-riding Ingram's 'My view has always been that he had nothing to gain by murdering Father. As for what he said to the police who arrested him, I don't know that I set much store by it. It sounds to me very much the sort of wild statement a badly frightened man might be expected to make. Naturally, it will have to be investigated—'

'Thank you, miss,' put in the Inspector, unable to control himself. 'Is there any other suggestion you would like to make?'

Ingram interrupted, ignoring this piece of sarcasm. 'You may not set any store by what he said, Char, but there are some of us who'd give a good deal to know just what Jimmy the Bastard knows that we don't!'

Faith found her voice. 'Ingram! Please!'

'Yes, it's all very well for you to object to a little plain speaking, Faith, but in your anxiety to shield everyone who might be suspected of having committed the crime, you're rather losing sight of the fact that it's *Father* who was murdered! I should have thought you'd be more anxious to bring the filthy swine who killed him to justice than to spend your time trying to hush it up! Damn it, he was your husband, little though you may have cared for him!'

'Shut up! Leave Faith alone!' said Charmian. 'It's no good expecting her to look at the thing in a rational light: you know perfectly well that she's incapable of reasoned thought. I flatter myself I can look at the whole question dispassionately, and I'm bound to say that I'm not wholly out of sympathy with Faith There is such a thing as loyalty, after all.'

'Yes!' retorted Ingram. 'And my loyalty was to Father, and it still is! I'm fed-up with all the hush-hush business going on in this house! I want Father's murderer brought to book, and I don't care who it is! An eye for an eye is my motto! When I think of the old man's being done-in like that, my blood fairly boils!'

Raymond smiled contemptuously. 'Why not say openly that you believe I murdered Father?'

'If the cap fits—!' Ingram barked.

'Don't answer him, Raymond!' Faith begged, crushing her handkerchief into a ball. '*I* know you didn't – didn't murder your father! Everyone who knows you realizes that you wouldn't dream of doing such a thing!'

'That would come better if we hadn't already had ample proof that Ray was perfectly capable or murdering him!' Ingram said with an ugly little laugh. 'I've mentioned no names, but this I will say! – I'd like to know just what it was that made you try to strangle the old man! And from all I've heard it seems to me that the one man who may be able to answer that question is Jimmy the Bastard!'

Faith rose from her chair, trembling so much that she was obliged to rest her hand on the back of it to steady herself. She was very white, but she managed to speak with a good deal of dignity, though in a husky, rather halting voice. 'Ingram, you forget that I'm – that I'm still mistress here. I won't have such things said. You're jealous of Ray. You've always been jealous of him. Ever since it – since it happened, you've come here day after day making trouble, trying to put the blame on to Ray, because you want to be Penhallow of Trevellin. But I won't have it. Please go! You have no business here, and you – upset me very much.'

'Well, I'm damned!' said Charmian, in an astonished tone. 'Talk about worms turning! Well played, Faith! You're about right, too.'

Ingram, at first thunderstruck by this unexpected attack recovered himself, and said: 'Of course, if I'm not welcome in my own home—'

'You're not,' Raymond interrupted. 'You've had your marching orders!' Get out!'

Ingram rose, very red in the face. 'By God, Ray—'

'I'll be getting along myself, sir,' interposed the Inspector tactfully.

Raymond turned towards him. 'As you please. In view of the fact that Jimmy at least shares with me the distinction of being suspected of murdering my father, I should be glad to hear from you as soon as you have seen him. I take it that you will be seeing him immediately?'

'Yes, sir. I expect to see him today,' replied the Inspector.

Raymond nodded, and moved across to the door, and opened it. The Inspector stood aside for Ingram to precede him out of the room, an after a moment's hesitation Ingram shrugged, and limped out. Raymond followed them both, and shut the door behind him.

Charmian stubbed out the end of her cigarette. 'I never knew you had it in you, Faith!' she remarked. 'If you'll allow me to say so, it's a pity you didn't assert yourself more long before this. There's nothing to look so scared about: Ingram is all bluster, and precious little bite. He won't bear you any malice.'

'It doesn't matter to me what he does,' Faith said, clinging to the chairback.

'No, I suppose not. I take it you don't mean to stay here, once we get things settled?'

'Oh, no! I couldn't! If only I could go now! I can't bear any more. It's driving me mad!'

'It's a great mistake to allow things to get on one's nerves,' said Charmian oracularly. 'Personally, I try to look at the whole affair as dispassionately as possible.

Faith's face twisted. She said wildly: 'Dispassionately! How can you talk like that? Haven't you any feeling? Oh, no, no! You never had! You were always hard and cold! Oh, don't talk to me! You wouldn't understand! You've never understood anything!'

'If you mean, my dear Faith, that I lack your faculty of persuading yourself into a state of exaggerated emotion, you are quite right,' replied Charmian dryly.

Faith gave a sob, and made blindly for the door.

Meanwhile, Raymond, having seen his brother and the Inspector off the premises, had walked down the long corridor to his office at the end of it. There were several letters on his desk, and he sat down behind it, and rather mechanically read them, placing them when he had finished them in one of the trays in front of him. The matter in them was not of immediate importance. He reflected coldly that Ingram would no doubt deal with them at some later date. He opened one of the drawers in his desk, and began methodically to go through the contents, destroying one or two papers, slipping rubber-bands round some others, and writing neat slips describing their nature. In that moment when he had so clearly seen the framework of his life crumbling, he had quite suddenly realized what the end to all the mental torment he was undergoing must be. Before many hours had elapsed, the police would be in possession of the story of his birth, for he could not doubt that Jimmy had overheard his last quarrel with Penhallow. He did not suppose that the police would wantonly publish such a disclosure, but he perceived that it must appear to them as a sufficient motive for the murder of Penhallow, and that they would be obliged to follow it up strictly. Sooner or later the truth would become known, and he thought that since there would be nothing left then worth living for it would be better to die now, while he was still, in the world's eyes, if not in his own, Penhallow of Trevellin. He was not in the least afraid of being convicted of murder, his father's death seeming to him so secondary a matter that he scarcely wasted a thought upon it. But he knew that he could neither face the scandal that would attend upon the publication of his illegitimacy, nor endure to see Ingram stepping into his place. Ingram would triumph; some others might pity him, and the pity would be as hard to bear as the triumph. He was no imaginative, but he was able to visualize with terrible clarity all the humiliations that lay before him, if he should choose to live.

He went on sorting the contents of his desk. Well, he thought, I'm not going to live. Whatever they say, I shan't hear. They'll think I murdered Father to stop his mouth. I don't mind that. It may even work out for the best. The police will drop the case, and Ingram won't let the truth leak out, once I'm safely out of his way. The police will probably tell him, but he'll see to it that it doesn't go any further. Or they might not even tell him. Jimmy would, though. Yes, Jimmy will try to get money out of him by threatening to broadcast the story. Well, that's Ingram's worry, not mine any longer. He'll deal with Jimmy all right.

He opened the bottom right-hand drawer in the desk, and took out the small service revolver which lay in it, in its holster. The revolver had belonged to Ingram, and was a relic of the Great War. Ingram had left it at Trevellin, forgetting all about it. It was typical of Raymond that, although he had never had any use for it, he should have kept it in good order. There was a box of cartridges in the drawer. Raymond drew the revolver out of its holster, broke it, and slipped in one cartridge. After that, he laid it down on the blotting-pad, and rose to open the safe that stood against the wall behind him. Here everything was in order, but he went through the contents, not so much because he desired to make things easy for Ingram, but because he had always prided himself upon his business-like methods. After a moment's hesitation, he took his keys out of his pocket, and, detaching the key of the safe from the ring, placed the others in the safe, and shut the door, and locked it.

He glanced round the room, trying to remember if there were anything he had forgotten to do. The accounts were all made up to date, he knew. He wished he could think that Ingram would keep his ledgers in the apple-pie order in which he would find them, but he supposed that it didn't really matter to him what Ingram did when he took command of the estate. He ran his eye along the shelf that held his files. Rents; Farm; Hunting-Stables; Stud-Farm; Pedigrees – he hoped the Demon colt would fulfil his early promise; he thought he would take a last look at the colt in which so many of his hopes had been centred: sentimental nonsense, of course, but he hadn't had time during the past three interminable days to visit the Upper Paddock, and he would like to see the colt again.

There were one or two matters that would require attending to in the course of the next few weeks: he must direct Ingram's attention to them, and also to the estimates for inch-elm for the new loose-boxes. He sat down again at his desk, and drew a sheet of notepaper towards him, unscrewed the cap of his fountain-pen, and began unhurriedly to write a letter to Ingram.

It was a strange, business-like communication, containing no reference to what he had made up his mind to do, no message of farewell, no directions for the disposal of his private property. Merely it informed Ingram where he would find various papers and documents; what business was necessary to be settled in the near future; and what was the safe-combination. He enclosed the key of the safe in this letter, slipped the whole into an envelope, and sealed and addressed it. He left it on the blotter, and rose, picking up Ingram's revolver, and putting it in his pocket. One of his pipes lay in a large bronze ashtray, some of the cold ash in it spilled from the bowl. He took the pipe in his hand, meaning to knock out the dottle, and to restore the pipe to the rack on the mantelpiece. Then it occurred to him that he would not smoke it again, and with a slight twisted smile he dropped it into the wastepaper-basket.

He cast one final glance round the room, taking silent leave of it. It would probably never look so neat again, for Ingram was an untidy man, and kept his papers in a perpetual state of chaos. It was so disagreeable to him to picture Ingram in the room that he had to tell himself again that it wouldn't matter to him what havoc Ingram created amongst his ordered files. All the same, he did hope that Ingram wouldn't quite undo his careful work. It hurt him so much to think of Ingram perhaps letting Trevellin down that he turned away abruptly, and left the room.

As he traversed the corridor again on his way to one of the garden-doors, he saw Martha emerge from the stillroom at the other end of it. He thought that she looked at him with hostility. She did not speak, and as he went out into the garden he thought: Yes, it's just as well that things have turned out as they have. Even if Jimmy had got away to America, I couldn't have stood it. Funny that I didn't see it before.

This reflection led him on to others. As he walked across the gardens towards the stables, he thought of all the hidden dangers that would have lurked on every side, waiting to pounce upon him, if he had decided to brave it out. He might at some time have had to produce his birth-certificate, and heaven only knew what that might not have led to. Or somewhere in the world there might exist some chance traveller who had met Penhallow, with his wife and his sister-in-law on that fantastic honeymoon. He would never have known from one day to the next when some unforeseen and devilish kink of fate might not have betrayed him. Oh, no! It was better to clear out now, before the worry and the suspense had driven him crazy. He had known an impulse to beg Ingram, in his letter, to do what he could to keep his secret, but he had been unable to force his stiff pen to write the words. Probably it was unnecessary, anyway. Ingram might dislike him, but he was too proud of his name to want such a shameful story to be made known. People might believe him to have been a murderer: he cared very little for that; but if he died now it was just possible that they would never know that he had been just another of Penhallow's bastards; and although, of course, that wouldn't matter to him in his oblivion, he couldn't help clinging to the hope that it would be as Raymond Penhallow that he would be remembered.

When he reached the stables, Weens came up to speak to him about several small matters requiring his consideration. Habit made him attend to Weens, but just as he was authorizing the head-groom to proceed with certain trivial alterations in the stable routine, he remembered that it was absurd of him to give Weens orders which Ingram might overset, and he told the man that he would think it over, and let him know later.

While his favourite hack was being saddled for him, he walked over to the loose-box which housed one of his hunters, and fondled him, pulling his ears, and running his hand down his satin neck. The animal, knowing well what he always carried in his pockets, nudged him, blowing softly down his nostrils. Raymond gave him a handful of sugar, patted him finally, and turned away. He hoped

Ingram wouldn't sell his hunters: he had loved them as he had never loved a mere human.

An under-groom led out his hack. He took a last look at the stables of his designing. Well! Ingram would run them, at least, as well as he had done: no use allowing himself to sentimentalize over them. He mounted the hack, nodded to Weens, and rode out of the yard, up the track that led to the stud-farm.

When he came to the Upper Paddock, he reined in, and sat watching the Demon colt. Yes, he had been right in thinking that he had bred a hit. It was hard to fault the colt. He had the long, muscular fore-arm that meant a strong action, a grand shoulder-blade, high, thin withers, and well-bent hocks. He was going to be a winner all right. A pity he wouldn't be here to break the colt himself. If Ingram were wise, he would put him in Bart's hands. He hoped he wouldn't let Con meddle; Con was no good at training horses: too impatient to be allowed to handle a nervous, high-couraged colt such as this one. Oh, well! No use worrying his head over the colt's breaking: probably Ingram would manage all right.

He turned a little in the saddle, and looked back at Trevellin. He had come uphill, and beyond the new roofs of the stables, and the screen of trees, he could just see the old grey house, sprawling in the middle of its haphazard gardens, its graceful gables and tall chimney-stacks lifting towards the cloudless sky. A wreath of smoke from the kitchen chimney curled upwards in the still air; and a glimpse of intense blue, caught through the foliage of the intervening trees, showed where the great bank of hydrangeas shut off the west wing from his sight. He let his eyes travel over all that he could see of his home, in a long, steady look; and then turned, and rode on, and did not again glance back.

He rode towards the Moor, as he had done a few days earlier. It seemed a very long time ago. He really didn't know why he had chosen to come again, or why he had a fancy to look at the Pool once more. He would probably find it infested by trippers, for the summer was advancing; and its old associations for him had been spoilt by the bitter hour he had spent beside it four days before. But he had always loved the Moor, and in particular that corner of it, and he thought that if he must blow his brains out somewhere he would like it to be there.

He was so fully prepared to find trippers picnicking on the banks of the Pool that he was surprised to find it deserted when he came to it. The waters were unruffled, and somewhere, high in the hazy blue, a lark was singing. He lifted his head to meet the slight breeze blowing from the east, and sat for a moment, looking towards the horizon. The sky-line was broken by great outcroppings of granite; not far away, a gorse-bush blazed golden in the sunlight; the breeze which so lightly fanned his cheek was laden with the smell of peat, and of thyme: nostalgic scents, which brought to his mind the memories of happier times spent on the Moor. Well, I've had close on forty pretty good years, he thought, dismounting, and pulling up his stirrups. Lots of fellows of my age were killed in the War. I was luckier than that. Good job I'm not married, too. Don't know what I should have done if I had been. Hell, I wish it wasn't Ingram!

He pulled himself up on that thought, and began to unbuckle the cheek-strap of the bridle. 'Think I'll unbridle you, old chap,' he said, giving the horse a pat. 'Don't want you to go breaking a fore-leg.'

The horse stood still, sweating a little, for it was very warm. Raymond drew the bridle over his head, bestowed a last, friendly pat on him, and started him off with a clap on one haunch. He watched him for a moment or two; then he thought that there was no point in hanging about, and took the revolver out of his pocket.

CHAPTER TWENTY-TWO

No particular comment was excited by Raymond's absence at tea-time. Bart knew that he had been at the stables, and supposed him to have ridden up to the stud-farm. Bart himself had gone to Trellick after lunch, to look over the place, and to decide what alterations would be needed in the house before he and Loveday could take possession of it. He wondered how soon it would be before Raymond could give the bailiff at present in charge of the farm notice to leave; and hoped very much that it would not be necessary to wait for probate. His father's death, followed as it had been by his quarrel with Conrad, had made Trevellin horrible to him. He would not enter the huge, deserted room at the end of the house, and could scarcely bear even to pass its closed doors. Even the sight of Penhallow's fat spaniel had upset him, but the old dog, as though aware that of all Penhallow's children he had most loved him, attached herself to him, waddling at his heels whenever he was in the house, and fixing him with a mournful, appealing gaze which touched his pity, and made him adopt her, and most forcibly veto Eugène's suggestion that she should be shot.

Clifford had motored up to Trevellin to see how the family did, but he had not brought Rosamund with him. He had come as near to quarrelling with Rosamund as was possible for a man of his sunny temper. Rosamund, never favourably disposed towards the Penhallows, was so shocked by the news that they seemed likely to be involved in a particularly unpleasant scandal that she had represented to Clifford in the strongest terms the wisdom of cutting all connection with the family. She told him that he owed it to his social position, and to his daughters' futures, to demonstrate to the world at large that he had no commerce with his cousins at all. Clifford was really angry with her, and he had gone off to his office that morning without kissing her good-bye, a circumstance which marked a milestone in their lives. Clifford, who had spent his boyhood under Penhallow's roof, was grieved by his death, and deeply distressed by the manner of it. He could not do enough, he said, to show his sympathy with his cousins; and as for casting them off, he hoped he was not such a sanctimonious swine as to consider doing such a thing for an instant.

What he had heard of the Inspector's investigations worried him very much. At first certain that Jimmy the Bastard must have murdered Penhallow, he had been forced to the reluctant belief that the crime had been committed by some member of the family: Raymond, or Clay, or even Faith, whose slightly hysterical behaviour on the day that she had visited his office he could not quite banish from his mind. He found himself thinking about what they must do if the worst came to the worst, and the police discovered sufficient evidence to justify the arrest of one of these suspects. We must brief the best counsel possible, he thought. No half-measures about it: thank God there's no lack of means to pay for the defence!

He had not heard about the arrest of Jimmy in Bristol until he reached Trevellin, but it was told him then by Eugène, who added that they were all breathless with expectation because of what Jimmy had said on being apprehended.

Clifford's round face was almost comic in its look of concern. He shook his head over this news, and said heavily that he didn't like it at all.

'Oh, don't you?' said Aubrey. 'That's probably because you're not implicated in this tiresome affair. You can have simply no idea what an appalling effect being a suspect has upon one's character. I mean, it's too daunting. Take me, for instance! The instant I heard that Jimmy had an important disclosure to make I felt ten years younger. I did really. Because though I don't know what ghastly secret he's going to divulge I do know that it can't be about me.'

'I wouldn't believe what Jimmy said on oath!' declared Bart, his brow beginning to lower.

'Wouldn't you, Bart dear? But isn't that because you've got this touching *idée fixe* about none of us being capable of killing Father? Or are you afraid that he knows something awful about Loveday?'

'No, I'm not!' Bart said, looking dangerous. 'And I'll thank you to keep your tongue off Loveday!'

Clifford intervened, telling Aubrey to shut up, and reproving Bart for rising to obvious baits. When the tea-tray was brought in, Faith and Vivian entered the room, and Clifford soon seized the opportunity to sit down beside Faith, and to ask her whether he was correct in assuming that Clay no longer proposed to enter his office. Before she could reply, Clay himself, who was standing close enough to overhear the question, said rather hastily that he hadn't made up his mind what he was going to do. Everyone looked rather surprised at this unexpected statement, except Aubrey, who said immediately: 'I do think Clay's efforts to avert suspicion from himself are too utterly arid! Anything more convincing, little brother, than—'

'Be quiet, Aubrey!' Faith said sharply. 'No, I don't wish Clay to be a solicitor, Cliff I – I don't quite know how things stand, whether I shall be able to afford – or whether Adam made provision for him?'

'Didn't uncle tell you?' Clifford asked. 'But you know the terms of your marriage settlements, don't you?'

It was so obvious that she had only the vaguest idea of what these might be that as soon as he had finished his tea Clifford suggested that she might like him to explain to her exactly how she stood, pecuniarily speaking. As she accepted this offer gratefully, they both withdrew to the morning-room, just as Conrad came in.

Conrad exchanged a brief greeting with his cousin, but waited until the door had shut behind him and Faith before divulging the news he had learnt at the stables. 'Look here!' he said. 'There's something damned odd up! Courtier's come in, without his bridle!'

'What?' said Charmian. 'Come in without his bridle? What on earth do you mean?'

'Just exactly what I said! Ray took him out this afternoon, not long after lunch, and they say at the stables that he rode off towards the stud-farm.'

'Peculiar,' said Eugène, reaching out his hand for a sandwich. 'But hardly worth all this suppressed excitement, I feel. One supposes that Ray decided to go farther, and sent the horse home. You will probably find that he caught the bus into Bodmin.'

'But Ray never did such a thing in his life!' Conrad objected. 'Besides, why shouldn't he have ridden into Bodmin?'

'Too hot,' said Eugène, yawning. 'I expect it would be *too* much to ask of Sybilla that she should send up some other sandwiches than cucumber. One would have thought that she must have known by now that cucumber is poison to me.'

Bart jumped up. 'To hell with you and your fads!' he exclaimed. 'Something's wrong! Something must have happened to Ray!'

'Well, I don't know,' said Clara, rubbing the end of her nose. 'It's a queer thing to do, but I don't see that there's any need to get in a fuss about it. If Courtier had had his bridle on, I should have said Ray had had a tumble, but if he took it off the gee, there can't be much wrong.'

'Ray may be hurt,' Bart said, hurriedly swallowing the rest of his tea in a couple of gulps. He glanced towards his twin, and his voice hardened. 'Did you send anyone out to look for him?'

'No, I didn't,' replied Conrad. 'Why should I? If Ray were hurt, he wouldn't have been able to unbridle the horse. Or if he was able to, then he must also have been able to mount him again. He probably had his reasons for sending Courtier home.'

Aubrey wandered across the room to hand his cup to Clara. 'My dear, how thrilling!' he remarked. 'Personally, I feel sure Ray has fled the country.'

'That isn't funny!' Bart rapped out.

'Oh, don't you think so? I find that there's something exquisitely humorous in the idea that Ray-the-Imperturbable may be fleeing from justice. Obviously, the news that Jimmy is about to divulge what he quarrelled with Father about has proved to be too much for his stoical unconcern.'

'You swine!' Bart said, through his teeth, and tried to knock him down.

Aubrey, who had been watching him closely under his lazy eyelids, saw the blow coming, and dodged it, closing with his young brother an instant afterwards, and grabbing his right arm. 'Now, Bart! Now, my little one!' he said soothingly. 'I should simply hate to break your arm, lovey, so don't struggle! I did warn you, didn't I?'

'Let go!'

'That's another of the Crown Derby cups gone,' said Clara, gloomily picking up the pieces. 'I wish you boys wouldn't be so rough.'

'Oh, what a good deed!' said Aubrey, letting Bart go. 'I do hope it was I who knocked it over? I can't think of anything as repellent as Crown Derby.'

'Damn you!' Bart said, massaging his arm. 'It's just like you to learn a lot of filthy Japanese tricks! I'm going down to organize a search-party!'

'Isn't that touching?' Aubrey said, addressing the room at large, as Bart walked out. 'Shall we get up a sweepstake on what has happened to Ray?'

'Come to think of it, it *is* queer,' remarked Clara, looking rather worried. 'What can have possessed him to go settin' his horse loose? I don't see any sense in it. Unless he's trainin' him for somethin'.'

'Training him for what, darling Clara? A circus?'

'No, he wouldn't do that,' Clara said decidedly.

'I wonder if Aubrey's right?' put in Clay. 'I mean, do you think he can possibly have got the wind up, and made off somewhere?'

'Do, for heaven's sake, learn to recognize a joke when you hear one!' begged Eugène wearily.

'Well, it's all very well, but I don't see—'

'Hush!' said Aubrey. 'Can't you see that your brothers are sick and tired of the sound of your voice, child?'

Clay said angrily: 'Considering I've only made one remark during the past twenty minutes, I call that rich! You seem to think—'

'One remark in twenty minutes is all we have patience to bear,' said Aubrey firmly.

Clay got up, scraping his chair aggressively. 'This place was bad enough before you came home, but it's absolutely *bloody* now!' he said, and stalked out of the room.

'Well, that's got rid of him,' said Aubrey, sinking into the most comfortable chair he could find.

'You shouldn't tease the boy,' Clara said, shaking her head. 'I daresay he won't be here much longer.'

'That is a very lovely thought, Clara love, and practically the only one that at all sustains me during this trying time.'

'I think I'll step round to the stables, and see what's happenin',' Clara decided, in her inconsequent way. 'The more I think of it the less I like the sound of it.'

Vivian, who had all the time been silent, watched her trail out of the room, and then glanced at Aubrey. 'Did you mean that? Do you really think it's got something to do with the police finding Jimmy? *Could* he have run away?'

'My pet, don't you think he would have taken his car if he had been running away?' suggested Eugène, tweaking her ear.

'Yes, I suppose he would,' she agreed, with a short sigh.

Clifford came back into the room just then, and announced that since there did not seem to be anything he could do, he thought he would be getting back to Liskeard. He wanted to know where his mother was, and when he heard what had taken her down to the stables, he looked rather startled, and said that he hoped to God nothing had happened to Raymond. 'Perhaps I'd better wait to see that he is all right,' he said. 'I'll go and see what they're doing about sending out to search for him.'

'He'll turn up all right,' replied Conrad indifferently.

However, Clifford continued to look grave, and took himself off to join Clara. They both returned half-an-hour later, with little to report, except that Bart had sent several grooms off in various directions, and had himself ridden up towards the Moor.

'One of the men saw him by the Upper Paddock, watching the colts,' said Clifford. 'But that was some hours ago! I can't make out where he can possibly have gone to. He hasn't been to the stud-farm, according to Mawgan. The whole thing is utterly incomprehensible!'

'Oh, I hope there isn't more trouble comin' upon us!' Clara said, her gaunt countenance wrinkled into lines of foreboding.

Charmian, who had been sitting apart from the others, reading a book, looked up to say dryly: 'Well, if you're wise, you won't say anything about this to Faith, until we discover just what has happened. Judging by what I can see of the state she's in, I should say that she'd go into hysterics on the slightest provocation.'

'Lord, Faith wouldn't worry her head over Ray!' Conrad said scornfully.

'Listen! What's that?' Clara said sharply.

'Only Ingram,' Conrad answered, recognizing the halting tread.

The door was thrust open; Ingram, his florid countenance strangely pale, and an expression of scarcely controlled excitement in his eyes, came in, and swallowed twice before he could manage to speak. 'My God!' he uttered, dragging his handkerchief from his pocket, and passing it over his face. 'Have you heard? No, I know you haven't. Gosh, I can't get over it!'

He was so obviously struggling under the burden of strong emotion that even Eugène was roused from his pose of languid boredom. 'Well, what is it?' he demanded. 'Don't stand there gobbling at us, Ingram!'

226

'Ray!' Ingram jerked out. '*Ray!*'

'Yes, dear, we've already grasped that you have come to tell us something about Ray,' said Aubrey kindly. 'Has he attempted to fly the country, or what?'

'He's shot himself!'

A moment's shocked, incredulous silence greeted this announcement. Conrad broke it. '*Christ!*'

Clara gave a moan, and collapsed on to the sofa, rocking herself dumbly to and fro. Charmian sprang up from her chair. 'It isn't possible!'

'I tell you he has! Good God, you don't think I'd make up such a story, do you? What do you take me for? It's true!'

'But how – where – when—?' stammered Conrad, almost as white as Ingram himself.

'Blew his brains out. Up by Dozmary Pool,' Ingram replied, still mopping his brow.

Conrad started forward. 'Bart didn't find him?' he cried.

'Bart? No! Some trippers – I don't know who they were. They drove straight into Bodmin, and reported it at the police station there. I don't know when it was. Really, I feel absolutely dazed! It was all I could do to take it in when that fellow – what's-his-name? the Inspector – rang me up just now. You could have knocked me down with a feather! Of course, it's obvious why he did it, but somehow I never thought that Ray, of all people on this earth – But he did: no doubt about that!'

'Look out!' Charmian said warningly.

Faith stood in the doorway, her eyes wide and questioning. 'Ray? What did you never think about Ray? Why are you all looking like that? What is it?'

No one answered her. She stared at Clara, at the tears coursing silently down her cheeks, and asked falteringly: 'Clara, what is it? Why don't you tell me, one of you? What has happened?'

'Ray's shot himself,' Conrad said curtly.

She stood rock-still, her jaw sagging queerly, her eyes fixed uncomprehendingly on his face. Charmian went across the room towards her, saying: 'Pull yourself together, Faith! It's no worse for you than for the rest of us. We shan't do any good by making fools of ourselves. Aubrey, go and fetch the brandy from the dining-room! She's going to faint!'

Even as she spoke, Faith crumpled up where she stood, with no more than a sigh.

'Go on, Aubrey, quick!' Charmian commanded, dropping on her knees beside Faith, and pulling open the neck of her dress. 'I knew this would happen! Do get out of the way, Ingram! I can manage perfectly well without your assistance. She'll be all right in a moment. It was the shock of hearing that fool Con blurt it out like that.'

'Oughtn't we to get her on to the sofa?' asked Vivian, hovering rather impotently beside Charmian.

'No, she'll come round quicker where she is. Anyone got any smelling-salts? Ammonia will do, if you haven't.'

'I've got some. I'll get them!' Vivian said, running out of the room.

By the time she had returned, Faith had come out of her faint, and was being forced to swallow a few sips of neat brandy. She was trembling from head to foot, icily cold, and a little dazed. She whispered: 'Did I faint? Why – what – I can't think what made me!' She lifted one shaking hand to her head. 'Oh, my hair! How stupid! I'm all right now. So silly of me! But what—' She broke off, as memory came creeping back, and turned her head sharply away. 'Oh, no! Oh, no!' she gasped.

'Steady!' Charmian said. 'Help me get her on to the sofa, one of you!'

Ingram bent to lift Faith bodily from the ground. 'Take it easy, now!' he recommended. 'Frightful shock, I know. Fairly turned me sick when I heard it, I can tell you. There! You're better now, aren't you?'

Clara, who had not ceased to rock herself to and fro, and had paid as little heed to Faith as to Clifford, who was clumsily patting her shoulder, said in a broken voice: 'He went up to see the Demon colt. He thought the world of that colt. I shan't ever be able to bear seein' it again. Poor boy, poor boy, goin' like that, all alone!'

'He killed Father, Aunt Clara,' Ingram said grimly.

'Shut up!' Conrad flung at him.

'No use blinking facts, Con old man.'

'Shut up, I said! It's too ghastly! Ray! *Ray!*'

Faith struggled up from the cushions on which they had laid her, pushing Charmian away in a distraught fashion. 'Don't touch me!' she panted. 'Let me go! Please let me go! I can't – I can't— Oh, no, no, no, no!'

Her voice rose so wildly that Charmian, fearing that she was going to fall into a fit of hysterics, took her by the shoulders, and shook her ruthlessly. 'Faith, stop it! Stop it at once, do you hear me? *Be quiet!*'

Faith caught her breath on a strangled sob, and stared up into her face, terror in her dilated eyes. 'Be quiet,' she repeated. 'Yes, I must be quiet. I mustn't say anything. This isn't real. None of it happened. It *couldn't* have happened. I'm not very well. I want Loveday.'

'All right.' Charmian spoke over her shoulder to Conrad: 'We'd better get her up to her room. Give her your arm, will you?'

Faith allowed herself to be lifted to her feet. She staggered, and clung to Conrad, but she was able to walk to the door. Charmian, arming herself with the smelling-salts and the brandy, prepared to follow, commanding Vivian, before she left the room, to find Loveday, tell her what had happened, and send her up to her mistress's room.

'I could wish that Char hadn't taken the brandy away,' said

Aubrey, when the little cortège had withdrawn. 'Really, I feel too dreadfully shaken myself! Because, if you want the truth, I never actually believed that Ray was the guilty one. And now I'm utterly dumbfounded at Faith's wholly unexpected reaction to the news. I don't want to be lewd, or even flippant, but is it possible that there was more between her and Ray than any of us guessed?'

'No, it isn't!' snapped Vivian. 'Though it's just like you to suggest it! I could very easily start screaming myself. I suppose *you* think it's merely funny!

'Not in the least funny, sweet one. Definitely un-funny, in fact.'

'Just keep quite, will you, Aubrey?' interposed Clifford. 'Ingram, I think I'd better go down to the police-station at once. There will be various things – I take it you'd like me to act for you?

'Damned good of you if you would, old man,' Ingram said. 'You'll know what ought to be done better than I should. Of course this puts the lid on the police investigation. Case is finished – and far better finished like this, than if – well, you know what I mean!'

'Did the Inspector tell you what Jimmy said, if he said anything?' asked Eugène

'No, I didn't ask him. I was so bowled over at the time I never even thought of it. It was only afterwards, when I was on my way up here, that I realized that that was what must have made Ray shoot himself. Knowing that Jimmy had been caught, and was going to spill the truth about his quarrel with Father, I mean. Well, I always thought that there was more to that than we were told.'

'Vivian, I wish you'd look afer Mother while I'm gone,' Clifford said. 'I'll be back as soon as I can, Mother!'

'You mustn't worry about me, Cliff. I shall be all right,' she replied. 'I don't want anyone to look after me. I think I'll go up to my room for a bit. But somebody must find Bart, and break it to him gently. He'll be very upset, for he was always the one who got on best with poor Ray. Oh, dear, oh, dear, that I should ever have lived to see such things happenin' at Trevellin!'

Upstairs, meanwhile, Loveday Trewithian had taken charge of Faith, who had begun to cry, in a gasping, hysterical way that made Charmian try to induce her to swallow some more brandy. But as she would do nothing but push Charmian from her, imploring her to leave her alone, Loveday respectfully asked Charmian to go away, saying that she could manage her mistress better without her. As soon as Charmian had left the room, she took Faith in her arms, and held her comfortingly close, crooning endearments into her ear, and patting her soothingly. She could not understand much that Faith jerked out between her shattering sobs, so choked and incoherent were the words uttered, but she did not think that this mattered much, and went on saying Yes, yes, and Never mind, until Faith had exhausted herself. After that, she undressed her, and got her into bed, and obliged her to swallow a couple of aspirin tablets. Too worn out to resist, Faith merely whispered: 'Don't leave me! Don't let anyone come in!'

'No, my poor dear, I won't,' Loveday said drawing up a chair, and sitting down by the bed. 'There, let me stroke your hand, and send you to sleep! It's been too much for you, and no wonder!'

'Loveday, Ray shot himself. Ray shot himself, Loveday! Because he thought the police were going to arrest him. Loveday, I never knew Ray had had a dreadful quarrel with Adam! Loveday, how could I have known that? No one told me! But what could it have *been*? There wasn't any need! If he'd only told me! Only he never told me anything. Loveday, I meant to be a good stepmother to Adam's children, but how could I be when they wouldn't let me? What shall I do? It's too late, too late, too late!'

'Hush, now!' Loveday said. 'There was nothing you could do to prevent it, my dear. You've nothing to blame yourself for. Shut your eyes, and try to get a little rest! You'll be better presently.'

The hand she was holding shuddered perceptibly; to her dismay, Faith began to laugh wildly, while tears streamed down her face. A knock on the door fortunately penetrated to Faith's ears, and startled her into silence. She said again: 'Don't let anyone come in!'

Clay opened the door, and showed a scared, white countenance. He checked, in obedience to a signal from Loveday, but said in a breathless tone: 'Has Mother heard? Does she know—'

'Yes, of course she knows, you silly creature!' Loveday replied. 'Go away, do! She doesn't want to be bothered with you now.'

'Of course, it's a frightful business, but at the same time, one can't help seeing that if Ray did it—'

'Will you go away, Mr. Clay, before you drive your mother out of her mind with your chatter?' said Loveday, with considerable asperity.

He looked a good deal offended, but since his mother paid no heed to him he withdrew, after a moment's hesitation. Faith lay quite still, her eyes fixed and haunted, her hand tightly grasping Loveday's. Loveday remained beside her until the sound of hasty strides on the gravel drive outside made her lift her head, and listen intently. She disengaged her hand gently, and went over to the window, and looked down. 'It's Bart,' she said. 'I must go down. He'll be needing me.'

'Oh, don't leave me!' Faith begged.

'It's Bart,' Loveday repeated. 'I must go. I'll come back in a little while.'

She crossed to the door, and went out, softly closing it behind her.

Bart had entered the house, and flung his riding-whip on to the table. Conrad came quickly out of the Yellow drawing-room, and started towards him, catching him by the arms in a hard grip. 'Twin! Twin, don't!' he said rather thickly. 'For God's sake, Bart—!'

Bart threw him off violently. 'Leave me alone, can't you?' he said, with suppressed passion. 'Keep off, damn you! I've got nothing to say to you!'

Ingram, who had followed Conrad out of the drawing-room, tried to intervene. 'Come, old chap, you mustn't give way! I know it's been a shock, and all that, but—'

'Get to hell out of my way!' Bart shot out, white as a sheet. 'A fat lot you care! A fat lot any of you care!'

'Bart-love!'

He looked up quickly to the stairs, where Loveday stood, one hand on the broad balustrade. His face twisted; he gave a dry sob, and went to the stairs, and stumbled blindly up them. She held out her arms to him, and folded him in them when he reached her, murmuring to him, stroking his black head.

'There, my love, there! Come along, then, my dear one, with Loveday!'

'O God, Loveday! O God, Loveday!'

'I know,' she said. 'Do you come with me, my love!'

He flung his arm round her, and went with her up the remaining stairs. Below, in the hall, Conrad stared after them, his face as white as Bart's, an expression of stark hatred in his eyes. Ingram said, in a maladroit attempt to console him: 'He's a bit upset, Con, that's all. He'll come round soon enough. I wouldn't worry about it, if I were you.'

Conrad looked at him with bitter contempt, turned on his heel, and strode out of the house.

Ingram went back into the drawing-room, shaking his head over it. 'Seems to be no end to our troubles,' he said heavily. 'Now it's the twins! Bart must have heard the news down at the stables. I can see I'm going to have my work cut out, keeping the peace between the pair of them.'

Aubrey looked up admiringly. 'Oh, isn't Ingram wonderful? I'm sure I should find it frightfully difficult to feel like a patriarch without a moment's warning, but you can see it comes quite naturally to him.'

Ingram cast him a glance of dislike, but was prevented from answering him by the entrance of Reuben, who silently handed him a letter.

'What's this?' Ingram said, recognizing the handwriting. 'Where did you find it?'

'It's a letter from Mr. Raymond, as anyone can see,' replied Reuben dourly. 'It was on his desk. You'd better open it, instead of standing there gaping at it.'

'Damn your impudence, you old rascal!' Ingram said cheerfully, and tore open the envelope.

The key of the safe dropped on to the floor; he stooped, grunting, to pick it up, before reading the letter. While he read, the others watched him in pent-up silence.

'Well, I'm damned!' he ejaculated, when he came to the end of the letter. 'Just like him! Gosh, he was always a cold-blooded devil, but this fairly takes the cake! Here, Eugène, what do you make of this?'

He handed the letter to his younger brother as he spoke, but as Vivian, Charmian, Aubrey, and Reuben all tried to read it over his shoulder, Eugène had some difficulty in mastering its contents. Charmian settled the matter by twitching it out of his hand, and reading it aloud. When she came to the end, there was a moment's silence. Then, to everyone's surprise, Vivian burst into tears.

'My pet!' exclaimed Eugène, putting his arm round her.

She groped for her handkerchief, and fiercely blew her nose, saying huskily: 'I never even liked him, but I think it's *awful*! To write a letter like that, m-making everything as easy as possible for Ingram, not even m-mentioning what he meant to do! Oh, don't you see how dreadfully tragic it is? Sorry! I'm a bit on edge. I didn't mean to make a scene.'

'Trust Ray to be business-like up to the end!' Ingram said, holding out his hand for the letter. 'Give it back, will you, Char? I shall have to show it to the police. Pretty conclusive, I imagine. With any luck, we ought to be able to get through this affair with the minimum amount of scandal.'

Vivian flushed angrily, and said, stammering a little: 'You call *Ray* cold-blooded! My God, what do you think you are? You stand there talking about the scandal, when this frightful thing has happened! As though that were the only thing that counted!'

'What you all of you seem to be in danger of forgetting,' retorted Ingram, 'is that Ray, on whom you're squandering so much pity, murdered Father!'

'I don't care if he did!' Vivian cried, unable to contain herself. 'It was the best day's work he ever did in his life, and I only wish he'd got away with it!'

CHAPTER TWENTY-THREE

BART was no more seen until dinner-time, but he put in an appearance then, and although he ate very little, and said less, he seemed to be quite calm. Ingram had stayed at Trevellin; and as Clifford had returned from seeing Inspector Logan, there was naturally a good deal of discussion on Raymond's suicide. Bart endured this in silence, only betraying by a folding of his lips how much he disliked the conversation.

Clifford thought there was no doubt that the police would now drop the investigation of Penhallow's murder; but he had no information to give the family on the nature of Jimmy's disclosures, the Inspector having made no reference to these, so that he did not even know whether he had yet had an opportunity to interrogate Jimmy. Charmian and Aubrey felt strongly that he ought to have made it his business to find out what Jimmy had said, but he told them that he had had other and more important matters to attend to, and would not, in any case, have thought it a part of his duty to try to pump the Inspector.

Clara did not come down to dinner, but Ingram made a point of visiting her room to assure her that whatever Raymond had intended towards her, he and Myra hoped that she would continue to make Trevellin her home. 'I'm not one to want to get rid of my family,' Ingram said, throwing out his chest a little. 'I always thought there was a lot to be said in favour of Father's idea of keeping us all round him. I mean, in these days, when people don't seem to care any longer for their homes and families— Besides, Trevellin wouldn't seem like Trevellin without you, aunt.'

'Thank you, my dear, I don't know, I'm sure,' she said apathetically. 'It's knocked me over, and that's the truth, Ingram. First Adam, and now Ray. I daresay I'll get over it, but I don't seem able to get my bearings just at present. You go on down, and don't let any of them worry about me. I'll just stay quietly where I am tonight. I know you never got on with him, but he was always very pleasant to me, and I don't feel somehow as though I could bear to see his empty place at table.'

So Ingram went down to dinner without her, and, after hesitating for a moment, took his place at the head of the table, saying that they might as well begin as they meant to go on.

'Speaking for myself,' said Aubrey, 'I mean to go on as far from Trevellin as I can contrive to be. Setting aside the unnerving nature of the late events, which have irrevocably spoilt the place for me, my spirit would become too utterly crushed by the platitudinous atmosphere in which you wrap yourself, Ingram dear, for me even to contemplate prolonging my sojourn here. I mean to say! – *too* corroding, my dear!'

'Wait till you're asked!' recommended Ingram brusquely.

'Oh, weren't you going to ask me?' asked Aubrey, with a maddening air of innocence. 'I quite thought you were. In fact, I made sure you'd begun to see yourself as a second father to me already.'

Ingram at once replied in kind, and the bickering might have grown still more acrimonious had not Reuben, who was handing the vegetables round at the time, called both combatants to order with a severity, and a total lack of respect, that made each one feel himself a schoolboy again.

When dinner came to an end, Bart curtly informed Ingram that he would like to have a word in private with him. Ingram took him by the arm with bluff friendliness, and marched him off to the library, telling him that he should have as many words with him as he liked. 'I know just how you feel about all this, my boy,' he said. 'Shocking business! But Time the Great Healer, you know! Got to keep our chins up, and face the world!'

Bart removed the grip from his arm. 'I don't want to talk about that. How soon can I have Trellick, Ingram?'

Ingram pulled down his mouth. 'Well, I don't know. Of course, we have to get probate, you see, and then—'

'I know all about that,' Bart interrupted. 'But I've got to clear out. I can't stick it here. It's all right for you. You loathed Ray's guts. I didn't. I got on all right with him. He was a darned good man to work for. I thought – I never dreamed— But it's no good going on about that. I know he killed the Guv'nor, but it doesn't seem to me as though the Ray I knew *could* have done such a thing! It's made Trevellin horrible! It's no use telling me I shall get over it: I dare say I shall, but I'm not going to stay here. I'm going to marry Loveday at once, as quietly as possible, and clear out. It was bad enough when the Guv'nor went: it's a thousand times worse now!'

'Yes, but look here, young feller-me-lad!' said Ingram, with hearty kindness, 'I can't get along without you, you know!'

'You'll have to. I'm through. I felt at first that I didn't even want Trellick any longer, but Loveday – well, anyway, I'll try to carry on, and I expect she's quite right, that I should never be happy anywhere else. But I'm not staying at Trevellin, Ingram. I should go mad!'

'Now, now, now!' Ingram admonished him, laying a hand on his shoulder. 'You're upset, Bart lad! You'll see things differently in a day or two.'

'No, I shan't,' Bart said, his voice cracking. 'I shall only see Ray going up there to take a last look at the Demon colt, and – and – O God, what did he *do* it for?'

He sank down into a chair by the table as he spoke, and buried his face in his arms.

'I'll tell you what it is, young Bart,' Ingram said, patting him clumsily. 'You want a good stiff drink, and a change of scene. I wouldn't rush into marriage, if I were you. Plenty of time to think about that. After all, old son, the Gov'nor's not buried yet. Got to think of what people would say.'

'I'll wait till after the – the funerals, but I won't wait any longer. Oh, I won't get married here! I'm going to take Loveday up to London. You can't stop me, Ingram'

Ingram heaved a sigh, and shook his head, but he saw that it would be useless to argue with Bart in his present mood, and merely said soothingly that he would see what could be done about installing him at Trellick as soon as possible, and that in the meantime he must try not to let things get on top of him. He disapproved profoundly of the projected marriage, but he could not help feeling that if Loveday could restore Bart to his senses there might be something to be said for it. He did not want to be deprived of Bart's services, at any rate until his son Rudolph was of an age to fill his place; and he hoped very much that Loveday would induce Bart to perceive the folly of abandoning at least his share in the management of the stables. As Reuben came in just then, to convey the information that Inspector Logan had come up, and wanted to see him, Ingram was obliged to put an end to the interview. Bart went upstairs to his own room, and Ingram went to join the Inspector in the morning-room.

Faith, meanwhile, had dropped into a deep sleep, as the influence of the aspirin she had swallowed took effect upon her system. She did not rouse until the evening was considerably advanced, and then it was to find Loveday beside her with a bowl of chicken-broth.

Loveday tidied her hair, and powdered her nose, and propped her up with extra pillows. She was resistless, and looked so ill that Loveday made up her mind to speak to Charmian about the advisability of requesting the doctor to call in the morning. When Loveday laid the tray on her knees, she said in a faint voice: 'I don't want it. What has been happening? Please tell me!'

'And so I will, my dear, but you must drink a little soup, or we shall be having you ill, and that won't do.'

She began to coax Faith to take a few spoonfuls of the broth, telling her, as she fed her, that there was nothing for her to worry about. 'You'll be going away soon, you and Mr. Clay, and then you'll be able to forget all this.'

'No,' Faith said, in a mournful voice. 'I shall never be able to forget it.'

'Yes, you will, then, my dear. Bart feels the same, for he thought a deal of Mr. Ray, and it has hit him cruel-hard, but he'll get over it, you'll see.'

'Bart!' Faith said, giving a little start. She turned her horror-filled eyes towards Loveday. 'I was forgetting Bart. Is he – very much upset?'

'Well, he is,' Loveday admitted. 'Bart's got a warm heart, and it hurts him bad to think of Mr. Ray's killing Mr. Penhallow. It's like he was being torn two ways, and he's not one as has known trouble, my Bart. But leave me get him away from Trevellin, and I know I can make him feel better about it all. Then there's Mr. Con. Bart won't come next or nigh him, and it doesn't make things easier, the pair of them living under the same roof at daggers drawn, as they say.'

Faith lifted a hand to shade her eyes. 'Even the twins!' she said. 'Everything spoiled for them too!'

'Well, it was bound to be different, once Bart and I were man and wife,' Loveday said sensibly. 'Mr. Con's that jealous, you see. But give him time, and he'll come round, and my Bart's not one to bear malice, I'll say that for him, bless him! I was thinking you should go away from here as soon after the funeral as you can, my dear, for I'll have to be leaving you, and you wouldn't be comfortable here with me gone.'

'Oh, Loveday, no! You can't leave me!'

'Yes, but I must,' Loveday said gently. 'Bart needs me, and my duty's to him. He'll go crazy if he's kept hanging about here, where every stick and stone reminds him of them that have gone. But I'll make him happy, never fear!'

'I hope you will,' Faith said wistfully. 'I think I could bear it better if I knew that it hasn't ruined everything for him. Have the police been up? What – what have they been doing downstairs?'

As Loveday had been shut up for the greater part of the time with

Bart, she was unable to give Faith much information on this point so as soon as the supper-tray had been removed from her knees Faith asked her to beg Mrs. Eugène to come up to see her, if she had not already gone to bed.

In a few minutes, Vivian tapped at the door, and entered. She said awkwardly that she hoped Faith was feeling much better, and offered to extinguish her cigarette, if the smoke bothered her.

Faith shook her head. 'No. Please sit down! It was so stupid of me to faint like that. I want to know – I want to know what has been happening.'

'Well, nothing very much, really,' replied Vivian, pulling up a chair. 'Dinner was pretty ghastly, I thought. Ingram took possession of Ray's place, which made it seem even more ghoulish, and Char held forth as usual, until one wanted to scream. You know, Faith, it's a funny thing, but I used to think that nothing could be as awful as those evenings we all had to spend in Mr. Penhallow's room, but ever since he was killed, everything has been ten times worse. It seems absurd to say so, but I almost feel as though I should be thankful if I woke up, and found that none of it had ever happened.'

Faith twisted her hands together. 'Yes, yes, I know. Go on!'

'Oh, there isn't much to tell! Bart's taking it frightfully hard. He swears he won't carry on with his usual job, and of course that doesn't suit Ingram's book.' She gave a bitter little laugh. 'And it doesn't suit mine either!'

'Yours?'

Vivian smoked her cigarette rather viciously for a moment. 'Yes, mine. It's quite funny, if you look at it in the proper light. I can see that. I mean, you know how I've always wanted to get away from Trevellin, and go back to London? Why, when I heard that Mr Penhallow was dead, I – I thought all my problems were solved!'

Faith regarded her with dawning dismay. 'Yes, of course. But you will go back to London – won't you?'

'Oh, no, I shan't!' Vivian replied. 'I'm going to be stuck down in the Dower House, where I shall have to remain for ever and ever – or at least until Ingram wants it for one of his boys, by which time I shall be past caring.'

'The Dower House!' repeated Faith. 'But why? Why?'

Vivian shrugged. 'Well, it's obvious that even if Bart were willing to carry on he wouldn't have the time to, once he's running Trellick. Ingram can't manage single-handed, and I suppose he doesn't want to engage a bailiff. Anyway, he's asked Eugène if he'll do all the book work – accounts, and that sort of thing and has offered to let him have the Dower House.'

'Oh, Vivian!' Faith cried pitifully. 'Oh, I'm so *sorry*! Can't you – can't you persuade him not to accept?'

'No, I— You see, he'd *like* it, Faith! And Mr. Penhallow didn't leave as much as he'd expected, and he just hasn't the health to be able to do anything very strenuous. I *can't* say I won't stay here when I know that there's nothing he'd rather do. It's just my rotten luck, that's all. At least we shan't have to live here any more. Of course, the Dower House is much too big for us, and I suppose I shall have to do half the work myself, but – it will be my own house, which is something.'

'I thought you would go away,' Faith said numbly. 'I thought everything would be all right for you.'

'Yes, that's what I thought. Only things don't happen to have gone according to plan. I suppose I ought to be thankful that I'm not being arrested for murder, which looked likely at one time. I never thought Ray had done it, though, did you?'

Faith shook her head, pressing her handkerchief to her lips. 'Is it certain – do they all think – the police as well as everyone else—?'

'Well, it's obvious, isn't it?' Vivian said. 'Why else should he have shot himself? Besides, he left a letter for Ingram—'

'Not saying he had done it!' Faith exclaimed. 'It isn't possible! Oh, this is a *nightmare*!'

'No, not mentioning his father's death, or even his own plans. I must say, I found it pretty upsetting. But it rules out any possibility of its not having been suicide. That's what I meant. He told Ingram where to find the keys, and all the papers and things, and – oh, don't let's talk about it! It absolutely haunts me!'

Faith gave a shiver. She saw how her hands were trembling, and clasped them tightly together. 'What was it – that Jimmy said?' she asked, almost inaudibly.

'I don't know. I didn't see the Inspector myself, and apparently he didn't tell Ingram. Ingram hasn't said anything about it, anyway; but to tell you the truth, he's so busy making glorious plans for the future, and thinking of all the grand things he'll do now he's Penhallow of Trevellin, that I don't really think he cares about much else. I can tell you, the whole atmosphere is fast getting me down. And to make it worse, that horrible old woman, Martha, is going about saying that it's all for the best, in a perfectly revolting way! Well, I was one of the people in danger of being arrested, but hang it all, I'm not such a callous beast that I could think Ray's death all for the best!'

'Horrible! horrible!' Faith whispered, burying her face in her hands.

'I oughtn't to have told you, really,' Vivian said, hoping uneasily that Faith was not going to start crying again. 'I expect I'd better clear out now, and leave you to get some sleep. Is there anything you want before I go?'

Faith shook her head. Vivian withdrew; and Loveday came in a few minutes later, and made her mistress ready for the night. She offered to sleep on the couch at the foot of Faith's bed, but Faith thought that she would rather be alone. She saw that it was nearly midnight, and with an effort thanked Loveday for sitting up, and told her to go straight to bed. Loveday left her with the lamp turned low on the table beside her bed, and for a long time she lay staring ahead of her, unable to marshal her thoughts, or to see anything but a vision of Raymond sending his horse home without his bridle, and then shooting himself beside the lonely Pool on the Moor.

At last the oil in the lamp began to run out. Faith roused herself to turn the wick down. Loveday had left the heavy curtains drawn across the windows, and the room became plunged in darkness. She tried to close her eyes, but she could not keep them shut, or remain for long in any one position in the bed. She was hot, and although her body ached with fatigue, she felt so wide awake that it seemed as though she would never sleep again. The image of Raymond remained with her so obstinately that it became an obsession which so possessed her mind that she could almost fancy him in the room. She began to talk to Raymond, as though from the unhappy shades in which his spirit might be wandering he could hear her. She wanted to explain to Raymond, to beg him to forgive her, to tell him that she had never meant to hurt him, and most of all to ask him why – why – why he had killed himself. As she rambled on saying over and over again the same things, she never thought of her husband. She had to make Ray's ghost understand why she had killed his father, and how it was that she had not dreamt that any-one would ever call that death in question. 'I couldn't know you'd quarrelled with him, Ray,' she said. 'You never told me. I didn't think anyone would think he hadn't died naturally. Ray, I thought it would make things easy for everybody! Why did you quarrel with him, Ray? But even if you did, they couldn't have convicted you! There was nothing to show who did it. Why did you lose your head like that, Ray? I wouldn't have let them arrest you! You must believe I wouldn't have done that! I didn't know it would all turn out like this. You don't understand, Ray! It was such a little easy thing to do, and I felt so desperate. It wasn't as though it hurt him, it wasn't even as though he was well, or would ever be well again. I didn't think of it as being a crime, really I didn't! He was making us all so wretched, and then there was Clay— But I wouldn't have done it if I'd known, Ray! You must believe I never meant you to suffer for what I did!'

She was roused from this endless monologue by seeing the door open, and a bar of light widen across the floor. She started up on her elbow, half-expecting to see Raymond himself. But it was Charmian who entered, with a candle in her hand.

'Are you all right, Faith?' Charmian asked her. 'I thought I heard you call.'

She sank back upon her pillows. 'No,' she said dully. 'I didn't call. I'm all right.'

Charmian looked at her narrowly. 'Can't you get to sleep? It's no good lying there thinking about it, you know. What's done can't be undone. It's pretty grim, I admit, but I've been talking to In-gram about you, and we both agree that the sooner you get away from Trevellin, the better it will be for you. He's perfectly prepared to advance you sufficient funds out of his own pocket to enable you

238

to go away somewhere with Clay. Of course, as soon as we get probate, you'll find yourself quite comfortably off, and you'll be able to send Clay back to College, or whatever you like. That's what you always wanted, isn't it?'

'I don't know. Are they sure – are they quite sure Ray did it?'

Charmian set down the candle, and began to straighten the rumbled bedclothes. 'Oh, yes, there's nothing for you to worry about, my dear! The police are satisfied it must have been Ray. So just you go to sleep, and stop fretting!'

She tucked Faith in securely, and went away, reflecting that such an exaggerated display of emotion was typical of a woman like her stepmother; and deciding that, upon the whole, Raymond's suicide was perhaps the best solution that could have been found to an appalling situation.

This feeling was not shared either by Inspector Logan, or by the Chief Constable. Raymond's death came as a shock to both these gentlemen; and the Chief Constable was inclined to blame the Inspector for having allowed such a thing to have happened.

'Sir, there was nothing whatsoever to go on!' Logan said earnestly. 'You know yourself I couldn't have detained Raymond Penhallow on the evidence I had! There wasn't a shred of real evidence against any one of them, nothing I'd dare put up to a jury, that is. I still can't make out why he did it.'

'There must have been something behind it that you never discovered, Logan,' the Major said heavily. 'I ought to have called in Scotland Yard.'

'Begging your pardon, sir, the cleverest detective in the world couldn't have found evidence that wasn't there. There *was* something behind it all; you're right there! Again and again I felt it, when I was working on the case. If you ask me, I'll tell you straight I've got a conviction that whatever it was, it was something ugly. Well, I'm not fanciful, I believe, but I got such a feeling in that house that there was a worse trouble hanging over it than I'd any notion of, that there were times when it fairly gave me the creeps.'

The Major shook his head, digging the nib of his pen into the blotter under his hand. 'I shouldn't be surprised. An old devil, Penhallow was. I don't know. Unprofessional, of course, but one can't help feeling that perhaps it's as well it ended as it did.'

The Inspector could not agree with this. 'I'd have liked to have got to the bottom of it, sir. If it hadn't been for the news of Jimmy the Bastard's arrest, and what he said leaking out, I might have had a chance. But we can't doubt that it was hearing that this Jimmy had something important to disclose which scared Raymond Penhallow into blowing his brains out. Whatever it may have been that he feared Jimmy was going to tell us, he couldn't stand up to. That finished him.'

'And the young man didn't throw any light on it, did he?'

'No, sir, nothing to help us. He thought the butler wouldn't have told us about the quarrel Raymond Penhallow had with the old man,

239

on account of his being so devoted to the family. He never heard anything worth mentioning, though I don't doubt he'd have had his ear to the keyhole a lot earlier than he did, if he'd known what was going on, for a nastier piece of work I hope I may never see! But all he heard was the old man saying: "*That's* where you are, my boy!" and then Raymond Penhallow saying: "You devil, I'll kill you for this, do you hear me? I'll kill you, you fiend, you devil!" Or some such words. I wish he *had* been in time to have overheard a bit more: I'd give a good deal to know what it was that passed between Raymond Penhallow and his father that made it necessary for him to take the risk of poisoning the old man, on top of having half-choked him to death. It must have been something pretty bad, sir, for, unless I'm much mistaken, Raymond Penhallow wasn't one to lose his head easily.'

'No,' the Major agreed. 'A horrible business, Logan, look at it how you will.'

'You're right, sir. A very unsatisfactory case,' the Inspector said.